# *Another Eden*

# Another Eden

## Patricia Gaffney

**THORNDIKE**
WINDSOR

This Large Print book is published by Thorndike Press®, Waterville, Maine USA and by BBC Audiobooks, Ltd, Bath, England.

Published in 2003 in the U.S. by arrangement with Leisure Books, a division of Dorchester Publishing Co., Inc.

Published in 2003 in the U.K. by arrangement with Dorchester Publishing Co., Inc.

U.S. Hardcover  0-7862-5808-X  (Americana)
U.K. Hardcover  0-7540-8700-X  (Windsor Large Print)

The text of this Large Print edition is unabridged.
Other aspects of the book may vary from the original edition.

Set in 16 pt. Plantin.

Printed in the United States on permanent paper.

British Library Cataloguing-in-Publication Data available

Library of Congress Cataloging-in-Publication Data

Gaffney, Patricia.
    Another Eden / Patricia Gaffney.
      p. cm.
    ISBN 0-7862-5808-X (lg. print : hc : alk. paper)
    1. Large type books.  I. Title.
  PS3557.A296A84 2003
    813'.54—dc21                                2003056353

*This book is for Joem Gaffney. Thanks for lighting the fire, Mom, and for aiding and abetting the dream.*

# One

Sherry's was crowded for a wet Thursday night. Alexander McKie sipped rye whiskey and scanned the dining room with a practiced eye. The attractive redhead at the banquette was watching him again. All he could see of her escort was the back of his bald head. Alex stared back in friendly appreciation until the girl looked down, trying not to smile, then up and away again with a charming blush.

Cheered, Alex made an effort to pay closer attention to whatever Bennet Cochrane was booming on about now. But a second later he found himself surveying the room again, transfixed with boredom. Cochrane was an imbecile. A gasbag, a flaming bore, a conversational bully. He was also the most important client Alex had ever had, the man with the power to lift him out of the anonymity of the drafting room and into a partnership, on the strength of one enormous commission. What matter that the house he wanted him to build was a joke, a monstrosity, a stone and marble palace of stellar, unrivaled, spectacular bad taste? Right now, Alex was in no position to choose his clients. Especially millionaire clients. But why did this one have to be such a nincompoop? He glanced across the table at John Ogden, his employer, who was clearing his throat and sending a warning signal from behind the thick lenses of his steel pince-nez. Immediately Alex straightened, sobered, and turned on Ben Cochrane a look of total absorption.

"I'm not saying workers haven't got any rights at all. This is the 'nineties — a decent wage for a decent day's work, that's fine with me. I'm talking about the goddamn anarchists who want to blow us all to hell so they can take over our factories and mills and railroads and banks."

*Rape our women, sodomize our children,* Alex added in silence, desperate to amuse himself.

"You know what they want now, what they're *demanding* these days?"

"Well, I've heard —"

"I'll tell you. Free love. Negro emancipation. Peace, temperance. Votes for women." He glanced around the table, as if looking for something to spit on. "There's a bunch of them trying to organize my

8

bakeshops right now — socialists and communists, talking to my people at night, stirring things up." He punched Alex's biceps with an angry forefinger. "I hear one word about strike, I'll fire 'em all, I swear to God. I'll set the militia on 'em. I'll set my *own* men on 'em."

"Bakeshops," Alex said mildly, easing back in his chair, out of reach. "I thought meatpacking was your game, Ben."

Immediately Cochrane mellowed; talking about himself always seemed to soothe him. "That's some of what I do," he explained, smug in his self-importance. "That's what I do in Chicago and St. Louis."

"Aha."

"Here in New York I do other things. A little of this, a little of that. Real estate, mostly. Banking, a little insurance."

"And bakeshops."

"Bakeshops, caskets, restaurant supplies. Asphalt. A little of this —"

"A little of that." Alex signaled the waiter for another drink.

Ogden cleared his throat again. "How did you get started in business, Ben? Are you a native Chicagoan?"

That set him off again. Alex listened with less than half an ear to an account of how, at the age of nineteen, Cochrane had invented a machine that could stun and kill a steer on a moving ramp in thirteen seconds; of how, two years later, he'd bought his first stockyard; of his relentless expansion into cattle ranching and meatpacking, the two extreme ends — birth and death — of his slaughterhouse empire.

The catalog of achievements went on, and Alex stopped listening entirely to study Cochrane over the rim of his glass. He was big and blunt-featured, barrel-chested, with slicked-back hair and wild, unkempt brows over shrewd eyes the color of Brazil nuts. His bullish chin had a deep, round cleft in the center, like a third nostril. He had an impressive kind of authority, though, there was no denying it, and it came from more than just money. There was something dangerous about him too, something coarse and not quite civilized under the veneer of good jewelry and expensive clothes. Alex remembered the first time he'd seen him, the day he'd walked into the offices of Draper, Snow and Ogden. "I need an architect," he'd announced to Travis, the office manager. He didn't look like a millionaire. The partners were all away that morning. Travis introduced him to the senior draftsman — Alex.

Two months ago, that had been. Since then he'd gotten to know Ben Cochrane a great deal better than he wanted to. The man already had a New York mansion; now he wanted one in Newport, on a lot he'd just bought on Bellevue Avenue. His specifications were vague but grandiose. He didn't have a clue about architectural styles, and he had no interest in aesthetics or comfort or domestic harmony. All he wanted was a house that blared out to the world that Bennet Cochrane was a success, and the only criterion he had for the blaring was loudness. Alex had never met a man as arrogant, ignorant, boorish, and vulgar.

Or as stinking rich. It was a compensating quality, no doubt about it. He glanced down at the sleeve of his new black suit and shot his cuff. Eighty dollars the suit cost, about three times more than he'd ever paid for a suit in his life. He'd picked it up from his tailor today on credit, in anticipation of the first installment Draper, Snow and Ogden would soon pay him out of Cochrane's commission. He pressed the crease in the knee of his natty striped trousers admiringly, thinking he didn't much look like a Salinas lettuce farmer's grandson. When anyone asked, he always said he came from Berkeley, as if his life had begun as an undergraduate. Which, he guessed, it pretty much had. Everything before that was mean and bleak and not worth remembering.

Cochrane flipped open his pocket watch for the third time in fifteen minutes. The first two times he'd done it, Alex had assumed it was to make sure he and Ogden knew the watch was solid gold. But his impatient scowl this time suggested that he really was annoyed, as he'd already mentioned two or three times, because his wife was late. "Let's order," he snapped suddenly, interrupting Ogden in the middle of a sentence, and raised an imperious hand toward the waiter.

Alex looked forward to meeting Mrs. Cochrane — or as her husband never tired of calling her, "the former Lady Sara Longford." She was just plain Sara Cochrane now, he also liked to say. Society gossip sniped that eight years ago Ben had gone to England in search of a titled wife, discovered Sara Longford at a debutante ball, and bought her from her mother, the impoverished Dowager Duchess of Somerville — a well-known drunk — for the sum of twenty thousand pounds. The idea had been that with his money and Lady Sara's blood, the Cochranes would take New York Knickerbocker society by storm.

But the plan hadn't quite worked out. Cochrane had made the *Tribune*'s list of four thousand American millionaires, but he'd never made the Social Register. And if Alex was any judge, he never would. Not if he married God.

"I beg your pardon, I'm horribly late, you must all be starving. No, please, sit down. I hope you haven't waited to order. How do you do — it's Mr. McKie, isn't it? And Mr. Ogden, how good to see you again."

For some reason, he'd thought she would be dark. She was fair. Average height, slim, fashionably dressed. She gave him her hand — cool and unexpectedly strong. Her eyes were smoky blue, her mouth wide, her nose a little too long. Cochrane stood up to help her off with her coat — hyacinth-blue wool, Alex noted with a connoisseur's eye for women's clothes. It proved to be lined in red satin, and he wondered cynically if she'd worn it to the table so that no one would miss that eye-catching surprise. Under the coat she had on a soft blouse of saffron cashmere and a long, full walking skirt of brown and copper silk. She wore no jewelry but her wedding band and a plain gold brooch pinned to her bosom. She was stunning.

They all sat down. Alex couldn't take his eyes off her. So he was startled when Cochrane noted snidely, without modulating his booming cannon of a voice, "You're late, Sara, but obviously it's not because you've been laboring over your dress."

Her perfect English complexion pinkened slightly. "No," she said, addressing Alex and John Ogden, "forgive me, I must look a sight. I came here directly from work instead of going home to change." Her husband snorted. She eyed him steadily. "There was a last-minute emergency and it kept me longer than I expected. I'm sorry I've kept you waiting."

A few uncomfortable seconds passed. Alex asked, "What is it you do, Mrs. Cochrane?" and she turned to him in relief, eyes warming.

"She plays nursemaid to a lot of Jews and Micks and Eyetalians."

He saw her lips compress whitely, but only for a second. "I volunteer a little time at the Forsyth Street Settlement on the Lower East Side, Mr. McKie. We try to

14

make the transition for new immigrants a little less harrowing. Mostly I teach English."

He liked her accent. But then, he reflected, the British could say anything at all and sound brilliant. He started to ask her more about her job, but the waiter came to take their orders, and after that Cochrane went back to monopolizing the conversation.

It was a struggle to listen, when what Alex really wanted to do was stare at Cochrane's wife. He contented himself with watching her hands as she folded and refolded her napkin. They were nervous, intelligent hands, slightly bony, the nails short and white. Was she listening to her husband's monologue? Had she realized long ago, as Alex was realizing now, that the cadence of Cochrane's speech was deliberately designed to wound and embarrass? When anyone tried to agree with him or ask a question, he ignored the contribution completely and began to talk through it as soon as he could think of something else to say. His politics were particularly abhorrent; they seemed more the views of a feudal tyrant than a quick-witted entrepreneur on the brink of the twentieth century. He spoke of the ruling class and the working class with all the sensitivity of a matinee villain. He truly believed that because he had started out shoveling blood and manure in a stockyard, that was a perfectly logical reason why workers deserved no sympathy at all. The man was a cartoon, a caricature; it was impossible to take him seriously. Hearing him try to elevate self-aggrandizement to the level of national interest was a joke. But as Alex watched the woman sitting beside him — tense, gravely polite, full of some quiet emotion that might be sorrow — it struck him that the joke wasn't very funny.

Cochrane's thick, bloody steak finally distracted him long enough to allow his wife to ask a question. "How long have you been practicing your profession, Mr. McKie?"

He almost smiled. Her husband had never thought to ask him that — a relevant inquiry, one would have thought, of the man who was going to build him a house in exchange for hundreds of thousands of dollars. "About four years."

"Alex is our brightest new man," Ogden put in quickly. "He got his engineering degree at Berkeley, and then took his Certificate at the Ecole des Beaux Arts. Which is, of course," he added thoughtfully for Cochrane's benefit, "the finest school for architecture in the world."

"Have you done many other large residential designs?" Mrs. Cochrane pursued mildly.

The answer, of course, was no; but how should he put it? Inspiration struck. "Nothing as large as this, but then, I expect there aren't too many architects in the country who've done one as large as this."

Cochrane exhaled gruffly, his version of a laugh, and muttered fervently, "Damn right."

His wife wasn't so easily flattered. Alex thought her blue-gray eyes looked faintly amused before she turned back to her plate. It made him defensive. "I might not be as experienced as some, but I think I'm qualified to design a house in the style your husband and I have discussed, Mrs. Cochrane. As John said" — it still felt strange to call Ogden "John," but he'd insisted on it, ever since Cochrane had hired Alex as his architect — "As John said, my early training is in engineering, so I like to think I'm well-grounded in the practical aspects of construction and design. Because of my Beaux Arts training,

17

I'm fluent in the academic vocabulary of the Gothic, the Romanesque, the Renaissance. My approach to design is eclectic, but my reverence for the classical is unwavering." He kept speaking, appalling himself, wondering if there was something about being around Cochrane that made people start talking like asses — some contagious speech disease. Only about half of what he was saying was true, anyway; his "reverence" for classical architecture had been doing nothing but waver for years. But she listened with care and courtesy and attention, which was partly why he kept nattering on. It was her husband — naturally — who finally shut him up by interrupting.

"That's fine, fine, but make sure I get a look at those blueprints or whatever you call them for the extra floor by next week. I'm leaving town on Tuesday."

Mrs. Cochrane looked at her husband, then back at Alex. "The extra what?"

Alex stroked his mustache. The enormity of what Cochrane wanted now, the surprise lunatic demand he'd made a few hours ago was still so fresh, so infuriating, he couldn't even bring himself to say the words out loud.

"Floor," Ben answered for him. "It's not

18

tall enough, I want it taller. More floors. Four seems about right. Yeah, four." He crossed his hands over his stomach and leaned back in his chair until it stood on two legs.

Mrs. Cochrane sat motionless, staring down at her plate. Alex watched her covertly while Cochrane launched into a new monologue on what was wrong with Tammany Hall. When she finally looked up, he caught her eye; in it he read sympathy and — this time there was no doubt about it — amusement.

Dessert came. Over coffee, Cochrane made an abrupt announcement that the gentlemen were going to walk up the street to Canfield's casino to continue discussing plans for his house. "Sara, you can get a cab home."

Alex looked away, embarrassed. Was there no limit to the man's rudeness? Then he remembered — damnation! — he'd told Constance he'd take her to an after-theater party at ten o'clock. She was already angry with him for not bringing her to this dinner. He hadn't quite known how to explain that Draper, Snow and Ogden considered it bad form to take one's mistress to a client meeting. Now he'd have to buy Constance something to placate her; otherwise, she'd sulk for days. Not for the first time, it occurred to him that he wasn't rich enough yet for a mistress. Not one with Constance's tastes, anyway.

"Well, now, that sounds fine," Ogden exclaimed heartily and, Alex knew, insincerely. Bleeding humbug.

Mrs. Cochrane spoke up quietly. "Ben, have you forgotten it's Michael's birthday? You were gone before he woke up this morning; he hasn't seen you yet. Perhaps Mr. Ogden and Mr. McKie would like to join us at the house tonight."

"No, of course I hadn't forgotten. This is business. I'll see Michael when I get back, give him his present tomorrow." He looked over at Alex and Ogden, grinning. "Got my son a shotgun for his birthday. Four-ten smoothbore, pretty as you please."

Mrs. Cochrane's coffee cup clattered against the saucer. "You must be joking."

He looked back at her, fleshy face bland, but behind the dark eyes Alex thought he saw a quick glitter of spite. "What's wrong with that?" he asked irritably.

"He's too little to have a gun! Ben, for God's —"

"No, he's not."

20

Awkward pause. Alex studied his thumb-nail intently.

"I say he's not," Cochrane pressed. "Seven's not too young for a boy to have a gun, is it?"

"Why, no," Ogden answered faintly. "No, indeed."

"See there, Sara? What do you say, McKie?"

Bloody hell, the son of a bitch wanted unanimity. Alex stared at him without answering until the silence stretched too tight. His mind went blank, and out of the absolute quiet he heard himself say slowly, "No, probably not. No, seven seems about right."

Cochrane thumped the table in triumph while Alex sat motionless, gazing at nothing. Ogden started talking about his four-year-old grandson. When he couldn't stand it any longer, Alex looked up. Mrs. Cochrane's eyes on him were cool and unsurprised, and in them he saw the recognition of a betrayal.

When the waiter brought the check, Cochrane and Ogden started to wrangle over it. Without pausing to consider, Alex asked Mrs. Cochrane if he could get her a cab, and she accepted. Everyone stood up. Cochrane reached for his wife's coat; she found it first and held it to her middle, tight-armed, stepping back out of reach. "Good night," she said to Ogden, "it was a pleasure seeing you again." She said something to her husband in a low voice, and then walked away. Alex followed.

The rain had stopped. Puddles glimmered blue and purple on the asphalt, lit by the electric glare of streetlamps stretching in either direction along Fifth Avenue. He signaled to the hansom coming toward them from Forty-second Street, but when the horse drew near, he saw that the cab was occupied. He stepped back onto the sidewalk with an apologetic smile.

The misty air was chilly; she started to put on her coat. He took it from her to help her with it. She wore her pale blonde hair up, but fine wisps had come down and spilled over the collar. "It smells like spring tonight," she said softly.

He was thinking it smelled like her faint, feminine perfume. "Yes. I saw geese this morning."

"That's always a good sign."

He nodded. A minute went by. "You're English," he noted, feeling uncommonly tongue-tied. Odd; he was usually glib with beautiful women.

"Yes, from Somerset."

"I spent some time in London when I was a student."

"Did you enjoy yourself?"

"Very much."

Another pause.

"I've not been back in eight years," she said.

"Is that how long you've been married?"

"Yes. Eight years."

He put his hands in his pockets and rocked on his toes, staring across the street at the bright entrance to Delmonico's, as if the sight fascinated him. "I grew up in California. I haven't been back in a long time, either. My people are all dead."

"I'm sorry." She looked away, down the broad avenue. "I lost my mother a year ago."

He said he was sorry to that. Then, because he was beginning to feel desperate, he said, "She was a duchess, wasn't she? I think I heard that from someone."

Unexpectedly, she laughed; the tinkling lightness of the sound was at odds with the melancholy in her face. "I wonder who that might have been," she murmured, almost to herself. "But as I'm sure you've also heard, Mr. McKie, I'm *just plain Sara Cochrane* now."

He couldn't think of a word to say to

that. He wasn't sure if he was relieved or disappointed when an empty cab came into view then. He whistled it over. Mrs. Cochrane told him her address, although he already knew it. He handed her in, saying, "I've enjoyed meeting you," and she repeated it back to him politely. "I should have some preliminary drawings ready by early next week with the changes your husband asked for."

"Ah, yes." This time her smile was genuine. "For the new *floor.*"

He was wary of smiling back, considering it politic to keep playing the game that Cochrane was a reasonable man, a man deserving of respect. "I can bring them to your house if you like," he said seriously.

"You're welcome to do that. But it's Ben's approval you'll need, not mine."

"You don't take an interest in the building of your home?"

She smoothed the collar of her coat with her long, thin fingers and seemed to think that over. "But it's not a home, is it?"

He looked blank. "Sorry?"

"It's a monument."

"A monument —"

"To my husband's accomplishments." Immediately she looked down, as if regret-

24

ting her words. "Yes, bring them if you like. Good night, Mr. McKie," she said briskly, and sat back.

"Good night." He closed the door and watched her out of sight.

Cochrane and John Ogden came out of Sherry's a moment later. Alex joined them without speaking, and they walked north a few doors along the wet sidewalk to Canfield's. Even inside, amid the noise and the adamant gaiety, he couldn't forget the irony in Sara Cochrane's comely, sad-eyed face for a long time.

# Two

"He's not asleep. If he looks like he's sleeping it's nothing but a sham — I caught him with his light on not ten minutes ago."

"That's all right, Mrs. Drum, thank you. I'll just tiptoe in and say good night."

" 'Tis probably all that hard candy he ate this afternoon. I could hardly credit what all he told me you'd bought him."

"Yes, you're probably right. Good night."

Mrs. Drum hitched her dressing gown belt tighter, sniffed, and went back into her room. Sara stood in the dark hall for another minute, waiting for her irritation to subside. She and Michael's nanny had disliked each other since the moment they'd met, five years ago. In spite of that, or more likely because of it, Ben had decreed that Mrs. Drum would stay. She was English; she had "class." But sometimes Sara suspected Mrs. Drum's true value to Ben was that she spied on her for him.

"Mummy?"

She pushed the nursery door open.

Michael was sitting up in bed, clutching the big speckled frog they'd made out of papier-mâché that morning. His flannel nightshirt swallowed him, making him look more frail and bony than he was. The slant of moonlight through the curtain brightened his pale hair to silver. He was so beautiful to her, she could have cried.

"So, it's all true, then — you're still awake and too cheeky even to pretend you're not." She sat beside him and kissed his temples while he giggled and snuggled back into his pillow. "Did you and Mrs. Drum have a nice evening?"

"Oh yes, there were ladyfingers for dessert." He was unbuttoning her coat so he could stroke the satin lining inside. "Where's Daddy?"

"He had to work tonight. He said to give you a big kiss and tell you he loves you very, very much. And — that your present is coming soon."

His enormous blue eyes widened in delight. "What is it?"

"Well, I couldn't tell you that, could I?"

"Is it as nice as yours?"

"Mm, you'll have to be the judge." She'd given him roller skates and a magic lantern. "Now, off you go to sleep."

"I'm not sleepy. I'm seven now. Tell me a

story, Mum. Where did you go tonight? Did you see any fire engines?"

"I went to Sherry's and ate dinner with your father and two architects. There wasn't a fire engine in sight." They had a running joke about fire engines, for as a very little boy Michael had been convinced that the smoking, sparking engines went around *setting* fires, and that if one ever stopped at his house he would have to give the alarm.

"What's an architect?"

"Someone who builds buildings."

"A carpenter, then?"

It never paid to be imprecise with Michael. "No, sorry, a carpenter builds the building after the architect decides what it's going to look like. Ahead of time. He draws pictures of it so the carpenter will know what to do."

"Oh, I've got a picture for you," he exclaimed, remembering. "On the table, see it? It's a present."

Sara went and got it. "What is it, love? I don't want to turn on the light."

"Turn it on, turn it on!"

"Honestly, darling," she grumbled, switching on the light, and in the sudden brightness she looked down at a crayon drawing of two — women, she supposed they were, one of them very tall, holding hands in front of a crowd of little black dots. She exclaimed over it with great enthusiasm while Michael scrutinized her face for signs of disingenuity.

"What is it?" he asked at last, calling her bluff.

"Why, it's two beautiful ladies. In a sort of snowstorm, I think, with —"

"No, no, no." He shook her arm, laughing uproariously.

"What, then?"

"It's you and the Statue of Liberty. See? And these are all your immigrant people."

"Well, of course! How perfectly lovely. I adore it, I'm going to put it on the wall in my — no, I'm going to take it to the settlement house and hang it up for *everyone* to see. Shall I?"

"All right," he muttered, shy. "Let's read our book, Mum."

"Sweetheart, it's so late."

"Please? Please?"

"Don't beg, darling, it's unseemly. Very well, but just for a little while, and only because it's still your birthday."

She unbuttoned her shoes and slipped them off while Michael plumped his pillow and settled the covers over himself tidily, tucking them under his chin. She found the place in their current bedtime book, the *Morte d'Arthur*, and began to read. Merlin was Michael's favorite, more so even than Gawain or Lancelot, but tonight the magician's adventures weren't enough to keep sleep at bay for longer than ten minutes. Even as she read, and watched him struggling to stay awake with all his might, Sara knew she would need to read everything over again tomorrow night, when he would insist he'd never heard it — which, indeed, he hadn't.

She laid the book aside and tucked his blanket around him — a needless attention since he was a neat sleeper and frequently woke up in almost the same position he'd gone to bed in. His face in sleep always undid her, for then his pale, exquisite beauty was purest. It hurt her heart and filled her with a sharp, nameless anxiety.

Ben wanted to give him a gun. A *gun*. "Never," she said aloud, softly. He'd have to shoot her with it first. God! The anger surfaced suddenly, quickly, familiar as bitter medicine to an invalid. She thought of how he'd coerced the two men at dinner tonight into taking his side. John Ogden's capitulation hadn't surprised her very much, but for a little while she'd expected better of Mr. McKie. Why? She'd heard of him before, though little more than society gossip — that he liked women a great deal and was considered to be quite a "catch." She pictured his clean, strong features, too handsome for his own good, and the silky-looking mustache he wore over his wide, rather eloquent mouth. It wasn't hard to see why a man who looked like Mr. McKie would enjoy cordial relations with a great number of women.

But he'd caved in when Ben had pressed him about Michael's present, merely to safeguard his fat architect's commission. He'd regretted it afterwards — she'd seen that in his face — but that didn't change what he'd done. She couldn't like him for it.

In the hall, the clock struck ten. She smoothed back her son's silver-blond hair and kissed him, whispering an endearment, then switched off the electric light and tiptoed from the room.

On the bureau in her own room, the housekeeper had left her a message. Miss Hubbard had called on the telephone at seven this evening; would Mrs. Cochrane please call back at her convenience? Sara would have loved to talk to Lauren, to tell her about Ben's "extra floor" — that would make her laugh — and to find out if her new art instructor was still as brilliant and fascinating as she'd thought a week ago. But Lauren lived with her parents, and ten was a little late for them. She would call her tomorrow.

She undressed in front of the wardrobe and put on her yellow nightgown and flannel robe — for in spite of Mr. McKie's prediction about the imminence of spring, it was chilly in her room tonight and the flannel dressing gown was welcome.

The maid had turned her bed down; it looked inviting in the lamplight, her book beside the pillow, sewing basket on the table. But she felt restless. Even though she was tired, she suspected this would be one of those nights when she wouldn't sleep. They had been coming more frequently lately, and she didn't know why. "What are you *thinking* about when you're just lying there?" Lauren had wanted to know when she'd told her about her insomnia. She honestly couldn't answer. She worried about Michael, of course, but not incessantly. She worried about the settlement house on Forsyth Street because the suffering and injustice she saw there every day went far beyond her puny ability to ameliorate. But it seemed to Sara that her sleeplessness arose more from a dearth, not a wealth, of life-concerns. Still, sustained unhappiness manifested itself in many subtle ways, and insomnia was probably one of the less alarming ones. No doubt she ought to count her blessings.

So. How would she occupy herself tonight? She had no letters to write; her book didn't really interest her. Then she remembered that Paren Matthews, who ran the Forsyth Street Settlement, had asked her to help him draft a request for aid from his alma mater, Dartmouth College. "You write so much better than I do, Sara," he'd wheedled; "you've got that English flair for the rhetorical." "You mean I tell lies better than you do," she'd countered. She smiled as she opened her writing desk in the alcove between the windows and sat down.

Her draft took much longer than she'd expected, but when it was finished she thought it was rather good. They ought to do much more of this. As it was, the settlement scraped by on desultory contributions from churches and charities. Who else could they dun? Companies, other universities. Social clubs. Why not Tammany itself? She started to make a list.

It was after midnight when she closed her desk, and a moment later she heard footsteps on the stairs. She rose to go to her dressing table and began to unpin her hair. The steps came nearer, along the hall now. She paused to listen, arms up, then started in dull surprise when the door to her room swung open. Ben stood in the threshold, swinging a dripping umbrella, still wearing his hat.

"Saw the light," he said, and came all the way in.

"I was just going to bed."

He sat down at the foot of the big four-poster and leaned back on his elbows, watching her in the mirror over the dressing table. The message from Lauren lay by his side. He picked it up, read it, made a sound of disgust, and sailed it across the room. "What's your anarchist friend want this time?"

Sara pulled a long blond hair from the brush and examined it under the lamplight. If she didn't answer, he would start a quarrel, and she was too tired to fight with him now. "I don't know, I didn't speak to her," she said levelly. Even from across the room she could smell the alcohol on him, and under it the hint of a woman's cologne.

"What did you think of McKie?"

She answered noncommittally. It wasn't

34

a question anyway, it was a formality, a conversational lead-in to preface his own opinion.

"Seems all right to me, maybe a little stuck-up. Can't hold his liquor worth a damn."

She looked up. "Did he get drunk?"

"No, he just quit drinking. Just stopped." He took off his hat and shook water from it onto the coverlet. "His firm's the best, though. They built Mark Workman's house on Bellevue."

"Cottage," she corrected dryly. "That marble Renaissance palace is called a 'cottage' in Newport."

He barked out a laugh. "That's right! A cottage!" It tickled him. "A cottage, can you beat that?" Then he sobered. "You'll have to spend the summer up there."

"What?"

"Supervising the work."

She turned around to face him. "But — I thought you would want to do that."

"Oh, really? When?"

She spread her hands. "I don't —"

"I couldn't get up except on weekends, for Christ's sake, and not even that half the time. McKie wants somebody there the whole time, to okay things. So you and Michael can rent a house or take rooms in a hotel for the season. It'll be good for us."

She knew he meant socially. She thought of the plans she and Paren had made for the summer at the settlement house — a young women's social club that would meet in the evenings, a children's theater group, a sewing class. How arrogant she had been to imagine that she was indispensable to any of them — she knew that, and yet she'd worked so hard to organize the programs and she wanted to know how they turned out. And she would be letting Paren down.

But she knew better than to say any of that to Ben. He despised her work, ridiculed it at every opportunity. As far as he was concerned, her only legitimate occupation was advancing the Cochranes socially. That was what he'd paid for, that was the deal — although she hadn't known it was the deal until after she'd married him. No matter. She knew it now.

"Maybe I'll buy a steam yacht," he was saying. "Vanderbilt's got one, parks it in the bay like a goddamn rajah. It's not like I can't afford one as big as his. Who the hell is he?" Sara didn't answer. "Minnie says to go slow, sometimes it's years before you 'take' in Newport."

She looked at him then. "When did

*Minnie* say that?" she asked, icily calm.

He had the grace to prevaricate. "Long time ago, I don't remember."

Liar. Minnie Russell had been his mistress — one of them — for nine years. They were 'protégées,' he'd told Sara when he'd introduced them, long ago. In a way, she had Minnie to thank for her marriage, for it was she who had advised Ben all those years ago to broach New York society by taking a titled, aristocratic bride. Disastrous advice, as it had turned out. What Minnie was to him now, Sara wasn't sure, but despite his denials she knew he still saw her and still listened to her counsel.

"So, anyway," he pursued, incapable of staying on the defensive for long. "You'll go up with Michael next month and take care of things."

"Very well, if that's what you want. But I've never even seen the plans for this house, you know."

"Whose fault is that?"

"Shall we not speak of fault, just once?"

He grinned nastily. "Sure." A moment passed. He stood up slowly and moved toward her.

She stiffened with premonition. By reflex, she spun back around to face the mirror. "I want to talk to you about Michael's birthday present," she said quickly.

Sly triumph flashed in his big, fleshy face. "What's the problem?" He put his surprisingly small, hair-covered hands on her shoulders. "The boy's old enough to learn how to shoot." He slipped his fingers inside her robe. "Don't worry, Sare, I'll take care of him. He'll be fine."

She fought to repress a shudder. "Ben, he's not. He's so little, and he's fearful, he's not like —"

"That's it, that's it exactly. He's a mewling little milksop."

"No! He's —"

"You've turned him into a coward. He's a sniveling little —" He pushed her down when she tried to jump up, and his hands slid around to cover her bare breasts. He leaned over and spoke in her ear. "I think I'll take him on a hunting trip as soon as I get back from Chicago. We'll go to Long Island, out to Montauk, maybe, and shoot some birds. Ducks, rabbits, whatever we can find."

"Damn you," she whispered. Tears burned behind her eyes.

"You want to talk about this?"

"Damn you —" She broke off; he was

pinching her nipples lightly, threateningly. She held very still.

"Want to talk about it some more? Do you?"

She nodded slowly, not looking at him.

Abruptly he released her. "Good. Let's talk." He unfastened his tie and whipped it out of his collar with a violent jerk, smiling at her. "I'll be in my room. Don't be long, Sare."

She heard the door close and glanced up. The sight of her face in the mirror appalled her; she hadn't seen that look in a long time — months. What had made her think he was finally through with her? What madness had made her forget that he loved to toy with her, to lull her into the illusion of well-being just before he sprang the trap? And always, always, he used Michael for the bait.

She stood up. It was only sex, after all. It was only her body. Except on special occasions, when he wanted to punish her, the worst was over as far as their marriage was concerned. Years ago, when they had both felt betrayed, it had been a fiery nightmare of rows, violence, and forced intimacy. But their mutual fury had finally burned itself out until only bitterness and cynicism were left — and bone-deep resentment. Lovemaking was no longer a violation, it was nothing. Two bodies temporarily connected — an abstraction. Not real. She had grown expert in making it not real.

She threw her hairbrush down on the dressing table and unconsciously started to button the top of her dressing gown — then stopped, thinking, *how foolish, he'll only take it off in a minute.* She wanted his hands on her as briefly as possible. Watching her reflection, daring herself to betray shame or revulsion by the slightest sign, she stripped her robe off, then her nightgown. She dreaded the look of possession and triumph she would see in his eyes if she went to him naked — but he would finish with her sooner that way. So it would be worth it.

# Three

"I'm sorry, truly I am. If there was anything I could do to change this, Paren, you know I would."

"Well, change it, then," Paren Matthews exclaimed with an artificial laugh. "I don't understand. You say you don't want to go, and yet you're going anyway."

"It's something I have to do, that's all."

"Have to do?"

Sara sighed with frustration. "Ben and I have decided it's something I should do. I'm sorry. We've worked so hard on these projects — believe me, no one wants to see them implemented more than I do, but there's nothing I can do. It's — for the whole summer, beginning in June." In dismay, she watched Paren turn his back on her, ostensibly to look out the window, but really to hide his displeasure. "Margaret can take my place, can't she? She's especially good with the sewing classes, and the children adore her." He didn't answer. She laid her hand on his arm. "Please don't be angry. It'll work out somehow, it always does."

He turned back, and his kind face behind the full red beard looked pained. "I don't understand," he said again. "We need you here, Sara. I know you're only a volunteer, you're free to do whatever you like. But you tell me you have to spend the summer in *Newport,* supervising the construction of a *mansion.*" He almost sneered the words, incapable of disguising his bewilderment and distaste. "Maybe I've made a mistake in thinking the settlement house mattered to you. If so, I apologize."

"Oh, Paren." She dropped her hand and backed away.

"I'm sorry," he said quickly. "That probably wasn't fair."

"No, that wasn't fair."

He ran his hands through his untidy red hair. "But — *why* do you have to go? Is your husband *making* you go?"

"Don't be absurd," she laughed, "of course not." The precise nature of her failed marriage was something she had never fully confided in anyone, not even Lauren. Paren was a good friend, and they had grown close over the last few years; nevertheless, to speak candidly to him about her relationship with Ben was unthinkable. The outcome of her reserve — or shame, or shyness, or maybe just habit — was intense loneliness, but she'd long ago accepted it as part of the price that had to be paid for the profound mistake she'd made eight years ago.

"Mrs. Cochrane? The English students, they are almost all here now. They are waiting for you downstairs."

"Thank you, Boris, I'll be right there," she told the little Hungarian boy who helped out at the house for five cents a day. She faced Paren one last time. "What else can I say to you? It's not for another month — I can train someone to take my place if you don't think Margaret is up to it. Whatever it takes, I'll do it. We *will* make it work, I promise."

"Yes, of course, I haven't a doubt of it. I'm just being selfish. I don't want you to go because I'll miss seeing you. It's as simple as that."

She smiled with relief. "I'll miss you, too."

He reached for her hands and held them tightly. "I mean it, Sara."

"I mean it, too!"

He let her go abruptly. "Go teach your class."

She moved to the door, disconcerted; he

seemed almost angry again. "Let's talk more about it later, shall we? Please?"

"Yes, yes." He waved his hand without looking at her, already sorting through a stack of papers on his desk. She went out frowning.

Her advanced English class met two evenings a week in the basement of the five-story brick building which housed the new, expanded quarters of the Forsyth Street Settlement. Her pupils — all but Mr. Yelteles — were fluent in English by now, and her class ought more aptly to have been called American culture. With very little direction from her anymore, the participants met to discuss anything and everything about this strange new land they'd come to, some fairly recently, some years ago. Today, as usual, they hadn't waited for her, and the painted brick walls resounded with a lively, raucous discussion already in progress. Mr. Yelteles was smoking again. Sara made a shocked face, and he dropped his cigarette on the floor and stamped on it as if it were a dangerous insect — their pleasant, unvarying ritual every time they saw each other. She took her seat in the center of the ragged semicircle of chairs and called out, "Good afternoon, ladies and gentlemen."

Eight voices echoed, "Good afternoon, Mrs. Cochrane," and immediately went back to talking, seemingly all at once.

"Where's Tasha?" she leaned over to ask Mr. Yelteles, who was smiling his beatific smile at her.

When he shrugged, his eyebrows almost reached to his high, silvery hairline. "Ain't comm yet. You need suspen'ehs? Cullah bottens?"

"How much are stockings today?"

"Six cents, such a deal."

"We'll talk later. Rachele? Let us all hear what you and Katrin are discussing, won't you?" Gradually the room quieted and the talk focused, as she had hoped, on roughly one speaker at a time. Konstantin went on at flamboyant length about the trouble he had to endure nightly to fend off the amorous advances of his employer's wife. Turkish and darkly handsome, Konstantin had arrived in America six years ago. He'd started out as a newspaper boy, with just enough English to shout the paper's name and enough arithmetic to make change. Now he worked as a waiter in a Russian tea room, soaking up the erudite harangues of the socialist literati who frequented it. His long-term goal in life was to attend City College and become a playwright. In the shorter term, he wanted to seduce Rachele, and he calculated that he was a little over halfway to the goal.

"Enough already," snapped Mr. Clayman, the upholsterer.

"Yah, enough," seconded his wife. They wanted to talk about whether Mrs. Clayman should give up her job in the cigar factory so they could start a family, or keep it so they could afford a better apartment. Everybody had an opinion and there were dozens of factors to take into consideration. The discussion ended the way they all did if related even remotely to personal money matters: Mrs. Cochrane was asked to make the final decision.

Sara never spoke of her personal life, never hinted at what it might be like on the days when she was not on Forsyth Street. She dressed simply; she took the Third Avenue Elevated to work. Nevertheless, somehow, she was never sure how, it had become common knowledge that Mrs. Cochrane was a very rich lady. She was, as a consequence, an object of great interest and speculation. For them she stood as a shining example of the typical successful American, no more and no less, and that she was an immigrant like them only enhanced her appeal.

How much were the Claymans paying now for their two-room apartment? she asked. Fifteen dollars a month, but it was a dump, a "stoop," and whores lived on the first floor. They wanted to move to a three-room flat on Chrystie Street because it had a range, a bath, and a water closet, but the rent was thirty dollars. How badly did they want to have a child? she asked directly — frankness was the order of the day in this class. Mr. Clayman said, "Well, you know, we'd like it, it's a thing we want, we have been waiting —" when all at once Mrs. Clayman burst into tears. She sobbed for several minutes while Rachele and Katrin patted her on the back and Mr. Clayman blew his nose.

"Well," Sara said faintly. Everyone looked sheepish. "I think that eliminates Chrystie Street. Mrs. Akers told me of an apartment house on Avenue A with two-room flats for twenty-two dollars a month. They have no water closets, but they're clean and respectable. Do you think you could afford seven dollars more a month? If so, you could quit your job and begin a family there."

This was greeted with great enthusiasm. No one could find any fault with the plan, and Mrs. Clayman said she thought she could make seven dollars a month at home, sewing lace on collars for the shirt-waist factory. Eight faces beamed at Sara, as pleased as if J. Pierpont Morgan had personally advised them on their finances. She shook her head at them and asked Rachele how things were going at the tailor shop.

She should have known that would open a can of worms. Rachele sat on the council of her local union, the Brotherhood of Tailors, and her opinions concerning management's greed and viciousness were growing more vocal each day. Sara was attempting to redirect the conversation when she glanced up and saw Tasha in the doorway. She motioned for her to come in, but the girl hung back. "Come," she called. "Tasha, come and join us!"

Conversation continued without a pause while Tasha sidled in and took her customary place next to Mr. Yelteles. Sara sent her a welcoming smile, but she ducked her head and huddled deeper into her shawl. "Are you all right?" she murmured. Tasha nodded vigorously, not looking at her.

But she wasn't; something was very wrong. Sara lost the thread of the discussion of a play at a new Bowery theater and finally dismissed the class ten minutes ahead of time. Mr. Yelteles wanted to "schmooze" with her, as usual, which meant standing outside and listening to his *mayselakh* — anecdotes — while he smoked cigarettes. She told him she couldn't "schmooze" today, and when Tasha got up to leave, she stopped her. "Stay and talk to me," she invited, holding on to the girl's cold hand while the others said good-bye and filed out.

"What's wrong? You look so upset."

"No, no, it's nothing." The lustrous black eyes slid away, evading her. "Sorry to be late today. I could not help it."

"Come and sit." Sara gestured to the wooden bench along the wall; the girl hesitated, but finally took a seat beside her. Sara watched her in perplexity. Tasha was always quiet, even aloof, but Sara thought they had become friends lately, and this unapproachability wasn't like her. "Are you ill?" She shook her head. "What, then? What made you late?"

Tasha's throat worked; she looked as if she was going to cry. Her shawl slipped. She reached for it — and Sara saw that the sleeve of her bright red dress was ripped to the elbow.

"Tasha! What's happened?" She took her

shoulders and forced the girl to meet her eyes. "Has someone hurt you? Tell me!"

"Yes, yes." She covered her face with her hands and mumbled rapidly in the hybrid mix of languages Sara now knew to be German, Russian, and Rumanian.

Sara seized her by the wrists and pulled her hands away. "Speak English, Natasha," she commanded sharply, giving her a quick shake. She judged her to be on the verge of hysteria. "Tell me what happened to you. *Now.*"

"Mrs. Cochrane, I'm so afraid!"

"Why?"

"A man — he follows me. Today he found me alone and he touched me. I ran, but he said he would get me!"

"My God! Who is it? Do you know him?"

"No. He is dark, he speaks like a Greek or a Russian, I don't know. He's strong — big —"

"What did he do to you?"

"He touched me, here." She indicated her breasts. "I was coming home from work, to eat something before the class. No one was in the lobby of my building and he caught me there."

Tasha lived alone in one tiny room in a Fourth Avenue tenement. "You say he's followed you before?"

"Yes, often."

"And you've never told anyone about him?"

"No. Never until today has he touched me, he has only — talked. Now I am afraid to go home." She hid her face in her hands again.

Sara put an arm around her shoulders and sat quietly until she stopped trembling. Then she pulled her gently to her feet. "Come, we must tell Paren, and then we'll tell the police."

"The police! No!"

"But they'll *help* you, Tasha." She read fear in the dark gypsy eyes. "Don't be afraid, I promise you it'll be all right. Do you trust me?"

"Yes, yes, you I trust, but —"

"Then come. We'll talk to the police together. They'll find this man, and then you'll be safe." She held out her hand. After a tense moment, Tasha took it, and the two women climbed the stairs together.

# Four

"Do you want some tea, Lauren? I can ring for it. Or a drink?"

"No, that's all right, don't make them do it twice."

"Well, why don't you just *stay* for tea, then?"

Lauren made a face which would have been indecipherable to anyone else, but Sara read it perfectly. It said: Not if Ben's coming, thanks all the same. "No, but I will stay long enough to meet this Mr. McKie. He sounds interesting. So, you were saying. You called the police — ?"

"We called the police, and they came and took all the information, and then they went home with Tasha to look around and make sure she was all right. I feel so awful, Lauren, so completely helpless. I gave her some money, I don't even know why — it was all I could think of. She wouldn't take it at first, until I made her."

"Maybe she'll find another place to live."

"Maybe. But if this man is really following her, what good will it do?"

Lauren shook her head in sympathy. "Have you talked to her since then?"

"No. It happened on Friday. I called Paren yesterday and again this morning, and he said Jonathan had stopped by her place twice to check on her."

"Who's Jonathan?"

"One of the residents — he lives at the settlement house while he goes to school to study social work."

"Is this girl really a gypsy? What's her last name?"

"Eminescu. Her mother was a gypsy; she says her father was a count." When Lauren looked skeptical, Sara smiled and shrugged her shoulders.

"Did she come here all alone?"

"Yes, about two years ago. She started out selling fish from a cart on Delancy Street."

"Good God."

"Now she works in a sewing factory. She does exquisite work — you should see her clothes. She makes them all herself, from scraps her employer lets her take home. She's a fashion plate!"

Restless, she got up from her chair and went to the parlor window. The May sky was cloudless, perfect. A house sparrow with a straw in its beak flew into the maple tree in a blur of gray and chestnut. Thirty-second Street was a quiet, clean, orderly bastion of respectability and wealth — and a world away from the teeming tenements of Fourth Avenue. What was Tasha doing right now? Sitting alone in her miserable little room, listening for a sound outside her locked door?

"It doesn't do any good to fret about this, Sara."

"No, I know. It's just that she's so helpless. She distrusts the police — and what can they do for her anyway?"

"I'm sure she'll be all right. This man probably just wants to scare her."

"I wish you could meet her. You'd like her independence. And she's so striking — not really beautiful, but once you see her you don't forget her."

"Come over here," Lauren said, patting the sofa. "Let's talk about *me* for a change."

Sara smiled, recognizing her friend's attempt to cheer her up for what it was, and went to sit beside her. "Yes, I do want to hear all about *you*. How is your painting class going?"

"Boring, boring."

"Really? But I thought you were in love with Mr. — Watson?"

"Whitson, and he turns out to be rather a limp rag."

"Oh, too bad."

"So I've decided to go to Paris."

Sara laughed — and broke off when Lauren didn't join in. "What? Are you serious?"

"Deadly."

She sat back weakly. "When?"

"In a few weeks. Well, you needn't look like that! After all, you were ready to abandon me for the whole summer while you go off to Newport."

It was absurd to feel this bereft — and this stupid urge to burst into tears. "You're absolutely right. But Paris is so far away!"

"But do you know, Sara, you can call there now on the telephone?"

"Yes, but Ben tried to place a call to London the other day, and he and this man just *shouted* at each other until they finally gave up and rang off." She waved her hand in the air; that was neither here nor there. "I'm glad for you, truly I am. What will you do?"

"Study. At the Louvre, with an artist named Jean Laucoeur. Oh, Sara, think of it — he's a genius, and he wants *me*."

"You never even told me you were thinking of doing this." She tried not to sound accusing.

"Because I never thought he would take me. It was such a daydream, the chance seemed so small. But he wrote me, *finally,* and he said my work has 'resonance.' Resonance!" She grabbed Sara's hands and squeezed them tight.

She had to laugh. Before she could reply, the maid announced from the doorway, "Mr. McKie, ma'am."

Sara rose to meet Mr. McKie in the center of the room. She'd forgotten how tall he was. His clothes were conservative in the extreme — a gray frock coat with silk lapels, plain trousers, and a broad knotted tie of a darker gray — but he wore them with such unself-conscious assurance, they seemed almost dashing. "How good of you to come on a Sunday," she told him, shaking hands. "I know my husband's schedule can sometimes be an inconvenience."

"Not at all, I was delighted to come." He smiled, and she noticed what she hadn't been able to see in the artificial light at Sherry's — that his eyes were intensely blue and his dark, blond-tipped lashes were nearly as long as a woman's.

She led him over to the couch, where Lauren still sat curled in the corner like a cat. "Lauren, this is Mr. McKie, our new architect. Miss Hubbard is an old friend."

Lauren stretched a hand up, with a look on her face that Sara knew well: full of charm and coy delight, it was the one she wore whenever she met a new man who interested her. Sara folded her arms while the two of them spoke pleasantly and easily, discovering within a few sentences that they had mutual friends. Did Mr. McKie find Lauren attractive? Well, Sara thought, what man wouldn't? She was small and petite, hardly taller than a child, but still unmistakably feminine. Huge, beautiful green eyes dominated her wry, intelligent face. If men were sometimes put off, it was because of her determinedly eccentric dress. Today she could have passed for a gypsy herself in a beaded smock of orange and yellow printed muslin. She'd wrapped an Indian scarf around her head for a turban, hiding the pretty brown hair she wore short in defiance of fashion.

When she and Mr. McKie ran out of conversation for a moment, Lauren unwound gracefully and stood up. "I hate to go, but I must — I've promised to watch some friends rehearse for a new play at the DeWitt Theatre."

It was the first Sara had heard. She looked at her watch. Nearly four; Ben would be home soon. He was infallibly rude to Lauren, so she avoided him whenever possible. Sara often wondered what he disliked about Lauren more — her ideological opposition to everything he stood for or simply that she and Sara loved each other, and their friendship was something he couldn't control?

"I'll call you, Sara," Lauren said, pulling on a fringed shawl.

"Yes, you'd better. I want to hear all about Paris."

"Good-bye, Mr. McKie, it's been a great pleasure."

"The pleasure was mine." They shook hands again, and Lauren glided out. A hint of her lemon-and-clove cologne lingered in the room after her.

"Please, sit down," Sara invited, and Mr. McKie took a seat on the just-vacated couch. "I can't think what's keeping Ben. He went to his office at noon, but he said he'd be home in a few hours. He knew you were coming to tea, of course." Indeed, he'd commanded her to invite him so he could see the revised plans for the Newport house before he left for Chicago. "I see you've brought your blueprints — is that what you call them?" She indicated the long cardboard tube he set on the floor at his feet.

"No, these are the design development drawings; blueprints come a little later."

"Oh, I see."

"And then we usually call them construction documents. That's when we convert the design concept into feet and inches, door swings, window frames, things like that. We're not quite to that point yet with your house."

"How long will it take to build it?"

"A lot depends on the weather. If we can get started in early June, it should be up by early autumn."

"So soon?"

"That's just the exterior. You couldn't move in before Christmas."

She could tell from his expression and the careful way he spoke that he was privately amazed that she didn't already know the answers to these questions. She could understand his confusion; it was her house — ostensibly — and she was the one who had been elected to supervise its construction. How could he know that Ben wanted her advice and opinions on his new architectural toy about as much as he wanted Michael's?

"Would you care to see the drawings?"

She hesitated. In a way, she was curious — about the house, and even more about this man's skill as an architect. But the ultimate pointlessness of it dissuaded her. "Let's wait for Ben," she suggested.

"Fine."

She thought he sounded faintly disappointed. The clock struck the quarter hour. "I'm sure he'll be here soon, but would you like to have some tea now?"

"No, that's all right, I'll wait."

"A drink, then."

"No, thanks."

She relaxed her hands on the arms of her chair and returned his disconcertingly direct gaze with studied casualness. His manners were perfect; he had never been anything but gentlemanly in their brief acquaintance. Nevertheless, the edginess she'd felt alone in his company last week returned now, and she wondered why.

"Have you lived in this house long?" he asked.

"Eight years."

"You didn't buy it together, then, you and Ben?"

"No, he bought it about a year before I met him." As he crossed his long legs and glanced around the drawing room, she found herself trying to guess what he was thinking. He kept his handsome face pleasantly bland and accepting, but she suspected it was a mask. She suspected he was a diplomat. What did he really think of her home — and of her?

Alex hardly knew what he thought. Mrs. Cochrane and her house presented a powerful paradox he wasn't yet able to reconcile. There she sat, cool and elegant, her bright gold hair upswept in that loose, effortless-looking, two-tiered affair so many women tried nowadays but few achieved. He liked her black silk suit and the humorously masculine waistcoat and tie she wore with it. Her skirt was the fashionable new "instep" length, so called because it revealed three-quarters of the shoes. Composed, genteel, unaffected, lovely — and she was sitting on an ugly chair in a pretentious room, surrounded by furnishings of surpassing stupidity. He'd thought of her often since their last meeting, and not only for the obvious reason — because she attracted him. The puzzle of her marriage intrigued him as well, keeping him pondering what life with a man like Bennet Cochrane might be like for such a woman. Now to that mystery he could add the baffling incongruity of this wretched house.

He stroked his mustache and asked innocently, "Would you mind giving me a tour? While we wait for your husband." He thought she hesitated, but then she said, "Yes, of course," rose to her feet graciously, and led him out to the hall.

They walked across its pinched, dark, uninviting width, past a sunken palm garden and into another drawing room, this one uglier and more grandiose than the other — something he would not have thought possible. Mrs. Cochrane pointed out, without enthusiasm, the most noticeable features — the English bog oak dadoes and wainscoting, the crimson stamped-leather wall coverings, the Spanish altar cloths of gold and garnet plush used as portieres to separate this room from the music room. On his own he took note of a Chinese ceramic pug dog standing knee-high beside the fireplace and a hideous gasolier hung over a damask-upholstered ottoman, the two creating a sort of static carousel that blocked traffic and devoured space.

"Who decorated the house?" he had to know.

"Parker and Stine, I believe."

That explained a good deal; Parker and Stine's specialty was ostentation and pretense. Still, even they had to have had an accomplice in the homeowner to commit an atrocity this flagrant.

She showed him the dining room and the conservatory, billiard room and smoking and sitting rooms, halls and salons. His favorite was Cochrane's combined office and trophy room, a truly horrible menage of stuffed ram and stag heads, a collection of vicious-looking medieval weapons, hunting prints of stunning mediocrity, leopard and bear and tiger skin rugs, hanging snowshoes, dead birds mounted on stalks — all against a background of black walnut woodwork, Beauvais tapestries, Oriental ceramics, Renaissance Revival bric-a-brac, and anything else that could possibly be crammed into the big, dark, stupendously depressing chamber. Even Mrs. Cochrane couldn't disguise her distaste for this room, and hung back in the doorway until he had looked his fill.

They wandered dispiritedly back toward the first drawing room, both pensive and silent. As they crossed the entry hall, the front door burst open and a small, yellow-haired boy barreled in. "Mum!" he shouted, then skidded to a comical halt at the sight of a strange man with his mother.

Alex's first thought was that the

Cochranes must have two children, for this could hardly be seven-year-old Michael. This boy looked closer to five than seven, with his spindly body and his big, intelligent head on a neck so thin Alex could have wrapped one hand around it. He was a tow-head blond with pale skin the color of skim milk, bony-shouldered, and sharp-kneed. But it was Michael because Sara said, "Hullo, darling, come and meet Mr. McKie. This is my son, Michael."

They shook hands solemnly. The boy had a pair of roller skates tied over his shoulder; the wheels left dust marks on the short jacket he wore over a white Russian blouse with knickers and black stockings. He'd come from the Lenox Lyceum, he told Alex politely but breathlessly, where he'd learned how to skate backwards. "You wouldn't care to see me do it now, would you?" he asked tentatively, then threw caution to the winds and yanked on his mother's sleeve, begging, "Oh, come out and watch me, Mummy, do, I'll stay on the sidewalk, I promise!"

A woman's irritable voice came through the open door — "I told you to *wait*" — just before its owner stepped over the threshold. She broke off when she saw the three in the hall, and Alex took note that

64

her ill-humored face matched her voice perfectly. Short, going soft as she approached middle age, she had gray-streaked blond hair that she wore in braids pinned on top of her head. "He ran ahead of me all afternoon," she informed Sara in aggrieved tones, pulling off a woolen scarf that was much too warm for the day and probably accounted for the perspiration beading her pink, discontented countenance.

The boy looked at his feet, whether with contrition or sullenness Alex couldn't tell. "That was naughty of you, Michael," Sara said evenly, "you must mind Mrs. Drum. Come and have your tea now, and after —"

"But don't you want to see me skate? I can do it, Mum, really I can, come and look —"

"He'll have to wash before his tea," Mrs. Drum interrupted imperiously. "He's covered with grime. I've never seen a child for dirt like this one. Come upstairs, young man, and get changed."

Sara put a light hand on the back of Michael's head. "You know, I think just this once he'll have his bath later. Thank you, Mrs. Drum, I'll send him up to you in half an hour."

Alex and Michael looked back and forth

at the locked gazes of the two women, both fascinated by the undercurrent of war going on between them. The battle was swift but bitter. Mrs. Drum's round hazel eyes turned muddy with resentment and her colorless lips thinned. "Very good, Mrs. Cochrane," she said with eerie indifference, then turned and trudged up the wide oak staircase while they all watched.

"Well," Sara said faintly. She could feel the flush on her cheeks. Her eyes sidled over Mr. McKie's interested gaze as she reached for Michael's hands to examine them. "Good lord, she's right," she murmured, and started to laugh.

Michael's infectious giggle prompted Alex to laugh with them. With their heads together, faces alight with the thrill of conspiracy, the resemblance between mother and son intrigued him. Had Sara Longford's hair been that brilliant shade of yellow-white when she was a girl? he wondered. It was honey-gold now in the light from the open door, heavy and rich and lush. They had exactly the same eyes, though — blue-gray and guileless, and full of mischief at the moment.

Sara straightened. "Really, darling, you are a fright. Go and wash your hands," she said in a no-nonsense voice, pointing

Michael toward the lavatory at the end of the hall. "Then come and join us — we're in the blue parlor."

"Okay."

"And put your skates by the door."

"Okay!"

He trotted off. Sara smiled at Alex, feeling more relaxed with him than she ever had. "Mrs. Drum can be a bit of a trial," she confided.

"So I see. Why do you keep her on?"

"Oh . . . we're used to her," she hedged. "And Michael's getting so big, it won't be long before he won't need a nanny at all." She went to the hall table and rang the bell for tea. When the servant arrived carrying a tray, Sara said, "Shall we?" to Alex, leading him back along the paneled hall to the drawing room.

After his tour, the blue parlor seemed almost subdued, or at least less relentlessly over-decorated than most of the other rooms; he suspected it was, for that reason, where Mrs. Cochrane chose to do her private entertaining. "I can't think what's keeping Ben," she told him again as she poured tea into porcelain cups so paper-thin he could almost see through them. He wondered if it was being English that just naturally endowed a woman with that courtly, impossibly refined manner of handing over a teacup. While he made casual conversation, his mind sauntered along its worn and familiar path whenever he contemplated a beautiful woman, turning over the pros and cons, the advantages and obstacles to trying to take her to bed. Would Sara Cochrane be easy to persuade? Her sour marriage would seem to be no deterrent. And although her behavior toward him was still somewhat reserved, experience had taught him that nothing was more deceptive than a lady's outward demeanor, or less compatible with her true character once she'd made up her mind to be indiscreet.

Nevertheless, his fine-tuned instincts warned him she would be a challenge. She was kind, for one thing — he knew it from her gentle manner, the way she tried to draw him out, the way she treated her son — and cold-blooded seduction was always harder — not impossible, but harder — for him to countenance under those circumstances. Constance, for example, had many fine character traits, but compassion for others wasn't noticeably among them. Besides kindness, though, Mrs. Cochrane had another quality — delicacy, perhaps; he hesitated to call it integrity because the thought was too daunting to his plans — that also tempered his expectations of success. At the very least, then, he would have to go slowly. And carefully, for he'd never broken his own stringent rule of staying away from the wives of clients. The rewards had never seemed worth the risk. Until now. Which was odd, since the rewards for making Ben Cochrane a happy man were much higher than any he'd ever been offered before.

Michael raced into the room, making skating noises. His mother's low-voiced admonishment transformed him into a gentleman in the blink of an eye. Wet comb tracks in his hair testified to the pains he'd taken with his toilette, evidently for Alex's benefit. He sat next to him on the sofa and politely devoured wafer-thin watercress sandwiches, cinnamon cookies, and little square sponge cakes, washed down with three cups of hot chocolate. Alex, who almost always felt uncomfortable around children, warmed to him immediately. He'd thought of being charming to Michael as a means of endearing himself to his mother, but clearly he was the one being charmed. He wasn't sure what it was about the child that appealed to him so strongly; his elegant shyness, perhaps, and his lightning-quick changes from earnest to silly and back again as he made a manly effort to participate in the grown-ups' conversation. He was impressed when Alex told him he was an architect, and begged to be shown the plans for "Daddy's new house" when he learned they were inside the long, intriguing tube of cardboard on the floor. "Oh, no, you needn't —" Sara started to protest when Alex agreed. He assured her it was quite all right, while privately contrasting her indifference with her son's interest in the house they were both going to live in one day.

Opening the tube, he spread his drawings out in the center of the sofa, anchoring the ends with pillows. Michael stared down at them until it occurred to him that some comment was called for, and then he said, "Very nice," in such a false, politely adult tone that Alex had to hold back a laugh. Obviously his drawings were a letdown. In the simplest terms he could think of, he began to try to explain what the neatly sketched plans and sections and elevations meant.

Sara stood up. Listening to Mr. McKie's careful, measured sentences finally piqued her curiosity, and she couldn't resist going closer for a look at his work. At first she could only sympathize with Michael's disappointment, for the drawings looked only vaguely like a house — more like webs or networks of wires with numbers and arrows scattered around at random. But her eyes shifted perspective when he explained that this one was a view from above, this from the side, this one a slice down the middle. "Why don't you just draw a *picture* of it?" Michael wanted to know. His shyness was drifting away, which meant he was becoming more direct.

"But I have," Alex insisted. "This is how I explain to all the different people who'll have to work on the house — the plumbers, painters, plasterers, electricians — what I want them to know. I use drawings to tell people what I want done, the same way your dad uses letters or reports."

"But I can't see it. What does it *look* like?"

Alex scowled, thinking. Then he flipped the top drawing over, took an odd-looking pencil from his inner pocket, and began to sketch. Michael was kneeling on the floor. He rested his chin on his crossed hands at the edge of the sofa and exhaled a sigh of satisfaction, watching expectantly.

Sara perched on the sofa arm above them, holding her empty teacup. She wondered if Mr. McKie's soft-looking brown hair had been blond in his youth, for it was still that color at the forehead and temples. He wore it in the fashionable new side part, without side-whiskers. She'd thought him handsome the other night at Sherry's, but she hadn't much liked him. Today she liked him very much. Because he was being so nice to Michael, of course. But no — not only that. He must have found the house shocking, atrocious, but he hadn't let on by so much as a raised eyebrow. She sensed that he took pride in his work, and an instinct told her he was good at it; so it must have taken a great deal of restraint — born of kindness, surely, and consideration for her feelings — to subdue his professional dismay and pretend that the monstrous edifice did not repel him.

She liked his manners, too, the easy way he talked and listened, his naturalness. She didn't need to be told that women found him charming; she found him so herself and was perfectly aware of a pull between them that was subtly but unmistakably sexual. It didn't concern her. Once in a great while she met a man she felt drawn to, one who, under other circumstances, in a different life, could have become important to her. But this was her life and these were her circumstances. And so it was possible to enjoy Mr. McKie's company, to take pleasure in looking at him — even to flirt a little — without engaging anyone's true feelings, hers or his, and without penetrating the deceptively pliant surface of courtesy and reserve she used to protect her inner life.

"Why do you move your hand like that when you draw?" Michael wanted to know. Sara wondered, too; he rotated the pencil in his fingers slightly as he drew each line.

"Like this? It keeps the lead sharp. You don't get any flat spots, so no wide, fuzzy lines."

"Neat. What's that?" He pointed.

"The carriage house and the stables."

"Oh. What's that?"

"Greenhouse."

Sara pressed her fingers to her lips. Just what they needed at their summer pied-à-terre on the ocean: a greenhouse.

"And that?" Michael prodded.

"Pool."

"*Pool?*" she exclaimed, taken by surprise. "But — isn't the house on the water? The Narragansett Bay?"

Alex made sure his voice stayed neutral.

"Yes, but Ben thought a pool would be nice for anyone who didn't like salt water. And it'll be heated, so you can swim year-round."

"Heated," she echoed weakly. Dear God.

"It's really *big,* isn't it?"

Out of the mouths of babes, thought Alex, still sketching. "Yes, indeed. Lots of rooms for you to play in."

"What will it be made of?" Sara asked dully.

"Limestone. Coral-colored."

Michael had finished counting the wings out loud — four — and was starting on the chimneys — seven so far. "It looks just like a castle," he noted with enthusiasm.

"It's a . . . sort of villa, isn't it? Italian?"

"Currently," Alex answered, then bit his tongue. It wasn't prudent to complain about the vagaries of the client's demands to the client's wife. Even if the client's wife would sympathize with him — and he suspected this one would.

"What's going to be on the new floor?"

Was there a twinkle in her eye now? He ignored it, in case he'd imagined it. "Servants' quarters. It's really a half-floor."

Then Michael wanted to know how the servants could live on a half-floor; would they have to bend over all the time? Alex started to explain, but the image of

74

doubled-up servants caught Michael's fancy all at once and he burst into laughter. He had a giddy, gurgling laugh Sara could never resist, no matter what silliness provoked it. It overcame him now and he slid to the floor, convulsed with mirth. He recovered enough to get up and demonstrate how the hapless servants would have to live, which struck him as doubly hilarious and started him off again.

Sara resisted for a few seconds, saying, "Tsk," and "Honestly, Michael," but his laughter was too contagious to withstand. Alex folded his arms, chuckling in sympathy, when she collapsed along the top of the sofa and gave in to it, all care for formality and decorum cast aside. The elegant, finishing school posture disappeared; her puffy-sleeved suit jacket fell open and her lush breasts, pressing against the couch, strained against the sheer, creamcolored blouse she wore. Her pale, aristocratic face turned pink, and a long golden strand of hair escaped her perfect coiffure. The source of Alex's enjoyment shifted. His smile froze. He stared.

Mother and son finally pulled themselves together. Sara apologized halfheartedly, wiping her eyes. "If you've finished your tea," she told Michael, "it's time to tell Mr. McKie good-bye and run upstairs. Yes, darling, don't be difficult. Mrs. Drum is waiting; she's probably run your bath and it will be getting cold."

After a commendably brief period of whining, Michael stuck his small hand out at Alex and said, "Good-bye, sir. Thank you for drawing the house, it's really smashing."

"I'm glad you like it." Afterward he would wonder what came over him, but he heard himself say, "Do you know what a skyscraper is?"

"A big tall building. Dad showed me one once next to his office."

"Would you like to see the first one ever built in New York City?"

The beautiful gray-blue eyes widened in excitement. "Oh, yes, could I?"

"I'll show it to you. And your mother," he added casually.

"How nice of Mr. McKie. Say thank you," Sara urged.

"Thank you. When?"

"Really, darling —"

"How about Tuesday?"

"I have to go to school."

"Afterward, I meant." In truth, he'd forgotten all about school.

"Can we, Mum?" She looked dubious,

and Michael tugged on her wrist to persuade her. "Can we? Why can't we? Please?"

"Well . . ." She didn't work at the settlement house on Tuesdays.

"We could have tea afterward at Dean's," Alex mentioned innocently.

"Oh, Dean's!" cried Michael, jumping up and down. "Dean's! Dean's!"

Sara knew she was outnumbered. "It's very kind of you, Mr. McKie. We accept." She interrupted Michael's triumphant crowing by sending him upstairs again, firmly this time. He scampered out, tossing "See you Tuesday!" over his shoulder as he went.

"That really was very nice of you," Sara repeated, getting up and going to sit in a chair, "but you needn't have done it. You must be very busy, especially on a weekday."

"I am; that's *why* I did it." They smiled at each other. "Michael's very special, isn't he?" And he wasn't even trying to flatter her, he realized; it was simply a statement of fact.

"Yes, he is. But of course, I can hardly be objective about that."

"Did he . . ." He hesitated to bring it up because the subject embarrassed him. But he needed to know the answer. "Did he like his father's birthday present?"

She sent him a long, level look. "Ben changed his mind," she said kindly. "He gave him a bicycle."

He had the feeling he'd just been forgiven. "Did he? Well, that's — good, I'm glad. You were worried, as I recall, and I was thinking afterward that you were probably right — seven's too young for a boy to have a rifle. So. I'm glad." He closed his mouth and told himself to shut up. Her sweet, knowing smile unnerved him.

The maid came in then and took away the tea things. Sara said, "I must apologize again for my husband, Mr. McKie," as she watched him roll up his drawings and slide them expertly back into the tube. "I can't imagine what's kept him. It was very thoughtless of him to ask you to come here —"

"Not at all."

"— on a Sunday, away from your office, and then not even to —"

"Don't give it a thought," he interrupted magnanimously, thinking he couldn't have arranged the afternoon better if he'd tried. "I'll just leave these here, if I may, and Ben can take a look at them when he gets a chance."

"Yes, of course." She stood up when he did, wishing he didn't have to go quite yet.

The telephone rang. The sound came from the hall, just outside the door, and after two rings Alex wondered why she didn't answer it — before recalling that the Cochranes had servants for everything. But after the third ring, Sara frowned, said, "Would you excuse me?" and dashed for the door.

It was impossible not to overhear her side of the conversation. When he realized the caller was Ben, he didn't try. He strolled over to a table near the door, on which a group of framed photographs was clustered artistically. "Yes, you've missed him, he's just leaving," she was saying. "Well, what did you expect?" The change in the tone of her voice chilled him a little; he wouldn't have thought it could sound so tense and brittle, so utterly devoid of warmth. He picked up the largest photograph, one of the Cochranes on their wedding day, and studied it while he listened. Sara looked young and fresh in her virginal white Worth gown, her beautiful face alight with hope and excitement — but not love, he thought. Perhaps it had never been a love match for either of them. Ben at thirty-five was leaner, more energetic, yet already that familiar self-satisfied look had begun to settle in his blunt-featured face.

"Yes, I'll explain it to him. Well, when *will* you be home?"

He put the photograph down and picked up another, this one of Sara, Ben, and Michael as an infant. Hope and excitement were both absent from her face now, replaced by a chilly sort of composure. Ben, standing behind mother and son, one possessive hand on his wife's shoulder, looked stern and smug and commanding. For some reason the picture repelled Alex; he put it down hastily. The rest were mostly of Michael at various ages. He saw that he had been a rather sickly child, but never less than physically beautiful, a skinny, tow-headed angel.

"Very well, yes. How many, then? Yes, all right, I said I'd take care of it." She rang off abruptly, and when she appeared in the doorway she hadn't taken the time to compose her face. Alex felt shock when he saw the strain and resentment and, under that, her desperate unhappiness. He looked away.

"That was Ben," she said with artificial ease, and when he looked back she was serene again. "He's so sorry to have missed you. He sends his apologies, but there was an unexpected situation at his office, it seems — I didn't get all the details — and he simply couldn't get away. He's so terribly sorry."

He admired her then — lying through her teeth for that son of a bitch, carrying on for courtesy and civility on behalf of a man who wasn't worth one of her little fingers. He moved toward her, wanting to touch her, but he stopped when he was three feet away.

"He asked if you'd leave the drawings, and he promised to look at them tonight. Unfortunately, he has to leave tomorrow now, not Tuesday, for Chicago. But he said he'd either call you with any new instructions or — or leave them with me."

"Well, that's fine. That's fine," he repeated, wanting to reassure her. "You could tell me what he says when I see you on Tuesday."

"Tuesday." Her somber face lightened as she remembered. "I'd forgotten — I'll see you on Tuesday."

There was a pause, while they dealt separately with the gladness they were both feeling because they would meet again on Tuesday.

"Well," Alex said. "Until then. Thank you for tea. I enjoyed it immensely."

"So did I." She went with him out into the hall. "Ben wondered if you could come to dinner on the twenty-seventh — that's Friday next."

"The twenty-seventh? Yes, thanks, I'd like that very much."

"He said to bring a friend. That is, if you'd care to. A lady, I think he meant."

She colored; he stared. It was the first time he'd ever seen her fumble in a social situation. "Thanks," he said smoothly, "I'll let you know, shall I?"

"Yes, all right."

She gave him her hand. As he held it, he wondered what she would do tonight, and whether she would accept an invitation to dinner in some discreet downtown restaurant. Too risky, of course; the moment slipped by. For just a few seconds he found himself thinking how different his life would be if he were married and had a child. She opened the door for him. He said good-bye and left her, walking west toward Fifth Avenue. At the corner he turned around. She was still there, illuminated by the house light, standing between the pretentious pair of stone lions and looking up at the pink sky.

# Five

"There it is!"

"That's it. It's called the Tower Building. How many floors does it have?"

Michael counted carefully. "Thirteen?" Alex nodded. "Wow! How does it stay up?"

"I was hoping he'd ask me that," he said, grinning at Sara. All three leaned back against the brick wall of a bank and gazed east across Broadway at Number Fifty. "How thick do you think the walls have to be to hold up a building that tall?"

"Thick!"

"How thick?"

Even Michael could see that this was a trick question, but he answered gamely, "A *mile* thick."

Alex laughed. "The whole building is only twenty-one and a half feet wide. How thick do *you* think?" he asked Sara.

Taking Michael's cue, she humored him. "Three or four feet?"

He shook his head, smiling with satisfaction. "Only twelve inches."

"Wow!"

"But how is that possible?" Sara asked leadingly.

"Well, it all started when a man named Stearns bought an empty lot on that spot about eight years ago. He wanted to put up an office building, but if he built a conventional stone masonry structure, the walls would have to be so thick he wouldn't have enough rentable space to turn a profit. It seemed as if he'd bought himself a white elephant."

"A white *elephant?*" Michael repeated, mystified. Sara explained; Alex continued.

"So he went to an architect, fellow named Bradford Gilbert. Gilbert thought and thought for about six months, and finally decided the solution was to build something like a steel bridge or a cage and stand it up on one end. That way the walls could be only a foot thick, and they wouldn't have to bear any weight at all."

"But how? What holds the *walls* up?" Michael wanted to know.

"Long steel columns sunk deep into a cement footing underground."

"It still doesn't seem possible," said Sara.

"That's what everybody thought. But Gilbert was so sure, he offered to move into the top two floors himself, and if the building fell down he'd fall with it."

"Are all architects so brave and intrepid?"

"Yes, all," he assured her, straight-faced. "And Gilbert got to prove his mettle one Sunday morning when the building was all finished except for the roof. Guess what happened."

"What?" prodded Michael.

"A hurricane hit."

"Gosh!"

"Stearns and Gilbert rushed over to see what was happening to their building. There was already a crowd around it, everybody yelling that the thing was damn well going to blow down. Darn well. The wind was gusting at eighty miles an hour and people started backing up, saying they didn't want to be crushed when it fell.

"Gilbert grabbed a plumb line and started to climb a ladder the workmen had left out the night before. Stearns was right on his heels. 'You fools, you'll be killed!' shouted the crowd, but they kept climbing. Stearns' courage gave out on the tenth floor; he sprawled full-length on a scaffold and started praying for his life. Architects are made of sterner stuff, though, as everyone knows, and Gilbert kept going." Alex glanced down into Michael's wide-eyed, open-mouthed face, intent on the building opposite and the scene his imagination was conjuring. "On and on he climbed, rung by painful rung, knuckles white from the strain, the wind blowing and battering at him like a son of a — unmercifully. Finally he reached the thirteenth floor and crawled on his hands and knees along the scaffold to that corner of the building there. See it?"

"Yes!"

"He pulled the plumb line from his pocket, got his frozen fingers around the cord, and dropped the leaded end down toward the sidewalk. And what do you think?"

"What?"

"There wasn't the slightest vibration. The building stood steady as a rock in the ocean."

"Gosh," Michael mouthed, awed.

"When Gilbert and Stearns got back to the ground, the crowd cheered them like heroes. They locked arms and started up Broadway, singing, 'Praise God from whom all blessings flow.' People coming out of Trinity Church were sore amazed."

While Michael ogled the Tower Building and hummed the hymn under his breath,

Sara murmured, "Mr. McKie, is any of that true?"

"Every word, Mrs. Cochrane. Architects never lie."

It was a warm, breezy afternoon with the smell of rain in the air. They started up Broadway, looking for a streetcar that wasn't already full of bankers and Stock Exchange men heading home from work. Sara realized she'd been more fashionable than wise when she'd chosen the feathered and flowered "cartwheel" hat that went with her beige walking suit; every few steps she had to reach up with both hands to keep it from blowing off in the wind. Finally a car came that they could squeeze into, but they had to stand all the way. "Look, a parade!" cried Michael, pointing through the window at a crowd of people marching toward them on Canal Street. Sara peered, but she couldn't read their placards at this distance. They weren't paraders, she explained, they were pickets, men on strike against their employer. "Oh," said Michael. "Daddy hates that," he confided to Alex, who nodded, thinking, *I'll bet.*

They got off at Union Square. "Where should we go now," Alex asked rhetorically, "to my office or to Dean's?"

"Dean's," Michael voted unhesitatingly.

"Is your office nearby?"

"Right there." He pointed to the five-story brownstone on the corner that was the unprepossessing headquarters of Draper, Snow and Ogden. He leaned down and looked Michael in the eye. "Are you saying you would rather go eat hot cross buns and ice cream than get a free tour of an actual architect's drafting room?" he demanded, which caused Michael to dissolve into giggles. "Oh, all right," he said with mock crossness. "Maybe another time."

"I hope so," said Sara, surprising herself because she meant it. "Do you live around here as well?"

"Not far. Tenth Street, over toward Sixth." She only nodded to that, making him wonder what she thought of his humble downtown address. At least he was on the West Side. The place suited him, for now; he could walk to his office, and his sixty-year-old landlady was in love with him. Constance wouldn't set foot in the place — she lived like a countess in Madison Square — but that was not without its advantages, too. Anyway, after the Newport house was finished, he could afford to move as far uptown as he wished.

Dean's was thinning out. It was really too late for tea, Sara knew, but a promise was a promise. Michael would never eat his dinner tonight, and Mrs. Drum would climb up on her high horse again. She sighed tiredly. But Ben would be in Chicago by now, and he was staying for ten days. The thought raised her spirits; she asked for ladyfingers with her coffee, and to hell with her figure.

They sat at a tiny table by the window, gazing out at the hurrying figures of men and women anxious to be home. London was far away and almost forgotten, but sometimes she contrasted its sedate, black-umbrella'd rush hour to New York's and marveled at how much busier, noisier, less *civilized* this one was. Which summed up everything she loved and hated about America, she supposed. She had lost as much as she had gained — in terms of a city to live in, that was. In personal terms — well, that was probably equal too. She'd lost her innocence and her expectations of happiness, and she'd gotten Michael. Did people get what they deserved? She didn't know. She added cream to her coffee and asked Mr. McKie what he thought of the so-called "modern" style of architecture.

He told her. Unpremeditated, even

against his will, but prodded by her skillful questioning and her genuine, unaffected interest in his answers, he told her. He even confessed his ambivalence — something he had not done with anyone before, and afterward he told himself that he'd done it with Mrs. Cochrane because he was brimming over with it and she was simply the first person to pry it out of him.

While Michael ate vanilla ice cream and gazed out the window at the passersby, Alex weighed in on his favorite complaint, that America was filling up with imitations. Where was originality in this slavish enthusiasm for Greek revival, Gothic revival, Romanesque, Queen Anne, French Renaissance, Italian Renaissance, even Byzantine? Where were directness, spaciousness, and freedom? The country was wallowing in columns, turrets, pinnacles, balustrades, mansard roofs, stained glass, arches, and gables. Grandomania, that's what it was. Had Sara visited the World's Fair a few years ago in Chicago? She said that she had. Well, what did she think of an exposition that declared there had been no advances since ancient Rome and that an architect's highest duty was to copy?

"What did any of it have to do with *Chicago?*" he demanded. "Chicago is stockyards and railroads and steel mills, not dignity and classical serenity. Did you see any Romans when you were in Chicago? What's it got to do with *America?* This country is young and democratic, industrial, dynamic — where are the buildings that express that?"

"Not in Newport, I don't think," she answered with a soft smile. That shut him up. He stared back moodily, uneasy because she'd put an unerring finger on the heart of things so quickly. "Why did you take my husband's commission if you despise the kind of house he wants you to build?"

"I don't despise it," he said defensively.

"No? I beg your pardon. I thought you were a modernist; you like the skyscraper we saw today, and you —"

"No, no, it's not that simple. I like the *engineering* of the skyscraper. I admire the technology that solved a problem of space and materials with such elegance and economy. But try to imagine a city with nothing *but* skyscrapers. And you might as well, because it's coming, it's inevitable. The telephone, the elevator, the price of land in the city — they've all conspired to make it inevitable. So picture it. Barbaric, isn't it? Dark, congested, lifeless. It's not ethical, it's not beautiful, and it's not permanent. It's a commercial exploit, an *expedient*. I don't want to live in that city."

But she would not be sidetracked; she wanted to talk about him, not his philosophy. Even as it made him squirm, he found her interest seductive. "Then what will you do?" she pressed. "How will you find a middle ground? Is there a compromise?"

"Maybe, but I can't see it yet. For me, the worst is the architect who tries to turn something like a skyscraper — which can be beautiful, I don't argue that — into what it was never intended to be. He treats it like a *stone* rather than a *steel* structure and smothers it with flying buttresses and parapets and spires and balustrades. He tries to impose, say, a Gothic sensibility on a building that has absolutely nothing to do with the Gothic *spirit*. Do you see? Do you call that a compromise?"

"Yes, I think I see. But what will *you* do?"

There was no shaking her. He took refuge in cynicism. "Oh, make lots of money, I expect. Exploit my not inconsiderable talent for classical forms, ride the wave of popularity for things ancient until it crashes, and then swim very fast to catch up with the next one."

Instead of repelling her, his answer made her laugh. "If I believed that, I don't think I would like you very much, Mr. McKie."

"How much do you like me now?" He relished this turn in the conversation.

"A little more than you deserve, I think."

"Ah, no, so little? I'm done for, then." But her answer pleased him enormously. For the first time, he'd coaxed her into flirting.

"Well, I like you a *lot*," Michael piped up. He'd finally understood a bit of the discussion, but misinterpreted the mock-serious tone. "I think you're *awfully* nice."

They all laughed, and Alex said he thought Michael was awfully nice too. After that, serious conversation didn't seem appropriate.

It was getting dark when they left Dean's, but it was still warm and the rain hadn't started, so they decided to walk the thirteen blocks to Thirty-second Street. Sara assured Alex he needn't accompany them; it was out of his way and they were quite all right on their own. Besides that, she could send his drawings — which she had stupidly forgotten to bring this afternoon — to his office by messenger the first thing in the morning. He wouldn't hear of it. As they walked up Fifth Avenue, Sara holding Michael's hand, all three speculated, at different times and in private, on the interesting fact that they must look like a family to anyone passing by. But no one spoke the thought out loud.

In the house, with very little coaching from his mother, Michael thanked Alex for a wonderful afternoon, after which he was told to run upstairs. Sara found the tube of drawings by the door where she'd left it — so she wouldn't forget — and handed it to him. "Ben liked the changes you made and said everything looked fine to him. He wondered when you would get started on the construction."

"I've been waiting for his final approval. Now I can go to Newport and supervise the site excavation. I'll also be looking around for a place to set up a temporary office."

"I see. Then we won't be seeing you for a while, I expect." She kept her face mild, but she felt a strong and utterly inappropriate dismay.

"Not for a while. But I'll be back before the twenty-seventh; I hope you haven't forgotten inviting me to dinner."

"No, I haven't, but I was afraid —" The telephone rang on the wall behind her. She jumped, then apologized, laughing. "I *can't* get used to that. Would you excuse me for one second?" She picked up the receiver.

He moved away to give her privacy, but spun back around when he heard the alarm in her voice. "What? I can't — Tasha, I can't understand you, speak English. Attacked! What do you mean?" She grabbed for the edge of the table. "Oh, God. Are you hurt? Have you talked to the police?" There was a long silence; she interrupted it twice with "Tasha — Tasha, I know, but —" With a visible effort, she forced her voice to sound calm. "Where are you?" she asked, while the hand clenched and unclenched on the table edge. "No, I don't know it. What street? Tasha, *what street?* All right, stay there, don't move, I'll come and get you. Are you sure you're not hurt, not — injured? All right, I'm coming right now, wait for me. It'll be about thirty minutes, maybe longer. Stay — Tasha, stay there, do you hear me? Don't move, don't go outside." Another pause. "I know," she said, and her voice almost broke. "I'm so sorry. I'll be there soon, I promise."

As soon as she hung up, she started shaking. But she moved purposefully toward the door. "I have to go out now, something's happened." She caught sight of herself in the mirror and took time to unpin her silly hat and throw it on the table. "Excuse me, I need to get a hansom —"

"Let me help you. What's happened?"

"It's someone I know, she's been attacked by a man. I have to go and get her."

"Yes, I heard that." He opened the door and held it for her. "I'll come with you. Where is she?"

Sara hesitated, but only for a second. "Thank you, I would be very glad for your company." They went outside together, walking east toward Madison. There were no cabs on the wide avenue, they saw quickly. "We're better off taking the El. My friend is down on the East Side, somewhere on Houston Street." Alex took her arm, and they set off at a fast walk toward Third Avenue.

They reached the top of the steep platform steps just as a downtown train was pulling in. They sat in the last car, nearly empty by now, grabbing onto the seat in front as the train started off with a neck-snapping jerk. Over the clatter and rumble of the wheels, Sara told Alex most of what she knew of Tasha Eminescu and the man who had been following her.

They got off at the Bowery and walked past a row of tenements and cheap amusement halls, a fake museum, a tough Irish saloon. At Houston they turned left and headed toward the river. Most of the pushcart peddlers were gone by now, the market booths empty but still redolent of fish and cheese and meat. A game of prisoner's base was breaking up in the street because it was too dark to see, but a gang of boys still played craps under the streetlight at First Avenue. The cobbled street was filthy, the sidewalk covered with litter. "Do you work near here?" Alex asked in amazement.

"Yes, on Forsyth," she answered, distracted. "Tasha's in a cafe, I think it's on this block."

"What's it called?"

"She didn't know. She was afraid to ask anyone. She said it's Russian, but there are so many — here, let's try this one."

They were walking past a dark, wooden building, scarcely fifteen feet across, which Alex would never have guessed was a cafe had he not been told. The only window was closed and curtained, and the only sign was in Russian. Inside, it was so dark and smoky, they could barely see across the room. As their eyes adjusted, they saw men sitting at tables, some playing chess, all drinking tea from tall tumblers, biting off bits of sugar from cubes. They were palefaced, tired-looking men, talking incessantly in Russian and Yiddish and German. "She's not here," Sara said, but Alex touched her shoulder and pointed.

"There?"

Sara squinted through the dense smoke into the darkest corner and saw her. Alone at a tiny table, staring straight down, stiff arms wound around each other, hands clutched between her knees. "Tasha," she breathed, and moved toward her.

Alex kept his distance and made no attempt to overhear their low-voiced conversation. No one paid any attention to him; even the white-aproned proprietor left him alone. He observed the girl named Natasha Eminescu and made out in the murk that she was young, probably not even twenty, dark-haired, with heavy-lidded black eyes and full lips. She had a generous figure, almost voluptuous, but strangely small hands, short-fingered and graceless. After returning Sara's first quick, hard embrace, she huddled back into herself and kept her head down while they spoke.

"Where did this happen to you? Tasha, I know it's hard but you must talk about it. Please." She touched the side of the girl's face gently. "Tell me."

Mumbling, not looking at her, Tasha said, "It happened in the alley beside my building, where I live."

"Tell me what happened."

"I was late coming home today because I didn't finish my piecework on time and Mr. Lehman said I must do it or I would lose my rate."

"Yes. And so — ?"

"So I stayed late and — the man, he was waiting for me. Hiding in the alley, in the dark." She stopped again, holding herself very still. "He grabbed me. He put his hand over my mouth, hard, so I couldn't scream." She touched her fingers to her lips gingerly, as if they hurt. When she started to cry, Sara put a hand on her shoulder.

"Did you see him?"

"No. Too dark, and he pushed me down. From behind. I couldn't move. Then he — did it. Talking the whole time. And when he finished —" She broke off, choking. Sara held tight. She had to whisper the rest. "He said it was just the first time, that he would have me again and again, as often as —" She covered her face with her hands and sobbed.

Sara felt hot and cold horror rush through her. She glanced up, searching for Alex, and he was beside her immediately. She reached for his hand and squeezed it, fighting for her own composure. "Tasha," she said, stroking the bent head, "this man is Mr. McKie, he's a friend of mine." She wouldn't look up. "He brought me here, and he's going to go home with us now."

She jerked up at that. "I cannot go back there! Please, I'm so scared, I can't —"

"No, no, you don't have to go there. You'll come to my house tonight and stay with me until we decide what's best to do."

Tasha's huge eyes filled. She seized Sara's hand and kissed it, wetting it with her tears. "Oh, Mrs. Cochrane," she began, then lapsed into a fast, voluble combination of languages Sara couldn't understand. The outburst of gratitude went on until her embarrassment was so acute, Sara drew her hand away and spoke almost sternly.

"Enough now, Tasha. Come, let's get away from here." She stood up. To Alex she said, "Do you think you could find us a cab?"

He shook his head; he had no intention of leaving them alone. "Not around here, I don't think. Come with me, we'll look for something on Third."

Tasha got up shakily. Sara put her arm around her waist and the two women went outside, Alex following.

There were no hansoms in sight on Third Avenue. They waited on the busy, teeming corner, staring southward, Tasha speechless, Alex and Sara saying little to each other. At last they gave up and caught a horsecar, riding it in silence all the way uptown.

Inside the house, Sara told Alex she was going to take Tasha upstairs. "You've been so kind, I can't thank you enough. If you like, I'll call you —"

"I'll wait."

"No, honestly, there's no —"

"I'd like to wait."

She was unspeakably grateful. "All right. I'm not sure how long I'll be. Thank you very much." A maid appeared in the hall; Sara asked her to come upstairs with her and Tasha. "Make yourself a drink, Mr. McKie, and — just — go anywhere." She wanted to be a good hostess, but her mind was so distracted.

"I'll be fine," he assured her, smiling slightly.

She almost smiled back, then turned away from him to help a silent Tasha up the stairs.

Alex wandered down the hall toward the blue parlor, turning lights on as he went. He remembered the liquor cabinet — a hideous rococo affair of laquered teak — and poured himself a strong scotch whiskey. He sipped it slowly, brooding. There was a door standing open at the far end of the room; it had been closed before — he'd thought it a closet, but now he could see it was a room. Carrying his drink, he went to investigate.

No light switch on the wall, just an old-fashioned gaslight sconce by the door. He turned it on. The room was tiny, hardly bigger than a pantry. The sole furnishings were a shallow desk built into a recess between bookcases on either side of a casement window, an armchair, a padded leather footrest, and a standing electric lamp. A Persian rug in bright shades of ruby and wine took up most of the floor.

The wall that wasn't covered with bookcases to the ceiling was covered with paintings and photographs. The photos were all of Michael, all unposed, some even blurred, as if they'd been taken with a box camera by someone more doting than talented. Sara, of course. The paintings were interesting, in themselves and in their variety. More than half were signed "L. Hubbard," and Alex remembered the eccentric-looking friend he'd met here on Sunday. They were landscapes and nudes, still-lifes and portraits, suggesting the artist hadn't settled on her true subject yet. What they had in common was exuberance and a muscular disregard for convention. There were also two small Corots, as well as a few of the Impressionist painters — Manet, Cezanne, a Degas. That was a rare sight in the homes of the American nouveau riche, Alex knew, where the safe and respectable Old Masters usually had pride of place.

He carried his glass to the bookcase closest to the chair, sat down, and perused the shelves. Another eclectic collection — Dickens, Zola, Twain, books in French on landscape gardening, Italian poetry, the sonnets of Shakespeare, all of Jane Austen, a dog-eared Henry James. All of them looked read, even reread, but he smiled to see that what was lying open on the desk this evening was the newest issue of *Women's Fashion Gazette*. He chose a magazine from the shelf at random, an old *Scribner's*, and began to read.

"So, you've found me out."

He lifted his head, surprised to see her leaning in the doorway; he hadn't heard a sound. She looked tired, but she'd repinned her hair and tidied herself up; once again she was neat and cool and composed. "You told me to go anywhere," he reminded her.

"Indeed I did."

"Besides, you can't hide secret rooms from me — I'm an architect."

"I should've known."

He gestured. "I like this room. It's my favorite."

"Mine, too."

"I know." He stood up slowly, holding her gaze, and moved toward her. She stepped back. "Let me make you a drink," he said smoothly, and passed by her in the doorway without touching.

"Yes, all right. Please."

"Sherry?"

"Anything. Yes, sherry." She followed him, restless.

"How is she?"

"She's stopped talking. She had a bath and now she's asleep. She fell asleep instantly," she said wonderingly, still amazed.

"A defense."

"Yes. A good one." Her low voice contained a touch of envy.

"Have you called the police yet?"

"No. The doctor, but not the police."

"Do you want me to call them?"

"Thank you — but no, I think it's better to wait until tomorrow. What could they do tonight anyway, except upset her even more? She says she never saw the man, couldn't even describe him."

"Did he rape her?"

She looked up quickly, shock in her eyes. But his steady gaze steadied her, and she nodded. "Yes." She swallowed what was in her glass and handed it back to him. In silence, he poured more sherry, then another whiskey for himself.

After all that had happened, they had little to say to each other now. But Sara found the stillness between them extraordinarily comforting. She walked to the windows, pulling the draperies across each one in turn. "I can't think what would have happened if you hadn't been here, Mr. McKie."

"I think you'd have been just fine."

"No, I doubt that. You must be starving — why don't you stay for dinner?"

"Thanks, no. I'll be going now."

"Oh. Yes, of course, you must have

things to do. . . ." She trailed off. Neither of them moved. "When will you be leaving for Newport?"

"Thursday, I expect."

She wanted to ask, *When will I see you again?* She didn't. "If there are any problems, you could call me on the telephone. I won't know the answers, but I can call Ben. Or" — the depressing thought just occurred to her — "I guess you could call Ben directly in Chicago. Do you have his number there?"

"Yes."

"Well." Finally she turned away and led him out into the hall, to the door. "Thank you again, you've been so kind."

He ground his teeth, tired of being thanked. He was used to her loveliness now, he realized, familiar with her cool expression and the warmth in her eyes that belied it. He felt as if he knew her much, much better than the short time they had spent together measured. Leaving her now with nothing between them but polite smiles and casual words — what a loss, what crude, regrettable hypocrisy. More than anything, he wanted to touch her. Not even sexually — or not exclusively. Would she allow it? He wanted to hold her slim white hands until they warmed and began to move in his. He wanted to massage the tension out of her proud shoulders. Run his fingers inside that prissy white collar around her throat. Listen to her sigh. And then slide the buttons open down the front of her jacket and touch her through the thin chamois blouse.

She put out her hand and he took it. Something flickered deep in her dark-fringed eyes, but all she said was, "Good night, Mr. McKie."

"Good night, Mrs. Cochrane."

"Have a safe trip to Newport."

"Thanks."

Their hands slid apart. He stood there for two more seconds. Then he turned, bounded down the four steps to the sidewalk, and strode away.

Sara remained in the doorway another minute, watching until he was out of sight. She wasn't naive; she knew where Mr. McKie's thoughts had wandered just now. Her own had followed him part of the way there, before skidding to a nervous halt and retreating. Nothing shocking in that — she had, after all, been the object of a man's admiration before now. Sometimes she found it pleasant, sometimes tedious, always meaningless. It was none of those things now, she realized. What was it, then?

Rather than answer that question, she closed the door and hurried upstairs to sit with Tasha until the doctor came.

# Six

There was no answer to Sara's light tap at the guest room door. She tried again, infinitesimally louder; at a faint response, she pushed the door open a crack and looked in. "Are you sleeping?" she whispered.

"No, no, please enter." Tasha sat up in the wide bed and sent her a wavering smile. "Oh, you have brought me tea. That is so kind."

"And some delicious scones with Mrs. Carrick's damson jam; no one can resist it." Since Tasha had eaten nothing for lunch except a few slices of orange, she hoped the tea would tempt her.

"Who is Mrs. Carrick?"

"She's our cook. Do you take cream and sugar?"

"Only sugar, if you please. Would you care to sit with me for a little?"

"Yes, if you like. Come, have one of the scones, Tasha, you've got to eat something." She sat on the edge of the bed and watched the dark-haired girl nibble obediently at a triangle of sweet bread. Her peach silk nightgown looked strange on Tasha, Sara couldn't help thinking; it was probably only the contrast with her olive skin, but somehow the gown seemed too young and childish, too — virginal. "Is your wrist paining you as much as before?"

"No, it's better, thank you. The binding the doctor put on makes it much better." But she still favored it and could not even lift a teacup with her left hand, Sara noted. Dr. Patterson had said it was a bad sprain, although there was no swelling, and that she should avoid using her left hand until all the discomfort was gone.

"We would not even have known you'd hurt yourself if the doctor hadn't discovered it by accident. It isn't good to be so stoical, Tasha, not now."

She looked down, crumbling the scone on the plate in her lap. "I don't know that word," she mumbled.

"Stoical? It means denying that you're in pain."

"Oh. But I'm all right now, I am not in pain."

"No?"

The downcast eyes evaded her. "Soon, perhaps tomorrow, I will be able to leave."

Sara shifted impatiently. "Nonsense, you're not ready to go home. You'll stay here until you're completely well."

"But I cannot! How can I impose on you in this way? You are so good, but I can't stay any longer, it's not right."

"We've been through this before. You can't work. You can't operate your sewing machine because of your wrist. Besides, where would you go? You're afraid to return to your old apartment, and I wouldn't let you go anyway because it's not safe. Why are you crying? Don't, it's all right, please don't cry."

"I can't help it," she whispered, burying her face in her hands. "Oh, Mrs. Cochrane, I'm so ashamed. I'm so ashamed."

Sara set the tray aside and took the girl in her arms. "Why?" she murmured, although she knew why. She knew everything about sexual humiliation.

"Everything is changed. Nothing can ever be the same again for me."

She sighed, unable to lie. "Perhaps that's true. But the important thing to remember — try to remember — is that you did nothing wrong. You were that man's victim. Nothing you deliberately did provoked his cruelty. It was out of your control."

Tasha pulled away. "I know this, in my mind I know it. But I'm still so sad. And —

shamed. I can't help it."

"I do understand. It's easy to share the blame because what happened has made you feel dirty. But listen to me, Tasha. You must not let that man's corruption poison you. The way to help yourself is to look deep inside your own heart and realize that you were innocent. Do you understand me? Remember what your life was like before this awful thing happened, remember what *you* were like. All your hopes and dreams, your faith that others were as simple and well-intended as you —" She broke off, dashing at the tears on her own cheeks. She had said too much, for Tasha was watching her intently.

"All I can tell you," she finished more calmly, "is that it does get better. Time helps us form scars. And then the pain is only a remembered thing, not constant anymore." She smiled a bit wanly. "It can even make you stronger."

They fell silent, and after a little while Tasha said she would like to try to sleep now. Sara took away the tea things and left her alone.

"That is a very stunning outfit," Tasha declared admiringly from the satin-covered chaise longue in Sara's bedroom. "Those colors are good for you; you are pale, but you can wear such a high contrast because you are tall. If you are short like me, it is better to wear the single color."

Sara studied herself in the wardrobe glass. She had on her new pink tulle blouse, sleeves puffed at the shoulders and narrow at the wrists, a black taffeta skirt with a perky pleated flounce, and a pink straw sailor hat trimmed in black maline. She liked to think her taste in clothes was sound, but her approach to fashion was much more intuitive than Tasha's, who always knew *why* something was good or not good. "You aren't short," she responded automatically, tightening the saucy black bow at her waist. "You're slightly below average."

"I'm going now, Mum," Michael called from the open door.

"Oh, darling," she said, turning, "is it time for your lesson already?" Michael's piano lesson had been moved up an hour this week. "Come and give me a kiss, then."

He came in, glancing shyly at Tasha and muttering a greeting. He regarded their new visitor as an oddity, staring surreptitiously sometimes but rarely speaking to her. Sara was sure he would loosen up soon, for he'd never yet met anyone he didn't like. Even Mrs. Drum, and that was saying something.

He gave her a quick kiss on the cheek. "Oh, I forgot — look what came for me in the post just now!"

"What, love? Tell me what it is, I'm in a hurry too, and my hands are full." She was back at the mirror, fastening her earrings.

"It's a postcard from Mr. McKie."

"Is it?" She turned around again. "Let me see."

"Look, he printed the message. He doesn't know I can read script."

"You shall have to write him back and tell him. Oh, it's a picture of the Casino at Newport. Read it, darling. What does he say?"

" 'Dear Michael,' " he read slowly, " 'have you seen this splendid building yet? A fine architect named Stanford White designed it. It has shops and a restaurant, reading rooms, a bowling alley, billy — billy — *billiard* parlor, even court tennis and a polo field. There's a gallery on the second floor, from which the resorters sit and gossip and look down on the towns-people below — whom they call rubber plants because they've got the aud . . . audacity to stare back.' " Michael laughed;

"rubber plants" struck him as funny.

"Is that the end?"

"No, it says, 'Tell your mother I'm looking forward to the 27th. Yours truly, Alexander McKie.' What's the 27th?"

"That's the night he's coming to dinner. Well, that was very nice of him, wasn't it?"

"Oh, yes. When do we go to Newport, Mummy?"

"In a few weeks. You'd better run now, darling, don't keep Mrs. Drum waiting. Have a good lesson!" she called after him.

"Bye!" And he was gone, taking his postcard with him.

Sara turned back to the mirror with a smile. Her expression startled her a little; she'd been about to pinch her cheeks for color, but now she saw it wasn't necessary.

"Mr. McKie," mused Tasha from the chaise longue. "Is that the gentleman who was with you that night you came for me?" Sara said it was. "He is a friend of yours, of your family?"

"He's our architect. We're building a house in Newport."

"Ah, Newport. Where the rich people go for the summer."

Sara raised her eyebrows at her in the mirror.

"This is a beautiful thing." She fingered

a flowered scarf of light challis Sara had tossed aside while she dressed.

"Take it," she offered. She and Tasha hadn't much in common, but one thing they shared was a love of beautiful clothes. Then again, perhaps they *did* have things in common — who knew? But Tasha would not talk about herself or her life before she'd arrived in this country. Instead she asked endless questions about Sara's life. She was fascinated by the way "the rich" lived, and she was hungry for news about plays and parties, concerts and the opera and the people who attended them. Yesterday she'd made Sara explain the complicated protocol of card-leaving when she'd found one in the foyer, left in Sara's absence, with one corner turned down. For the most part, Sara found her curiosity touching and was glad of anything that helped bring her out of her dark, brooding melancholy. It astonished her to learn that Tasha was an avid reader of "Town Topics," a weekly scandal sheet that was the terror of New York high society, and it amused her to hear her drop the names of the Bradley Martins, the Hamilton Fishes, the Astors, and the Vanderbilts with comical familiarity in her slow, beguiling Slavic accent.

"Thank you," she said now, folding the scarf with great care, "but I could not. It is not possible."

She was also proud, Sara had discovered. "Why not? It would look nice on you, Tasha."

She compressed her lips and shook her head, briefly but finally.

Sara shrugged. "I have to go to work now. What will you do while I'm gone?"

"Study my English. I am enjoying this book, this *Trilby* you have lent me."

"Good. Ring for tea when you want it and have a nice lazy afternoon. I'll be bringing some of your things back with me, and Paren says he'll send the rest." Tasha bowed her head and started to say, "It isn't right," when Sara interrupted with a cluck of the tongue. "Enough already, as Mrs. Clayman would say. Your employer says you may stay away until you're well, without losing your piece rate —"

"Only because you called him on the telephone and spoke him into it."

"Talked him into it. As for your apartment, what sense does it make to pay seventeen dollars a month for a place you aren't using and probably won't be returning to anyway?"

"Then where will I go?" she wailed. "I

117

am so stupid, I can only do one thing — sew — and my hand is still too weak to do it! I have no money put by, I am a useless burden to everyone —"

Sara went to her before she could start to cry. "Stop that. You're not a burden and you know it. Listen to me, Tasha." She took her firmly by the chin and made her look up. "Today, after I'm through at the settlement house, I am going to visit Lockhart's."

In spite of herself, Tasha smiled. "How nice."

Sara laughed. "No, I'm not going to buy clothes, silly. I'm going to speak to Mr. Lockhart himself and ask if his shop needs the services of the most talented, most fashion-smart seamstress I've ever met." She waited for a reaction, expecting euphoria, but Tasha's face was a study. "Aren't you glad?" she asked uncertainly.

"Yes . . . oh yes, I am glad. Again, you are much too kind."

"But — ? The pay will be very small at first, I know, but the working conditions will be so much better. And after a while, when Mr. Lockhart sees how good you are, your wages will improve and you'll be able to afford a nice place to live. What's wrong, don't you want me to ask him?"

"Oh no, I think it is wonderful. By all

means. I was only thinking that perhaps I am not good enough for such a fine establishment."

"Rubbish, you're a genius. One day you'll *design* clothes for Mr. Lockhart that will rival anything in the city." She gave her a bracing pat on the arm, saying, "Leave it to me," and stood up. "I'll be late if I don't go now, and Mr. Yelteles will glare at me all afternoon. I'll give them all your regards, shall I?"

"Oh yes, give everyone my best wishes." She settled back against the chaise and opened her book, using her good hand.

A few days later, Sara sat in her tiny study, penning a menu for the cook in preparation for Friday's dinner three nights hence. The casement window was open and a soft breeze that smelled more of summer than spring fluttered the papers on her desk. Behind her in the blue parlor, she heard Tasha set her coffee cup down and turn a page of the *Evening News*. Her spirits seemed better lately; she was still quiet and kept most of her thoughts to herself, but her natural curiosity was beginning to return. Everything about the Cochrane household interested her — as Sara imagined the living conditions of a

Rumanian family would interest *her* as something completely new and unknown — and she was alternately amused and touched by the girl's artless questions. Now if she could only overcome her tiresome guilt feelings and the need to express near-constant gratitude because she believed she was a "burden," she might even be happy for the time she was here.

A thumping noise out in the hall made Sara lay her pen down and listen. Michael had been in bed for an hour, so who — ?

"Well, well, who might you be?"

Sara jumped up and hurried into the parlor. "Ben! What a surprise — I wasn't expecting you for two more days." She smiled to hide her dismay; she could guess his reaction to Tasha's presence and had wanted some time to prepare him for it before they met. She went to him and offered her cheek — something she never did and found herself doing now purely for Tasha's benefit, because it seemed the sort of gesture a wife would make to a husband she hadn't seen in over a week. Tasha had stood up and was clutching her hands at her waist. "Tasha, this is my husband," she said casually. "Ben, I don't think you've met my friend, Natasha Eminescu. Tasha has been staying with me for a while."

They shook hands. "It is so much a plea-sure to meet you," Tasha said sincerely. "Your house is very, very beautiful, and your wife has been an angel of great kind-ness to me, Mr. Cochrane. I am so hon-ored to be allowed to visit with you these last days."

Ben frowned to hide his perplexity. "Well, that's fine," he muttered, studying her narrowly. Sara watched them, trying to see Tasha through Ben's eyes — her still, watchful face, the black eyes that seemed to know secrets. Her voice was soft and smoky, intriguingly foreign, and sometimes she had a fascinating quality of stillness, the capacity to be physically motionless, like an exotic statue.

"Well," Ben rumbled, dropping Tasha's hand and turning brusque. "You ladies excuse me, I've got work to do."

"Did you have dinner?" Sara wondered. "I can ring —"

"Yeah, I ate on the train," he answered on his way out, not turning around.

She went to the sofa and picked up Ben's topcoat where he'd thrown it, folding and refolding it across her arm to cover her awkwardness. She was aware that Tasha was watching her in her silent, assessing way. What an odd couple they must seem to her. "Will you excuse me?" she said brightly. "I have to — I'd like to check on Michael. I'll be right back." Tasha nodded and watched her go.

She found Ben in his office. She visited him there as infrequently as possible because the room oppressed her with its dead, staring animals and cruel-looking weapons, displayed as proudly as fine art. Already he was on the telephone, booming into it to some underling about stock quotations and market shares and what he wanted bought and sold first thing in the morning. He looked tired. He needed a haircut, and his dark eyes were red-rimmed with fatigue or harassment. The blunt fingers drummed monotonously on the desk while he spoke. She was thinking how much she hated his hands when he hung up abruptly and looked at her. "Well?"

"I'd like to speak to you about Tasha."

"Who is she?"

"I'd like her to stay with us for a while, Ben. She's had a misfortune, an — accident, and she needs our help."

"Who is she, I said?"

"She's someone I've known for quite a while. She's not employed right now, but I've spoken to Mr. Lockhart — he's a *very*

122

fashionable couturier on Fifth Avenue, everyone goes either to him or to Worth's — and although he doesn't need anyone right now, he says in a month or two —"

"She's one of your goddamn immigrants, isn't she?" he exclaimed wonderingly. "Well, I'll be goddamned."

"She's foreign, yes —"

"I want her out of here."

"But why?" Her hands behind her back balled into fists. "She has no place to go. She's not hurting anyone here —"

"It doesn't look right, having a foreigner staying with us. She's probably even Jewish. Is she?"

"I have no idea, I never —"

"Well, I want her out. Give her some money if you have to, but get rid of her."

She fought to keep her voice calm. "Listen to me, no one even knows she's here — it's not as if she makes social calls with me. She needs a place to rest for a while, a safe harbor until —"

"I don't have time for this," he warned, coarse fingers drumming again.

"She's an aristocrat." He looked up sharply, and even though there was suspicion in his eyes, she knew her impulsive comment was inspired. "She comes from old European royalty; her father was a count." No point in mentioning her mother was a gypsy and never *married* the count. If the count even existed. She could see Ben wavering, and it almost made her laugh. But her contempt for him was too strong for laughter.

"Aristocrat? Blue blood, ha. Yeah, but what kind of blue blood, blue Jewish blood?"

She shrugged. "Blue Rumanian blood."

"Rumanian." He reached for a sheaf of papers and spread them out in front of him. "Leave me alone. I'll think about it when I get time."

She stayed where she was. She supposed she had won, but she felt little elation. Once it had exhilarated her to defeat him in petty domestic battles, but anger was the only pure emotion he evoked in her anymore. "Michael's stomachache is better," she said softly. "In case you were worried about him."

"I told you on the 'phone it was nothing."

"That's right, you did. Well. I'll let you get back to your work." She walked out, feeling his cold eyes on her. At least now he was angry too. That was something.

# Seven

"Here, McKie, have a drink."

"Thanks." He almost added, "I can use it," but that might have tipped Cochrane to the fact that he'd found the second tour of this pretentious, relentless, overbearing domestic museum of a house even more oppressive than the first. And this time he'd had to listen to a long, self-important story about every Egyptian water bottle, Japanese vase, Thuringian cup, and cloisonné paperweight in sight. Constance had ooh'd and ah'd incessantly, but she was good at social subterfuge, and Alex looked forward to hearing later what she really thought of the place. The Donovans, Harry and Lucille, were simply floored; they'd run out of superlatives early, suffering the bulk of the tour in silent and apparently genuine awe.

Now that they were all back in the "crimson drawing room," as Ben called it — Alex thought of it as the "bullfighting room" because of the blood-red leather walls and the Mexican saddlecloth drap-

125

eries — he wanted to know where the hell Mrs. Cochrane was. He could understand if she'd had the good sense to absent herself at tour time; no sane person could hold that against her. But he'd thought about her every day for two weeks, and now he wanted to see her. Badly. Wanted it so much, in fact, that he hadn't yet taken the simple expedient of asking Cochrane where she was, because to do so might give too much away. That was extraordinary in itself, considering that he was a past master at counterfeiting innocence for the benefit of potentially suspicious husbands and lovers.

"So, McKie, how's everything going up in Newport?"

"Things are going well, Ben. We've worked out a delivery schedule for the materials and equipment that we can live with, and the contractor's all set for a June start. I've set up a base of operations in —"

"I want a June third groundbreaking."

"June third? Well, I'm —"

"That's a Saturday. I'm throwing a party, every swell in Newport's invited, and it's on the third. Doesn't matter if you're ready or not, we can just stick a shovel in the ground for the ceremony. The party'll be at that Casino place afterward."

The *ceremony?* "I see. Well, that shouldn't be a pr—"

"You'll be there, of course, and Ogden says he's going to try to make it. He damn well *should* try, shouldn't he? It'll be good advertising for his company, and I told him so."

Alex nodded, imagining his employer's reaction to being told that Draper, Snow and Ogden needed Ben Cochrane's "advertising." "Yes, I can be there. It sounds like —"

"Say, Harry, what's this about you guys voting to send inspectors into the slaughter-houses to check up on kosher killing? What the hell is that?"

Alex gritted his teeth and clenched the glass in his hand harder as Cochrane turned his back on him and walked over to where Donovan was sitting with his fat wife. Donovan was a city alderman; rumor whispered he was comfortably nestled in Cochrane's pocket, as well as those of a lot of other New York real estate moguls. "Ben, we had no choice, the butchers on the East Side —"

"What do you mean, no choice? That's the Jews' job, the rabbis take care of that. They're strict, too, you wouldn't believe the rules they've got." His voice got louder, signaling he wanted Constance and Mrs. Donovan to stop talking and listen. "They call it *shechitah,* the way they do it, and the guy who does it is the *shochet.* He sticks a knife into the steer's throat and it bleeds to death. But if he doesn't do it exactly right, say if he tears loose the windpipe or the gullet, or even if the knife has a little knick in it, the rabbi who's sitting there watching everything says it's not kosher and they throw away the whole animal. Then it's only fit for us Gentiles."

"But there were complaints, Ben," Donovan protested, "people were saying the meat wasn't always kosher even though —"

"Well, Jesus, Harry, who the hell cares? Do you think a Jew sitting down to a nice Porterhouse steak knows whether the steer bled to death or got his skull smashed in? It's just another example of the government trying to horn in on the natural conduct of business. Let the buyer beware, that's what this country's — Well, well, look who decided to show up."

"Hello. I'm awfully sorry to be late, you must think I'm terribly rude. My son didn't want to have his bath tonight. Mrs. Donovan, so good to see you again, and Mr. Donovan. You must be Mrs. Cheyney. How do you do. I'm Sara Cochrane."

Alex set his glass down and moved toward her, some instinct making him want to put himself between her and Cochrane. Christ, she was beautiful, slim and elegant, fashionably chic in a gown of midnight blue silk, her bright hair swept up in some neo-Greek style he'd never seen before. But there was tension in her face as she smiled and greeted her guests, the kind of strain that had been absent two weeks ago when he'd had her to himself. A dozen times he'd thought of calling her on some trumped-up pretext, but he never had. Had she thought of him, too? It was impossible to tell; her expression held nothing but cool friendliness as she gave him her hand and said his name.

Her husband handed her a glass of sherry, demanding to know, in what was for him a discreet tone of voice, what the hell had kept her. She murmured something Ben didn't like and Alex couldn't hear, then moved away to talk to the ladies.

Leaning against the overwrought marble mantel, pretending he was listening to Cochrane and Donovan discuss utility investments, Alex contemplated the interesting spectacle of Constance and Sara together. What a contrast they made, one dark and one fair; one earthy, the other

129

elegant. Coarse and refined. No, that wasn't really fair; Constance was not coarse. At least, not in comparison with any other woman. He hadn't wanted to bring her tonight, but when she'd discovered he meant to spend his first evening in town without her after a two-week separation, she'd made things so unpleasant that he'd had no choice.

He couldn't have said exactly *why* he hadn't wanted her along. She was a perfectly presentable dinner guest, after all — young, attractive, respectable. She'd been left exceedingly well off by the late Mr. Cheyney, a trial lawyer who had dropped dead in the New York Court of Appeals during closing arguments. His wife had been too much for him, Alex always theorized, not completely in jest. Hell, she'd seduced *him* not two hours ago — sent the maid out and had her way with him on the brocade sofa in her drawing room. She'd missed him, she said. She was a noisy, athletic bed partner, hot and responsive and uncomplicated. Everything a man could want.

Sara laughed at something Constance said then, and the unself-conscious sound pulled at him and made him smile. He wanted her very much, wanted to solve the mystery of her. With other women, he accomplished that by taking them to bed. But with Sara, he sensed that might not do it — the mystery might remain unexplained afterward. Still, a man had to start somewhere. What would she be like? Cool and quiet? Quiet — yes, perhaps, but he did not think she would be cool.

She turned around, and he followed her smiling gaze to the doorway, where Michael stood, wearing pajamas and a plaid nightrobe, hand-in-hand with the formidable Mrs. Drum.

"Darling, come in and say good night to everyone."

The boy advanced shyly, heading straight for his mother. There were admiring exclamations from everyone, which increased his embarrassment; when he reached Sara he ducked his golden head and hung onto her hand. She whispered something and he pulled himself together. Constance wanted to know how old he was. He told her in bashful, gentlemanly accents, calling her "Mrs. Cheyney" when his mother prompted him. Mrs. Donovan said she had a boy at home almost his age, he would have to come over and play with him sometime. He thanked her politely, his serious face indicating that he would take the suggestion under advisement.

He shook hands with the men next. When Alex's turn came, he reached into his pocket and handed Michael the Indian arrowhead he'd picked up on the site in Newport and wrapped in a piece of drawing paper. As the boy gazed down, bemused, at the rough piece of flint, Alex caught the clean smell of soap and sun-dried flannel, and had a most unexpected urge to put his arms around Michael and give him a hug. Instead he explained what the gift was, to the child's highly gratifying amazement and delight. They were speculating on the age of the artifact and the tribe it might have come from when Cochrane interrupted with brusque, sense-less severity that it was past Michael's bed-time and he wanted him upstairs *now.*

Alex's eyes flew to Sara's, surprising a quickly hidden look of distress. Instantly obedient, Michael spun around and ran to his father. Cochrane put his beefy arms around him in a bear hug that looked more like a punishment than a demonstration of affection. Alex looked away, reaching for his drink and pushing back dark, long-ago memories best left buried.

Michael went away with Mrs. Drum, and soon after Sara stood up and announced that dinner was ready. Alex put his glass down and moved toward Constance, but Cochrane beat him to her, offering his arm with a fatuous smile and leading her out of the room. The Donovans followed. Sara waited beside the door with her hands clasped together, smiling tensely.

More than anything, he wanted to make the smile real. He said, "I almost called you. A number of times."

Her gray-blue eyes softened, and he came closer. But then she asked, "Why?"

Three or four answers sprang to mind. All of them would change everything, alter for good the fragile friendship they were sharing. Tentative as it was, he found he didn't want to risk losing it. "I wondered how your friend is, and if the police found out anything."

"Ah." She turned aside before he could discover if the new look in her eyes was disappointment. The girl named Tasha was still living in the house, she told him, recovering slowly; she hoped to find her a job soon, sewing clothes for a New York couturier. The police had discovered nothing and had no clues.

He said something sympathetic. Then, "Have you been all right? I thought you might be looking a little tired."

"Oh no," she said quickly, "I'm quite all right. How did you find Newport?"

"A bit empty yet. Ben tells me you'll be spending most of the summer there."

"With Michael, yes. We're looking forward to it."

He studied her tense cheeks, the strain in the fine blue-white skin around her eyes. He didn't believe she was looking forward to it, nor that she was quite all right. But they didn't have the sort of relationship that would have allowed him to challenge her.

As if she sensed his skepticism but had no resources to deal with it, she turned aside, murmuring about dinner and the other guests, and slipped through the door. Following, he took her arm in a gentle clasp. They moved down the hall together without saying anything more.

Dinner was skillfully prepared, beautifully served, and as strained a meal as Alex had ever sat through. Later that night Constance would tell him how pleasant she'd found the evening — an amazing reaction until he considered that he was beginning to perceive things that went on in the Cochrane household through Sara's eyes and ears. He sat in uncharacteristic silence throughout most of the meal, but he watched and listened, and against his will he learned.

Bennet Cochrane was a bully. He'd known that for months, but tonight he discovered that he was also dangerous. He wasn't the callous, blunt-spoken ruffian Alex had taken him for — or not only that. There was method in his cruelty and finesse in his insults, and he was capable of surprising subtlety. He could also be charming to women, a quality Alex had not expected and found disquieting to watch. Although no one was exempt, Sara was the target of his rawest malice — but even that was disguised. Instead of addressing her directly, he spoke generally of "the English" as stupid and supercilious, a snobbish, cold, incompetent breed who used rank to get what brains and ability got "over here." And he had a knack for drawing people into these veiled attacks as accomplices; Alex listened in astonishment when the Donovan woman agreed with him and even offered a recent example of pomposity in an Englishman of her acquaintance. It was as if Sara's heritage was unknown to them, or they'd all suddenly developed amnesia.

But Cochrane saved his sharpest barbs for his victims' poorest-defended vulnerabilities, and in Sara's case that meant her work with foreigners and new immigrants. There was no talk of "Jews, Micks, and Eyetalians" tonight; instead the focus was on the economic harm these unnamed ethnic groups were perpetrating on "real Americans" — anyone born in the United States, presumably. Jobs were being lost, neighborhoods degraded; the very spirit that made this country great was being tainted by the corrupt influence of foreign blood. Because he was a forceful, bullish speaker and because he was powerful and filthy rich, people agreed with him. He managed to make ethnic hatred sound patriotic. Even Constance was nodding when he talked about the systematic destruction by "aliens" of everything that had once made lower Manhattan livable and attractive.

Sara somehow managed a taut, smiling civility through most of it. Alex's newly sharpened senses witnessed nuances of self-restraint that impressed and dismayed him, and churned up an absurd desire in him to rescue her. But even her rigid control faltered when Harry Donovan took up the complaint, seconding Ben and deriding the recommendations of something called the "Tenement House Committee Report."

"But surely," she remonstrated with disarming gentleness, "no one could quarrel with a study that finds tenement house living conditions in need of improvement."

"Maybe," Donovan conceded, "but this report goes way too far." He looked to Ben for approval, and got it in a series of deep nods. "You fix things up for these people, Mrs. Cochrane, they just wreck them again. Believe me, I've seen it happen over and over." He was a burly, fair-haired man with pink cheeks and pale eyes. His wife's brother owned a number of laundries, a *growing* number since Donovan had been elected alderman and — a coincidence, surely — his brother-in-law had become the recipient of so many city contracts for laundry service.

"But we're not talking about luxuries," Sara pursued, "we're talking about things such as light and air. I'm sure you don't oppose a recommendation that new tenements occupy no more than seventy percent of an interior lot. Or better fire safety measures for existing buildings, or more drinking fountains and public lavatories. Simple, basic human necessities —"

"You can't build a profitable building on less than seventy percent of a lot," her husband snapped. She started to disagree, but he talked over her. "Anyway, where does it say honest taxpayers have a duty to provide these so-called basic necessities to people nobody asked to come here anyway? Who provided *me* with 'basic necessities' when I didn't have a nickel to my name? Nobody, and that's how it's supposed to be. If you can't make a living in this country on your own, the way the rest of us did it, through hard work, competition, and free enterprise, then you damn well ought to go back where you came from."

"I've got to go along with you on that, Ben," Donovan chimed in.

Sara spoke quietly, fervently. "Three-quarters of the people in New York live in tenements. The Eleventh Ward has almost a thousand people to every one of its thirty-two acres. The only city that even comes close to that is Bombay. The buildings are fire traps without sanitation or ventilation, the stairs choked with garbage, common privies constantly stopped up —"

"Who's making them —"

"Hundreds of people crammed inside tiny rooms, poverty-stricken newcomers who have no alternatives, no choices —"

"Then why don't —"

"— and from a safe distance uptown, the owners count their profits and stuff *more*

138

people in, *more* rent-paying tenants —"

"Let 'em leave, then!" Cochrane boomed, finally drowning her out. He laughed falsely to break the tension. "What did they come here for, a handout? How do they *expect* to live, bunched up down there like ants? It's a big, wide country," he said, spreading his arms and smiling with odious magnanimity, "there's room for everybody. Let 'em move west, or south, wherever they want. It's the land of opportunity, isn't it? Everybody starts out the same, am I right?"

Nods and murmurs of agreement. Alex watched Sara turn a teaspoon over and over on the cream lace tablecloth; her face was smooth, but the long fingers pinching the spoon were white from strain. "Of course, that's a little easier to say if one is sitting in a Louis XVI chair, dining on lobster and tournedos at one's Venetian Renaissance table." She softened the words with a smile that made the others titter in self-conscious amusement.

Cochrane didn't smile. "And that's easy to say if 'one' doesn't have to lift one of her dainty little fingers to live like a goddamn queen."

"The lobster is excellent, by the way," Constance put in diplomatically when the silence went on too long. "Maine, isn't it?"

Sara sat back in her chair. The tension seemed to drain out of her, replaced by fatigue. The brittle look she sent her husband down the length of the table was a combination of weariness, contempt, and spite. Alex saw it; if anyone else did, they gave no sign. It made him shiver.

A little later, a maid came in and spoke quietly in her ear. She put down her fork, smiling in apology. "Would you excuse me for just a few minutes? It's Michael."

"Is he ill?" worried Mrs. Donovan.

"No, it's only a nightmare. He's been having them rather frequently. I'll just run up —"

"Leave him be," Cochrane commanded. "The only problem Michael's got is that he's spoiled. As long as he knows you'll come running, he'll keep on having his dreams."

"Carla says he's been crying for twenty minutes, Ben. I really think I should —"

"Leave him."

A pause. Sara folded her napkin with great care and laid it beside her plate. "Do you know," she said slowly, looking at no one, "I think I'd better look in on him just for a moment. Please don't wait dessert on me." She rose and went from the room.

Alex spoke up into the new silence, talking on about Newport, hardly aware of what he was saying. Cochrane's dark eyes narrowed on the wine glass he spun in slow half-circles beside his plate. Alex took unwilling note of his small, fleshy hands and beefy forearms, the round, powerful breadth of his shoulders. A prickling sensation started at the back of his neck and crept up his scalp. He was glad Sara had won that battle of wills — the thought of Michael sobbing alone in childish terror was not to be borne. But he wondered what price she would pay for the victory later.

It was her usual punishment, crude and unimaginative. He hadn't inflicted it on her in more than a year, but neither of them had forgotten anything. At least it came swiftly — but tonight she had known it would. She preferred it that way. Sometimes he postponed his retribution, and the anxiety she suffered waiting for it added to his satisfaction. She had infuriated him tonight, though, and he didn't have the patience for delay.

His timing was flawless. He pushed the door open — it was unlocked, of course; the one and only time she had locked it

141

he'd broken it in — at the moment she was extinguishing the lamp beside her bed. In the sudden blackness he was invisible, but she could hear him moving and she knew what he would do. She made a clear target in her white nightgown. His hands clamped on her shoulders. She gave an involuntary cry, a pointless, nearly mute protest, hearing the tearing of cloth and the quick whistle of breath through his nose. Her hands flew up, flailed, pushed.

"You had a lot of opinions tonight," he panted, backing her into the bed. Why was she fighting him? She couldn't not fight him. His sweating weight crushed her against the mattress. "You tried to make a fool out of me." She cut off his string of curses by whispering, "I didn't have to try, you did it so well yourself!"

His hands slid into her hair. Backing up enough to turn her, he thrust her face-down into the sheets. There was no need to muffle her mouth. He knew she wouldn't scream — Michael would hear. She only gasped when he shoved himself into her, using his body like a sword. This was the moment when her mind usually shut down. She would fix on an image of anything, past or future, and not let go until it was over. But tonight she couldn't stop fighting. The pain, the bruises, none of it mattered; she had to throw the vile weight of him off her, she didn't care if it killed her.

He didn't hit her — he hadn't hit her in five years — but he had a better way. He hauled her up, hands mashing her breasts, his hard sex buried deep, and grunted into her hair, "We're sending Michael away to school."

"No. No."

"Do him good. There's one in Germany I heard about. Military academy."

"Please!"

He almost climaxed then; she could feel his obscene excitement. "It's what he needs. They'll make a man out of him."

She started to curse him. He pulled her head back by the hair and she gasped again.

"In the fall. He'll go away in the fall." When he felt the wetness of her tears on his wrist, he couldn't hold back. "Sara," he ground out like an oath. The slap of his thighs against hers was loud and ludicrous, the sound of victory; but she welcomed it, thanked God for it. He shoved her down again and pulsed into her, groaning, teeth grinding.

When it was over, he kept her pinned a

little longer, stroking and squeezing her buttocks in a travesty of after-play. "Good night," he whispered in her ear. As soon as his hands left her, she jerked upright. But her legs gave out; she dropped to her knees beside the bed. She saw his broad backside outlined for a second in the dim hall light when he opened the door. Hot loathing brought bile up into her throat.

She used the sheet to haul herself up and collapsed on the bed. He's bluffing, she thought, he has to be. If he sent Michael away, he would have nothing left to use against her. It was a trick. When chills racked her, she dragged the covers over her head and tried to stop shaking. A trick, another torture, that's all it was. Maybe he wanted something from her. What? Something she had, something she could barter for Michael. She turned her head into the pillow to muffle a soft, desolate scream, because there wasn't anything left.

# Eight

Alex snatched a glass of champagne from the silver tray of a passing waiter while Mullaly's String Orchestra struck up another waltz. The waiter, poor bastard, was rigged out as an English footman, complete with knee breeches and powdered wig. It was that kind of a party. Alex calculated that the cost of the food, spread out under the stars in the Casino's Horse Shoe Piazza, amounted to about half his yearly salary. And this was only the first supper; at midnight, there was to be a second one, even more elaborate.

If enough people stayed around for it. From the look of things, the Cochranes had been expecting at least two hundred people — "every swell in Newport," he recalled Ben prophesying — but so far only about forty had shown up. About half that number had bothered to attend the "ground-breaking ceremony" earlier; swells indeed, overdressed and uncomfortable, standing around a great sandy ditch in the middle of Cochrane's lot and listening to him christen his new home "Eden."

*Eden,* for God's sake. Alex thought of how Sara's careful smile had wavered when she'd heard that; but she'd kept her eyes on the ground, seemingly fascinated by the hole her husband was digging, his patent leather evening shoe looking ridiculous against the shovel's muddy edge. Alex had willed her to look up so that he could smile at her, send her a message that said, *No one who knows you believes you had anything to do with any of this.* But she never had. She probably knew it already; she'd probably worked out long ago that if she worried about what people thought of her solely because she was Bennet Cochrane's wife, she would drive herself crazy.

Still, he wondered how she was taking the spectacular social failure this evening represented. Renting the Casino for the night must have cost Cochrane a small fortune; at eleven, they were to be entertained by a troupe of dancers he'd hired and had sent up *en masse* from a Broadway revue. Each guest had been given a "favor" — pearl brooches for the ladies, diamond stick pins for the gentlemen. Orchids and camellias and hothouse roses tumbled over everything, banked in masses or twined in

146

the pine-green lattice along the long, curving walkways. Clearly, the evening was intended as the Cochranes' grand debut into Newport high society. What was equally clear was that Ben couldn't have chosen a better way to demonstrate the pathetic improbability of being allowed so much as his big toe in the door.

If it weren't for Sara, Alex might have relished his host's mortification. But he felt her chagrin as he glanced around at the empty tables and empty chairs, the legion of liveried waiters standing around with no one to wait on. Sara was dancing with Ben now; from this distance, in the romantic glow of candles and rose-colored lantern light, her face looked serene. But he knew by now how eloquent her masks could be. Did she think of this night as a personal humiliation, or had she known in advance what would happen and now only worried about Ben's reaction? He suspected she had few illusions left. Rising in society was her husband's goal in life, not hers. Alex thought of her tiny room, with its books and pictures and photographs. She would be happier living a quiet life, he was sure of it. This one didn't suit her. But then, maybe he was deluding himself; maybe she was past being able to live a "simple" life, because all the luxuries and accouterments that surrounded her were so constant and unremarkable by now that she took them for granted.

He sipped his wine moodily, watching her. Her low-cut evening gown was of rich, imperial purple; she'd caught up the long train in one hand to dance. She wore a diamond stomacher whose price he could only guess at, and around her slim throat blazed a dazzling necklace of sapphires and more diamonds. No doubt she traveled to Paris twice a year, like Constance, to buy a completely new wardrobe. She had on enough jewelry right now to finance a small Baltic country for a couple of years. For the first time he wondered if she did her settlement house work at least partly out of guilt. If so, it was an admirable but misguided motive. It wasn't her fault her husband was a capitalist millionaire. And somehow he was sure it was Ben, not Sara, who found charm in the idea of weighting her down from head to toe with precious stones.

"Not dancing, Alex? What's wrong, are you sick?"

He hadn't noticed John Ogden standing beside him until he'd spoken. "Maybe later." He smiled, setting his drink down on a convenient break in the lattice grille he was lounging against.

"Never knew you not to take advantage of so much feminine pulchritude, my boy. And think of the daughters' dowries."

Alex stroked his mustache and tried to decide if he'd just been insulted. Not that it mattered — he would, of course, return a bland smile in either case — but it was worrisome to think that his mating habits, so to speak, which he thought he handled with admirable discretion, might be so well understood by the man who employed him.

"I wanted to speak to you about this office you've set up, Alex," Ogden said, his tone shifting from jovial to serious.

He'd been half-expecting this. "You surprise me if you don't approve, John," he said diplomatically. "It's not just convenient for me, it's also efficient." He'd rented a house on Pebble Drive about a half mile from town, half in the woods and half on the water, and he'd turned part of it into a drafting room. "It's got a telephone, so I can call New York in minutes if I need —"

"I know all that. And I don't say I wouldn't like something like it myself if I had to spend the whole summer up here.

But it's certainly no public endorsement of the firm, is it? You're invisible out there in the middle of nowhere."

"Oh, I'd hardly call it —"

"You should've taken something on Bellevue, or Narragansett Avenue or Thames Street, something public. We're building a million-dollar house here; it would've been good for us to have our local office in plain sight for the duration."

"You're probably right, I didn't think it through." This was a lie; he'd thought it through, then chosen a place he could stand to live in for the next three months. "But Newport's incredibly tight-knit, you know, John, and word of mouth is still our best advertisement. If Cochrane ends up with a good house, I don't think we need to worry about people not knowing who built it for him."

Ogden grunted. "Maybe," he conceded. "I still wish you'd consulted me first. But that reminds me — I already know of someone who's watching the progress of Cochrane's house with more than just casual interest."

"Who?"

"Marshall Farley."

Alex pursed his lips in a silent whistle. Marshall Farley was the textile king of the

East Coast; he was so rich and owned so many mills that there was always some government investigation going on into his business holdings, trying to ferret out monopoly trading.

"He wants a Newport 'cottage.' He told me so himself. If he likes what he sees going up on Bellevue Avenue this summer, there's every likelihood he'll come to us — to you — to build it for him. And he's about four times richer than Ben Cochrane." Ogden paused, watching him. "Well, I see you're able to contain your enthusiasm pretty well."

"No, no," Alex protested, laughing to cover his unease, "it's wonderful news. I'm very glad to hear it. Very glad. It'll be good for the firm, and it goes without saying that it'll be good for me."

"But?"

"Nothing. Really, I'm delighted to hear this, John."

Ogden took off his steel pince-nez and began to polish them with his handkerchief. "I've been in this business for about thirty-two years, Alex," he said, squinting up at him. "I can tell the difference between flash and substance, and I can separate competence from genius. As far as I'm concerned, you're one of the most brilliant natural architects working today. You're inventive and eclectic, and you're not so mired in the classical past that you're afraid to take advantage of technology if you think it'll get you where you want to go. I've never known anyone who's better at combining practicality with — well, for lack of a better word, with what I'll call mysticism. You're unique."

Alex could feel the heat of emotion rising to his cheeks. He blushed only on rare occasions, and this was one of them. "Thanks, John," he muttered gruffly. "Means a lot."

"I haven't finished."

That broke the tension, and he laughed. "You mean there's more?"

"It looks like your reputation is about to take off in a big way, assuming things go well here in Newport. Naturally, I'm delighted for you. What concerns me is that your professional dedication won't have time to keep up with it."

He stiffened. "My professional —"

"Poor choice of words, sorry. What I meant was, you haven't figured out yet what kind of architect you want to be. Because of that, if you don't mind my saying so, you've got a big chip on your shoulder. There's not a damn thing wrong with the house you're building for the Cochranes — about ninety-nine percent of the people in the world would cut off an arm to live in a place like Eden. But look at you — you can't help it, you sneer when you even hear the word."

"I'm sorry, I wasn't —"

"On the other hand, you're almost as full of contempt for the new styles, the modern architecture. You're skeptical about that on aesthetic grounds, but I suspect you ridicule Eden because you're a snob."

"*I'm* a snob — !"

"Yes, in reverse. Listen, Alex, take my advice. You don't have anything to prove anymore. Your future's assured, if you want it to be, so what you need to do is forget about your own past. You don't say much about it, and that's your prerogative, but I think it's holding you back. Understand what I'm saying?"

Yes and no. Alex cleared his throat. "It's good of you to take an interest, John. I appreciate it, and I'll certainly give a lot of thought to what you've said."

"You do that. Oh, I almost forgot." He pulled an envelope from his inside coat pocket and handed it over. "The partners decided you deserve a bonus. Maybe this'll help clear up some of that fuzziness in your thinking, eh?" He gave him a friendly pat on the arm. "Just keep doing what you've been doing, and in a year or two I wouldn't be surprised if you were one of us. Wouldn't that be something? A partner by the time you're thirty. Christ, Alex, I envy you. You've got the world by the tail."

"John — I don't know what to say. I'm very grateful."

"Then that's all you have to say. Look, I'm going to try to sneak out of here before the entertainment starts — if I leave now, I can just make the last ferry back to the city. Make sure we hear from you every few days — that's in addition to mailing in your reports, of course. And I expect you'll be coming to town once in a while as well, won't you?"

"Yes, sir, every couple of weeks, I should think."

"Good, good." They shook hands. "Well, carry on."

"I will. And thanks again."

Ogden gave him another slap on the shoulder and took his leave.

Alex reached for his drink and sank back against the vine-covered spindle screen. Fumbling the envelope open, he glanced at the check inside. Blinked and looked again. He slid the envelope into his pocket and finished off his warming champagne in two swallows.

No doubt about it, money like that had a way of clearing out ambivalent debris in a man's mind and helping him see his way. Yes, indeed. He glanced down appreciatively at his new three-button cutaway and dark blue trousers, the fancy vest surrounding his carefully knotted Waterfall necktie. In Bennet Cochrane's vernacular, he looked like a million bucks.

Closing his eyes, he replayed Ogden's words of praise in his head. He especially liked the part about combining practicality and "mysticism." It made him chuckle. He knew he was good at what he did, had always known it, and the exciting thing was that he knew he was getting *better*. But to hear the sentiment expressed by someone else, someone he respected — that was a deep and abiding satisfaction.

"Putting you to sleep, are we, McKie?"

His eyes snapped open. Ben Cochrane was bearing down on him, holding on to his wife's arm. "Ben!" he exclaimed with false heartiness. "Just catching my breath. Watching all that waltzing tired me out." They made small talk for a minute, about the party, the perfect weather, the Casino. Sara said nothing; Alex thought she seemed upset under the veneer of her tireless poise.

Once the amenities were out of the way, Ben got down to business. "I've changed my mind about the back yard."

"The what?"

"In back of the house, down to the Cliff Walk. I never liked that idea of just letting it go natural. I've decided I want an English garden. Formal, you know? Rows of things all lined up, and maybe one of those whatchamacallits, those things you get lost in."

"A maze?"

"Maze, right. So, what do you think?"

His hands in his pockets squeezed into fists. "Well, it sounds fine, Ben, except there's not enough room. You told me you wanted the house near the water."

"Yeah, well, move it back."

"Move it back?" For a wild second he thought he meant the water. "Move the house back?"

"Put it on a little hill, so it'll be up high and look out over the gardens and the cliff and the ocean."

"A little hill." He sucked his lips in and bit down. "We've already broken ground. We're almost finished digging the foundation."

"Well, we'll have to fill it in and move the thing back. The lot's big enough for it. I want the house closer to the street anyway. What's the point in spending all this money if nobody can see the place?"

Alex didn't trust himself to answer. He glanced at Sara, but she was looking away, her rigid profile motionless against the twinkling lanterns behind her. "We can do that," he said carefully. "It'll delay the commencement of construction by at least a month, and there may be trouble with the ordinance. All the plumbing and electric will have to be recalculated, and we'll have to start over again as far as scheduling the delivery of supplies and equipment and materials. A lot of them have already arrived, so there'll be extra warehousing costs, more —"

"That's your department. Money's not an object. I told you before. You just do it, and I'll pay for it." He looked over his shoulder. "Jeez, people are leaving already. There's Walter Fallon, I have to go talk to him. See you later, McKie." He dropped Sara's arm and strode off.

The ensuing silence was long and embarrassed. Alex was too angry to speak anyway. Finally Sara broke the impasse by saying, "I'm terribly sorry," in a low, hopeless voice.

He looked down at her. She was massaging her hands in her long white gloves, her quiet gaze intent on his face. His irritation drifted away, irrelevant. "Never mind." He leaned toward her and asked, "How is just plain Sara Cochrane this evening?"

It might have been a trick of the light, but her troubled expression seemed to relax and a lovely warmth shone in her silvery eyes. She smiled. Then, just as subtly, the softness receded. Her mouth trembled and her eyes welled with tears. "Sara," he whispered in alarm, reaching for her hand. For the space of a heartbeat she allowed his touch; then she stepped back, murmuring, "Excuse me, I'm quite all right," and turned away as if to watch the dancers.

He stood beside her, staring straight ahead. What was wrong? Had Cochrane been browbeating her? Did he blame *her* for this debacle of a ground-breaking party? Her distress was acute, he could sense it; but he knew she would not allow herself his comfort, or even overt concern. For all that, a moment later he heard himself say, still without looking at her, "If there is anything I can do for you, now or ever, I hope you won't hesitate to tell me."

"That's very kind of you," she said, so softly he could barely hear. "Thank you, Mr. McKie, I won't forget that."

What frightened him was that she hadn't denied she needed help. A minute passed; he could feel her pulling herself together.

"So," she said finally, facing him with a bright, painfully artificial smile, "Ben tells me you've moved into a sort of shed in the middle of nowhere, with no conveniences but a telephone. Do you think that's sending quite the right message to this most sociable of towns?"

"Ah, but you're mistaken," he said lightly, "Newport's the most *social* of towns, not sociable."

"You're right. I stand corrected. It's quite the reverse of sociable, isn't it?"

"Exactly. That being the case, what does it matter where I set up shop? The Drexels and the Goelets and the Goulds aren't going to invite me to dinner anyway, so I may as well please myself."

"And does it please you to live in the wilderness?"

"Mrs. Cochrane, I see you've been misinformed. My house is all of half a mile from the center of town. It's comfortable — you might even call it picturesque — and I've got every amenity a man could want — no, that *anyone* could want. I invite you to come and inspect it. Anytime, at your convenience." She smiled again and shook her head slightly, murmuring a polite thank-you. He saw he'd been rash, that she would never come to his house because of the impropriety, and that the very suggestion was a subtle insult she was too much of a lady to acknowledge. "How do you like *your* new house?" he asked quickly.

"Oh, I love it," she answered with real enthusiasm. "It's on Elizabeth Street, close to everything, and yet the houses are far apart and wonderfully private. At least, they seem so to me after the city."

"And do you like the house itself?"

"It's lovely, it's — perfect. I can't understand why the owners would want to let it to strangers, even for a few months. If it were mine, I'd never leave."

"I like it, too."

"Oh, do you know it?"

"Yes. It's rather well known, in fact, as one of the finest of the old shingle houses built in the '60s and '70s, before Newport became —" He stopped, chagrined.

"Weighted down with stone and marble," she finished, eyes twinkling. "Well, we'll say no more about that, will we?"

"No, indeed."

"Except that it's a wonder the southern tip of the island hasn't fallen into the sea." He laughed, and she laughed with him, both of them relieved to have it out in the open. "There's even a swing in the back-yard for Michael," she went on, "and so many rooms and porches and balconies, it will take him half the summer to explore them all. And he'll be pestering you every day at the building site, I'm quite sure, since it's only three blocks away."

"I'll look forward to seeing him. Did you know you've got a famous next-door neighbor?"

"Really? Which side?"

"The limestone house with the pillars. It's Daisy Wentworth's; she lives there year-round."

"Who is she? I don't know the name."

"You must not read the scandal sheets."

"Oh, but I *do*," she confessed, smiling. "Then you must've taken a holiday from them about two years ago when they were full of Daisy's scandalous divorce from her banker husband."

"Ah. He had an outside interest, I take it?"

"No, no, *she* did. He sued her on grounds of adultery and won. She got that

161

house and some unspecified amount of money, and now they say she's turned into a recluse."

"What happened to her lover?"

"Went back to his wife."

"Were there children?"

"I don't think so."

"Thank God for that," she said fervently.

She looked sad again, as if she'd taken his trivial story too much to heart. Something was wrong; he'd never seen her like this, so full of sorrow and poorly hidden distress. "What's happened to Natasha — I've forgotten her last name," he asked to divert her. "Your friend from the settlement house."

"Oh, Tasha is doing very well."

"You told me she might have a new job."

"That's been postponed for a little. She's working with a tutor now, perfecting her English."

He could guess who was paying for the tutor. "Did she find a new place to live?"

"No — actually, she's going to be staying on at our house for the summer. Ben's moving to his club," she added hastily, seeing his expression. "It's really a boon to us to have someone there while we're away. Now we won't have to close the house. And we're scheduled to have some work done to the plumbing — rather a major overhaul, I understand — and now someone can be there to let the workmen in and out and so forth."

"I see." But he wasn't sure he did. The orchestra began a new melody, and he thought of inviting her to dance. As much as he would have welcomed a legitimate excuse to touch her, caution held him back. He had designs on Mrs. Cochrane, no doubt about it, but oddly, they weren't quite the kind of designs he usually had on beautiful married ladies. In truth, he wanted to dance with Sara a little too much, and his eagerness served as a warning that made him careful.

But she was wearing fresh gardenias in her hair and the sweetness was subtly enticing. Her bare shoulders gleamed palely in the lantern-lit darkness. She was as regal as a queen, but she softened her English hauteur in some mysterious way so that it impressed but never offended. He wanted very much to know what she thought of him, and if she was kind to him because she liked him or because she was evenhandedly kind to everyone.

"You're beautiful tonight. You're always beautiful."

She went still, and looked away. He

could see her trying to decide what to say — how to feel. He'd taken a chance and he didn't regret it; in fact, he felt euphoric in the wake of his words. "Sara." How lovely to call her that. Caution flew away like a bird let out of a cage.

"You must not," she said almost inaudibly.

"Must not what?"

The look she sent him then contained so much sad tenderness, his heart stopped beating. "Spoil it," she said.

He looked up at the sky, breathing deeply. "No, you're right. Please forgive me. I'm sorry I said you were beautiful and that I uttered your beautiful name. It must be the — no, please, don't go." He touched her shoulder with urgent lightness. "I'm drunk. I most humbly beg your pardon." She kept her face turned away. "I would do anything not to spoil it." Her troubled eyes mirrored indecision. His only hope now was her generosity. "Am I forgiven?"

The wait was intolerable, but at last she murmured, "Of course. Now if you'll —"

"I thought I might see Michael at the ground-breaking," he interrupted quickly, to keep her beside him. "Is he all right? Not sick, is he?"

Her jaw muscles contracted and her

pretty mouth turned into a thin line of pain. "No, he's fine. His father decided it wasn't the place for children."

Another subject that was off limits. Talking to her was like walking on eggs tonight. The solution came to him all at once, although he thought it might not strike her in the same way. He held out a gentle, perfectly impersonal hand. "Mrs. Cochrane, would you care to dance?"

She hesitated. Time warped, gnarled, stretched grotesquely. He became fixated on her mouth. The tip of her tongue touched the dainty surface of her top lip. "I —"

"Sara!"

He jerked his hand away like a criminal caught in a theft.

"Come and say good night to the Kimmels!"

Now her face was truly unreadable. For an instant he saw regret. But no, now it was amusement — and now it was sadness again. "Another time, I hope," she said kindly. "Thank you, Mr. McKie. Will you excuse me now?"

He'd run out of ways to keep her. He made her a bow and watched her glide away in the direction of her husband.

# Nine

One afternoon a week later, Sara was sitting on her side porch — or *lanai,* as the rental agent insisted — sipping iced champagne with her new next-door neighbor. They had met the day before under less than ideal circumstances when Michael inadvertantly crossed the boundary line between the Cochrane and Wentworth properties, climbed into Mrs. Wentworth's brand-new flowering dogwood, and snapped its main branch in half. Too frightened to confess to the deed alone, he'd run home and gotten his mother. Sara had been hoping for days for a glimpse of the notorious Daisy Wentworth, divorcée; she was glad to return with Michael to the scene of the crime and coax him through a full confession. She had yet to meet the woman who could resist Michael in the midst of one of his sincere apologies, and Mrs. Wentworth proved no exception. Within minutes he'd been forgiven, his offer of recompense brushed aside, and invited to play anytime he liked with Gadget, Mrs. Wentworth's adolescent dachshund.

In the face of such magnanimity, Sara had extended an invitation to Daisy for tea the next day, and now they were sitting comfortably on the porch, already on a first-name basis, shifting their chairs every few minutes to follow the afternoon shade, while Michael and Gadget played on the steps at their feet.

"You're not at all what I thought you'd be like," confided Daisy. She was on her second glass of champagne, which she had brought over herself, "to inaugurate our friendship." Sara had felt obliged to join her out of politeness, even though champagne made her sleepy and it was not quite four o'clock in the afternoon.

"No? What did you think I'd be like?"

"Snooty. Stiff." She flashed one of her acrid half-smiles. "Obnoxious."

"Oh, dear." She'd discovered already that her new neighbor didn't mince words. "Is that my reputation these days?" she asked lightly.

"No, not yours. I'd say it's more by association."

Tact wasn't her strong suit, either. Sara sipped her wine and said nothing.

"But you're nothing like that, thank God. Do you know you're the first person in Newport to invite me to anything in months? Oh, they'll call me on the telephone sometimes, but only because they want some bit of gossip and they know I know everything. But heaven forbid they should be seen with me out in the world." Her lips curled down at the corners, turning her smile bitter. She was forty, she'd confided a few minutes ago, but to Sara she looked at least five years older. Her skin had a sallow, unhealthy cast, and her gray-flecked dark hair needed a wash. Her body might have been graceful once, but now it was too soft, as if the bones were melting into her flesh.

It was pointless and somehow insulting, Sara decided, to pretend she didn't know what Daisy was talking about. "You mean, because of the divorce."

"Yes, of course, what else?" She stared down into her glass, intent on the bursting bubbles. "I made a mistake and got caught, and I've been paying for it ever since."

"Do you like living here?" Sara asked after an awkward pause. "It's a beautiful place. I love the sea, and the weather is so —"

Daisy made a sound very like a snort and fixed her with a baleful eye over the rim of her glass. "You don't think the appeal of this place for the resorters has anything to do with the sunshine and the fresh sea air, do you?" Sara raised her brows in a question. "My dear, the real sport is Exclusivity. You'll notice there's no culture, no business, no charity or philanthropy to get in the way of what people really come here for — to snub each other in public. It's the only game in town."

"If that's true, then why do you stay?"

Daisy sighed, and her ample breasts rose and fell heavily. "Why, why, why. I ought to go. I keep saying I will, but then I don't. Frankly, I haven't got the energy. Besides," she cackled, "who would they talk about if I left? I serve a vital social function."

"Why do you suppose they *care* so much?" Sara mused a moment later. It was a question that frequently nagged her. "Snobbery takes so much work, and the rewards are so petty. I should think they'd all be exhausted."

"Don't be naive. The great thing about being admitted into Society is that you're finally allowed to help keep everyone else out. That's the whole *point*. Why else do you think they stayed away from your perfectly nice party last week in droves?"

Sara wasn't surprised that her neighbor

knew about that fiasco; she imagined all of Newport and most of New York had heard of it by now. There had even been a nasty piece in the Newport *Observer* that, although it named no names, had managed to devastate all the same. Predictably, Ben blamed her for the miserable failure of their Newport debut, and it was only because he'd had to return to the city so soon the next day that he hadn't thought of some way to make her pay for it. Yet.

"What's high society like in England?" Daisy wanted to know. "And don't tell me it's democratic, because I won't believe you."

"No, of course it's not. It's not the same as here, though. Money's important, but it's not *worshipped* quite so much. And the aristocracy seems to have more fun with all its privileges. I'm not sure why — perhaps because morality isn't quite so strict, so — puritanical, perhaps. Oh, I don't know." She heard herself sigh as heavily as Daisy had, and wondered if they were getting drunk.

The older woman set her empty glass down and clasped her hands behind her head. "Americans are insecure. No matter how rich we are, we still feel gauche. So we buy these ostentatious mansions and try to make them look as European as possible."

Sara smiled, thinking Mr. McKie would certainly agree with that. "Yes. You particularly admire the English, but if you don't mind my saying so, you have a very peculiar idea of what English manners are supposed to be. *Stiffness* is the prominent feature, you think, and so you've adopted stiffness as the highest mode of social conduct."

"That's right," Daisy agreed, nodding and reaching again for the bottle. "You're exactly right. Oh, but you should've seen Newport thirty years ago, Sara, before the Vanderbilts and the Astors got their hands on it. I used to come here when I was a girl with my family, and it was such a lovely place. The houses were all wooden and rambling, with wide verandahs and porch swings, picnics, and rides on donkey carts. Swimming anywhere you liked, no 'Bailey's Beach' to separate the upper class from the vulgar masses. Maybe that's why I can't seem to leave it now — I remember so clearly what it was like before it all turned to stone."

Sara felt her neighbor's melancholy settling over them like a subtle fog. Even Michael seemed affected by it; he wrapped his arms around Gadget's neck and stared up at his mother with worried, searching eyes. She felt a disproportionate relief when the screen door squeaked open and the maid announced that she had a long distance call from New York.

Daisy heaved herself up. She'd better go home, she said; she was feeling in need of a little nap. They bade each other quick good-byes, then Sara rushed into the house.

There was only one telephone, in the foyer at the foot of the staircase. The operator identified the calling party — Lauren, thank God, not Ben — and then her friend's strong voice came through as clearly as if she were in the room.

"Sara! Hello, how are you? Can you hear me?"

"I can hear you perfectly. How are *you?*"

"I've just come from your house. I took Lulu over in a cardboard box and gave her to Tasha. I think it was love at first sight for both of them." Lulu was Lauren's cat; Tasha was going to keep her while Lauren was away in Europe. "Now I've got just a little bit more packing to do, and then I'm off. The boat sails at six this evening."

"Are you excited? I can tell you are."

"Manic! I'm looking at myself in the mirror right now, and my cheeks are so red

I look like a clown! I can't keep two thoughts together. Won't it be interesting to unpack this suitcase tonight and discover what bizarre things I've put into it?"

Sara laughed, although she felt like crying. "I wish I were going with you."

"God, yes, then it would be perfect."

"What did you think of Tasha?"

"I liked her a lot. She's very sweet, isn't she? So simple, and yet very strong, I think. But to tell you the truth, I'm amazed that Ben is letting her stay there. It doesn't seem like something he would do."

"Yes, it was a surprise." He'd made the decision suddenly and without explanation. Sara's private theory was that he had a new mistress, and that he'd realized he could consort with her more freely from his club than his home, away from the watchful eyes of his own servants. So the offer to move out for Tasha's sake was really a fine piece of hypocrisy.

"How's Michael?" Lauren asked.

"He was sick for the first three days — nothing serious this time, just a cold. But now he's well and running around everywhere. We have an interesting next-door neighbor and he's made friends with her dog. And he loves to visit with Mr. McKie at the site."

"That's that beautiful man I met at your house?"

"He's the architect you met, yes."

"Don't you think he's beautiful?"

She laughed again. "That's not quite the word I would choose."

"I would. I'd love to paint him — What? Yes, Mother, I know. Sorry, Sara, I have to hang up, Mother says it's time to go. She's trying to scare me, but I should probably finish packing now anyway. I just called to say good-bye. I'll write to you all the time."

"I'll write to you, too."

"The address might change, but for now it's the one I gave you. Take care of yourself and have a wonderful summer —"

"I hope Paris is everything you want it to be, Lauren, everything you deserve —"

"Give Michael a kiss —"

"I will, and be *careful*, don't do anything silly, don't be *reckless* —"

"I will be careful, and you stop sounding like my mother. I love you."

"I love you — good-bye!"

"Good-bye!"

"Bon voyage!"

The line went dead. Sara held on to the ear-piece for a long moment before finally cradling it and getting slowly to her feet. She despised good-byes and had never been any good at them. And this was how bereft she felt because Lauren was leaving: what would it be like if Ben made good on his threat and took Michael away from her?

But it wouldn't happen — she was almost certain he'd only been trying to frighten her. The day after he'd brutalized her and told her of his spiteful plan, she'd forced herself to confront him, despite her fear and a cowardly hope that by not dealing with it at all it might go away.

"If you send Michael away," she told him, dry-eyed, in his study the next morning, "I'll leave you."

He smiled, taunting her. "No, you won't. You'll never leave."

He was right. She knew it then, she knew it now. If she left him, he would find her and take Michael away from her for good. Because he was the one with the power. He was the American millionaire, she the penniless foreigner, and although he was an adulterer ten times over, she could never prove it.

Hating herself, she'd wept in front of him. And that was the victory he'd been craving all along; after that he could pretend to be generous. "We'll discuss it later," he said softly, eyes glittering with

175

triumph. "There's no hurry to make a decision yet. I've been in touch with this school — it's in Heidelberg, by the way. They say they'll take him as late as September, so —"

"Why are you doing this?" she burst out. "Damn you, how can you hurt your own son just to get at me? How, Ben? What kind of a man —"

"You're the one who's hurting him," he retorted, irate, "turning him into a damned sissy —"

And so on and so on, an ancient, poisonous argument they both slipped into with the ease of habit. But no more was said of the German military school after that. All she could hope was that it was another weapon of torture he would hold over her for the rest of the summer, then let go. He'd perpetrated similar cruelties before, after all, too many times to count. And this one would hardly be the last.

"Mummy!" Michael ran into the room, skidded on the just-waxed floor, and careened into her, nearly knocking her back on her chair. "It's four-thirty," he announced breathlessly, backing up.

"Thanks very much," she said when she'd caught her balance. "I guess I won't be needing my watch anymore."

*"Four-thirty,"* he insisted. "Mr. McKie says that's a good time to come and see him!"

"He does, does he?"

"Yes. And he wants you to come with me."

"Indeed. And when did he say that?"

"I can't remember. But one time he said, 'How is your mother today, Michael?' and I said, 'Fine,' and he said, 'Sometime you must ask her to come along with you,' and I said, 'Yes, sir,' and so — and so —"

"And so you're asking me."

"Yes. So — will you?"

It was time for her to go to the site, to see how her own house was progressing. Avoiding Mr. McKie was childish and self-defeating. She ought to have gone immediately after the Casino party, not put it off day after day, adding weight to his inevitable speculation that the things he'd said to her that night had affected her. They *had,* but she might have hidden that if she'd possessed the wherewithal to confront him sooner. Now it would be awkward. But not as awkward as it would be if she procrastinated even longer.

"Yes," she decided quickly, to Michael's delight. "Give me two minutes to put on better shoes for walking, and then we'll go."

Alex saw them through the open door of the contractor's hut, where he was rescaling a section of the first-floor elevation for the master carpenter. He threw down his pencil and jumped up, dragging both hands through his hair to comb it, grimacing at the dirt on the knees of his trousers. He had no idea where he'd left his coat. He looked like one of his workmen, and Mrs. Cochrane looked, as usual, as if she'd stepped off a page of one of her fashion magazines. Michael was pointing at the hut and dragging her toward it, so there was no sense in prolonging his useless toilette; he made a halfhearted loop in his tie, tucked in his shirt, and stepped outside.

"There he is!" shouted Michael. He dropped his mother's hand and broke into a run, not stopping until he'd slammed full-tilt into Alex's hip. Used to this welcome by now, Alex countered it by seizing Michael under the arms and swinging him around in a wide arc, making aeroplane noises while the boy shrieked with glee.

Sara stopped in her tracks, amazed by the degree of familiarity the enthusiastic greeting implied. When had this happened?

"I've brought my mum!" declared Michael once he was on the ground again.

"So I see." Alex wiped his dusty palm on the pocket of his trousers, then took Sara's outstretched hand. "I was hoping you'd come," he said simply.

"I meant to before now, but — I've been so busy." She almost made a face at herself. Seven days to come up with a good reason for her cowardly absence, and all she could manage was "I've been so busy"? Shocking incompetence. She consoled herself with the thought that she *might* have fashioned a really clever, believable lie, but she couldn't have used it anyway with Michael standing beside her, listening to every word.

She took her hand back and glanced around. "You're much further along than I thought you'd be. To tell the truth, I expected a great hole in the ground and very little else."

Each time they met, her English accent took him by surprise for a few seconds. He folded his arms across his chest and stopped staring at her long enough to follow her gaze. "That's where we would've been if Ben hadn't changed his mind." *Again,* he added to himself.

"Yes, I heard about that."

179

The latest design was for a house with two fronts, one facing the street and one facing Cliff Walk, which got nearly as much pedestrian traffic as Bellevue Avenue. Ben had settled on leaving the building where it was once that had been pointed out to him. Now, though, he wanted a new, more castle-like facade for what had originally been conceived of as the back of the house, including double studded oak doors from a Spanish cathedral, nine feet wide and a foot thick. Alex, who had expected him to demand a moat and a drawbridge next, considered he'd gotten off easy. This time.

"Come on, Mum, I'll show you everything," offered Michael, tremulous with responsibility.

"Mind if I come along?" Alex asked solemnly.

"No, you can come," he answered in the same tone.

"But you were working," Sara started to protest, "we don't want to take you —"

"No, I was finished. Really. And Michael gives a wonderful tour; I should know, I've taken it several times myself." She laughed — a light, lovely sound that offered forgiveness and forgetfulness and made Alex feel blessed — and they all set off across the bumpy ground. It seemed natural to take her arm so she wouldn't stumble, and he did it with gratefulness and almost motiveless solicitude. The sunlight was kinder, the fresh air sweeter, now that he'd gotten back what he'd nearly thrown away. He told himself he would never be so rash again.

Michael made a bee-line for his favorite piece of equipment, the huge, steam-powered crane used for moving heavy steel beams and unwieldy piles of materials. The crane was idle now; so when he begged to be allowed to sit in it, Alex obligingly hoisted him up into the controller's seat.

"He can't turn it on, can he?" worried Sara in a low voice.

"I think he could do anything he set his mind to." He laughed at her expression. "No, of course not. Not from up there, anyway."

Relieved, she turned in a slow circle, surveying the site. Most of the workers had gone home, even Mr. Perini, the building contractor, whom she'd met at the groundbreaking. The sandy yard was strewn with neat stacks of lumber and metal and glass; Michael pointed at them from his high perch and told her what they were all for

— a recital which gave her a strong clue as to the sort of pest he'd made of himself in the past week. The house's foundations had been dug, and cement footers laid along their bottoms. Rudimentary floors already lay over about half of the partitioned spaces, so that it was possible to discern shapes and forms even though no walls had been erected yet. "Tell me where the rooms are going to be," she said, curious now in spite of herself.

"I will!" cried Michael, clambering down from the crane with Alex's help. "Come over here, this is the front."

He showed her the main entrance and pointed out the future location of reception rooms, drawing rooms, parlors and sitting rooms, as well as an immense ballroom that would run along the whole rear section of the main wing. Beyond it was a courtyard, and beyond that, she learned to her horror, was a separate building that would house "the kitchens."

"You're joking," she said to Alex in disbelief.

He shook his head. "He's modeled it after Castello Firenzuola, a castle in —"

"Italy. Yes, I've heard of it. It's a *medieval* castle." She put her hand on her forehead. "My God, it's worse than I thought."

"No — I mean yes, it's — not good, but it could be worse."

"How?"

"Well, he wants a tunnel, and a sort of conveyer belt constructed inside it in order to transport food between the house and the kitchens, and then dumb waiters down to the cellars —"

"Oh, please. Stop."

She'd turned away; she was hugging herself and her shoulders shook. He thought she was crying. "Sara —" Just then she let out a strangled whoop, and he realized she was laughing.

Michael heard, and ran around to face her. "What's funny?" he wanted to know, already laughing with her. "What's funny, Mum?"

She wiped her eyes and pulled herself up straight. "Nothing, I'm just being silly. Tell me where your room is going to be." She found her handkerchief in her pocketbook and used it, sending Alex a private look of chagrin.

"Well, it's not on *this* floor, of course," Michael explained with exaggerated patience. He took her hand and led her over toward one of the drawing rooms he'd just pointed out. "It'll be *above* this room right here."

"How nice; you'll have a tree to look at out your window. It's a copper beech, isn't it? I'm glad you could leave that," she told Alex.

"We left as many as we could."

"And *your* room will be there," Michael went on, gesturing, "and Daddy's is down there. This is a corridor and his is at the end. See?"

"Yes, I see. Very nice."

"Mummy, why don't you and Daddy sleep in the same room?"

First she flinched, then she turned pink. She opened and closed her mouth once, but nothing came out. Alex wanted to look away from her embarrassment, out of courtesy. At the same time, he was dying to hear her answer.

"Charlie O'Shea's mum and dad sleep in the same room," Michael pursued doggedly, "and Charlie says they even sleep in the same bed. The same *bed,*" he repeated, mystified. "Why don't you and Daddy —"

"Michael."

"Yes, sir?"

"Do you know the difference between a trabeated roof and an arcuated one?"

"No, sir."

"Come over here and I'll show you."

"Oh, *boy.*"

184

While Sara waited for her cheeks to stop burning, half a dozen brilliant answers to her son's question leapt annoyingly to mind. She unfurled her parasol with a vexed snap and walked over to watch Mr. McKie demonstrating something to Michael with a handful of small sticks. They were crouched together, perfectly at ease, faces displaying identical interest in whatever it was they were making. The picture moved her in an odd way. For reasons she would never understand, Ben wasn't able to play with Michael in this simple, good-hearted way. He must love him — she had to believe that — but he was incapable of showing it. And yet Michael loved his father, with a generous, uncomplicated love that broke her heart because she was afraid that someday Ben would use it to hurt him.

Alex looked up and grinned at her. She moved closer, smiling back. He was in shirtsleeves and suspenders, his shoes caked with mud, tools sticking out of his pockets. The summer sun had bronzed his skin and gilded his hair. He looked strong and healthy, muscular and male, and as much in his element kneeling there in the dirt as he did in evening clothes at Sherry's or in her drawing room. All the cloudy, unconfronted reasons she'd been avoiding him became perfectly clear then, and focused in the sharp but simple truth that she wanted him. Wanted to have him for her own.

And she never could.

Well, that was all right, then. Sad, too bad, maybe even a tragedy — but not dangerous. It was hopeless, and so it was safe. Nothing would ever come of it.

That was why, when Michael asked if Mr. McKie could come with them tonight on their walk — an evening ritual they never missed, although they trod the fashionable Cliff Walk at an unfashionable hour — Sara said yes. And when the invitation was later extended to the next night, and the next, and then wasn't extended at all because it was simply assumed by all three that he would, of course, accompany them, she felt no alarm. Only a little stab in the heart, and she was used to that.

Alex helped to further her perception of safety by treating her at all times with the most meticulous propriety, so much so that she began to wonder if perhaps, that night, he really had been drunk. It all seemed like a dream to her now, or a misunderstanding whose importance she had foolishly overestimated. Mr. McKie was courteous, agreeable, mannerly, and obliging — the perfect gentleman companion in a community that would have rooted out the merest semblance of improper behavior and happily torn its perpetrator to shreds. He was also charming and amusing, and unfailingly kind to Michael; she couldn't have asked for a more congenial friend. And if, once in a great while, some wayward, outlaw longing stirred the quiet surface of her content — well, she simply forgave herself. She was a woman, not a block of ice. Such thoughts were natural. Natural — but pointless. And hurtful. But because they hurt no one but her, she tolerated them.

The month of June passed quickly. Ben never came. She'd known he wouldn't visit every weekend as he'd promised, but she'd thought to see him at least once or twice. But he never came, and so for Sara the long, idle days were also a reprieve from the strain of worry and distrust and foreboding. They spoke on the telephone, and she would report on the progress of the house — steady despite his continuing demands for changes; Michael's health — perfect; the status of her social advancement — never fast or grand enough to suit him. From him she learned that he was comfortable at his club, business was good, and that the one time he'd stopped by the house to pick up something he'd forgotten, Miss Eminescu seemed to have everything under control.

She had deduced the same thing from the letters Tasha wrote to her. Her English lessons were going well, she related. She was keeping busy by doing a little sewing, not only for herself but for Sara, who had been so kind as to say that she might alter and experiment with a few of her beautiful winter garments. Sara considered this a good sign, since it meant Tasha's wrist must be healed by now. It wouldn't be long before she found steady employment in a fine New York dress shop — if not Mr. Lockhart's, then someone else's. Meanwhile she made a convenient housekeeper while the family was away, taking calls, relaying messages, and dealing with the workmen who came and went to service the new plumbing. All in all, it seemed a fortuitous arrangement for everyone.

The lazy, sun-drenched days slipped by. To please Ben, she dutifully accepted all the invitations that came her way, and was privately glad because there weren't very many. Mr. and Mrs. Kimmel, business friends of Ben's from the city, were particularly solicitous and always included her at dinner parties and teas and excursions into the country. But otherwise she saw few hostesses more than once or twice, and entertained sparingly herself. Instead she spent most of her time with Michael. How lovely to have him to herself, without Mrs. Drum's interference! They did everything together. They went to Bailey's Beach each morning at eleven for the "ladies' swim" — only for an hour, because at noon a flag was run up to announce the gentlemen's turn, when the ladies must disappear. She watched his hair turn nearly white from the sun, his skin a deep golden brown, and sometimes she swore she could *see* him growing taller. In the afternoon they did lessons, then played cards or games. Or she would read a book on the terrace while he and Gadget ran each other's legs off in Daisy's front yard. Mrs. Godby, the cook, liked to go home at five o'clock, so they either went out to dinner in restaurants or made sandwiches and ate them at the kitchen table.

Daisy dropped by almost every day — to "schmooze," as Sara put it to herself. It was a surprise to discover that the champagne she'd brought over that first day wasn't a one-time, celebratory bottle after all;

rather, it was part of Daisy's daily ration of alcohol, and often she started on it as early as two or three o'clock. But the only effect it seemed to have was to sharpen her tongue and darken marginally an outlook that was already sardonic in the extreme.

And every evening at six o'clock, while fashionable Newporters were drinking tea on the lawn or starting to change for dinner, Sara sat on a rock at Anchor Point and waited for Michael to fetch Mr. McKie from the building site. Then the three of them would amble the length of Cliff Walk and back, taking their time, stopping to stare at the "cottages" or to watch the late slanting sun dance on the ocean. It was a time to tell each other what they'd done that day, or what they'd thought, or said, or heard someone say. They looked forward to it as the hour that rounded things out, smoothed over the complexities of the day, and put everything in perspective. If the walk had to be canceled — because Sara had a social engagement or Alex had to go to New York — they all felt cheated, and the day seemed oddly unfinished.

One Saturday Alex invited Michael to go with him to Bailey's Beach for the "gentlemen's swim," and after that it became a regular weekend outing for them. Sara was intrigued by Michael's unbounded delight in the arrangement. He enjoyed going to the beach with her, of course, and they always had fun — but going with Alex raised the experience to a completely different level. Had he missed male companionship that much? It ought not to surprise her; Ben rarely did anything with him alone, purely for enjoyment. But she sensed something in Michael's happiness in being with Alex that went beyond the simple pleasure a seven-year-old boy might take in spending time with a kind, funny, indulgent older member of his own sex. She couldn't have put it into words, but sometimes she felt there was a kinship between them, some connection that existed on an unspoken, hardly conscious level and manifested itself in their speedy and remarkably easy friendship. She had deep, complex feelings about the situation. But it was summertime; she felt more relaxed than she had in years. She put off sorting her feelings out because she was lazy and they were too complicated.

On an afternoon early in July, thick, gunmetal clouds rolled and writhed over the bay, signaling a storm. Michael could see his walk being washed out, and he was longing to show Mr. McKie the model battleship he'd spent all day constructing out of toothpicks. Sara finally gave in to his cajoling and let him carry a message to the site, asking Alex to meet them, if it rained, at the house instead of at Anchor Point. What was wrong with that? Mr. McKie was in her employ, they'd been seen together in public countless times, Michael was always with them — just as he would be today. She could see nothing wrong in it, no social decencies flouted. At four o'clock the heavens opened up, and at four-fifteen Alex slogged up the front steps under an umbrella and knocked on the door.

At five, the sun was shining, and Sara, Alex, Michael, and Daisy were eating salted nuts and playing cassino on the side porch. Alex had never met Mrs. Wentworth and wasn't quite sure what to make of her. Her manner was cynical and lethargic; he thought she might be a little drunk, and she kept giving him what he could only describe as "the eye." She was nice to Michael, though, and Sara seemed fond of her. Right now, she was explaining to Sara why she — Sara — could never hope to rise in Newport society unless she made some radical changes in her style of life.

"First of all, you don't ride. Anyone with serious social intentions — I won't call them pretentions — rides every morning on the common from nine to ten. In, I hope I need hardly say, a new and different riding habit each day. Second, and if anything worse, you don't own a pony phaeton or indeed any other sort of equipage at all. But a phaeton is the *preferred* carriage, because it has low sides, thus allowing more of one's costume to be seen by the vulgar herd of pedestrians as one rolls along behind one's matched pair to visit the Casino.

"And that's another thing, my dear. You're not seen nearly often enough at the Casino. It's no wonder Mrs. John Shirlington did not invite you to her little *fête champêtre* last week in the country. Didn't you hear about it? It was quite a rustic affair, just a tent for fifty, champagne, her best linen and crystal, four wigged footmen — oh, and my favorite touch — half a dozen rented sheep."

The mention of sheep reminded Michael of horses. "Guess what!" he exclaimed, laying his cards down face-up — a disconcerting habit no one had been able to break him of.

"What?" said Daisy, since he was looking only at her.

"Mr. Oliver Belmont keeps his horses in his house!"

"No! I don't believe it."

He was still hardly able to believe it himself. "It's true! He does, doesn't he, Alex?"

Daisy continued to feign amazement, although there wasn't a soul in Newport who didn't know about Belcourt Castle, the fifty-two-room estate on Bellevue Avenue that housed, among other things, the owner's horses.

"The whole first floor is a stable," Michael persisted, "and each stall has a gold plate with the horse's name on it! And every night the horses get bedded down in Irish linen sheets."

"With the Belmont crest embroidered on them," Alex added for color. "And what's he got upstairs?"

"Two *stuffed* horses!" Daisy reacted with an appropriate mix of horror and fascination. "And he's got *dummies* sitting on 'em, dressed up in medieval armor!" Even Michael thought this was going too far. But the idea of letting your horses live in your house with you seemed wonderfully logical to him, an idea to which more grown-ups ought to give serious consideration.

The game progressed in fits and starts,

not unlike the conversation, which shifted suddenly to costume balls. Daisy told of a fancy masked ball in Newport a few years ago, when a wealthy couple had attempted to explain their costumes to the announcing footman at the entrance to the ballroom. The husband was dressed as Henry IV, his stout wife as a "normal peasant."

"Henry the Fourth!" shouted the footman. "And an enormous pheasant!" The story sent Michael into one of his laughing fits, which convulsed the others and put an end to the game once and for all.

"Mr. McKie, I'm having a small party next Friday night at my house," Daisy announced over her third glass of sherry. "I would be so delighted if you could come. It's mostly a family affair, an engagement party for my niece who lives in Boston, and quite informal. Will you be in town that evening?"

Sara watched him, wondering what he would say. She was aware that Mr. McKie had "social intentions," as Daisy would phrase it, and Daisy herself was now *persona non grata* in true society because of the scandal in her past. She'd already invited Sara to the party, with great casualness — "My dear, it won't be anything at all, mostly outside, you ought to come just so the music won't drive you mad. But if you can't make it, I'll understand perfectly, it won't matter in the least —" And so on, until Sara finally had to interrupt to say she would love to come. Daisy's gratitude had been painful to witness.

"I have to go to New York tomorrow," Alex answered, "but only for a few days. I'll be back Thursday evening, and I'd like very much to come to your party."

Under cover of her lashes, Sara sent him a soft, grateful look. *How kind of you,* she signaled.

It was the sort of look that could make Alex forget about breathing for a heartbeat or two. Sometimes she had that effect on him without any effort at all, just by turning her head in a certain way or laughing at something he said or dropping gracefully to her knees so that she could look her son in the eye. It hardly bothered him that what he ought to be feeling was self-reproach, since she'd completely misread his gesture to Mrs. Wentworth — not that he ever intended to correct her. Kindness had nothing to do with it: he'd accepted the invitation so that he could be near Sara.

"I'm hungry," Michael announced.

"Impossible," said Alex. "You just ate a pound of nuts single-handed."

Sara glanced at her watch and saw that it was indeed time to start thinking about dinner. "Why don't I make something for us here? Mrs. Godby left a roast, I think. Or possibly it's a turkey." Michael and Daisy exchanged looks. "What? Don't you think I can do it?" Their faces remained skeptical; she turned to Alex. "I assure you I can cook, Mr. McKie. I can do eggs now, and I can make vegetables that just need boiling —" Michael interrupted with simulated gagging sounds. She frowned and opened her mouth to reprimand him.

"Too bad Mrs. Wiggs isn't here," he said to divert her.

"Who's Mrs. Wiggs?"

"Alex's landlady. She makes cornbread that melts in your mouth. Sometimes she brings him his breakfast in bed. Right, Alex?"

"Right." Daisy and Sara were looking at him with identical expressions of interest. "She's sixty," he mentioned helpfully.

"Why don't you all come to my house?" Daisy suggested. "Unlike Mrs. Godby, my cook stays to make dinner. Whatever she's making, I'll just tell her to make more."

"Why don't we go out to a restaurant?"

Alex chimed in. "Shoal's is good, or Terrier's, that new one on Bay Street."

Daisy looked thoughtful; Michael was all for it. Sara was privately weighing the proprieties involved in such an outing when they heard a carriage stop in front of the house. Michael bounded down the steps to investigate, and a second later he shouted from the yard, "Daddy!"

Sara pushed back her chair. "Oh," escaped her involuntarily, but she cut herself off before the "no" could follow it. Her eyes flew to Alex's. In that brief, urgent contact he saw alarm as naked as a cry for help, before she beat and bullied her emotions back in line and composed herself. Her steely, smothered calm was worse. Helpless, he watched her stand up and say, to no one in particular, "Well, what a nice surprise."

A minute later Ben rounded the turn in the flagstone walk and strode up the steps, Michael trotting behind him. Amid the greetings and introductions and expressions of surprise, Alex took note that the Cochranes never touched each other. "Why didn't you call?" Sara asked with a now-pleasant, wifely smile.

"Didn't have time. I ran into Martin Keynes on the street in New York this

198

afternoon and he invited me for dinner. So we came up together on the boat. It starts at eight, Sara, out in the harbor on his yacht. Better start getting ready."

"Can I come too, Dad?"

"No."

"Ben, Mrs. Wentworth and Mr. McKie and I were just starting to make plans for dinner. Perhaps we could all go out —"

"Look, I've already told him we're coming. Sorry," he said shortly to Alex and Daisy, who began to assure him it was quite all right; he interrupted by telling Sara, with a look of heavy meaning, "Keynes says the Shermans and the William Whitneys are coming, too."

"Oh, the Shermans and the William *Whitneys*," she repeated with exaggerated emphasis, then gave a quick, artificial laugh. "Ah well, in that case, you two had just better be running along, hadn't you?"

She hated the embarrassed silence that followed, hated herself even more for losing control to the point of resorting to the cheapest kind of sarcasm. And she'd made Ben angry. The consequences of that might be anything.

Alex spoke up hurriedly. "I wish I'd known you were coming, Ben. I've got to

199

go to New York tomorrow, otherwise I'd have shown you around the site. I guess I could put it off a day, or you —"

"It doesn't make any difference, I have to get back myself first thing in the morning. You taking the eight o'clock? We can talk about it on the ferry together."

"Well, I'll be going," said Daisy, surging to her feet. "A pleasure, Mr. Cochrane. I've heard so much about you."

"That so?" His eyes flicked over her rudely. He reached into his vest pocket, found his watch, glanced at it, and snapped it closed. "I've heard about you, too."

Sara reddened with anger. "I'll call you," she told Daisy, touching her arm. "Thanks for coming today. I'll see you soon." Daisy squeezed her hand and turned away without a word.

"Well," Alex began. "I'll be —"

"No reason why *you* couldn't come to this thing, McKie," Ben said suddenly, not bothering to lower his voice. "You know Keynes? Banking and real estate, mostly; do you good to meet him. Want to come along?"

He ought to say yes. Ogden and the other partners would value the new connection; they'd also expect him to spend a social evening every once in a while with his most important client. "Thanks, Ben, I appreciate it. I think I'll pass this time, though — I've got packing to do, some phone calls to make before it gets too late." He gave a few more reasons, all stupid, but at that moment he didn't give a damn what Cochrane thought. The bastard had his arm around Sara's shoulders, and she was staring straight ahead at nothing, stiff and subdued. Michael stood between them, gazing up at his father with his heart in his eyes. Alex had to get out.

He could hardly look at Sara, and he cut her off in the middle of wishing him a safe trip. "So long, Michael. See you in the morning, Ben." He whirled, hurried down the porch steps, and rounded the curve in the flagstone path almost at a run. He walked fast in the fading evening light, and he was home in fifteen minutes. A new record.

His house was a roomy shingled bungalow on the beach, jutting out from a thick pine woods that started at his back door. An open verandah ran across the long front of the house; he spent most of his non-working time there, watching the ocean from a chair or stretched out on the rusting glider. The living room had a wide front window, nearly four feet across, and so he'd turned that room into his bedroom, relegating his office to what had formerly been the dining room. There was a bathroom upstairs, as well as two other rooms he never used. The sparse furniture was old but adequate, the bed comfortable. He had no visible neighbors. The place suited him perfectly.

But tonight it depressed him. He turned on all the lights and rummaged in the kitchen for something to eat. Out of inertia, he settled on a can of beans, opened it, and carried it out to the veranda. Sitting on the railing, one leg stretched along its wooden length, he ate cold beans with a spoon and watched the moon rise.

The rough wash of low tide splintering on the shore gradually calmed him. The reasons for that prickly, nearly panicky awareness he'd felt for a few seconds while watching the Cochranes together began to elude him. It was absurd and probably arrogant to think Sara needed him for anything, especially protection. She was a strong woman, and she'd lived with her bully of a husband for eight years. He thought it unlikely that she needed anyone.

But he was beginning to wonder if he needed her. The past weeks had been extraordinary, like no other time in his life. Contentment wasn't an emotion he had ever been able to sustain for longer than a matter of days, and that rarely, usually inspired by the completion of some long-planned seduction. Seduction wasn't even on his mind these days — astonishing in itself — and yet he'd been content. He would go so far as to say he'd been happy. Why? Because a woman and her son had graciously invited him into their lives, and for the first time ever, he'd felt as if he was part of a family.

But it had all been a dream, and Cochrane's return had precipitated his rude but overdue awakening. Long overdue. He understood now that there was a price to pay for the privilege of knowing Sara, and it was the obligation to know all of her. He hadn't bargained on that. It was past time to back up, disconnect, because things were getting too complicated. Not long ago, the idea of an affair with her had seemed simple and neat and clean, satisfying and finite, a sharp, short-term pleasure. In and out like a prizefighter or a burglar or a quick surgeon. But now he knew too much. Felt way too much. Even Michael was a problem; if he severed the ties now, he would regret Michael's loss very nearly as much as Sara's. How had this happened?

He'd been a fool to let matters progress so far. His excuse was that he was in novel surroundings, everything was slightly skewed, and he'd lost his bearings. He'd let himself be seduced by Michael's charm and Sara's sweetness. But tomorrow he would be in New York, and by this time tomorrow night he would undoubtedly be with Constance, in bed with her if he wanted to be — stretched over her on her damn dining room *table* if he wanted to be. Then why was it so hard to even remember her face?

Constance was perfect — clever, uncomplicated, passionate, discreet; and she had the added advantage of not being in love with him. He'd made a career of accommodating women like her for years, not to mention something of a name for himself in New York society — lady-killer, gay blade, man about town. He wasn't vain, but he could admit that he was probably a little spoiled. Mothers trusted him, though, because he didn't go around seducing virgins; he was charming and kind to innocent girls, who usually responded by falling in love with him. But he played by the rules and only took willing widows and wives to bed. When the time came to settle down and marry, he intended to choose wisely: some gorgeous debutante with an impeccable background, a compliant nature, and a great deal of money. If he was in love with her, all the better, but he'd never made that a prerequisite. Cynical, maybe. But then, the only model he had of conjugal happiness was his grandparents. It didn't inspire romantic idealism.

So what the hell was he doing with Mrs. Bennet Cochrane? She put him off his stride, she cramped his style; all his courtship habits, his venerable, time-tested moves were wrong with her, irrelevant. He'd lived like a monk for four weeks and he hadn't even minded. Well — he laughed out loud, face turned up to the darkening sky. No sense getting carried away. He'd minded. Not a day passed when he didn't think of making love with her. For once, though, he could see a distinction between lovemaking and seduction. As much as he wanted her, he wasn't willing to compromise her, because she had become too dear.

And now he could add a new torment — sexual jealousy. A few months ago he'd found watching the Cochranes together fascinating; later it had irritated him; now it was intolerable. He knew too well what he himself would be doing tonight, right now, if Sara belonged to him and he hadn't seen her in a month. A lurid picture flashed in his mind's eye — of her naked, locked in passion with her bullish husband. It was an obscenity. He came away from the porch rail and bolted down the three steps to the mottled beach that was his front yard. Sara didn't love her husband, she didn't even *like* him. But — what if she found pleasure with him physically? What if his big, coarse body satisfied her?

Intolerable. His hands clenched as he swung his arms out, striding fast. The shoreline looked dirty to him, the graying waves angry and cold. Even the streaky sunset was niggardly-looking, a skimpy, grudging show that made him feel mean. He wasn't accustomed to backing himself into corners and losing the controlling edge he maintained in his relationships with women. But here he was, infatuated with a woman he couldn't bring himself to seduce, and driving himself crazy because she was spending time tonight with her husband.

The solution was obvious: forget about her. Retreat slowly, carefully, so no one got hurt — Michael, he was thinking of — and then forget about both of them. He'd done it before, often enough to know exactly how, which move to make first, which to delay, at what pace to proceed. He could start immediately. This trip to New York was perfectly timed; he could use it to inaugurate his strategic retreat. When he got back he'd be different, distant — but just slightly, subtly. If he did it skillfully enough, they would hardly even notice his withdrawal until it was done.

But the whole prospect made him feel tired. He had no energy for it. He didn't want to give anything up; he wanted more, not less. Since he couldn't have it, why not compromise? Maintain the status quo, neither advance nor retreat; be a steady, faithful friend to Sara and an engaging, summer-long companion to her son, no more and no less. Where was the harm in that? That's what he would do. No need to take matters to such extremes. Moderation in all things: that was the key.

He'd reached the point where the giant sea rocks tumbled out of the water to the thickening forest line, blocking the beach. He was glad to turn back anyway, because he was hungry again. The retreating surf was erasing all the shoals left by the high tide, but the sucking erosion of shell and shale no longer depressed him. The dregs of the sunset looked peaceful, not petty. The moon would be almost full tonight. And in four days he would see Sara again. At Daisy's party.

# Ten

"... I pray the Lord my soul to take. God bless Mummy, God bless Daddy, God bless Mrs. Drum, God bless Mr. McKie, and God bless Charlie O'Shea." Charlie was Michael's best friend. "Mum, is it all right to ask God to bless a dog?"

"I can't think why not."

"God bless Gadget. Oh, and God bless Mrs. Wentworth." That was the end of the prayer; to his mother he added, "Even though sometimes she smells funny."

"Michael," Sara admonished, but not very severely, because he was merely stating a fact, without malice, and he was far too polite ever to hint of such a thing to Daisy herself.

She tucked the covers around him and combed the silvery hair back from his forehead. "You like Mr. McKie, don't you?"

"Oh yes, I like him a lot. Don't you?"

"Yes."

"I didn't think of God-blessing him until what he told me, though."

"What was that?"

"Well, first of all, what's the worst thing that can happen to an architect? The very worst thing?"

"Mm, I can't think."

"The building falls down!"

"Of course. No question, that would be the worst."

"So do you know what they used to do if it did? They *killed the architect!*"

"Gracious."

"This is back in B.C., during the time of King Hanner — Hammer —"

"Hammurabi?"

"Yeah. So that's why I'm God-blessing Mr. McKie. Just in case."

"Good idea. Go to sleep now, sweetheart."

"Mum, you look so pretty."

Sara cocked a skeptical eyebrow; Michael was a seasoned staller at bedtime. "Thanks."

"Are you going to dance tonight at Mrs. Wentworth's party?"

"No, probably not."

"Why not?"

She didn't want to tell him, not right now, that she wasn't going to Daisy's at all. "I don't know, sweetie. Maybe I will."

"What's that?" he asked, pointing to the flower in her hair.

"A camellia."

"Let me smell. Mmmm. Mummy?"

"What."

"You're sad sometimes, aren't you?"

Her face went very still. "Oh," she said evenly, "everybody's sad once in a while. Why would you ask me that, darling?"

"Because I told Mr. McKie you were sad a lot. I told him I try to cheer you up, but sometimes you just pretend to be happy."

She leaned over to kiss him, whispering so he wouldn't hear how close she was to tears. "I love you very much. You make me happy, and you *always* cheer me up. What would I do without you?"

"I don't know. Mummy, do you think Dad loves us as much as we love him?"

"I know he does. I just spoke to him on the 'phone and — he said so."

"He did?"

She nodded, swallowing hard. "Now off you go to sleep."

"Will you see Gadget tonight?"

"Yes, and I'll tell her you said hello." She kissed him again and stood up.

"Mr. McKie's back, isn't he? Will we go on our walk tomorrow?"

"Yes, and yes. Now, go to *sleep*. Good night."

"Night. But don't close the door tight, okay?"

"Have I ever?"

"Night, Mummy."

"Good night, my love."

Leaving his door ajar — because he was afraid of the dark, and she always left the hall light on for him — she tiptoed out. As she passed one of the maids on the way downstairs, she said, "I think I'll go outside for a while, Maura."

"Yes, ma'am."

"I'll just be in the back — in case Michael wakes up and calls me."

It was a perfect night — warm, starflecked, with a brilliant three-quarter moon coasting between wisps of cloud as sheer as gauze. An old stone wall separated Sara's backyard from Daisy's; above it Japanese lanterns winked in the branches of the beech trees. The party was beginning; Sara could already hear the murmur of voices, and now the high, light sound of a woman's laughter. Soon there would be music.

Sitting in Michael's swing under the willow tree, she smiled down at the useless extravagance of her new dress. Another evening gown was the last thing in the world she needed, but she'd bought it anyway at Worth's boutique in the Casino, because she'd wanted something special to wear tonight. Now no one would see it. She stroked her hand over the soft skirt of buttercream duchesse satin, sighing and feeling a little sorry for herself. It was for the best, though, it really was, because the secret vision she'd entertained all week — of herself dancing with Mr. McKie on Daisy's lawn in this beautiful gown — was an illicit one that richly deserved its sad fate: oblivion.

Tears sprang to her eyes as she thought of Michael's ingenuous question tonight, not for herself but for him. The grave error she'd committed eight years ago in marrying Ben had turned her life into a penance, but she'd refused to let Michael pay it with her. She had vowed at his birth that he was going to be a normal, happy child, and that she would not allow Ben to spoil anyone's life except hers. But, perhaps inevitably, Michael had become the battleground on which their marriage was fought, a consequence that filled her with intense and terrible guilt. What kind of family model was she exposing him to in the name of stability and normalcy? He was an astute child, preternaturally so; he must realize that something was tragically wrong between his mum and dad. But he was also unfailingly and exquisitely polite; delicacy or good breeding, bone-deep and pathetically inappropriate, had always prevented him from acknowledging the essential wrongness of his home life in any way. Or maybe it was kindness. Or fear. Or hope that by not paying attention to it he could make it go away. Her heart broke for him; she wanted to cry and cry for days.

She heard a soft rustling, incongruous with the sounds of merriment next door, and looked up. A man was walking toward her from the house. Her spirit shriveled during the instant when she thought it was Ben — then soared when she realized it was Alex. She waited for him without moving, feeling the sudden leaping race of her pulse. Tall, lean, dressed in formal black, he moved with a panthery sleekness she never tired of watching, the set of his shoulders delineating masculine elegance under his expensive jacket. Even when he reached her, she didn't speak; she was content just to look at him and to marvel, a little fearfully, at the deep pleasure she felt in being with him.

Her silence unnerved him. He'd heard she was ill, but that couldn't be true — he'd never seen her more beautiful. Her face, so grave in repose, softened with a slow, bewitching smile, and he wanted to touch her, pull her to her feet and kiss her long white hands and then her lips. "Sara," he said, softly, forgetting that that intimacy had been forbidden him. She whispered, "Alex," and then he did touch her, just the side of her face with his fingertips. Her skin was silky and cool — then warm. She lifted her hand, but dropped it again, quickly, before it could touch his. He stepped back.

"Are you all right? Mrs. Wentworth said you weren't feeling well."

"Oh — no — I'm sorry, did you come here from Daisy's? I'm not ill, I . . ." She wavered, then decided to tell him. "It's Ben."

"He's here?" he said sharply.

"No, no. He called, a little while ago. I mentioned I was about to go next door to Daisy's party and he — asked me not to."

"Why?"

She thought of making something up, but what was the point? "He doesn't approve of her. He suggested I make an excuse, and so I did."

They regarded each other grimly across a moonlit, four-foot distance. "You could go anyway," Alex said, aware of a simmering anger.

"No, I've told Ben I won't."

"Do you always do what your husband tells you to do?"

She felt his anger and smiled softly to defuse it. "No. I always do what I say I'll do." He shoved his hands in his pockets, but gradually his stiff posture relaxed. She hadn't known, hadn't allowed herself to suspect how much she'd missed him until this moment. But he shouldn't be here; she should send him away. Instead she asked, "How did you find the city?"

"Hot. Busy." Meaningless.

"Is Mrs. Cheyney still in town?" Now, what had possessed her to ask that?

"Yes, I believe so."

His tone was so casual, she knew immediately that he'd seen her. And she already knew that they were lovers, had known it since the moment she'd laid eyes on the beautiful Constance. Jealousy was a brand-new emotion to Sara. It felt like hell.

"My grandfather's dying. I found out yesterday."

"Oh, no. I'm so sorry." She stood up uncertainly. "Does he live in New York?"

"No, California."

to burst. "My mother and father never married. He died before either of them knew she was pregnant." He sagged against the rough trunk of the tree in horror. He had never so much as hinted of that truth to anyone, ever. And now he'd told Sara. It was as if he'd deliberately jumped from a high building, or stuck a gun in his mouth and pulled the trigger. He felt nauseated, sick with remorse.

She touched his sleeve, but he wouldn't face her. So she spoke to his dark back. "Alex." It felt right, calling him that — but of course, in a few minutes she would have to stop. "I'm so sorry. I know how you feel." She couldn't help smiling when he let out a sharp, rather rude sound of disbelief. "I do, actually. My mother married my father for his money — she thought. He was a duke; she could be excused for thinking he was wealthy, I suppose. She got herself pregnant on purpose, and he did the gentlemanly thing." Alex turned around in slow motion. "But the joke was on her, because his fortune turned out to be nonexistent. And then he added insult to injury by getting himself killed in a horserace a year after the wedding."

Her ironic smile turned wistful. "I like to think that he saw me, knew me, during the first five months of my life. The last five of his. When I was little, I used to imagine him holding me and feeling an amazed sort of love for me, a warmth he couldn't resist, even though he must've known his pretty wife had tricked him."

She backed up and sat down in the swing again. "So. A few more months and we'd have *both* been born on the wrong side of the blanket. Shocking, isn't it?" She laughed softly. "Don't tell anyone about me, will you? Especially Ben. It would tarnish his image of me. Or rather, of just plain Sara Cochrane."

Alex felt like sitting down. So he did, on the ground in his evening clothes, forearms dangling between his knees, back against the willow tree. Sara laughed again, he suspected at him, and this time he laughed with her. "Why did you tell me that?"

"So you would feel better."

He digested that. "And no one else knows it?"

"God, no. I thought I would take it to my grave."

The willow leaves threw delicate moving shadows against the pale oval of her face. It was the finely arching brows that gave her that look of quiet composure, he decided — that and her straight, unsmiling mouth. But he was learning that she was a mixture of open-heartedness and deep cynicism, kindness and extreme wariness. "What was it like growing up?" he asked. "Were you happy?"

Later she could worry about the dangerous intimacy of this conversation; for now, she would allow herself to be seduced by his interest in her, and by the striking and rueful fact that no one had ever asked her that question before, not directly, not even Lauren.

She found she couldn't answer it directly, either. "My mother wasn't a very strong person," she said slowly. "She found she didn't like being a duchess after all, but she lacked the initiative or the energy to do anything about it. She was unhappy. She . . ."

"Drank."

"Ah. You've heard."

"I'm sorry, it was just —"

"It's all right, I don't know why I'm surprised."

Ben's attitude toward her "aristocratic" background was a lethal mixture of contempt and grudging admiration, and he took perverse pleasure in maligning it at the same time he took advantage of it to elevate himself socially. Her mother had been a target of his public ridicule from the beginning, not only because her weaknesses were easy to sneer at, but also because vilifying her was a clever and economical way to wound Sara.

"Yes, she drank. She'd been left with nothing but a molding, decaying estate she wasn't allowed to sell and a five-month-old baby. She was allowed to sell the furnishings, though, so she did that, bit by bit, and scraped by on the yearly pittance that was all my father's will had left her. By the time I was ten, his ancestral home was nothing but an empty, echoing barn, stripped of everything of value to pay for my mother's secret vice."

"What was it like for you, living like that?"

"It was . . ." She resisted the deep, gentle sympathy in his resonant voice and didn't say the word *lonely,* or *frightening,* or *dreadful.* "I was lucky, because my father provided quite handsomely in his will for my education. Yes — it's odd, isn't it? I'm sure my mother shared your surprise when she learned of it. She wasn't allowed to touch that money, which must have driven her crazy. Very prescient of my father, don't you think? Anyway, there were governesses when I was little, and then rather grand boarding schools until I was sixteen. So you mustn't think it was just my mother and me shut up together at Kell Hall, getting battier together year after year."

He stared owlishly back at her feeble attempt at a smile until it faltered and she looked away. "And were you happy at these grand boarding schools?"

She got up from the swing and walked a few steps away before turning around to face him. "No, of course I wasn't. I was lonely, poor as a churchmouse, my shyness was taken for arrogance, I had almost no friends." Which accounted for her excessive sensitivity today — according to Lauren — to being thought a snob. She overcompensated, Lauren claimed, by befriending the likes of Tasha Eminescu and working to exhaustion at the Forsyth Street Settlement.

Alex stood up too and came toward her. Music had begun to drift on the air. Daisy's lanterns twinkled like fireflies in the tree branches. Overhead, the moon rode behind a long, thin cloud and then broke free, showering down silver. Sara's hair caught icy fire in the radiance; her quiet eyes glowed. She looked like a straight, slim goddess to him in the colorless moonshine, cool and warm, marble and flesh.

"What?" she said softly, misinterpreting his look. "Are you feeling sorry for me? You needn't, I assure you."

"Because you're happy now? Ben rescued you and now you have everything?" He regretted the words as soon as they were out of his mouth. Her face crumbled, went from proud to distraught in the space of an instant — he had to reach for her hands to keep her from turning away. "I'm sorry, that was a stupid thing to say. I *don't* feel sorry for you — how could I? Look at you, you're —" He broke off; that wasn't the way. "I've never met anyone like you, no one with your courage, your goodness —" He held tighter when she tried to wrench her hands away. "There's no meanness in you, none. Do you know how rare that is?"

"Oh, Alex, you don't know me!" She half-laughed, a bitter sound, as she pulled harder at his hands. "You don't know anything about me."

"I know all about you. You're sad most of the time, you've given up hope for your own happiness, but you never stop trying to make other people's lives better. The work you do at the settlement house —

even your husband ridicules it, but you don't stop. Women in your circle soothe their social consciences by putting on all their jewelry and dragging their husbands to charity balls, but you —"

"*Please* stop."

"Why? Why does this embarrass you?"

"Don't you know that nobody's motives are ever completely pure? That's not cynicism, it's just a fact. Even a *saint's* reasons for doing those selfless-seeming deeds would very likely not bear scrutiny — and I can assure you I'm not a saint!"

"Well, I'm relieved to hear it. Now you don't scare me so much." Her helpless laugh heartened him. His hands slid gently up her bare arms to her elbows where, under his thumbs, he could feel the quick flutter of her pulse. Ambivalence clouded her fine gray eyes. She started to speak — to say, he was sure, something like, "You mustn't touch me like this" — when he forestalled her. "Mrs. Cochrane, would you like to dance with me?"

Her indecision was thick, palpable. The silence went to foolish lengths, and she began to feel silly. "Mr. McKie," she said with perfect truth, "I'd love to."

They moved into position too slowly, their skimming hands too much like caresses. Sara stiffened her spine and waited for him to begin. He didn't move, didn't move — she lifted surprised eyes — and then he did, a slow, smooth glide that brought them closer. She closed her eyes, and immediately his scent, a subtle, lemony cologne, shockingly intimate, began an insidious assault on her senses. If she lifted her left thumb from its discreet resting place on the back of his collar, she could touch his curling, gold-tipped hair. She did, and reveled secretly in that soft, cool thrill. They were moving to the slowest of waltzes, paying no attention to the brisker tempo of the orchestra next door. She had a poignant awareness of her own body and the pleasure it took from the pressure of his steady hand on her waist, his warm breath on her hair, the light press of her breasts against his chest. The sizzling rustle of her skirts against his long legs seemed more erotic to her just then than the sounds of lovemaking. When his hand tightened at the small of her back to bring her closer, she didn't resist. But nerves made her break the risky silence that was stretching between them like a thin, tight wire. In a murmur she said, "Michael blessed you in his prayers tonight."

"Did he? I'm sure my wicked soul can

use it. What a nice boy he is, Sara."

She wondered how wicked Alex's soul was. Not very, she thought. What she sensed in him was the restlessness and confusion of a man who didn't know himself yet. Was it arrogance or only naiveté that sometimes made her think *she* knew him, and that there was greatness in him if only he could find it?

"What are you thinking?" He drew away to look at her. Her eyes were deep and mysterious, and her soft, serious mouth told him nothing except that she was sweet. He already knew that. His deepest wish was to touch her body with his mouth — anywhere, her hair, her lips, her throat. The soft, dark cleft between her pale breasts.

"I was thinking . . ."

"What?"

"That Michael is making something for you that's a surprise."

The carnal fragrance of the flower in her hair was making his head swim. "What is it?"

"Well, I can't tell you, of course." Now she could feel his breath on her lips. They were dancing much, much too close, they had almost stopped moving at all. "Did you tell him what kind of house you'd like to live in someday?"

He sighed. It was difficult to talk, and he understood perfectly why she kept at it. "Yes, once. Is he building it for me?"

"I didn't say that. You did not hear that from me."

He smiled with his eyes closed. He stopped dancing, or the pretense of dancing, and put both hands on her waist. "Sara."

It wasn't fair to back away from something she wanted and had conspired to get at least as much as he. But he had a choice and she did not, and for some reason the moment had just come, belated but inescapable, when she remembered it.

"Forgive me," she whispered, and stepped out of his arms.

He blinked in disbelief, hands outstretched, mouth open. A vision of his own foolishness restored his composure, but it was cold comfort. He teetered on the edge of anger, but toppled instead into regret. "Do you want me to go?"

"Yes," she answered immediately. "You must go."

"Right." Then it was anger, pure and simple. "Right. I'll leave. But don't be an idiot. Don't think this —" He stopped; he had no idea what he was talking about.

"Sorry. I'm going. But don't —" What? He cursed violently under his breath, and she just stared at him. This was crazy. "Sara —"

"No, it's better if you go. Please let's not talk anymore, not right now. I don't know how this happened. I do beg your pardon, but you must go."

He looked up at the black sky, stalling for control. He didn't understand how it had happened, either. He remembered his careful plans for a "strategic retreat." If he was serious about withdrawing from her, he ought to let this night's work stand, for it had accomplished all of his alleged goals in a fraction of the time. But he heard himself say, "I apologize if I've offended you, Sara. I assure you there will be no repetition of my behavior tonight. You're perfectly safe from me, in other words. And so if you were thinking of avoiding me from now on, I promise you it won't be necessary. I promise." She was squeezing her hands together and staring up at him with odd, painful intensity. He couldn't think of anything else to promise without making an even bigger fool of himself. He made her a short, formal bow and escaped.

# Eleven

"Tasha? Is that you? Hello, it's Sara."

"Mrs. Cochrane! Yes, this is Tasha speaking, I can hear you. How do you do?"

"I'm fine, how are you?"

"Thank you, I am very well!"

Sara held the earpiece away from her ear because Tasha was shouting. "Is it raining there?"

"No, the sun is shining. It is very hot! It rains there?"

"Yes, all afternoon. How are things at the house?"

"Things at the house are very good! The plumbing men have finished their work. Everything is fine now."

"Good, I'm glad that's over. What have you been doing?"

There was a pause. "Today I went to church."

Sara smiled. "Yes, we went to church, too. I meant, how have you been keeping busy?"

"Have I been keeping busy? Oh yes, yes, I have my lessons every day. I read quite a

228

lot, and in the evenings I sew. And the little cat, she keeps me company!"

It didn't sound like much of a life. "Are you able to work yet, do you think? How is your wrist?"

This time the pause was longer. "Mrs. Cochrane."

"Tasha?" The girl's voice had dropped almost to a whisper. "Tasha?"

"I'm ashamed."

"What's wrong?"

"How can I tell you? You will think me lazy and stupid."

"Nonsense," Sara said sternly. "Tell me what's wrong. I'll think you're stupid if you *don't* tell me."

She laughed, but there was a little catch in her throat. "I'm not — I can't —" Another pause. "I do not go out of the house. I just can't. Yet."

Sara bowed her head. "Because you're afraid."

"Yes. Yes. I know it's foolish, but the man — I'm still so scared of him!"

"I do understand. I wish I could help you, I wish you could come here." But when she'd suggested it to Ben, he'd laughed at her. "Listen, Tasha, I've told you before, you're welcome to stay as long as you want. And my husband says the

229

same." Miraculously.

"You are so very kind. Someday I will repay you, I swear it!"

"Never mind that, the important thing is for you to get better. I've told Paren — that's Mr. Matthews at the settlement house — that you're there by yourself, and he says he'll call sometimes just to make sure you're all right." Tasha started to thank her again; she cut her off quickly. They spoke for a few more minutes, then Sara hung up. She stood with her hand on the receiver, staring into space. Something troubled her about the conversation, but she couldn't put her finger on it. She was still puzzling over it when the telephone rang again. It was Daisy.

"What are you doing?"

Daisy never slurred her speech when she drank, but in some indefinable way Sara could tell from those four words that she was tight. "I'm looking out the window at the rain," she answered lightly, "trying to decide whether to finish my book or take a nap."

"Oh, boring! Come over here and talk to me. Take an umbrella and walk around to the side; you'll hardly even get your shoes wet. I've got some lovely Madeira, we'll sit on the porch and have a nice —"

"Oh, I don't think so, Daisy. I'm just too lazy. And Michael's playing outside, he's probably wringing wet."

"Outside!"

"Yes, well, it was so warm, I said he could. He wanted to play with his new umbrella."

"Oh, come on, dry him off and bring him with you. We'll have a good time."

They went back and forth a little longer. But Sara held out and Daisy finally rang off, disappointed.

Sara wandered into the kitchen. The house was dead quiet; on Sunday afternoon, all the servants were on holiday. It was murky, too; she ought to switch on the light. But the watery dimness suited her mood. She poured a glass of water from the faucet and drank it over the sink, staring blankly out the window. Should she have gone to Daisy's? She'd been restless for two days, ever since she'd sent Alex away. Yesterday she'd made up an excuse to explain to Michael why their walk had to be cancelled; today, luckily, she wouldn't need to because of the rain. He would be disappointed, she knew; yesterday he'd wanted to call Mr. McKie on the telephone — "I haven't seen him for a *week*, Mummy, a *week*. I've got this *model* and he hasn't even *seen* it." His attachment to Alex had seemed harmless and natural in the beginning, even desirable, but now it worried her. What had happened on Friday evening called into very serious question the likelihood that she and Alex could simply go on as they had been, in what she'd told herself was a casual, friendly relationship, one whose sexual undertones always stopped dead at the level of mild flirtation. To believe that now was worse than naive, it was irresponsible. She couldn't afford it. The time had come to open her eyes and see what a perilous game she'd been playing, for the consequences were real and terrible: If Ben ever suspected she was interested in another man, he would punish her in ways she couldn't even imagine. All of them involving Michael.

So. She had learned a hard lesson, and it was a blessing. A good thing. Long overdue. For two days she'd been trying to see it in that light — so far without success. Daisy's invitation beckoned seductively. What an easy solution to this ache she carried inside all the time. An unopened bottle of cognac was gathering dust in the cabinet over the icebox. She thought of lying on the sofa in the living room with a glass of brandy and the serialized novel in the newspaper, and letting the rainy afternoon slip past in a steadily thickening fog.

It could be done. She'd seen it done a thousand times. One of the things she hadn't told Alex was that her job as a child, when she wasn't away at school, had been to take care of her mother — to keep her from falling and hurting herself, to try to make her eat, and most of all to keep the truth of their dreadful domestic situation a secret from the rest of the world. She'd fallen into the conspiracy with no thought that she had a choice. Her mother had turned her into a crafty accomplice, and she'd chosen her ally wisely. With Sara in charge, she could relax and do whatever she wanted. And what she wanted to do was drink.

It was the picture of her mother in a stained dressing gown, oily blond hair awry, sunk in a chair or passed out on the sofa, that turned Sara firmly away from thoughts of brandy and oblivion. Much better to be good and miserable than to choose that path, because she knew exactly where it could lead. Even if she didn't care what happened to herself — and she did; thank God it hadn't come to that yet! — she could never do to Michael what her mother had done to her.

Thinking of Michael made her wonder where he was. She'd told him to stay in the backyard, but if he was out there now she couldn't see him. She decided she would make him his favorite supper — cold chicken and graham bread sandwiches. Yesterday Mrs. Godby had taught her how to make mayonnaise — how *incredible* that it only had three ingredients — so she would make that and a pitcher of lemonade. Some carrots and celery sticks, if she could get him to eat them. She started to wash her hands. Condensation had fogged the window; she wiped it with the dish towel and saw that the yard was empty. Perhaps he'd gone over to Daisy's to see Gadget. A movement caught her eye, high up in the willow tree. Bright red — his new umbrella. She froze for two seconds, then shouted *"Michael!"* through the half-closed window. Her scream merged with his when he fell. His body struck the lowest branch, slithered off, and hit the ground with a silent thump that jolted through her like an electrical shock.

She went blind. Rain on her face roused her from a sick, waking faint. Over the roar in her ears she couldn't hear herself screaming when she collapsed on the sodden grass beside his still, crumpled body. His arms felt like cold, wet rubber and his face was the color of smoke. She held him tight to her chest and called out for help, help, shouting at the dripping sky, empty-headed with panic.

Time snarled, tangled; she would never know how long it took Daisy to find her. But all at once she was there, kneeling, shaking her shoulder and shouting something in her ear. Then she was alone again and the meaning of the words sank in: Daisy was going to call the doctor.

Doctor. The concept galvanized her. She gathered Michael's heavy, lifeless weight in her arms, stood up, and staggered toward the house. Daisy met her at the door. She took his legs — so thin and bony! the left shin scraped and bleeding — and together they got him into the day parlor and laid him on the sofa.

"The doctor's coming, he's on his way. Where is he hurt?"

Where! She didn't know! She started to cry. Daisy stilled the futile fluttering of her hands over Michael's body and examined him herself.

"His arms aren't broken," she declared, moving them. "Legs are fine."

"Why can't he wake up?" Sara whimpered. Stroking his wet hair, she felt it — a lump nearly the size of a tennis ball on the left side of his head. "Oh my *God*, my *God*."

"I don't think it's so bad," Daisy said quickly. She pulled the afghan from the back of the couch, spread it over him, and tucked it in at the sides. "Sit down now, Sara, you're going to make yourself sick. There's nothing to do but wait. Honestly, I don't think it's that bad!"

She stayed where she was, kneeling on the floor by Michael's head, holding his hands. His face was so pale, his lips white. The shallow rise and fall of his narrow chest became the focus of all her senses. "Darling," she kept whispering, and "Please God, please, please, please, God."

The doctor came. She didn't hear his name. He told her to move back, please, and she scooted sideways on her knees a few inches. He pulled a chair close to the couch and sat down. He was big and burly, white-haired, and she winced every time his enormous, blunt-fingered hands touched Michael's body.

"That's a big one, isn't it?" he rumbled, gently skimming the bump on Michael's temple with his fingertips. "Round as a goose egg. He'll have a little headache from that, won't he?"

She was literally biting her knuckles; she couldn't form a question because she was too terrified of the answer.

"Has there been any vomiting?"

She shook her head violently.

"That's good, that's a good sign. Well, well, what's this?"

"What?" she croaked.

"Look here. He's broken his collarbone, hasn't he? Now, don't worry, that's all right, that's not serious." He glanced around for Daisy and sent her a warning look.

She went to Sara and put her arms around her shoulders. "He's all right, honey, the doctor's saying he's *all right*. You have to try to stay calm."

She gathered up all her courage. Her voice shook ludicrously, but she got it out. "Why won't he wake up? Please, please, tell me the truth."

"Hush, Sara, let him listen."

The doctor was pressing his stethoscope to Michael's puny chest. Next he opened the boy's white eyelids and stared down into his pupils. He looked at his teeth, moved his jaw carefully, then his head, palpating the vertebrae at the back of his neck. "What's that, now?" he said when he'd finished, pulling his glasses to the end of his big nose and peering at her. "Why won't he wake up? Because he's got a bump on his head and he's not quite ready to. Shouldn't be much longer, though. Stand back a little now, I'm going to straighten this bone."

It was the setting of the bone that woke Michael up, with a lusty howl of pain that sent Sara veering toward hysteria again. She shook off Daisy's restraining arm and ran to him, oblivious to the doctor's grumbled, "Here now, give him some room to breathe, can't you? Oh, all right, I'm finished."

Her tears dried up at the sight of Michael's. She smeared his cheeks with her fingers and her lips and smiled down at him. "How do you feel, darling? You're all right now, the doctor says so. Do you remember what happened?"

"Fell out of the tree."

"That's right. That was a silly thing to do, wasn't it?"

He nodded, then flinched. "Head hurts, Mum."

"I know." She pressed a soft, soft kiss to his forehead. "Better?"

"Yes." He tried to smile, but his eyes flickered closed and he drifted off again.

She threw a look of panic at the doctor.

"He's fine," he assured her as he straightened the contents of his black bag. "He fell out of a tree, bumped his head, and broke his clavicle. He'll be running around like a wild Indian in six weeks."

No need to stir the boy up again tonight, the doctor told her; he'd return in the morning and put a bandage on to immobilize that shoulder. Meanwhile, keep him quiet and keep the room dark. Call him if she observed vomiting, convulsions, or severe headache. Now, now, he didn't expect any of that, but those were the things she should watch for. If the boy got hungry, feed him, whatever he would eat. But he'd probably sleep most of the time, and that was the best thing for him.

After the doctor went away — Buell was his name, she finally heard — she moved a chair to the head of the couch and sat down in it to wait. Daisy sat with her at first, but Sara couldn't talk yet and she couldn't eat any of the food Daisy offered to make her. So after an hour or so, Daisy gave her a hug and went home.

A little later Sara roused herself to call Ben. He wasn't at his club or his office; she finally reached him at home, where he'd gone to pick up some papers, he told her.

He took the news of the accident unemotionally — perhaps because Sara was numb and exhausted and her recitation of it was unemotional. She felt glad to hang up and go back to Michael.

At eight o'clock he woke up again, complaining that he was thirsty. She gave him a drink of water, then coaxed him into eating a half slice of bread. Every bite he swallowed was like a weight being lifted from her shoulders. "I was trying to keep the birds dry," he muttered drowsily.

"What, darling?"

"There's a nest in the willow tree, Mum. I put the umbrella over it so the birds wouldn't get wet." Then he fell asleep.

Sara cried for ten minutes. Then she felt like laughing. That scared her, so she got up and went to the kitchen to find something to eat.

On the way, she heard knocking at the front door. Halfway down the hall, she saw who it was through the glass, in the glow from the porch light. Her footsteps quickened and she threw open the door. "Alex! Thank God!"

It wasn't the greeting he'd been expecting. "I should've called first," he began. "I won't come in, I just wanted to see you and tell you —"

"For God's sake, come in."

She took his sleeve and pulled on it. He thought she wanted him inside so that no one would see him from the street, because his coming here could compromise her. Then he saw her face — flushed with illness or excitement or something else, eyes red-rimmed, her mouth drawn with tension. "What is it, Sara, what's wrong?"

"It's Michael! No — he's all right. He's hurt but he's going to get well." She reached for his hands when she saw the fear in his eyes. And at last, after all the hours of worry and torment, a little comfort began to seep into her soul and warm it. "Come and see him. Please — would you like to? He's in the back parlor." It was important to her for some reason that Alex see him. Holding his hand, she led him down the hall to the rear of the house.

She'd put a cloth over the lamp on the table to shade it. In the soft yellow light, they stood over the sofa together, watching Michael's sleeping face. Sara whispered the terrible story in short, halting sentences, using the words of fear and desperation she hadn't been able to say to Ben. Alex felt chilled to the bone. He gripped her hand tighter as he saw it all in his mind, and he found it impossible not to

241

think the unthinkable, imagine a different and horrible ending. "I wish I'd been here," was all he could say when she finished, and she whispered back immediately, "I wish you had too."

She bent over to brush the pale hair back from her son's forehead, reluctant to leave him yet. "They say you don't know how you'll react in a crisis until you're in the midst of one," she murmured, straightening. "Well, now I know. I fell to pieces, Alex. I was completely useless. If it hadn't been for Daisy, I know I'd still be rocking him in my arms in the back yard right now. In the rain."

"No, you wouldn't. You'd have pulled yourself together and done everything that needed to be done."

"You can't know that. How do you know?"

"Because you would have."

"That's no answer." But it comforted her immeasurably.

She kissed Michael one last time. She felt startled, and strangely moved, when Alex bent down and kissed him too, with a gentleness she'd never seen in him before. Then she led him out of the parlor and into the kitchen.

"I was about to make some tea. Will you

have a cup with me?" He said yes, and she set about lighting the gas stove and putting the kettle on. But her hands shook so severely when she took the cups and saucers down from the cabinet that she almost dropped them. "Goodness!" She laughed shakily, surprised; she thought she'd finally gotten her nerves under control.

"Sit down and let me do it," he ordered, pulling her away from the counter and backing her toward the big kitchen table.

"All right. I won't sit down, though." She wrapped her arms around herself, shivering.

"Are you cold?"

"No, I couldn't be. It's stuffy in here."

"But if you're cold —"

"No, it's stuffy. Open the door, will you?"

He did, and the moldy scent of wet earth wafted in through the screen. The rain had stopped, but the sound of water in the gutters was still a soft, steady gurgle.

She told him where the milk and sugar were, the tin of biscuits, the plates and napkins. She apologized for not having any lemons. He worked smoothly and efficiently, more at home in a kitchen than most men would be, she imagined. She liked to look at his hands; they were lean and strong and sensitive-looking — an artist's hands. "Do you cook for yourself in your little house on the beach?"

"Sometimes."

"Too bad you don't have your Mrs. Wiggs to cook for you. Michael loves your house, by the way. Did you know he rode his bicycle all the way out there by himself about a fortnight ago? To leave you a message about our walk. Oh yes, of course you knew, you must have gotten the message." She put her hands on the sides of her face and pressed.

"What do you take in your tea?"

"Sugar. I'll do it — oh. Thank you, yes, one. Ben takes four, can you imagine? Sometimes Michael drinks 'cambric' tea — I tell him that's what it is but really it's just hot water and sugar. And lemon."

"Will you sit down to drink this?" He held out a steaming cup.

"I won't, if you don't mind. I'm too keyed up." Leaning against the table, she set the saucer aside and held the hot cup in both hands because her fingers were freezing. "I wonder if I'm still in shock."

He thought she was. He took a sip of the hot, strong tea. "When I was about eight, Sara, I thought it would be a fine idea to jump on the freight train that rode so slowly — I thought — past my grand-father's lettuce farm every day at noon. So one day I did it."

"What happened?"

"I broke my leg in two places, fractured my hip, and punctured a lung."

"Alex!"

"The thing is, in three months I was fine again, perfect, as if nothing had ever happened to me."

She set her cup down carefully. "I know, children are wonderfully resilient. Even the doctor says in six weeks Michael will be completely well. I know all that, and I know accidents happen to everyone's children and you can't — let — yourself fall apart. But this hurts. This hurts too much. Oh lord, I'm starting again. I *hate* to cry." She dashed at her cheeks with the back of her wrist. "I protect him too much, I know it. I'm not a good mother."

"Don't be ridiculous."

"No, it's true, you don't know. I love him too much, it's not good for him. When I thought he was hurt, when I thought he might die, I wanted to die too. Because he's all I have. So I — try to shield him from everything, and it's wrong, but I can't help it. And he's so good, he's so kind and loving —" she turned around, struggling not to cry but unable to stop talking. "He deserves the best, the absolute best of everything, and all I can do is love him, it's the *only* thing I can give him —"

"Sara, don't do this." He hesitated, just for a second, then put his hands on her shoulders. As soon as he did, she dissolved into helpless weeping. Her whole body shook with deep, racking sobs, and she kept saying something he couldn't understand. He turned her gently and put his arms around her. For a second she stiffened, but then she leaned into him heavily, hands fisted against his chest, shuddering. Finally he made out what she was saying.

"Ben's going to send him away."

He stroked the wet hair back from her cheek. "What do you mean? Send him where?"

"To Germany. A mil-military school." Her mouth felt gluey; she could hardly talk. She swallowed painfully. "I think he's lying. I *think*. I think he's trying to sc-scare me. Oh God."

He held tighter, appalled. It couldn't be true; Cochrane couldn't send his own son away without Sara's consent. He'd terrorized her somehow, that was it. Alex murmured against her hair and pressed his hands gently up and down her backbone. Gradually she quieted, but the tears wouldn't stop. He took out his handkerchief and put it in her hand.

"Pardon me," she muttered. "You must think . . ." She stopped to wipe her eyes. "I don't know what you must think." She put her hand to her throat; it ached, and there was a lump there too big to swallow.

He pushed her hand away and put his fingers on the warm skin of her throat, stroking softly. "Put your head back," he whispered. "Relax your shoulders." She obeyed, more out of exhaustion than trust, he knew. He soothed her with his fingertips in slow, feather-light circles, one arm around her waist to steady her, and after a moment the tautness in her body began to soften. Her eyes closed. When she sighed, he put his lips on her throat where his fingers had been. Breathing softly, not moving. Her scent was lilac; she'd put some here, right here. His hand widened at the back of her head, tangling in her hair, cradling her. He moved his mouth to her jaw and followed the fine, fragile line to the base of her ear. A stray tear still glistened on her cheekbone. He touched it with his lips, tasted it. She said, "Oh," indistinctly. Then she craned her neck, pushed against him, and twisted out of his arms.

She went to the stove and pretended to do something with the kettle and the gas ring. That could not have happened, she told herself; she'd misunderstood, misinterpreted his touch. And if she hadn't, she must behave as if she had, because anything else was beyond possibility. But her body was in rebellion; her senses had misunderstood nothing. Physical desire might be unfamiliar to her, but it was not unrecognizable. So she fiddled with the tea strainer and kept her back turned, trying to think of something to say. "Would you care for —"

Alex put his hand on her arm. She made a half-turn toward him, and he pulled her the rest of the way around. In her eyes he saw all the reasons why he must not keep on with this. "Sara," he breathed. A plea and an apology. Then he bent his head and kissed her.

She could have broken away again; he wasn't forcing her. Each moment, each second, she made a new decision not to move. Shy, her hands crept to his shoulders, his neck, caressing him for the first time. His lips were warm and sweet; they tasted like tea. The feathery softness of his mustache tickled her. He kissed her in tender little sips, slow and savory, and the secretive sucking sounds his lips made did something extraordinary to the muscles in her abdomen. They held each other tighter in a quick, hard embrace, then relaxed again.

His restraint calmed her, although she sensed it was hard-won. The kiss that had never stopped started again. His fingers drifted to her temples, the hollows of her cheeks, her eyebrows, stroking her with such tenderness that she was afraid she might start to cry again. He whispered her name, and when his lips gently urged her, she opened her mouth to him, submissive at first, then hungry. It amazed her that they wanted the same things, that what gave him pleasure pleased her, too. She had never been touched like this; her most womanly fantasies had never taken her this far. The seductive lure of surrender beckoned from a place inside she couldn't even recognize. *Anything,* she thought with the part of her mind that could still think. *Anything.*

He had her pressed against the wall between the pantry door and the spice cabinet, and for the rest of his life he would think of her whenever he smelled the combined musks of thyme, marjoram, and cardamom. He heard himself humming to her, saying, "Oh, Sara," and "Ah, lovely, lovely," silly lover talk that he would not have thought could pass his lips. It was because he couldn't believe he had her, that she was letting this happen. She was all and nothing that he'd thought she would be. He deepened the kiss, deliberately drugging her, his hands slipping down, down, caressing her throat and sliding lower, surrounding her breasts. He began a slow, concentrated exploration, thigh to thigh, stomach to stomach, his fingers teasing and soothing the heavy softness of her breasts in the scant space of warmth he'd left between them. Her quickening pants lured him on. She was like a virgin, so surprised at each sensation he gave to her. He felt himself spinning, dizzy, speeding toward something beyond his control, but he couldn't let her go. He wanted to possess her, lose himself in her. At last it was prosaic necessity that made him murmur against her soft throat, "Sara, love, I can't do this much longer standing up, is there someplace we can go?"

Too much. Too much pleasure, too new. And suddenly too much like pain. "No," she said, pushed his hands away, and stepped out of his arms.

Reason flooded back in cold waves as

soon as she was alone again, transforming what had just happened from inevitable to incredible. The temptation to blame him tugged at her for a moment, then skulked away, embarrassed. "Alex, I'm sorry," she got out thickly, "I made a mistake. I beg your pardon. Shouldn't have happened. My fault." She waved all her fingers in the air, to erase it.

His emotions were too chaotic to sort out. He turned his back on her, to avoid saying something hurtful, or humbling himself, or making things worse.

"I've ruined it, haven't I?" she said when he didn't answer and she could speak again. "Now we can't even be friends."

"I don't know what we can be."

"I'm sorry," she repeated. "If you could believe that I want . . . exactly what you want. . . ." She despaired. "But it's not possible."

"Why not?" He was looking for an opening, a weakness; he already knew why not.

"You know," she answered, reading his mind, smiling with great tenderness.

"I'd make you happy, Sara."

"I know that. It's beside the point."

"I can't stand the life you lead."

"Thank you. But you can't help me." He reached for her, touched her cheek, but she slipped away again. "Go away, Alex. Leave me, please, you must."

"And then what?" He felt thwarted and angry. "What do we do then, Sara, pretend nothing's happened? See each other whenever you'll allow it — only in public, of course — and pretend there's not a damn thing between us?"

"Yes. Exactly that."

"Well, I can't."

She smiled again, hugging herself. "Alex," she whispered, "don't make it harder. It's already —" She made another futile gesture. *"Please* go."

He walked away, found himself standing in front of the sink. He slid his hands restlessly along the gleaming metal spigots, the sleek line of the spout. Each second that passed widened the gulf between what he wanted and what he could have. When he faced her again, she was standing in the same posture, but it was as if she had faded, diminished. Burned down. "All right, Sara. Since I don't have a choice, I'll do what you want. But will you at least let me know if you need me? Ever, for anything. If I can do anything for Michael. Or if you just —"

"I will." She nodded vigorously. But she was reaching the edge of her endurance.

"I never meant to do this to you. Don't tell me again that this was your fault, because we both know that's a lie." It hurt to look at her any longer. "Good-bye, Sara."

She listened to his footsteps fade, heard the front door open and quietly close. Silence flowed back, heavy as snow, smothering her. She swallowed a mouthful of cold tea and nearly gagged. The cup clattered in the sink, startling her. She went into Michael's room. Looking at him brought her comfort of a sort; she didn't cry again. Every few minutes she touched him — light fingers on his cheek, a soft kiss on his grubby hand. Hours later, she fell asleep in her chair.

Michael lay flat on his back for five days. Sara ordered a cot moved into the room so that she could stay with him at night. Keeping him entertained and quiet exhausted her and challenged all her maternal resources; by the fifth day she was as glad as he was when Dr. Buell said he might get up. Alex never visited, but each day the post brought an amusing note with the gift of a book or a game or a puzzle. His thoughtfulness moved her, even while it deepened her despondency.

Ben didn't come either — his business affairs were too pressing right now; besides, the boy was fine, wasn't he?

Ten days after the accident, Sara decided to go home. She didn't ask Ben's permission; she sent a note to his club announcing her decision and the time of her arrival. She let the servants go, but kept the lease on the house for the rest of the summer — Ben might make her return, after all. For now, though, whether he liked it or not, she was taking Michael home.

She could have written to Alex to tell him they were leaving, or called him, even gone to see him at the site. She delayed doing any of those things until the morning of the last day, with less than an hour before the Fall River steamboat left for New York. Then she picked up the telephone and called him.

From the sound of his voice, she knew she'd awakened him — and for the first time she realized that it was Sunday and not quite seven o'clock in the morning. She spent the first minute apologizing, giving away the full extent of her nervousness. Then she explained why she was calling. Michael was improving, but he was such a handful these days, she really needed help. And he missed his friends quite a lot; it would be good for him, especially now, to see them again. They might come back later in the summer, who knew, but right now it seemed best to return home, where they could both rest and recuperate from the accident.

It didn't sound very logical in her own ears, and she kept rattling on in hopes of achieving credibility by sheer volume of words. But finally she ran down and thanked him for his kindness — and told him good-bye.

There was a lengthy pause. She imagined him raking his disheveled hair with his fingers and rubbing the whiskers on his cheeks. Did he sleep in pajamas? she wondered irrelevantly. A nightshirt? Naked? "Sara," he said in a husky voice. "This isn't necessary." She started talking again, repeating herself, pretending not to know what he meant. His heavy sigh cut her off. In the new silence he asked, "How are you?" and at once all of her defenses crumbled.

"I'm all right. No — I'm tired. Oh, Alex. How are you?"

"I miss you."

She squeezed her eyes shut.

"I'm sitting here trying to figure out if it'll be better or worse if you leave. Worse, I guess."

"Please," she whispered. This was exactly the conversation she had wanted to avoid. He was quiet for a minute; she could hear his slow breathing. And she sensed his frustration, because from the beginning she had forbidden frankness between them, and anything approaching intimacy. She'd had no choice.

"Don't forget what I said, Sara. If you need me for anything, call me. I'll always be here."

"But I don't want you to be. Don't make promises to me, I don't want them."

"It's not a promise, it's a fact." His voice lost its edge and turned gentle again. "You don't have to worry. About me. I won't do anything to hurt you or to put you at risk. Do you understand what I'm saying?"

"Yes."

"I'd like to be your friend."

Her friend. She almost laughed, but she managed to say, "Thank you. I'd better go now. Michael sends you his love."

"Give him mine."

"I will."

The next pause was interminable.

"Sara."

"Yes?"

"Take care of yourself."

"Yes, and you too." She hung up abruptly.

It was good that she was leaving, she saw that clearly now. In trying to reassure her, Alex had actually clarified the danger. She ought to feel grateful to him. But what she wanted to do most was cry.

But she couldn't afford the luxury. And through the window she saw Daisy toiling across the yard in her paisley dressing gown, hair swaying from side to side in a graying plait down her back. Sara got up to say one more good-bye.

# Twelve

". . . his name is Claude Reynauld, his father and mother are both painters, and he's an artist to the bottom of his soul. We met in my life class. The first thing he said to me was, 'Mademoiselle 'Ubbaird, you have a very mandarin sense of style.' Naturally I fell in love! No, but truly, Sara, I think I love him. We're together all the time, and it's hell for me when we're apart. For him too, I believe. No one has ever made me feel this way; I can hardly describe it. He's so good and noble and kindhearted — and funny too. We're always laughing. He wants very much to have a *complete* relationship, and of course it's what I want too, but I hang back. He says I'm bourgeois, that I'm still a child listening to my parents, that convention is the death of passion and art and personal growth. Oh, Sara, I'm so tempted! Tell me what to do! We're nearly the same age, but I've always felt years younger than you, and *decades* more foolish. In my head I agree with Claude, and I long to be everything to him. But I'm afraid, I can't even say of what. Is it women's curse always to be the cautious ones? What are we protecting? Is there some *evolutionary* motive that keeps us chaste, something beyond 'morality' or the simple need to run away from what's new and unknown? Oh, my friend, I'm so confused. . . ."

Sara almost knew Lauren's letter by heart. She refolded it and put it back in her desk drawer. Each time she read it, she had a different response. This time she was struck by the quotation marks Lauren had put around "morality." Like tongs, they held the word at a distance, demeaned it and made it sound fatuous. Was that Lauren's conviction now — or merely the influence of noble, kindhearted Claude?

Poor Lauren. If she expected sage advice from her best friend on this subject, she was going to be disappointed. Sara had no idea what to tell her. Her own upbringing had been fairly conventional, if not strictly "moral" in any religious sense; her first reaction was to urge Lauren to *marry* this man if she truly loved him. Why not marry him? If Lauren knew how lucky she was to be in a position to make that free, joyous choice, she might not be so quick to decry it as "bourgeois."

But perhaps kindhearted Claude didn't

want to marry *her;* perhaps he was afraid such a commitment would put an end to his "personal growth." Then what would she advise Lauren? Spit in his eye — that's what. But envy lurked at the root of that reaction, and well she knew it. Besides, she was thinking of M. Reynauld in the abstract. If she personalized him, if she imagined him to be, for example, someone like Alex McKie — then everything changed. Black and white turned gray, and her rules flew out the window. For the truth was, if not for Michael, she might have become Alex's lover.

She thought of him constantly. He'd been right — it was worse, infinitely worse, not being allowed to see him at all. But her memories were acute. She remembered things he'd told her weeks ago, fragments of conversations about his work, his friends, his likes and dislikes. And she caught herself in the midst of shockingly erotic daydreams, fantasies that began with kissing him in the kitchen and ended with desperate lovemaking somewhere in her imagination. This was new to her, this incessant physical longing for a man. She fought it, because it served no purpose except to intensify her unhappiness. She'd given him up, told him "no" without coyness or equivocation, so it was stupid now to wallow in regrets and useless wishing for what might have been. She felt like a goose. And yet, try as she might, she couldn't let go of her dreams. Thoughts of Alex — calm or sexually charged, lyrical, philosophical, contemplative or salacious — were like flashes of lightning in a pitch-black sky, the brightest moments in a round of days full of manufactured gaity, duty, and dreary responsibilities.

A knock sounded at the closed door to her study. "Come in," she called.

"Excuse me for disturbing you, but I thought you'd like to know."

She heaved an inward sigh. "Come in, Mrs. Drum." Michael's nanny always prefaced her reports of harmless childish misbehavior in this portentious way. When Sara didn't respond with sufficient outrage, Mrs. Drum had a way of communicating her disappointment behind a guilt-inducing wall of icy, silent reproach.

But Michael's transgressions weren't on her mind today. "I've come to speak to you about Miss Eminescu. There've been complaints."

"Complaints about Tasha? From whom?"

"The servants."

"Why?"

Mrs. Drum drew herself up to her full height, which was not considerable, and pushed out her narrow shelf of a chest. "She orders them about as if she lived here, like *she's* the mistress here instead of a guest in the house."

Sara was flabbergasted. "I beg your pardon, but she does not."

"I beg *your* pardon, but she does."

"Mrs. Drum —"

"You're not here when she does it, so you don't know. She waits till you're gone to your settlement house or wherever it might be, and then she starts ordering people around."

Sara tapped her fingers on the desk and eyed the nanny with veiled dislike. "Perhaps the servants have misinterpreted things. Tasha's foreign, and her ways aren't the same as ours. And of course she's not used to the presence of servants at all; it's possible she takes a certain tone to them that's not quite appropriate and has been misconstrued."

"No, ma'am, nothing's been misconstrued. I know because she's done it to *me*. She's tried to send me on errands for her — 'tell the maid to do this, tell the cook to fix that.' But I'm not having any."

Now they were getting to it. Wounded

pride, that's what this was about; Tasha had used the wrong tone of voice, and Mrs. Drum had taken umbrage. "I see. Well, I'll speak —"

"The servants don't know where she stands, so they don't know how to act. Some of them do what she says and some don't. Is she a guest or not? That's what they want to know."

"Thank you for telling me this. I'll certainly —"

"There's something else."

Sara sighed again. "Yes?"

"Yesterday morning while you were out, Mrs. Kimmel paid a call."

"Oh, did she? She didn't leave a card."

"No, ma'am, she didn't. That's because Miss Eminescu entertained her in your absence."

She smiled. " 'Entertained' her?"

"That's right — sat her down in the drawing room, ordered tea, and talked to her like she was you for thirty minutes. The parlor maid said so, and the housemaid verified it."

"I see. Well, I'm sure there's an explanation for that, Mrs. Drum. I'll look into it. Is that everything?"

"Yes, except Charlie O'Shea's mother called just now to say that they'll meet you and the boy in the park at four. I said I'd convey that to you."

Sara's eyes narrowed in irritation. There was nothing she disliked more about Michael's nanny than her persistent habit of referring to him as "the boy." "Thank you," she said shortly.

"It's not for me to say, of course, but in my opinion the boy isn't ready yet for roughhousing in the park with his little friends. He could hurt himself all over again."

"I appreciate your concern. It's been more than six weeks since the accident, however, and Dr. Patterson says Michael's ready to resume his normal activities. Now, Mrs. Drum, have we finished?"

The nanny sniffed, said, "Yes, ma'am," and took her leave.

"Tasha? May I come in?"

"Yes, of course, come." Tasha sat up — she'd been lying across the bed, reading the newspaper — and sent Sara a welcoming smile. The remains of tea lay on a tray at the foot of the bed.

"You're not ill, are you?" Sara asked.

"No — why? Oh, because I'm not dressed! Yes, I was feeling odd this morning, not ill but not myself, do you know? So I didn't put on my clothes yet. Forgive me — it offends you?"

"No, of course not."

"Ah, good. I am just reading something of interest here, perhaps you have seen it already. This tells the story of Mrs. Cornelius Vanderbilt II's great house-warming in Newport last week. 'The Breakers,' they have named their new house. It's quaint, is it not?"

Sara laughed, but she wasn't amused; the subject of "The Breakers" had been a source of friction between her and Ben for weeks. "I doubt you would choose the word 'quaint' if you could see the house."

"Yes, I'm sure you're right. The article describes it here — 'a stately dining room two stories high, most opulent and breath-taking of all the formal dining rooms in Newport. The grand salon is also resplendent, constructed in France, disassembled and packed, shipped to America, then reassembled.' There is a sixteenth century fireplace in the library, it says, purchased from Chateau d'Arnay-le-Duc in the Loire Valley. How exquisite it all sounds! You've seen it, then?"

"Yes, certainly. No one could avoid it." The seventy-room "cottage" dominated Cliff Walk, dwarfing its neighbors.

"But you did not go to this 'house-warming'?"

"You know we didn't. We were here."

"But — why, I wonder? So many people went." She went back to her newspaper. "Where is the place . . . ah, here. 'The doors of this grand American palace were thrown open in a combined housewarming and coming-out ball for the Vanderbilts' beautiful daughter Gertrude. Dinner at 8:30 was reserved for a small gathering of thirty of Gertrude's friends, while the grand assemblage of over three hundred began arriving at 11:00 for the formal cotillion. A special stage was erected in the great hall for a private theatrical event for the entertainment of another two hundred and fifty guests —' "

"Yes, I read it," Sara cut in brusquely. "The reason we didn't go is because we were not invited."

Tasha's luminous black eyes widened in astonishment. "But —" She halted, apparently realizing that to ask "why" again might be tactless. "Oh, I see. What a shame. This makes you sad, does it not?"

"Not particularly." Sara folded her arms and regarded Tasha with interest, trying to discover if the new look on her face was pity. And she'd noticed something else while the girl read the newspaper story to her: her speech was different nowadays. She still spoke with a heavy Slavic inflection, but she pronounced her words with a decidedly British, not American, accent. Odd, since the tutor Sara had hired for her was a native New Yorker. Was Tasha unconsciously imitating her? The speculation made her uneasy.

"I should feel sad to be excluded from my own . . . what's the word? My own peers," Tasha said positively.

"Would you?"

"Yes. I would wonder what was wrong with me."

"How interesting. Speaking of that, Mrs. Drum has mentioned to me —"

"Sara?"

She blinked in surprise; she had repeatedly asked Tasha to call her by her Christian name, but until this moment she never had. How strange the word sounded on her lips now. Almost like a presumption.

"If I may say this to you, you don't look well these days. You seem tired, and not so happy as usual. Perhaps you are working too hard?"

It was on the tip of her tongue to ask Tasha if she herself hadn't put on a little weight lately. But how petty — Tasha was only being kind. "Yes, perhaps," she answered with a smile. "But it's a busy time at the settlement house. I'm sure I'm not the only one who's tired and a bit over-worked."

"I hope it's only that. I hope there is no other reason that you seem so sad."

"No," she said slowly. "No, there's no other reason." How ironic that their roles seemed to have reversed. Once she'd tried to draw Tasha out, but she'd remained quiet and remote; now it was Tasha who wanted to draw *her* out, and she was the one resisting. But Tasha's thoughtful over-ture blunted her enthusiasm — not strong to begin with — for investigating Mrs. Drum's complaints about her treatment of the servants. Instead Sara asked, "And how are *you* these days? I don't mean phys-ically — you look wonderful, healthier and stronger than I've ever seen you."

"Oh, thank you." Tasha beamed. "It's because you take such good care of me."

She waved that aside. "I wonder. . . . Have you given any thought lately to finding a place of your own?" Tasha's face fell. Sara said quickly, "Of course we love having you here, and you know you're wel-come to stay as long as you like. But — do you think it might be time to start thinking about becoming independent again?"

Tasha didn't answer. Sara sat on the edge of the bed and put a soft hand on her shoulder. "I've been thinking. How would you like to have a shop of your own? A boutique, somewhere on the Ladies' Mile. You'd sell only the finest, most fashionable, most *expensive* ladies' dresses in the city. You could employ seamstresses to work for you while you concentrated on design. You'd probably need a business manager, someone to help you with things like book-keeping and the actual running of the shop — Ben could advise you there, and he may even know someone who'd be interested in becoming your partner." Tasha kept her face averted. "How does that sound? Does that interest you? I'd help you in any way I could, Tasha. Your talent is real, you know; with the right backing, I don't know why something like this couldn't work out well for you."

She put her fingers on Tasha's chin and gently pulled her head up. "What's wrong?" The full lips began to tremble; tears filled Tasha's dark, heavy-lidded eyes and spilled down her cheeks. "Oh, no," Sara whispered, "don't, Tasha, don't cry, it's all right." She wound her arms around her and held tight, soothing her as she

269

would have soothed Michael. "Shh, I'm sorry I've upset you. We won't talk about this now, all right? It's too soon — I didn't realize. It wasn't a good idea —"

*"No, no, no,"* Tasha broke in, wiping her wet cheeks with the sheet, "it was a good idea, it *was*. And you are an angel, I don't deserve such a friend! But please, please, don't make me do this. I'm still so afraid, please don't make me go yet, I can't, I just can't —" She broke down again, covered her face with her hands, and sobbed.

Sara's arms went around her again automatically; she rocked her and said calming things while Tasha wept on her shoulder. Gradually the girl's sobs diminished and she quieted, but she stayed where she was and didn't move. A little later, limp and relaxed beneath Sara's patting hand, she made a low, satisfied noise deep in her throat. It sounded like purring.

"What? Say that again, I must not've heard right."

Sara dropped her packages on the elephant-foot Indian settee in the entrance hall and reached up to unpin her hat. The mirror over the settee was not a friend; it told her what she already knew — she was exhausted and she looked like hell.

"Now? You want paid now, this minute? No? Well, what the hell *do* you want?"

And Ben was angry at someone, she could hear his booming fury all the way from the red drawing room. That meant he would be *more* irritable, *more* insufferable tonight after his unlucky visitor went away. The last few weeks had been so awful, it was hard to imagine the domestic environment getting worse. He wouldn't confide in her, of course — it would break some masculine code of honor to speak frankly to a woman, or at least to her — so she couldn't be sure exactly what was causing his agitation. Labor unrest was the likeliest culprit, for lately it seemed as if the workers — the "communist mob," he called them — were striking every business he owned. Things weren't going well politically, either, and each night he came home with a new grudge against the city aldermen, the reformist mayor, or "that liberal bastard Cleveland." Now it sounded as if money was a problem as well. How very interesting, she thought, laying her hat on the hall table. In all her years with Ben, money was probably the only thing that had never been a problem.

She had one foot on the staircase when the voice of his visitor came to her clearly.

271

She stopped short and whirled around. Alex! It was as if she had conjured him up, for he'd been in her thoughts all day — more so even than usual. But why was he here? What could he and Ben be arguing about? A dreadful possibility occurred to her. But no, that couldn't be. *I would never do anything to put you at risk,* he'd said, and she believed him.

It would be insane, supremely foolhardy to go to him now, in Ben's presence. She should run upstairs as fast as she could, and pretend later for Ben that she hadn't known he was here. *Don't,* she told herself, shaking her skirts and patting at wisps of her hair. *Don't, Sara,* she warned as she made her way down the hall toward the drawing room. The sound of voices was louder now, and angrier.

"No one's suggesting anything of the sort. It's a matter of demonstrating to the partners —"

"Well, that's what it sounds like to me. Look here, McKie, you can tell Ogden and the rest that they're not the only architects in this town, and if they don't like my business I'll take it somewhere else. Got that?"

"All they're asking for is a show of good faith. It's been six months, and in all that time —"

"Good faith? They want a *show* of *good faith* from Ben Cochrane? You listen to me, sonny, I made a million dollars before you were out of short pants. I'll give 'em a show of good faith! That pile of crap can rust through to China for all I care. Tell 'em *that*. And tell 'em —"

"Ben? I thought I heard your voice. Mr. McKie, what a surprise, I thought you were still in Newport." She moved farther into the room, smiling, pretending the tension in the air wasn't as thick as smoke. "Ben, you haven't ordered any tea for our guest. Or perhaps you'd prefer something stronger, Mr. —"

"Our *guest* was just leaving," Ben snarled.

"Oh?" She feigned surprise. "In that case, I'll show Mr. McKie out, shall I?"

"You do that." He turned his back rudely and started to light a cigar.

Sara risked a glance at Alex. His anger was poorly hidden. "I'll give Ogden your message," he said tightly, staring at Ben's back. "I expect he'll be in touch." When Ben didn't respond, Alex stalked out.

She followed, high heels echoing on the parquetry floor as she almost ran to catch up. But in the foyer he stopped and waited for her, leaning against the ugly split-bamboo wainscot. She slowed as she neared him, twisting her hands. Embarrassment and an excess of feeling tied her tongue. She'd thought about him incessantly for four weeks. To see him now, like this, Ben's ugly words still ringing in their ears —

"What the hell is that?" He jerked his chin at something over her shoulder.

She glanced around. "What?"

*"That."*

"Oh. That. It's new." It was Ben's latest decorative addition: two gas fixtures mounted on the newel posts at the bottom of the stairs. Carved oak griffins, they were, with chains in their mouths supporting a nest of four curling serpents each. From every serpent's mouth a gas burner protruded. When it was lit, the flames looked like flickering tongues. "You mean you don't like it?"

He looked at her in blank amazement. The twinkle in her smoky eyes was subtle at first, then blatant. She had a dimple on the right side of her mouth; it quivered now as she tried not to laugh. His anger vanished into thin air — a mist burned away in the bright sun. "I love it," he said tenderly. "It's so . . ." She raised an arch brow. "So Ben."

She couldn't help laughing. It was disloyal, patronizing, everything she'd resolved never to indulge in with Alex because he was dangerous, and he tempted her so powerfully, and this sort of intimate badinage between them could sow the seeds of her destruction as effectively as forbidden kisses. But she couldn't help it: it was funny.

Her laughter enchanted him. He smiled back, savoring it. He wanted to ask, *How did you save yourself, Sara?* She could have become someone like Daisy Wentworth, a sardonic, self-involved drunk. But she hadn't. Because of Michael? What might she have been like if she'd never met Ben at all?

He stopped staring at her to ask, "How is Michael?" because it seemed the safest subject.

"He's fine, completely well. Did you get the letter he sent, thanking you for all your nice gifts?"

"I did. I thought I recognized his mother's hand in that."

"No, no, it was his idea, I only addressed the envelope."

"Ah. So he's all well, is he?"

"Oh yes, he's even looking forward to school starting again."

"What school?" he asked deliberately.

"That — hasn't been decided yet." She should never have told him of Ben's threat; she saw that clearly now. That was one of the private nightmares she wasn't used to sharing with other people. Telling someone else, even Alex, made her feel even more vulnerable, more at risk. "How are you?" she asked quickly. "How have you been?"

"I've been looking for you." She frowned. "Sometimes I think I see you, on the street or in a restaurant, riding by in a cab. But she turns, and it's never you."

She took a deep breath. "Alex, please —"

"I've got a new commission," he hurried on. "I'm to build another house in Newport, this one for Marshall Farley. Sara, you ought to hear what he wants. It makes Eden look like the caretaker's lodge."

"Oh, dear. Ben will be very cross when he hears that. But that's wonderful for you, Alex! Congratulations." She looked at him quizzically. "Aren't you glad?"

"Yes, of course, it's wonderful. As you say."

She couldn't see beyond the bland impassivity of his beautiful eyes to know whether he meant it or not. And they couldn't speak frankly to each other because she'd decreed too many subjects off limits. "I'm sorry about Ben," she said

quietly. "He can be terribly rude sometimes. He's been under a lot of pressure
lately —"

"Don't apologize to me for him, Sara.
Ever."

"No, but — I take it he owes money to
your firm. Would you mind telling me if
it's a lot?"

He hesitated. It would be stupid to
alarm her; but on the other hand, she had
a right to know the facts. "I'm sure it's
nothing to worry about. I mean, I think he
could pay if he wanted to. And, yes, it's
rather a lot. All the firm wants is a gesture
at this point, a fraction of what he owes to
prove his good faith."

"And he won't pay them anything at
all?"

"He wants to delay. The building contractor is in the same position we are, so
work on the house has stopped. For now."

"Good lord. I had no idea."

He studied her while she looked away,
digesting his news. She looked more
intrigued than worried. "You don't seem
all that concerned," he noted, curious.

"At the prospect of Ben going broke?"
She put her fingers to her lips, trying to
imagine it. She couldn't. "Frankly, I can't
make it real. But the money's always been

an abstraction to me — I suppose because there's so much of it. Not that I don't enjoy spending it." She smiled, gesturing toward the Lord & Taylor shopping bags on the settee by the door. "Anyway, I'm sorry you haven't gotten paid. It doesn't affect you personally, does it, Alex? I mean, they still pay *you*, don't they?"

"Most definitely," he assured her, smiling gravely.

"Well, that's all right, then."

And that seemed to be that as far as her interest in Ben's finances was concerned. Alex could think of nothing to say. It was obvious that he ought to leave. Standing in her foyer like criminals, trying to say everything and not being allowed to say anything at all — he felt stupid and thwarted and resentful. The only dignified thing to do was go away. She probably wanted him to go but was too polite to say so. "How have you been?" he asked, stalling. "You look well." She didn't quite roll her eyes, but her disbelief was obvious. "More than well," he insisted. "You look beautiful."

"Alex." She shook her head with a pitying smile.

She wasn't being coy, he realized, she really didn't believe him. He would have given anything to be allowed to convince her. "Doesn't he ever tell you that, Sara?" She gave a little laugh, and he had his answer.

"How long have you been back in the city?" She could stall, too.

"A week. I leave again in a day or two."

"Oh? But not for Newport, I take it, not if work on the house has stopped."

"No, I'm going to California."

"California? Is it because of your grandfather?"

"Yes, he's dead. Finally."

"Oh, no. Alex, I'm truly sorry." She reached for his hand impulsively and surrounded it with both of hers. "You told me he was ill —"

"I also told you not to feel sorry for me."

"That's right, you did." She studied him curiously. "May I feel sorry for him?"

"Sure. I like him better myself now that he's dead."

His flippant tone didn't fool her. "What did he do to you, I wonder," she said softly.

"Maybe I'll tell you someday."

She dropped her eyes. A sharp sorrow stabbed through her without warning. "Yes, maybe." But he would never tell her, because she could not allow such an intimacy. Everything she wanted from him was forbidden, everything she wanted to

279

give him. Years ago self-denial had become a way of life, but she'd never been tested in quite this way. This was too hard.

"Sara." He brought her clasped hands to his chest. Her sadness made him feel desperate. "Sara —"

"Oh — excuse me."

She jerked out of his grasp and stepped back in haste.

Tasha stood at the foot of the staircase, poised motionless between the spitting serpents' tongues. The look in her gypsy eyes was dark and unreadable. "It's Mr. McKie, isn't it? How nice to see you again."

He wanted to say something smooth, something casual, to lessen the intense awkwardness of a situation that seemed to have turned Sara to stone. But he couldn't think of the woman's damned foreign name, so he only muttered inaudibly and bowed to her. She returned a slow, deliberate nod, then moved off down the dim corridor and out of sight.

Immediately Sara turned her back on him and walked to the other side of the foyer. In the mirror over her head, he saw that she'd gone deathly pale. She clamped one hand over her mouth and shut her eyes tight. He went to her but didn't touch her — touching her was what had brought on this catastrophe. "Sara? Sara, I'm sorry, that was all my fault. What does it mean? What's going to happen?"

She spun around. Color returned to her cheeks like two slap marks. "I don't know! Nothing. Nothing *did* happen. Oh, Alex, for God's sake, go away." He turned to obey, and she clutched at his arm to stop him. "I'm sorry, I don't even know what I'm saying!"

"What will happen?" he repeated. "She won't say anything, will she? To Ben, I mean."

"No — no. How could she? There's nothing to say."

"Are you going to be all right?"

"Yes, of course."

He ground his teeth. "I can postpone this trip, there's no reason —"

"Don't be silly. You must go, of course."

The mask of her composure slipped back into place so easily, he wanted to shake her. "Let me write to you."

"No."

"Sara —"

"*No,* and I can't see you again. You have to go now, Alex, don't you see?"

"Sara, this is —"

"Please, if you care for me at all — !"

"All right." There was nothing else to

say anyway. He opened the door, but when he looked back her mask had slipped a little; for a fleeting second he saw all the hopeless tenderness in her eyes. And so, for once, he said the very thing he was thinking at the moment he was thinking it. "I'm in love with you."

Her eyes went liquid with sorrow. He saw his truest emotions mangled and twisted into weapons that pierced to the heart, and knew he'd committed the ultimate unkindness. He couldn't bear it. He pulled the door closed, blocking out the sight of her.

Sara stood still for a long time, staring at the pattern in the oak door frame, listening to the soft hiss of the gaslights. Finally she turned — to go upstairs, she thought, but her legs gave out and she found herself slumped on the settee beside her shopping bags. The comforting numbness retreated, and all at once tears blinded her. She groped for her handkerchief. A "broken heart," they called this. She felt broken. Split. Alex had ripped open all the scarred-over hurts that had been sleeping for years, and she was bleeding. Why, why hadn't he left her alone?

She couldn't stay here where any passing servant might see her — Ben might see her, or Tasha. No — Tasha had already seen her. But she must get up, pretend nothing was wrong. As much as she longed to take refuge in her room until she had her emotions in check, she had to be seen, now, no matter what it cost. She got up and crossed to the mirror — and gasped softly when she saw her face. True panic brought sweat to the palms of her hands. How could she explain this? Maybe it was better to hide after all, run upstairs and escape. No. A stronger instinct warned her she had to see Ben now, without further delay.

She used her soaked handkerchief again. No need to pinch her cheeks — they were already flushed. She took several deep breaths, squared her shoulders, and tried to arrange her features into a look of self-possession. It might serve. It had to serve.

Halfway down the hall, she could hear voices from the drawing room; but when she paused in the doorway, they abruptly stopped. Her nerves jolted. Tasha sat on the scarlet brocade sofa, her sewing in her lap; ten feet away, Ben stood beside the liquor cabinet, mixing a drink. She glanced between them, straining to gauge the atmosphere. But she could read nothing in their faces, hear nothing ominous in the silence between them.

She often came upon them together in this room in the evening. It was the family gathering place, to the extent that there was one at all. Or, she thought cynically, to the extent that they were a family. Ben liked the "crimson" drawing room's garish, overdone opulence. He said good night to Michael there when Mrs. Drum brought him downstairs at eight, clean and combed and sweet in his nightrobe and slippers. Tasha sewed there. Sara forced herself to act wifely there when she longed to go to her little room across the hall and read a book or write a letter or think her own solitary thoughts.

Ben finished the whiskey and soda he'd just made and poured another. She wanted a drink, but if she asked him to make her one and he came close enough to hand it to her, he would see too much in her forlorn, red-eyed face. Tasha looked up and smiled at her — an odd smile, she thought. Was she being fanciful? She tried again to interpret the younger woman's dark silence as she plied her needle to the sewing in her lap, but it was impossible. Deliberately taking a seat beside her on the sofa, Sara asked, "What are you making, Tasha? That silk is lovely."

She looked up. Absurd to read anything sinister in the black, uncanny stillness of her bottomless eyes. "A shawl for you. Do you like it?"

"It's beautiful. Thank you."

"You are welcome, Sara."

Again the familiarity almost made her wince. She looked across at Ben. He was watching both of them over the rim of the glass of his third drink. Presently he came and sat in the chair opposite, slouching down in it on his spine. He rested his glass on his belt, knees spread wide, glaring. "Who the hell does he think he is?"

"Ben, do you think this is the —"

"Goddamn son of a bitch, who the hell does he think he is? Does he think I *can't* pay? I could buy everything he owns right now with the change in my pocket."

Sara fingered the lace at her wrist, wondering why she wasn't used to his vulgarity by now. And what was he thinking of, to speak of money in front of Tasha? Still, before she could stop herself, she snapped, "Well, why don't you pay him, then?"

His bloodshot eyes narrowed dangerously. "I'll pay him when I'm goddamn good and ready. 'Show of good faith,' he says." He muttered another curse, obscene and vicious, and Sara tensed. Tasha sewed on in silence. "Ogden got him into the New York Club."

"What?"

"Ogden got McKie into the New York Club. Can you beat that?"

Ben had been trying for six years to find someone influential enough to sponsor him for membership in the most exclusive men's club in the city, probably in the country. And now they'd admitted Alex. It was too delicious; in spite of everything, Sara had to pinch her lips to keep from smiling.

"You know why, don't you? The bastard sleeps with Ogden's wife."

"That's absurd," she bit out, furious and unable to hold her tongue. "Why would you say such a thing?"

"Because he sleeps with anything that moves. Christ, everybody knows it, don't look so surprised. His favorite is other fellows' wives."

"You are ridiculous. That's a lie and you know it." *Stop!* her brain shouted. But she was shaking with anger, incapable of keeping silent.

"The hell it is. I bet he's had every man's wife in his whole damn firm."

She jumped up, but managed to conquer the impulse to shout at him. She couldn't stay in the same room with him, though. She muttered something about dinner and started to stalk past him. His hand flashed out and he grabbed her arm. *"Let go."*

"Stay here, I've got something to say to you."

She couldn't break his grip on her wrist. She kept her face a rigid blank and said quietly, "Very well. Tasha, would you mind leaving us alone for a few minutes?"

"No, certainly." She put her sewing away carefully, and so slowly that Sara wanted to scream — for Ben's hold on her arm was excruciating and he was not going to relax it until they were alone. "I will see you at dinner, then," Tasha murmured, obsidian eyes scanning them languidly as she passed Ben's chair and went into the hall.

As soon as she was gone, Sara gave a violent yank to free her arm and moved out of his range. "You bastard," she whispered; despite her best effort, tears of pain and fury streaked down her face. "What is it you want to say to me? Say it quickly."

As usual, the sight of her weeping had a sedative effect on his temper. He crossed his legs and sent her a nasty smile. "I want you to go back to Newport, and I'm tired of arguing about it. You're going."

She blinked at him, then spread her

hands in genuine bafflement. "Why? It makes no sense for me to go back — especially if work on the new house has stopped." She shouldn't have said that — Alex shouldn't have told her!

But Ben didn't seem to notice her gaffe. "It'll start again as soon as I send them a check. I'll send it in the morning."

"But why?" she repeated. "Why do you want me gone so badly?" It seemed he'd been trying to get rid of her since the day she'd returned. She had been uncommonly adamant in her refusal, using Michael's injuries as an excuse. But the real reason, of course, was Alex.

"I don't want you gone, Sara," he answered innocently. "I'm thinking of Michael. It'll do him good, all that fresh air and exercise."

That was such an obvious lie, she almost snorted. "You really have got a bloody cheek. Michael goes back to school in ten days, and you know it. It's a woman, isn't it? You want a free rein while you carry on with your latest whore."

He finished his drink, not looking at her. "Don't be stupid."

"Why bother to deny it? God, Ben, do you think I *care?*"

He got to his feet and came toward her

slowly, and all at once she realized he was drunk. "Listen, Sare."

"Don't touch me." She backed up until she felt the liquor cabinet behind her. "I mean it, don't touch me."

He reached out with one beefy hand to stroke her cheek. "Come on. Come on, Sare, don't be like that. Jeez, you're soft." His bloodshot eyes watered lugubriously.

"Stop it."

"Be nice, Sare, c'mon. Don't you like me? Jeez, look at you. Come on, let's —"

She batted his pawing hand away and jerked sideways. "Just *don't,*" she ground out, shuddering with revulsion. Once in a great while, and only when he was drunk, this kind of maudlin sentimentality replaced the callousness he usually showed her. Once, a hundred years ago, she'd mistaken it for real feeling. Now she hated it as much as his brutality, maybe more — an honest blow was almost preferable to this mawkish, grotesque affection.

Snarling, he dropped his arm. He lurched against the liquor cabinet, cursed, and started to make another drink. "You're going to Newport." His voice was ugly again. "You're going, that's it."

She could go, she realized, now that Alex wouldn't be there. She could even make it seem like a concession.

"All right," she said, facing him. "If it means so much to you, I'll go. But only on one condition." Bleary-eyed, he gulped his drink and waited. "Michael goes to school *here*, Ben, in New York. There won't be any more talk of sending him away — not this year, not ever." Heart pounding, she fixed him with a firm, falsely confident stare. "Do you agree?"

"No."

All the blood drained from her face. "Damn you! I mean it, Ben, I won't —"

"Shut up. He can stay here — for now. We'll give it six months. That's fair. After that, we'll renegotiate."

*"You bloody bastard!"* She wanted to hit him, she realized. She spun around, trembling, afraid to look at him.

He laughed, then tossed off the rest of his whiskey and made a grab for her arm. She tried to jerk away, but he gave her a savage warning shake that made her teeth clash, then solicitously tucked her hand into the bend of his elbow. "Dinner's ready by now, Sare. Come on, we don't want to keep Miss Eminescu waiting, do we?" He guided her out of the room, smiling down at her, patting her hand.

# Thirteen

Matthew Holyfield's new grave still had no headstone. The Blessed Brethren must be waiting for the deceased's kin to cough up enough money to buy one, Alex thought as he stood over the convex dirt rectangle with hands clasped and head bowed. He wasn't praying. He was trying to decide on an appropriate epitaph for his grandfather. The Brethren expected something cheap but unctuous, no doubt — "He sleeps in peace" or "His life was a prayer." But Alex had other tributes in mind. "He tolerated no human frailty" was one. Or "He was congenitally incapable of forgiving." What about "His family feared him all his days"? or something really basic, like, "His grandson despised him"?

He swore at himself under his breath; even dead, Matthew could still bring out the worst in him. What he ought to do was *forgive* the son of a bitch. Then, if his grandfather was right and there really was a hell, Alex could watch him burn in it from a safe distance away in heaven for the rest of eternity.

He moved sideways, past the inconspicuous marker on his grandmother's grave to the one over his mother's. *Susan Holyfield*, it read. Nothing more, not even the dates. But that was probably just as well; if Matthew had wanted a message carved on his daughter's tombstone, it would've been "Wretched Sinner." That's what he'd called her often enough while she lived.

Alex knelt to lay his bouquet of bright poppies at the foot of his mother's grave. If she'd lived, she'd have been forty-eight years old today. He didn't even know, not for certain, what had killed her. One day when he was seven, she'd "taken to her bed," as the family put it. But not for long; within a few weeks she was gone. The funeral sermon, preached by his grandfather, had been so full of her shame and sinfulness that Alex had been embarrassed to show his grief. But he'd mourned her in secret, keeping her memory alive in his heart during the dreadful decade that followed. And then, at sixteen, he'd run away, just as she'd been driven to do twenty years earlier. Sometimes he thought she must have been looking out for him during those first years on his own because, unlike her, he'd never been forced by circumstances to return.

"Well, bless my soul. That's Alexander Holyfield, ain't it?"

Alex shot to his feet and pivoted. An old man stood on the path twenty feet away, shielding his eyes from the sun with a veiny, gnarled hand and peering at him. He wore rusty black trousers and a collarless white shirt; a sweat-stained straw hat was jammed down over his forehead.

"Don't you remember me, boy?" He started forward at a loose-jointed amble, talking all the while. "Reese Melrose, over to Cider Creek. I was deacon in your grampa's church for a time. You recollect me now, don't you? Law, you've done changed a mite, ain't you?" He wiped his palm on the side of his pants and stuck it out to shake.

"How do you do. I'm sorry, but I don't remember. And my name's McKie now."

"McKie? Hah! Changed it, did you?"

"It was my father's name."

"That's right, I recollect that now."

I'll just bet you do, thought Alex, amazed at how all the anger and resentment could return in the blink of an eye, strong as ever and still as bitter as alum.

Grinning, Melrose stepped back and swept him with a good, long look, head to

293

toe. " 'Pears to me like you done pretty good after leaving outa here all sudden-like. How you been, boy? Didn't show up at your grampa's funeral, did you? Some o' the Brethren wondered about you. Glad to see you're not dead. What you been up to?"

In spite of himself, Alex almost smiled. He picked the old man's last question at random and answered, "I'm living in New York now, sir. I've become an architect."

"An *architect*. Well now, ain't that something. What would ol' Matthew have to say about that, I wonder?"

"Something about the devil's handiwork, I expect, or the sins of the father being visited. Something on that order."

Melrose whacked his thigh and whooped out a laugh. "Wouldn't he, though? Yessir, that's just what he'd say. You got that right, Mr. Alexander *McKie*."

Now Alex did smile. "How's your daughter, Mr. Melrose?"

"Ha, so you do remember me! I knew it."

"How's Charlotte?"

"Charlotte's good. Got four kids, lives over in Monterey. I'll be sure to tell her I run into you. Reckon she'll remember you pretty good."

"I reckon she will." He wasn't likely to forget her. When he was fourteen, she thirteen, he'd gotten her back behind the school building and kissed her. She'd told her mother, who had told his grandfather. Matthew had made him "confess" in front of the whole congregation of Blessed Brethren, then beaten him with a strap until blood ran down his legs.

"Why'd you come back, boy?" Melrose asked, squinting at him. "You miss the place?"

Alex looked off across the flat yellow distance, inhaling the sunny smell of summer. He'd asked himself that question many times since boarding the train from New York. He owed his grandfather nothing, and he could've hired someone to see to the disposition of Matthew's "estate." "Miss the place?" he repeated. The drone of bees off in the seared clover was as familiar to him as his own voice; the high summer sky was a burning shade of blue that he'd never seen anywhere else in the world. "How's the crop this year?" he asked instead of answering. "Things are looking pretty dry."

"Terrible year, terrible. I give up on lettuce about four years back — got too old for all the bending. Just do sugar beets and a few pear trees now." He pushed his straw hat back to scratch the top of his bald head. "Matthew quit planting altogether after you left. You know that?"

"No, sir." And he didn't care. "Why?" he asked anyway. "Couldn't he afford another slave?"

Old Melrose pushed his lips out a few times consideringly. "Don't know if it was that or not. Got kinda peculiar, we thought. Kept to himself more. Kept preachin', o' course; nothing could make him stop preachin'. He took to carryin' on about sin in the big city and such-like, couldn't let go of it. Course, he knew you was up in San Francisco by then, so we all figured that's what was behind it. You go to school up there or something?"

"That's right." It was satisfying to think of Matthew getting crazier and crazier because of some sick notion about Alex living a life of sin and degredation in the city. Not too long ago he'd felt a compulsion to confront the old man, to rub it in his face that he'd gone out and gotten every damn thing he'd sworn to him thirteen years ago he would get. But maybe this was better; if thinking of his grandson consorting with the devil in that cesspool of wickedness and vice — Oakland — had finally driven the miserable bastard around the bend, Alex couldn't find it in himself to feel sorry.

"How are the Blessed Brethren these days?" He took care not to sneer the name of the congregation; Melrose, he recalled, was a true believer.

"It ain't the same without Matthew. That's what everybody says. Course, some of us say that ain't all bad," he added with a wink.

Alex grinned. "What brings you out here, sir?"

He pointed with a long, sun-browned arm. "Lucille, my wife. Over yonder by that spittal pine. Passed on about nine years ago now."

"I'm sorry to hear that."

"I make it up here about onct a month. Talk to her and all, tell her what's going on with the children and what-not. Reckon she can hear me?"

"I — um —" he stammered, taken off guard. "It wouldn't surprise me, sir. Not a bit."

Melrose grinned slyly. "Then I reckon Matthew can hear you. Hah? I'm gonna get on now, boy, got things to do. You stay and think o' something to say to ol' Matthew, you hear?" He tipped his hat and started to shuffle off, still grinning. "Make

297

it a good one, now, you hear? Nice talkin' to you! You're looking very prime, Mr. Alexander McKie!"

Alex laughed and held up a hand in farewell. The old man waved back, then disappeared around the first turn in the path.

Still grinning, Alex looked down at his grandfather's grave. Melrose's idea appealed to him. "Well now, let's see," he said experimentally. He never talked to himself; his voice sounded strange with no one around to hear it. "You were a mean son of a bitch your whole life, Matthew Holyfield. Nobody in the world is sorry you're dead. Nobody misses you. If you're in hell now, it's no more than —"

He stopped, sheepish. What the hell was he doing? He glanced behind him nervously, but there was no one around.

"It's no more than you deserve," he resumed confidentially. "You ruined my mother's life, you tried to ruin mine. Your wife you just beat down to nothing, so that nobody even knew she was there. When she died, we hardly even noticed."

His throat closed; all at once he felt like crying. It came back in a hot rush, how it felt to be twelve years old and full of impotent rage. "Do you know how many women I've had, Matthew? I can't even

298

count — maybe a hundred. Sinners all. And I'm *rich*. These shoes cost thirty dollars. Every two weeks I pay a man to cut my hair. I live in New York City, and I belong to a club that's so exclusive, they wouldn't let you in to clean the toilet." He swiped at his eyes with the back of his hand. "Here's a promise: I'm coming back in ten years so you can see how much richer I got. And I'll put flowers on *Melrose's* grave."

He laughed, then sucked in his breath and closed his eyes tight. "You're nothing, old man, you can't touch me anymore. I beat you. And I can't waste any more time thinking about you." He knelt down swiftly and put a hand on his mother's grave, a hand on his grandmother's. Then he stood up and walked away fast, not looking back.

"Good-bye, Mr. McKie, it's been a pleasure talking to you." George Mitchell's boyish face pinkened. "And — an honor."

Alex shook hands. "The pleasure was mine." Behind Mitchell's shoulder, he saw Professor Stern wink at him in amusement.

"It's really nice of you to offer to look at my drawings. Shall I send them to New York, sir, or to your hotel in San Francisco?"

"Since I'm not sure how much longer I'll be here, why don't you send them to New York. Professor Stern can give you my address."

"Very good, that's what I'll do. Thanks again, sir, it's awfully nice of you."

"Don't mention it." Bemused, he watched the professor open the door for young Mitchell and see him out.

When Professor Stern turned back, his mild gray eyes were twinkling. "Mitchell's never found talking to *me* an honor," he noted, leading the way down the hall toward his study. "Martha, don't do that now — leave it till morning and I'll help," he called to his wife as they passed by the archway to the dining room.

Mrs. Stern flapped her hand and resumed clearing the dishes from the table. "Go sit down, the coffee's almost ready."

Stern shrugged and kept moving.

In the study, at the professor's insistence, Alex took the place of honor — a soft, worn leather chair whose back reclined at the touch of a button on the wooden arm rest.

"Brandy?"

"Thanks."

"What did you think of Mitchell?"

"I liked him. He seems very bright."

"He is bright, the best student I've got this year. He was thrilled when I told him you'd be here — don't be surprised if he asks you for a reference. He wants to study at the Beaux Arts. Following in the master's footsteps, don'tcha know." Alex laughed as he took the glass Stern handed him. The professor sat down on the sofa opposite and set about lighting his pipe. "So," he said, puffing cloudily. "Tell me what you really think of my new house."

"I've already told you — it's magnificent, it's splendid."

He blew out a deprecatory puff of smoke. "Come, come, you've no need to flatter me now; I haven't graded a paper of yours in about ten years."

"Nine," Alex corrected. "And I got an A."

Professor Stern guffawed. "I don't doubt it! Not a bit!" He crossed his short, stocky legs, revealing an inch of hairy skin between trouser cuff and stocking top. "I never had such a stubborn, single-minded pupil as you, Alex. What were you when you showed up in Oakland, seventeen? Eighteen?"

"About that."

"Not many boys know what they want at that age as surely as you knew. Or else they think they want to run off to sea, or be cowboys, or outlaws. You don't find too many runaway seventeen-year-olds with a burning desire to become architects."

Alex smiled. "All I knew was that I wanted to have clean hands and wear suits and walk on city pavements. With women my grandfather wouldn't approve of."

"Well, I guess you got all that, didn't you?"

"Yes, sir, I got all that."

"That's not it, though," Stern said after a moment, turning serious. "That's not what you wanted. You could've been a banker if it had been, or a politician. No, no, you wanted to be an *architect*. You've got to admit, that's rare at that age."

That age? Alex thought, sipping the rich California brandy slowly. He'd known what he wanted to be from approximately the age of five. He'd never told Stern why, though. "Did you know my father studied engineering here, sir?"

Stern raised his white beetle brows. "Why, no, I didn't. You never told me that. In fact, you never told me much of anything about yourself. And you were the kind of young fellow who discouraged people from asking questions."

Alex had no reply to that.

"When was your father here?"

" 'Sixty-six and 'sixty-seven."

"He didn't graduate, then?"

"No, sir, he died. In a boarding house fire."

"Well, now, I'm sorry."

"He wanted to be an architect — that's what he was studying for."

"Did he?" Professor Stern peered at him shrewdly through a haze of pipe smoke. "You must've been very young when he died."

"As a matter of fact, I wasn't born yet. It was my mother who told me about him." Told him, almost every day until the end of her life, all of Brian Alexander McKie's hopes and dreams. She'd made his father as real in Alex's imagination as if he'd never died.

"Well, now. Wasn't it lucky that your ambition and your talent happened to coincide so neatly? Not many men are so fortunate."

"I often think of that, sir. But I was lucky in other ways too."

"How's that?"

Alex smiled. "We both know that if it hadn't been for you, I'd never have made it through my undergraduate studies."

"Oh, now, that's —"

"But if by some miracle I *had*, I'd never

303

have gotten accepted into the Beaux Arts without your help and influence and political backing. Not to mention a sizeable loan."

"Well, that might be true — I say it *might* be true, but only because they're such a hidebound, backward lot. They think if an American boy hasn't gone to a fancy eastern prep school, he's got no business studying architecture in Paris. But the rest of that, my friend, is pure hogwash." His pipe sputtered out. He stood up and busied himself with pouring more drinks.

Alex sighed, familiar by now with his old teacher's dislike of gratitude in any form, except maybe high-scoring examination papers. But the debt he owed Stern was real, whether the professor chose to acknowledge it or not. Alex thought of the day he'd appeared on Stern's office doorstep — seventeen years old, penniless, scrawny, hungry, and claiming he wanted to study engineering so he could become an architect. It didn't take Stern long to ascertain that he had a lot more practical knowledge of lettuce farming than descriptive geometry. Nevertheless, and for no particular reason Alex had ever been able to determine then or now, the professor decided to help him. Within days, by what must have been legerdemain, he'd gotten him enrolled in the college. After that, he found him the easiest, highest-paying campus jobs, tutored him personally, guided, encouraged, and occasionally comforted him, and finally bullied the department committee into granting him a full scholarship.

Alex raised his glass in the air. "To hogwash," he said fervently.

Stern smirked. "Hogwash." They drank.

"So, Alex. You're a big New York architect now, designing mansions in Newport. How do you like it at Draper and Snow?"

"I'd better like it. They've offered me a partnership."

"No!" Stern smacked his knee. "I'll be damned! Say, that's wonderful. Congratulations."

"Thanks. It just happened last week — took me by surprise. I knew they were considering it, but I assumed it was a few years off." He shifted, uncomfortable himself now under Stern's respectful gaze. Professor Stern was supposed to be his mentor, not his admirer. But he knew a sure way to distract him. Glancing around the room, he asked, "How long did it take you to build the house, sir?"

"Three years, start to finish. Martha

almost left me about six times. So you really like it?"

"Of course. It's bad for business, though."

"Bad for business?"

"Sure. People are going to take one look and say, if a lowly engineer can design a house like that, who needs an architect?"

Stern laughed delightedly. "It must seem pretty simple to you, though, compared to what you've been doing, the materials you've been working with. This Eden you were telling me about — now, that's a *house*."

"No, sir. I don't know what it is, but it's not a house." A monument, Sara had called it. That probably came closest. "Have you seen some of the homes going up now in the Berkeley hills? I took a walk around there yesterday. Have you seen them?"

"Some, yes. What's your opinion?"

"I think they're amazing, completely unique. There's nothing like that on the east coast as far as I know."

"It's this English movement, isn't it? This 'arts and crafts' thing you hear about —"

"No, it's different. Maybe it started with that, but what I saw yesterday goes much

306

further. It's not so plain, it actually allows ornamentation." He sat forward, intent. "They're using redwood almost exclusively. The colors are incredible — some of the houses are practically invisible, they blend in so cleverly with the trees. The work in stone is good, too. There's one made of stucco and shingles on St. Claire Street — have you seen it? It's not finished, they're still working on it. I walked around to the back — nobody was there — and I swear they're throwing buckets of muddy water on the stucco just to get the right shade of brown."

Stern chuckled. "You like that, do you?"

He sat back. "Yes, I do. I like to get my hands in what I'm making. I like the feel of wood. I like to see things change."

Professor Stern sucked rhythmically at his pipe, blinking alertly through the smoke.

Alex crossed his legs and folded his arms — a defensive posture. "Of course, there's no money in that, and that's not what we do at Draper and Snow. We work in stone, primarily, and fine marbles, occasionally brick. Steel. We don't just build mansions for the rich, though; we design stores, schools, churches, gymnasiums —"

"You'll have to specialize, though, won't

you? Since you're a partner now, won't they expect you to pull in more clients for the big, expensive houses? I don't know, of course, I'm just —"

"Yes, probably," Alex said shortly. "For a few years, anyway." He massaged the arm of his chair, running his fingers lightly over the smooth, oiled wood. Marshall Farley, he'd just heard, was going to name the house Alex built for him in Newport "Kubla Khan." The professor would enjoy that, would laugh if he told him. But for some reason he kept it to himself.

A few minutes later, Mrs. Stern came in with a tray of coffee and pastries and fruit. "Only two cups?" Stern noticed. "Get one for yourself and sit with us, Martha. Alex has been telling me how wonderful our house is. You need to hear this." He sent Alex a wink while he tugged on his wife's hand until she had no choice but to set her wide rump down on the arm of the sofa, and then he put his arm around her waist. They looked alike, Alex realized — both short, rotund, white-haired, and gentle-faced.

"Why do I need to hear somebody else say how wonderful it is when I've got you to tell me the same thing several times a day?"

"Yeah, but Alex is a very important architect. Him you might believe."

"Don't you like the house, Mrs. Stern?"

"Of course I do," she answered, laughing. "But for Walter, you see, it's not really a house, it's more like his first-born son. As far as he's concerned, nobody can ever like it *enough*."

"I can't deny it," the professor admitted, giving her a squeeze.

She ruffled his hair and stood up. "I'll leave you two to your coffee." Alex rose and took her hand when she offered it. "Good night, Mr. McKie. I hope I'll see you again before you go back to New York." He said the same and thanked her for dinner. She sent her husband a wry, affectionate look and bustled out.

Alex watched her go and realized that she reminded him of Sara. Not because of her appearance, certainly, or anything else tangible. Just the fact of her, the soft, kind-hearted essence of her.

Professor Stern was leaning toward him, elbows on his knees, face alight with an exciting secret. "There's a room upstairs I didn't show you and young Mitchell," he confided in a conspirator's voice. "At the end of the hall on the west side — you probably thought it was a closet. But it's not. It's a bedroom. We go there . . . every once in a while. Know what I mean?"

Alex nodded, and raised his eyebrows in imitation of the professor's touchingly lecherous leer.

"There's a skylight and a bed, that's all. Oh — and a gramophone. We put on Mozart and . . . well . . ." Modesty prevented him from continuing.

Alex was charmed. "That's very . . . nice," he said inadequately. "Very, very nice. How long have you been married, sir?"

"Thirty-eight years."

Stern leaned back and crossed his arms over his chest with a slightly complacent smile. "So, Alex. When do you go back?"

"Sooner than I thought. A few days, I'm afraid."

"Oh? I thought you meant to stay for a while and sell your grandfather's farm, settle his affairs."

"I've hired an agent to take care of all that."

"Can't wait to get back, eh?"

"It's not that. One of my clients has decided to pay us what he owes us, which means I've got to go back to work on his house."

The prospect demoralized him. "Eden"

was a joke to him now, a rich vulgarian's megalomaniacal celebration of himself. But what Alex hated even more about the house was that Sara was going to live in it with Ben for the rest of her life, and there wasn't a damn thing he could do about it. Part of him had rejoiced when construction had halted — even though Cochrane's financial problems affected Sara and he had no way of knowing how serious they were. But designing rooms for her to walk and talk and sit and eat and sleep in with Ben had become an obscenity to him, a travesty of his expertise and a perversion of his feelings. He wanted to build her a house she could be happy in, but when he pictured Cochrane in it with her, he wanted to sabotage it.

"You don't look too enthusiastic," Professor Stern noticed.

Alex rested his head on the back of the chair. "Someone I knew during the first phase of building this house — won't be there this time," he explained cryptically.

"Ah. A woman?"

He nodded.

"Ah," he said again. "The sort of woman your grandfather would disapprove of, I take it?"

His smile was cynical and hopeless.

"Most definitely."

The professor swirled the brandy in his glass, then abruptly set it aside. "Alex, Alex, what are we going to do with you? Spend six weeks in this house — the second-floor guest room is yours, take it — and I promise you Martha will find you a wife and have you married off before Thanksgiving. It's a sure thing; I won't even take your money by suggesting a bet on it."

"That's a handsome offer, sir. I'll certainly give it some thought."

"I'm serious! Oh well, I can see you're not interested. But if you think it couldn't happen, you're underestimating my wife's powers of matchmaking. Believe me, they're formidable in the extreme. I would go so far as to call them supernatural. Oh — you're leaving? It's early yet, do you have to go?"

"Yes, sir, much as I hate to. It's been wonderful seeing you again." But he'd suddenly had enough of conjugal bliss, secret lovemaking rooms, and Mrs. Stern's supernatural marriage-brokering prowess. He shook hands with his old friend warmly, thanked him for his hospitality, and promised to be a better correspondent in the future. They said good-bye at the door, and Alex made the professor smile by telling him the entrance to his house was a triumph because it expressed welcome at the same time it gracefully ensured the Sterns' absolute privacy.

Instead of hiring a cab, he walked back to his hotel. It was a long way, but the chilly, misty evening reminded him of a thousand undergraduate nights and he couldn't resist it. San Francisco was still magical, still pulled at him; and yet, as dreary a prospect as Newport was, in some ways he would be glad to leave California. Melancholy had descended on him the moment he'd arrived. There was something here for him, some truth he needed to learn, but so far it had eluded him, and he sensed that he was still a long way away from discovering it.

He wasn't used to introspection. His life had been forward-looking and goal-centered for the last thirteen years; this new contemplativeness made him edgy. Memories he'd avoided were coming back fast, so fast he had no time to filter or censor them. By almost anybody's standards he was a success now; he'd surmounted rotten odds and gotten everything he wanted by defeating his grandfather and becoming all the things his father had wanted to be. He'd *won*. The dream was fulfilled. So what underhanded trick of fate had decreed that he couldn't be happy?

It wasn't only that he'd fallen in love with a woman he couldn't have. He'd also missed something, lost sight of an ideal he'd once had, something strong and clear that had sustained him through the worst of times. He didn't want to name it, that goal, because at the same time he missed it he was glad it was gone. It was too messy, it confused things. He was on a straight and narrow path to fame and fortune. *Fame and fortune.* They weren't just words, a cliche that applied to unknown, abstract others. They were real and possible and imminent, and he would be the world's biggest fool to take some sentimental wrong turn now.

He walked home in the mist, thinking of his mother, of his grandfather, of the rich Salinas soil. He thought of John Ogden and the New York Club. Of Professor Stern and his wife and their lovely secret room. Sara. And Michael. The monstrous house he had to finish for them.

Maybe that was it — maybe Eden was the key. If he could finish the damn thing, be done with it once and for all, maybe his life could get back on that neat, tidy track he could just barely remember it had once been on. If he couldn't have Sara, his career would console him. That was no tragedy; that was the way he'd always seen his life unfolding — success in his work paramount, a loving wife and family shadowy seconds, standing behind him like figures in some old-fashioned daguerreotype, sepia-colored and a bit faded.

Eden was the key, then. He'd even stop putting scornful quotation marks around it in his head. "Ninety-nine percent of the people in the world would cut off an arm to live there," Ogden had lectured him. Damn right. Hell, yes. He'd finish it and get on with his life. He had work to do, a reputation to make.

Striding home, invigorated, he forgot all about the stately pleasure dome he'd promised to build for Mr. Marshall Farley.

# Fourteen

*Newport*
*September 2*

My dearest Michael,
   I'm sitting on the big rock at Anchor Point while I write this, thinking of all the evenings I used to wait here for you and Mr. McKie before we took our stroll along the Cliff Walk. I loved watching the people go by, trying to guess what their lives were like. Nowadays there's hardly anyone to watch, though, because the season is over and everyone's gone home. I had no idea what a tiny town this was without the resorters! The streets are quiet and the beaches are bare; most of the grand houses are closed up and empty now except for the caretakers. Yesterday I let all the servants go except for Mrs. Godby and one maid — do you remember Maura? — and they both go home by five in the afternoon. So you can see what a quiet life I'm leading!

I haven't been to the new house in a few days, but I'll walk by this evening when I finish this, and either add a postscript or tell you in my next letter how it's progressing. With Mr. McKie in California, I've been dealing with a Mr. Cronin; he's called the "clerk of the works" in architects' language, which means he's Mr. McKie's assistant. The last time I looked, the house had all its floors and some of the roof, but no walls yet. If Daddy can get away, I hope you and he can come up for a weekend soon to see it. Don't pester him about it, though, darling. I've asked him already, and he's going to tell us when it's convenient.

Mrs. Wentworth says to tell you that Gadget got the crayon drawing of the cat you sent and enjoyed it very much. And thank you for your last letter. I'm glad to hear that you like Miss Roberts and that you're finding school so easy this year. It's also nice to hear that you've inherited your mum's spelling expertise. But for your sake, darling, I hope you haven't got her facility with numbers; much better to have inherited that from your father, I assure you. By the way, I had a note from Mrs. Drum, who says you're studying hard and minding her very well. Do you know how proud I am of you? If I were there, I would give you a big mushy kiss and a giant smothery hug and then I would TICKLE you until you begged for mercy! I miss you every day, my sweetest boy, and I love you very, very much.

All my love,
Mummy.

Sara folded her letter and slid it into her pocket. She wrote Michael every day. at least a postcard but more often a letter, usually enclosing a little gift — a drawing of her own, a photograph, a tiny shell. The pain of missing him was physical, a steady, aching hurt deep inside, unlike anything she'd ever experienced. He missed her too, and told her so with unabashed frankness; and although he wasn't above saying such a thing purely out of kindness, she knew it was true. Still, she worried that her incessant letters and gifts and telephone calls might oppress him sometimes, make him feel smothered with mother-love. But she couldn't stop. Newport was a banishment she had willingly accepted for his sake, but she hadn't known and couldn't have imagined how lonely her exile would be. Michael was all she had, the only person she was allowed to love; without him, she might as well turn to stone.

Rather than sit there contemplating the rest of her life, which she could see unfolding in a succession of humiliating bargains with Ben over Michael, she stood up, brushed at her skirts, and began to walk along the sandy path toward Eden. The setting sun on the water was blinding; she adjusted her enormous feathered hat — her "three-story hat," Michael called it — to shade her eyes. There wasn't another soul on the path behind or in front of her. Out to sea, a quartet of fishing boats bobbed on the horizon, heading inland at day's end. On her other side, the clipped and coddled lawns of the "cottages" rose above the uneven cliff-walls, stretching to the far-off backs of the opulent palazzos, hunting lodges, chateaux, and manor houses. At the bottom of a short flight of makeshift wooden steps that led up to her own house, she paused for a second to stare.

Eden looked more like a medieval castle every day as the sandstone crenellations rose higher and the mullioned windows proliferated. Ben had been persuaded to abandon the majority of his more outlandish follies, but no one had been able to talk him out of his "maze." American shrubbery wouldn't do, they had to be *Italian* yews, fully grown and imported at spectacular expense, along with an ill-tempered, effete English landscape architect to supervise the installation. Picking her way across the rough, rubble-strewn yard, Sara eyed the completed maze with dislike. The tight-packed yews looked black and aggressive, dark swords stuck upright in the ground for no reason except to intimidate. She had no intention of ever setting foot in the thing. Michael liked it, though. He liked the idea of learning its secret and then flaunting his superiority in front of his lost and baffled friends. But Michael was a child. It was depressing to think Ben's infatuation with the shrubby puzzle derived from exactly the same childish expectation.

"Mrs. Cochrane! Nice to see you!" Mr. Cronin was bearing down on her from the direction of the house. He swept off his hat en route, revealing his shiny, totally bald pate, and stuck out his hand to shake. Fiftyish, finicky, always nattily dressed, he struck Sara as someone who ought to be counting out money in a bank, not building houses. Sometimes she wondered how it set with him to take orders from a man twenty years his junior.

"Hello, Mr. Cronin, how are you? I haven't seen you in a few days."

"A week to the day, Mrs. C.," he corrected.

"Oh dear, has it been that long? I didn't realize." She glanced around dutifully, scanning the progress. "My, it's really coming along quickly now, isn't it? That whole wing is under roof," she noted, pointing.

"Yes, indeedy. You'll be moved in by Christmas, I shouldn't wonder."

"Lovely." The very thought made her feel tired. "You asked me about the door frames for the reception room, Mr. Cronin — I hadn't forgotten. I spoke to my husband, and he's chosen to have the casings of Carrara marble, carved in the pattern you suggested."

"Very good. If you'll tell Mr. McKie that, he'll take it from there."

"Well, but — he's in California."

"No, ma'am," Cronin laughed. "He's right over there."

Sara suffered a small, devastating explosion in the chest while her heart stopped and restarted. Following Mr. Cronin's pointing finger, she looked across the yard and saw Alex talking to three men in work clothes, all four hunched over a drawing or a blueprint spread across two sawbenches. She barely had time to compose her features before he straightened, turned, and looked directly at her. From this distance she couldn't read his expression precisely, but she thought it looked impassive and unsurprised.

Mr. Cronin was saying something, but Alex was walking toward her and she went deaf. Shock, gladness, worry, and nerves tumbled and rolled inside, finally canceling each other out until there was nothing except unbearable excitement. The sight of his tall, striding body, hard-muscled and lithe, filled her with a dangerous delight. She went dumb as well as deaf until he shook her hand, and then she came alive. He said something casual, she wasn't sure what, and she managed to greet him with words that sounded halfway appropriate. For Cronin's benefit, she added, "I didn't expect you back from California so soon, Mr. McKie. Did your trip go well?"

"Yes, thanks, it went fine."

"I was just mentioning to Mr. Cronin that Ben finally made up his mind about the marble he wants in the first-floor reception room."

"Well, I'll leave you two to that," Mr. Cronin decided, clapping his hat back on. "A pleasure seeing you again, Mrs. Cochrane, as always. You ought to come around more often."

"Yes," she answered faintly, "I certainly will."

Then he was gone and she and Alex were alone. The living, breathing reality of him still overwhelmed her. "Hello," she said, wary and unreasonably shy, but unable to stop smiling.

"Hello."

"It's good to see you." He said nothing to that. "How long have you been in Newport?"

"A week."

"A week! But —"

She bit back the rest, but he could tell she was hurt, confused, and put out. He came closer. "Do you think I didn't want to see you, Sara? Do you think this was my choice?" He took her arm almost roughly. "I can't talk to you here. Come into your new house."

She let him lead her across the rocky yard, stepping smartly to keep up with his long-legged gait. They went around the gigantic rear section of the house, still framed with scaffolding, and crossed a bare, unfinished courtyard to the main wing's back double doors — massive studded oak barriers offering the opposite of welcome. Inside, once her eyes adjusted to the dimness, she found herself standing in a huge square hall leading to a wide alabaster staircase at the far end. "What is this? I don't remember it in the plans." Her voice echoed hollowly off the cold, glistening surfaces.

"No, it's new; Ben thought of it right after we finished laying the parquet floor. It's a sculpture gallery. All marble, as you can see."

She nodded in glum agreement. Marble floor, marble wall panels, marble ceiling slabs. Marble lintels, cornices, and Corinthian columns.

"What keeps it all up?" she asked dispiritedly.

"Fireproof brick partition walls from the basement to the roof," he answered shortly. "Mortared floors over brick-arch construction supported by iron joists. It's not going anywhere."

His tone of voice put her on guard. He stood away from her, hands on his hips, cool blue eyes narrowed. "It's good to see you," she said again — and once more he didn't respond. "Michael asks about you all the time." What a timorous thing to say, she chided herself.

"Where is he?"

"In New York."

"Not Germany, then."

"No. Ben changed his mind."

"Good. But I never thought he'd do it anyway."

"Didn't you?"

"No. Not even Ben could send his own son away without your consent."

"Is that what you think?" But there was no point now in telling him what Ben was capable of. She pressed her hands together tensely, bewildered by his mood.

"Do you want to see the house?" he asked suddenly.

"No. I'm sorry. No, I don't."

"It's all right." He came toward her, and now she saw the first sign of softness in his expression. "How are you, Sara? You look . . ."

"What?"

"Sad."

Instinctively she backed away. "No, I'm all right."

"What happened that day, after I left?"

"Nothing. Tasha didn't really see anything. Anyway, who would she tell? I was upset, I made too much of it. It was nothing."

"Nothing. That's right. You must be used to it by now, men telling you they're in love with you. How tiresome for you —"

"Alex!" He turned his back on her. "Why are you angry with me?"

He walked a few steps away before turning around to face her again. "Sorry."

But there was no sincerity in his voice, and nothing but antagonism in his face. She was on the edge of anger herself, and she had no idea why. "What is it you expect from me? What do you want me to do? Have an affair with you?"

"I'd like you to be honest with me."

"I've always been honest with you!"

"With yourself, then."

"What does that mean? That's just *words*, Alex. No, what you want is to seduce me."

" 'Seduce' you?"

"Yes. Don't laugh at me! Am I the first woman who's ever resisted you? Is that the appeal, is that why you won't leave me alone?"

"Won't leave you alone?" Incredulous, he came close enough to seize her by the arms. "I didn't even know you'd be here. What are you doing here anyway? Why the hell didn't you stay in New York?"

"I'm here because my husband insisted on it. He's got a new mistress and he wants me out of the house." The sudden sympathy in his eyes didn't comfort her; for some reason it made her even madder. "Why can't you leave me alone?" she repeated illogically. "Every time I turn around you're there — *touching* me like this —"

"Damn it! I've done everything you ever asked me to do. That night Michael was hurt, you told me you wanted me, Sara. Unless it was a lie" — he pulled her back when she pushed at him and tried to escape — "Was it a lie? I didn't think so then. And some men might have tried to take advantage of it, but I never did, I let you —"

"And that's something you're *proud* of, that you didn't take advantage of my feelings?"

He ground his teeth. "All I'm saying —"

"That must have been hard for you, not at all what you're used to. Unhappily married women are your specialty, aren't they? Other men's wives? I'm sorry I've proven such a difficult case — surely you must be ready to give up on me."

He dropped his arms. "I must be.

Because if you care for me, Sara, then you're a coward. If you don't, you're a liar. Either way, I've made a mistake."

She was blinking fast, ready to cry. "How dare you call me a coward. You don't know anything about me."

"If that's true, it's because you don't give anything."

"I can't! You *know* I'm in love with you. Why do you treat me this way? It's cruel, Alex, and it's selfish —"

He reached for her again. "You love me?"

"Let me go, it doesn't change anything. You knew it anyway."

"Sara —"

"Stop, don't!" She pushed at him violently until he released her. "I can't stand this. Don't talk to me anymore." She stalked to the heavy doors and hauled on one until it opened. "Mr. Cronin has been keeping me informed about the house perfectly well. I want to continue to deal with him, not you. He can relay messages back and forth between us."

A plasterer's trowel lay on the floor at Alex's feet. He kicked it hard and sent it sailing toward the marble staircase, where it landed with a sharp, echoing clatter.

Sara jumped. "Do you think that's cowardly of me? All right — I don't care! Leave me alone, Alex, don't come near me. I can't bear it."

She wasn't by nature a door slammer, but anger and frustration seemed to have localized in her arm muscles. She stomped over the threshold and gave the heavy oak portal a push that rattled the amber glass in the windows and startled the workers laying tiles in a fourth floor bathroom.

Mrs. Godby had left potato soup, tomato aspic, and a piece of grilled chicken in the icebox for Sara's supper. She picked at it, sitting in the kitchen, while she read the note from Michael that had come in the afternoon post. Sometimes his letters cheered her up, sometimes they deepened her despondency. This was one of the latter kind, even though it was full of his lovely, irresistible silliness. He wanted her to start eating lots of oatmeal and sending him the flag card inside the box; if he got the full set of twelve flags, he was entitled to a handsome prize of large but unspecified value. Instead of making her smile, his letter made her weepy.

What had she done? Although she'd replayed the scene in her head a dozen times by now, she could still hardly believe what had just happened. She felt ashamed and filled with sadness and regret. She *loved* Alex. She wasn't that mean and shrewish to *Ben*. What had gotten into her? Him, too — he'd been furious with her almost from the moment they'd met. She kept trying to see what had happened as for the best, a blessing in disguise, but she couldn't. Now it just seemed wrong.

She stood up and went to put water in the kettle for tea. What if she apologized to him? Would that only make everything start over again? Not if she did it right, if she controlled it and just said she was sorry and nothing else. She owed him that much.

The telephone was in the front hall. "Four-oh-one-one," she told the operator, and after a few seconds it rang. And rang. She waited a full minute before banging down the earpiece and going back to the kitchen. Her depression turned black. Where was he, what was he doing? She'd imagined him at home, alone, as miserable as she. But he wasn't, he was *out* — probably dining in a restaurant, talking to people, not thinking about her at all. Not enough, anyway.

Oh, what a bitch she was turning into. Was this what love did? She'd been much nicer to Alex before she'd fallen in love with him. She began to pace, restless. On one of her circuits she stopped before the cabinet over the icebox and took down the bottle of brandy that had been there since June. She opened it and poured some into a glass. The pungent fumes startled her. It was a good brandy, but the first sip made her shudder. All at once, without a thought, she tossed the rest into the sink. Why had she done that? she wondered helplessly. Silly — she wouldn't have gotten drunk, she'd only wanted a drink. One drink wouldn't have turned her into her mother. It made no rational sense; she only knew she'd have gagged if she'd tried to finish the brandy in that glass.

She made tea instead. Staring at her reflection in the black window over the sink, she remembered the night Alex had kissed her. Here — right here where she was standing. She touched her fingers to her lips, eyes closed, filled with yearning. And today she'd accused him of trying to "seduce" her, as if she were some chaste, innocent victim — as if he had ever touched her when she hadn't been longing for him to. *Hypocrite.* He was wrong — she wasn't a coward or a liar, she was both. She set her cup down with a clatter and marched back into the hall. She snatched up the telephone — and whirled with it in her hand at a knock at the door.

She hadn't turned on the porch light, so she hoped but didn't know it was Alex until she opened the door to him. "Oh, Alex —"

"Sara, listen —"

"Come in!"

"No, this won't take long. I should've called, but —"

"Will you please come in? I can't talk to you like this."

He came in. He looked wary. She could understand why — two hours ago she'd told him to leave her alone, not to come near her.

"Will you come in here?" she invited, leading him into the sitting room. Even now, he couldn't help looking around with his architect's eye, she noticed. "It's a beautiful room, isn't it?"

"Yes."

"Would you like to sit down?"

"No."

"Would you like something to drink, some —"

"Damn it, this isn't a social call."

"No, of course not. What is it, then?" He moved away, to fiddle with a soapstone candlestick on the mantel. It wasn't fair to make him speak first. "I was trying to call you," she said softly. "I had the telephone in my hand when you knocked."

"Really? Why? To fire me?"

She sent him a look. "Are we going to fight again?"

"No — I'm not, anyway. I came here to apologize."

"Did you?" She went closer, smiling with relief. "But you didn't do anything."

"I don't know why I was so angry. I've been wanting to see you for days, ever since I found out you were here. But I stayed away because I thought that's what you wanted. Then when I saw you, I guess all I could see was what I'm not allowed to have. I said things I didn't mean, and a lot of things that were out of line, none of my business. I'm sorry if I hurt you. I just wanted you to know."

"Alex, don't go. Don't you want to know why I was calling you?"

"I already know. You felt guilty because you thought you'd hurt my feelings. You wanted to try to make me feel better by saying you hadn't meant it. That's it, isn't it?"

She held out a helpless hand. "Well — yes. Wait. Alex, please!" He stopped again, hands shoved in his pockets. "You're still angry, aren't you?"

"Yeah. But not at you. I want something to change, and nothing can. Let me go, Sara — now I'm the one who can't bear it."

"But — how can you just go? Nothing's settled, it's the same as before. When I see you again, everything will be exactly —"

"You won't be seeing me, you'll be seeing Cronin."

"Oh, Alex, I didn't mean that. That's only one of the things I didn't mean. Of course I'll see you, it's inevitable. We have to settle this between us!"

"How?"

"I don't know!"

"Sara, for God's sake, don't cry."

"I'm sorry, I know, I'm not —" She wiped her eyes briskly. "I'm all right now. How stupid, I hate to cry. Every time I see you — I'm not saying it's your fault," she added hastily.

"No, no. Purely a coincidence."

She tried to smile. "What are we going to do?"

"Nothing. I'm leaving."

"Oh." She followed him out into the hall. "Can't you — can't we talk? I don't even know how you are, what happened in California —"

He turned around so abruptly that she ran into him. His hands gripped her shoulders hard. "Sara, what I'd like to do is marry you, but I can't. Failing that, I'd like to have an affair with you. *Seduce* you, as you say, carry on with you behind your husband's back for as long as you'll allow it. I can't do that, either. My distant third choice is to take you to bed now, tonight, and then again whenever it pleases you. But there's one thing I find I can't do. I thought I could, but I can't, and no doubt it's a deep flaw in my character. I can't be your friend."

He let her go, even though she was crying, and left her standing in the hall. Unlike her, he didn't slam the door behind him.

# Fifteen

Maybe this was his grandfather's God's punishment for a life of sin and sexual debauchery, Alex thought as he dove naked into a cold, salty avalanche of dark water. If so, it was surprisingly effective; before now he wouldn't have given any God of Matthew's credit for so much imagination. Or such a fine appreciation of irony. He had to admit, the punishment suited the crime. After making love to a hundred women he didn't love, he'd finally fallen in love with the one he couldn't have.

Out here the waves were gentler; he treaded water and watched the moon shimmer toward him in a widening V, a dancing silver delta that covered and quieted the sea. He couldn't see the future beyond this minute; couldn't imagine the rest of his life, the banal, changeless passing of day after day, without Sara. How had this happened? She didn't belong to him, never had, so when had this monumental presumption that their fates were somehow tied together begun? He thought he knew, but the answer didn't flatter him. His associations with women over the last ten years had set him up perfectly for this catastrophe, because until now he'd been allowed to have whatever he wanted, *whomever* he wanted. When, once in a while, a woman resisted him, he'd given a mental shrug and passed on unhesitatingly to someone more willing. The experience had given him a somewhat egocentric view of reality — for which he was now paying. Which brought him back, full-circle, to Matthew's God's revenge.

Muttering obscenities, he dove under the pewter surface of the waves and swam, froglike, toward shore for as long as he could hold his breath. Surfacing, he saw how far downshore he'd drifted by the dimness of the lights of his house far, far away. Because he was tired, he struck out for the near coast. When he reached it, he trudged through the soft, wet sand for home.

He'd told Sara he couldn't be her friend, but now he saw that he'd made a bad mistake. Because the alternative was not seeing her at all, or worse — running into her on rare occasions at social functions. Shaking hands with her while Ben watched; asking how Michael did these days. And never knowing the truth, never being allowed into her confidence. To know she was unhappy and not to be able to help her — that was the hell he'd just consigned himself to out of anger and frustration. He snatched up the towel he'd left on the beach and scrubbed himself with it until his skin burned.

He was twenty feet from his front porch when he saw her. She was just a shadow in front of the window until she moved into the moonlight, her shoes echoing on the wooden porch floor. He saw that she wore a dark cloak or cape over a dark dress. After a long, silent moment, she turned her back on him, and then he remembered he was naked. He pulled the towel from his shoulder and tied it around his hips.

She turned around again when she heard him on the steps. "I — I —" She swallowed. She felt a little mad. "I'm not trying to make you crazy, Alex. I don't want to be so difficult. If you send me away, I'll understand perfectly."

He laughed in amazement. Closing the distance between them, he touched her shoulder, to make sure she was real. "Darling —"

"This is all I can do," she rushed on, compelled to speak her peace. "I wish I could give you more, I wish I could give you everything. But this — this is your distant third choice. Just tonight. If you want me."

"If I want you." He gathered her into his arms. In seconds they were both trembling. "How did you get here, Sara?" he murmured, still astounded.

"I walked."

"You walked? By yourself?"

She looked at him humorously. "No, I asked Mrs. Astor to come with me, just as far as your turnoff."

Smiling, beguiled, he kissed her. "I should try to talk you out of this," he whispered halfheartedly. "I coerced you tonight, I made you cry."

"No, don't say that. I'm not a child, I made this choice. I told you once before — I want exactly what you want. Let's just be happy tonight, Alex. I love you so dearly." She put her hands on his face and brought his mouth down. "I love you." He whispered it back, and then she couldn't help adding, "I love your mustache. I've been wanting to tell you that for months."

He hugged her, laughing with delight. "Come in, come inside." He opened the door and pulled her in. He felt euphoric, jubilant, drunk. "If you knew how many times I've thought of you here —" He shook his head in wonder. "Are you hungry? Are you thirsty?"

She'd stopped just over the threshold. "This is your bedroom."

"Yes."

The unexpected intimacy startled her. She took it in with a quick, darting glance — the quaint old furniture, the comfortable clutter. A book lay open on his unmade bed; the clothes he'd worn today hung neatly from the back of a chair. His wardrobe door was ajar; she could see his tweed jacket inside, the one she always thought made him look English. He was watching her. "Are you going to get dressed?" she faltered. If so, she felt she ought not to stay here, watching him.

"Should I?"

"I don't know. It seems . . . unnecessarily . . ."

"Unnecessary."

She almost giggled. "Alex, I'm so nervous, I can't stand it."

He grinned with relief and came to her. "How do you think I feel?"

"You're nervous?"

He put her hand, palm down, in the center of his chest. "Feel."

She was too overwrought to feel anything but cold. "You're cold." He shook his head slowly, hypnotizing her. Now she could feel the strong beat of his heart under his still-damp skin. She took his hand and brought it to her lips, then pressed it to her own heart. "Feel."

He spread his fingers, watching her eyes close. They flew open when he slipped the fringed black cloak over her shoulders and let it fall to the floor behind her. She had on a dark blue military jacket with epaulettes over a plain white, high-collared blouse. He smiled, charmed as always by her effortless chic. "I don't know anyone who dresses like you, Sara. But . . ."

"But?"

"But right now you make me feel a little under-dressed. Can I help you off with some of your things?"

She caught her breath. So they weren't going to talk at all first. His long, skillful fingers played over the buttons at her throat. If she'd ever had doubts about the extent of his worldly experience, they were humbly laid to rest by the miraculous speed with which he managed to open, without seeming to hurry, the whole front of her shirtwaist.

"A corset," he exclaimed, much surprised.

341

" 'All deficiency of development supplied,' " she breathed with her eyes closed.

He smiled again. Not that it mattered, but he could see from the soft, womanly swell of bosom over the undergarment's lacy edge that Sara's development had been wonderfully efficient. He kissed her between her breasts while he unfastened her skirt at the back and pushed it over her hips. She had on a marvelous petticoat, white with rosettes and lace flounces and ribbons running merrily in and out. He divested her of it quickly, but took his time with her corset, savoring the new view every unsnapped hook afforded. Then there was nothing left but a short chemise and thin white cambric drawers. And black silk stockings.

His burning hot gaze turned her cheeks scarlet. "Alex," she admitted breathlessly, "I'm scared to death."

His fingers traced her cheekbone gently. "Why?"

"Don't let's talk."

"No?" He put his lips on her temple. "Just get it over with as fast as possible?"

"I didn't mean that." His soft breath on her face was intoxicating. "But — Alex?"

"Mm?"

"Don't let's talk about Ben tonight, all right?"

"Sweetheart. I didn't have any intention of talking about Ben." He took her hand and led her to the bed. She sat down on the edge, back straight, knees together. Her shoes were high-heeled red leather. He thought he might die if he couldn't have her soon. "Shall we leave the light on?"

"Oh, um. No, I'd rather we didn't."

Somehow that didn't surprise him. "What about a candle?"

"All right. Just one."

He lit the candle in the holder on his bedside table, turned the lamp out, and came to sit beside her. "Are you cold?" He slid his arm around her shoulders. She shook her head. He started to unpin her hair. "When I first saw you today, I thought to myself, all that hair, all that *hat*, how does she keep her head up on her long, beautiful neck?" He kissed her behind her ear, feeling her smile, and then tugged gently at her earlobe with his teeth. "Sara." What a lovely word to whisper in a woman's ear. His fingers drifted down her throat, her chest, inside her shift to caress her shoulder. "Take this off for me, Sara. I'm dying to see you."

Her breath was coming in difficult little

jerks. The trembling in her fingers slowed her down, but finally she got her chemise unlaced. She hesitated for the space of two heartbeats and then shrugged it over her shoulders. He made a noise in his throat she'd never heard before, a growl of almost animal satisfaction; but his hands were gentle on the back of her neck as he brought her close and kissed her. She embraced him, pressing her breasts against the cool sleekness of his skin and combing his wet hair with her fingers. His silky mustache was a soft, exciting caress on her face. He coaxed her mouth open and touched his tongue to the soft inner surface of her lips. She moaned. He took her down, down, and she felt the bed on the bare skin of her back. In the center of a deep, drugging kiss, she cried, "Wait! I have to tell you something."

A long golden strand of her hair was trapped between their mouths. He lifted his head and pulled it gently away. "What?"

"I — I'm not any good at this."

"Not any good at what?"

"You know. This."

" 'You know, this'?" She didn't smile back. He watched her for another second. Then he put his mouth on hers lightly, and

344

at the same moment he began to stroke the soft underside of her breast in slow, rising crescents. Her lips parted, but he resisted the urge to sleek his tongue inside. "You mean this?" he murmured. She moved against him restlessly. The silky play of his hand avoided her nipple even when she arched up, wanting it. He whispered, "This?" and nipped at her lips; when she groaned and put out her tongue, he sucked it into his mouth. Her hand clamped on his and urged it higher. He used all his fingers, all at once, ministering to the tight spike of her nipple until she writhed under him, her head twisting on the tangled sheet. "I said I wouldn't talk about Ben," he managed to say, breathing hard. "Otherwise I'd ask who told you you weren't any good at this."

Sara felt like laughing. A rare, uncontainable joy was rising fast and high, and some new, dangerous, unimaginable freedom was coming closer. "I love you, Alex! I've wanted to tell you for so long."

He wound his arms around her and rolled, pulling her on top of him. They kissed until she sat up, straddling him, panting. She dragged her fingers through her hair and licked her lips, tasting him. His body tightened. "I don't understand why you still have on all these clothes." He pulled on the little tie, and the front of her drawers opened. He'd never seen anything as wanton as Sara in shoes, stockings, gaping drawers and nothing else, sitting splay-legged on his thighs. They reached for each other at the same moment and rolled over again. He lost his towel. She looked down, said something indistinct. He found her awed gaze intensely gratifying. Without ceremony he got her undressed once and for all, and then he lowered himself over her. His seeking fingers told him she was soft and wet and ready. "Darling," he got out, and entered her sleekly.

She went stiff; she all but winced.

He froze. "Sara? Does this hurt you?"

She hesitated, then said, "No — no."

The unmistakable surprise in her voice chilled him. He didn't like her tone or her hesitation. "Listen to me," he told her, eyes intent, framing her face with his hands. "If we ever do anything that hurts you, you must tell me." She nodded. "I mean it."

"Yes, I will." She smiled tenderly, hiding the rough edge of sadness that nudged through her. He didn't believe it yet, she knew, but there would be no other times for them. Just now. "Love me, Alex," she whispered. "Make love to me."

Sighing her name, he began to move in her, slowly at first, his long, sensuous strokes urging her higher. His deep, hot kisses consumed her; she forgot everything except the way her body felt, abandoned to his. It had never been like this for her; she could hardly believe how good it was. "Alex, this is so . . ."

He agreed completely. But he could tell that her pleasure was still a long time away. "What do you like?" he said against her lips.

"What?"

"Tell me what you want, love."

"I don't know what you mean," she admitted, embarrassed. "I told you, I'm not any g—"

"Shut up." He kissed her softly, inwardly cursing her husband. "Do you ever come, Sara?"

"Come —"

"Spend. Climax."

"Oh. No, I don't think so. Maybe. I'm not quite sure." She was blushing furiously. She wished he would stop talking and continue. It had been so lovely before, but now she felt stupid, and almost ashamed. When he pulled away from her and lay on his side, she wanted to weep. "It's no good, is it? I'm sorry, I knew —"

He kissed her again to silence her. Leaning over her, braced on his elbow, he said, "Do you know how beautiful your body is? You have beautiful legs, Sara, long and strong, such a lovely shape." While he spoke, he caressed her thighs.

"You're beautiful too, Alex, your —"

"Thank you, but we're talking about you. I like your feet."

"My feet?"

"English feet. Long and skinny and aristocratic." They looked down at her feet; she flexed her toes self-consciously. "This line of hip here — now, this is lovely." He ran his hand over her hip bone, between waist and thigh. "Not voluptuous. Gently feminine. Just right." His hand slid to her belly. "And this. You look beautiful in your clothes, Sara, but you look even better naked. That's rare. Women would kill for this navel." His hand moved again. "This is the most feminine pelvic bone I've ever seen."

She lay still, wide-eyed, bemused, ready to laugh but utterly fascinated. He spread his fingers, tracing the delta on either side of her thighs to the apex in the middle, ruffling her pubic hair with each soft pass. What would he say about *that*, she wondered hazily.

Nothing. But he kept his hand there while the rest of his attention wandered to her breasts. He kissed her nipples, once each, then raised his head, relishing her quick gasps. "Such pretty breasts, Sara. But even that son of a bitch must've told you that sometime."

"Alex —"

"Sorry. Sorry. But it's like going to the Grand Canyon and then forgetting to tell anyone the view was nice."

Sara snorted, a rude, unladylike explosion in her throat that made Alex bark out a loud, delighted laugh. They kissed wetly, their smiles colliding. She had almost forgotten his hand, which twitched to life between her legs then. Once in a while Ben caressed her like this — no, not like this. No, not in the least like this. She arched, wincing. "Alex!"

But this time he knew he wasn't hurting her. It wasn't pain, it was the newness that stunned her. He kept on, watching her face, anticipating every response. But she couldn't let go. Twice he brought her to the brink; both times she stopped, physically stopped, as if she feared the thing that might happen next was much too perilous and unpredictable to risk giving in to.

"Sara," he murmured against her throat.

349

She couldn't speak. "I'm going to kiss you here."

Her eyes opened. His stroking fingers told her the place he had in mind. "Alex, you can't be serious."

"I love the way you talk," he mentioned, touching his lips to her chin. "I've never appreciated it as much as now, though. The incongruity."

"The what?"

"The disparity. Between the accent and the sight of you, legs open, enjoying my tongue on your pretty little quim."

"Alex," she groaned, unable, and completely unwilling, to stop him from spreading her thighs wide and putting his mouth on her in the place he'd been teasing with his fingers. Her "quim"? What a funny — she groaned again, so loud she felt his sharp breath on her, exhaling in another of his gleeful laughs. "Oh Jesus — bloody hell — Alex!" She clamped down on her lips with her teeth. Stupid to think she wouldn't have picked up a curse of Ben's after eight years — but funny she'd never used one until now. Another of Alex's chuckles vibrated through her, driving her higher. "What — are — you — doing?" She had to know; her body was a wreck.

He loomed over her suddenly. "Let go,

Sara. It's definitely time."

"I don't even know what you're talking about."

"You've got a pretty good idea, though. Let go, love. Follow me. Trust me. I'm going back now."

This time she laughed, a helpless sound cut short by the prompt and dutiful fulfillment of his promise. His clever hands slid softly across her stomach and the insides of her thighs with sweet, endless patience, while his tongue fluttered light and insistent against the most sensitive place on her body. She didn't even hear it — he knew because he would ask her, later — but for the rest of his life he would remember what she said next. "Oh, okay." Then she exploded. He held to her tightly, sharing the ride, glorying with her in her deep, powerful, surprised release. When it was over, he thought of all the lewd, luscious things he could have done to prolong it. Next time.

He climbed up her damp, shuddering body, panting with her, until their faces touched. She hadn't opened her eyes yet; she was still tense, savoring it, her throat muscles corded and tight. He kissed her with slow, thorough finesse until she pulled her mouth away to look at him. He wanted praise, he realized; not thanks — praise. She smiled dreamily at him, breathing, "Oh, my," and he guessed he'd gotten it.

"Poor Sara," he crooned to her. "What a shame you're not any good at this."

She put her arms around him and squeezed. "What did you do to me? Am I still alive?"

"Well, let's see." He fondled her left breast, tweaking the nipple until it tightened. "Seems to be a little life left here. Over here, too."

Snickering, she wrapped her legs around him. He groaned. She jumped. "What? Have I hurt you?"

"Not exactly."

"Oh. Oh. I beg your pardon — now it's your turn. Do we ever do this together? Go ahead, do anything you'd like, I want you to."

"Well, thanks very much, that's very accommodating of you. Oh, sweetheart — I'm not laughing at you."

"You are, though. This is *new* to me, Alex."

"I know. I know." He soothed her with kisses and sweet, whispered compliments. He'd never in his wildest imaginings thought to find her so innocent; long ago he'd made an assumption that she was at least as worldly as she looked. "That's never happened to you before?" he probed gently.

"No, never."

"Not even touching yourself?"

"Not even *what?*" Her shocked mind raced.

He smiled, sad as well as amused. "I'll explain later."

She hoped so. "It happens to —" She stopped.

"To Ben," he finished grimly. "I'll bet it does. It happens to Ben every time and never to you. What's wrong with this picture, Sara?"

"We said we wouldn't talk about him," she reminded him unhappily.

"Believe me, the last thing I want to talk about is your husband."

She stroked the harsh line between his brows with her fingertips, then kissed it until it went away. "Make love to me the other way, Alex."

"The other way?"

"You know."

"No, how?"

"You know. Using . . ."

"What?"

"Alex."

"What?"

Finally she saw his game — he wanted

her to touch him. She smiled, a slow, seductive smile, totally new, and obliged him. His head fell back; he drew a quick breath through his teeth. How different, caressing him like this, from what it was like when Ben made her touch him. She loathed being forced to give him pleasure. She smiled down into Alex's face, watching his closed eyes, the rather tortured-looking smile stretching his lips. Stroking the thick, silky length of him excited her unbearably. "What do *you* like?" she whispered.

"I'm easy," he whispered back, "I like everything."

"Indiscriminate."

"Agreeable." He hummed his deep satisfaction. "What I would like right now . . ."

"Yes?"

"Is to be inside you."

She shut her eyes tight. "Oh, yes."

He shifted, moving over her, sweeping her body with his hands. He loved the feel of her thighs parting under his, so eager and giving. He came into her carefully, alive to every subtle shade of her response. But this time their slow joining was a deep, arousing connection that reminded Sara of nothing and had no antecedents. And for the first time, she knew how it was supposed to end. In awe, she monitored her body's glad rise toward the new and delicious goal. Gratitude distracted her; she kissed him passionately, murmuring fervent thanks. "I didn't know, I didn't know. Oh, *Alex*."

"What, love?"

"That it could *be* like this." The rightness of it erased all the shame from an act that for years she'd found lifeless and degrading. "I love you, love you, love you," she chanted, while tears welled in her eyes, blurring his face.

He filled his hands with her hair, let it fan out across the pillow. "Golden Sara," he named her, stopping the tear that slid down her temple with his tongue. It had never been like this for him, either. The distinction between loving and lovemaking had always seemed irrelevant. Now it was nonexistent, and he was connected at last to his deepest feelings; he was home.

Their clasped hands tightened; desire drove them up higher until their kisses became artless afterthoughts and every sense narrowed and focused on the extreme objective just out of reach. He thought fleetingly of holding back, of deepening her pleasure by delaying it, but such cunning was beyond him now. Her body trembled on the edge. When she gasped into the air over his shoulder, "Shall I wait for you?" he had the full measure of her innocence. He smothered a gusty, euphoric laugh in her hair. "No, dear, don't wait," he advised kindly, groaning. "You never want to wait." They kissed for the last time, and then the storm broke. Sara felt her body shatter into slivers of bright light and disappear. She might have been frightened, but her lover was with her this time in the weightless black void, sharing her intense pleasure. When it subsided, when their bodies finally reformed and rested against each other in exhaustion and gratefulness, they found that the light had moved into their hearts. For good or ill, no matter what came next, they knew it would never go out.

"What are you doing in there? I thought you were supposed to be my helper." Alex pushed corned beef hash, fresh from the can, to the side of the black iron skillet and cracked four eggs into the empty space. "Want more coffee?"

No answer.

He picked up the pot and carried it across the kitchen to the room he used as a studio. In the doorway, he had to stop. Sara Cochrane, millionaire fashion plate, was leaning over his lamplit drafting board in nothing but his shirt. It was a sight he had never allowed himself even to dream of. "Pretty lady," he said softly. She looked up and smiled. Her hair, down and loose around her shoulders, looked like spun gold in the lamp's glow. She had long, beautiful legs, and he'd meant every word about her elegant English feet. She was cupping her coffee mug in both hands, the long sleeves of his shirt pushed up past her elbows. "What's got you so enthralled?" he wondered. "The framing plans for Ben's solarium? Section elevations for the Roman bath?"

"No. This."

Moving to her, he saw with surprise the sketch she'd found, probably at the bottom of his stack of drawings.

"If you hadn't been an architect, you could've been an artist. Alex, this is beautiful."

He poured coffee into her cup, then set the pot down on the drafting table. "Thanks."

"Do you always do a watercolor drawing of the houses you design?"

"No, not always. Only when color is important."

"This *is* a house, isn't it?" she asked,

suddenly unsure.

He chuckled. "I like to think so."

"Yes, of course, but — I've never seen anything like it."

"What do you think of it?" he asked, with great casualness, sliding two fingers up and down either side of her spine. "That bad?" he prodded when she hesitated.

"Oh no, I think it's — magnificent. It's made of wood, isn't it?"

"Redwood. And this is stucco."

She stared at the sketch, drawn first to the warmth of the colors — ochre and chocolate and rich umber browns — and then to the rash, exuberant design. "I've never seen anything like it," she said again. "There's so much glass — how light it must be inside. The colors are amber and — I can't even describe it. So beautiful. Are these tiles?"

"Colored stones."

"And these on the sides, they're so —" She had no words again to describe the clean, whimsical, trellis-like structures on either end of the house that seemed to be functional as well as decorative. "Imagine living here," she said wonderingly. "Who is it for, Alex?"

He pulled a long lock of her hair away

from her ear so that he could kiss her. "No one. It was just an exercise."

"Oh." She felt oddly disappointed. "I can't imagine it in New York. At least not in the city."

"No. If I built it anywhere, I'd build it in California."

"Would you? Would you like to live there again?"

He shrugged, and dropped his hand. "New York is my home now. Come on, let's eat — I thought you said you were starving."

They ate dinner in bed. "Alex, this is wonderful. How do you keep the eggs from breaking? You're a much better cook than I am," she said sincerely.

He thanked her without mentioning that, according to what Michael had once confided to him, man to man and in great secrecy, that probably wasn't saying much.

"I've never eaten in bed before," she admitted, biting into a piece of toasted bread. "I can see I've been missing out on one of life's deepest pleasures." He smiled at her; she could tell he was thinking, as she was, that that wasn't the only one. They had opened the door and the windows; the sea was a soft, steady roar and the salt tang of the breeze smelled fresh and clean. "Are you sure no one ever walks by here?" she worried, a little unnerved by the well-lit spectacle they would make for anyone who did.

"Never. We might as well be on an island."

"Why do you like being an architect?" she asked directly, setting her plate aside.

"That's easy. I'm trying to achieve immortality."

She was fairly sure he was joking. "Is it because you like being rich?"

He paused in the chewing of a mouthful of toast and looked at her. Her face contained nothing but curiosity and the question wasn't weighted with any moral judgments; she honestly wanted to know. Her candor prompted him to respond in kind. "I've never been rich, so I don't know if I'd like it or not. I assume I would. But that's not why I became an architect. Anyway, most architects die poor. It's the contractor and the realtor and the building trades unionist who get rich."

"I see. What, then?"

He had to think for a second; no one had ever asked him the question in quite this way before. "I like to organize space."

He paused, and she thought he was finished. She said, "Oh."

"And I like to try to figure out how things will go — how people will act and react in a space. What they need. What they want. And then I try to give it to them in a way that's so functional and satisfying and beautiful, it makes them happy." He grinned, hearing the arrogance in his answer. But it was the truth.

Sara smiled back serenely. She heard it too, and was equally unconcerned. "I think you're going to be a great man."

"You do, huh?"

"Yes, I do." She began to peel a banana for dessert. Snuggling closer, she rubbed her cheek on the soft gray silk of his robe. "Now tell me about California."

"Not much to tell."

"Was it hard, burying your grandfather?"

"No, it was easy." He looked down at her patient face, her gray-blue eyes gone soft with sympathy. "I wish my mother could've known you, Sara. And you can believe I've never said *that* to another woman."

That led her to a digression. "You've had lots of women, haven't you?"

He stroked his mustache, stalling. "Sweetheart —"

"It's all right, I don't —" She gave a little laugh. "I was going to say I don't mind, but that wouldn't be quite true."

He kept quiet.

"How is Constance?" she asked, forcing the words out, hating herself for them.

"I don't see her anymore."

"Really?"

"Yes."

"Why?"

He rolled onto his hip, facing her. "Because I'm in love with someone else."

She touched his face. "Did you used to be in love with her?"

"No." He turned his head to kiss her hand. "I have known a few other women, Sara. I liked them all. I didn't love any of them."

"Why?"

He thought. "Because they weren't you."

"Oh, Alex. You don't have to take such good care of me. I won't break if you tell me the truth."

"I am telling the truth. There's no one but you."

They reached for each other. She pressed her face to his throat, inhaling his clean scent. Finally she pulled away, flicking her fingers at the wetness on her eyelashes. "Tell me about your mother. When did you lose her?"

"When I was seven."

"It must have been awful." He nodded slowly. She sensed that he wanted to talk, but it was hard for him. "Do you look like her?"

"She said I look just like my father."

"But you never knew him."

"No."

"I never knew mine, either."

Alex put a hand on her stomach, fingering the buttons of his shirt as he spoke. "They met in Oakland, my parents. He was studying engineering at the college — he was going to be an architect — and she had a job as a maid in the boarding house where he lived. She'd just left home and come to the city, she had no money, and it was the only job she could get. She didn't mind it, though; she said the work was easy and the students were nice to her. If you could've seen her, Sara, you'd believe that — she was so pretty. At eighteen, she must have been beautiful."

She smiled, stroking his hand. "And your father? What was he like?"

"Oh, she said he was tall, handsome, brilliant. Charming. She fell in love with him on sight, though, so I had to take that on faith."

Still, she noticed, his voice was proud when he spoke of his father. "What was his name?"

"Brian McKie."

"Oh. So she named you —"

"I was Alexander Holyfield until the day I ran away from home. Then I took his name. They loved each other — he'd have married her if he'd lived, and then it would've been mine legally." He paused, then said bitterly, "But I'd have taken 'Smith' or 'Jones' or 'Rappaport' by then. I didn't want anything that had ever belonged to Matthew Holyfield."

"Why, Alex? What did he do to you?"

Keeping her hand, he shifted onto his back again. "You don't need to know this, Sara."

"I'd like to, though. What did he do that you can't forgive?"

Habit, not desire, prevented him from telling her, he realized. His past shamed him; he kept it a secret. Until Sara, he'd never been tempted to reveal it to anyone. "It wasn't just me," he said carefully, feeling his way. "If it had been, I could've stood it, because I was a tough little beggar. It was what he did to my mother and my grandmother. And a lot of other people in his congregation."

"His congregation? He was a minister?"

"Self-appointed. 'Preacher' is a better word — 'minister' sounds too much like he cared about people. He didn't. He took their faith and used it to set himself up as their judge, their conscience. There was nothing he liked better than a sinner he could save. His specialty was leaping on some poor bastard who'd made the mistake of confiding in him, standing him up in front of the whole congregation of Blessed Brethren — that's what he called his church — and making him confess his pitiful 'sins.' But when you finished, you weren't forgiven, you were just humiliated. Then he was satisfied. There wasn't any charity in his heart, only meanness."

She'd heard the change in pronouns. "Did he do that to you — make you confess?"

"Sure. I was a terrible sinner. I was up there almost every Sunday, baring my wicked soul."

She shuddered; she could think of few crimes uglier than humiliating a child.

"Being a child of sin, I was doomed from the start — my vicious ways were only what you'd expect from a boy conceived in lust and born of a harlot. That's what he called his own daughter, Sara, every day until she died."

"Why did she stay there?"

"She had nowhere else to go. She didn't

know she was pregnant until after my father burned to death in a fire in his boardinghouse. His people were all dead. She had no money, no skills, not much education. All she had was me. So she went back home and let my grandfather abuse her for the last seven years of her life, for my sake."

Her arms tightened around him. He put his fingers in her hair, gently massaging her scalp. "My mother's death left a big hole in Matthew's life. My grandmother didn't have any fight in her by then, so she was no good to him. That left me. Satan's spawn."

He stopped. In dread, Sara finally asked, "What did he do?"

"He believed in two roots of all evil, not one — money *and* sex. That made poverty and absolute chastity the highest moral goals. And I'll say this for him, he wasn't a hypocrite — he practiced what he preached. In our house, that meant there wasn't enough to eat, among other things."

"What other things?"

"Stupid, grinding poverty that served no purpose but to degrade us. I wasn't allowed to have shoes. The house could never be heated. My grandmother was fifty years old, and he wouldn't let her have a *coat.* God put us in California; the sun and the earth's bounty were His blessing. If you wanted more, you were selfish and ungrateful and you'd burn in hell for it."

She knew there was more; she could even guess what it was. His hand, tangled in her hair, had turned into a fist; if she moved her head, he would hurt her. Slowly, gently, she disengaged his fingers, then kissed them one by one. "Did he hurt you?"

After a long time, he said, "Yeah."

"Tell me."

"Why?"

She waited, as tense now as he.

With a defeated sigh, he told her. "I got a beating almost every day from the time I was seven years old. Usually he used his hands. He was a big, strong son of a bitch. I was faster, though, so I could outrun him. I'd sleep in the fields or hide in the barn for a night or two, but in the end I'd always have to go back. And he was always waiting. He never forgot anything."

"Alex," she whispered, horrified.

"If I'd been really wicked, he used a strap. My grandmother never tried to stop him. I think my mother would have. When I was sixteen, I fell in love with a girl named Shelly. She lived in Salinas; her father ran the livery. We used to sneak off to this place called Deep Creek as often as we could. It started out innocently, nothing but holding hands and a few kisses. But before long we were making love. I guess we seduced each other. It was — magic, something I'd never felt. Not just the sex, either. The cherishing. The caring. It was as if she was healing me."

"And then?"

"Salinas is a small town. No secrets. My grandfather found out." Suddenly he had no stomach for going on with this story. "I ran away that night," he finished, skipping the worst, his voice clipped. "If I hadn't, he'd have killed me, beaten me to death. Or I'd have killed him. I never went back. Once I wrote to my grandmother, but there was no answer. I found out that she died about a year later."

Aching, Sara lay still, wondering what words she could possibly say that would comfort him. "Perhaps he was unbalanced, Alex, his mind —"

"I don't care about that," he said harshly, sitting up and turning away from her. "Do you think that changes anything, whether or not he was deranged? I don't give a damn. It makes no difference to me, understand?"

"I understand that you're not ready to forgive him."

"No, and I'll never be. I haven't told you half — a *quarter* of what he did. He's rotting in hell now, there's not a doubt in my mind, and he deserves it." He stood up, cursing violently. "Son of a bitch, he can still do this to me. Christ, I wish I could let it go." He turned back. "Sara, I'm sorry. How the hell did I get started on this?"

"Let's go for a walk."

"What?"

"Do you want to?"

"Now?"

She threw the sheet off and got up. "Why not?"

# Sixteen

A lovers' moon coasted high in the blue night sky, racing the clouds, raining ghostly showers on the sea and the sandy beach. Low tide sucked monotonously at the rubble of the surf, then hurled it back shoreward with a violent slap again and again, incessantly. Sara leaned back against Alex's chest and pulled his arms tighter around her. The salt breeze was steady but warm, a late-summer gift. "I wish we lived here. You and Michael and I. I wish."

He wished it, too. He rested his chin on top of her head, blind to the moon on the water and the crashing waves. *Leave him, Sara.* He almost said it out loud. But that would lead to an argument he didn't want to have, not yet. "I was thinking of you and Michael, how different you are from my mother and me. I was all she had — like you and Michael — but you're stronger than she was. And Michael's a bright, happy boy. Open and full of life."

"I hope he's happy." But he was too sensitive, too much like her. She was afraid

370

her melancholy would infect him.

"My mother was miserable. And I was angry all the time, especially after she died. Sullen and rebellious, closed up. Ben never hits Michael, does he, Sara?"

"No, he never hits Michael. But Michael never gives him any reason. Michael *loves* him, and that baffles Ben, I think. He's impatient with his frailty and his ill health because they frighten him, and when he's frightened he can become aggressive. Michael's a sort of pale mystery to him, I think. He looks more English than American, and that irritates —" She broke off when he turned her around forcefully and gripped her shoulders hard. "Alex, what — ?"

He'd heard nothing after, "No, he never hits Michael," because the odd inflection froze his blood. "Does he hit you, Sara? Does he?" He gave her an urgent shake when she didn't answer. *"Tell me."*

She pulled his hands away and stepped back. "Alex," she said as calmly as she could, "we're lovers for now, for this night. But you can't have my past or my future. I'd give anything to change that, but I can't. So don't ask me such questions — that part of my life isn't for you, isn't for us. Please." She turned from him and

371

started to walk.

He grabbed her back after two steps. "My God. He does, doesn't he?"

"No."

"You're lying."

*"No."* She wrenched away again. He was so upset, so close to violence himself, that a shrill blare of alarm sounded in her brain. "I'm not lying. You misunderstood what I said — I'm sorry! Some things are worse than hitting — coldness, absolute withdrawal. Other things. Insensitivity beyond a certain point is a kind of sadism. I have a bad marriage, Ben and I don't suit" — the understatement made her laugh — "but he doesn't hurt me physically, I swear."

"Are you telling me the truth?"

"Yes. Alex, I would tell you if he did."

"Would you?"

"Yes." She waited, feeling the battle he was waging between what he feared and what he wanted to believe. "It's true, I swear," she said again. She put her arms around his waist and drew him close. "What kind of woman do you think I am? I would never allow Ben to hurt me. Believe it, Alex." She felt the tension draining out of him as his hands came up to hold her. *Forgive me,* she begged in silence. But she didn't regret the lie.

He sighed with relief, and an odd kind of weariness. "Why did you marry him, Sara?"

She hid a sad smile against his shoulder. "I was wondering when you would finally ask me." She took his hand and they started to walk again, bare feet sinking deep in the soft sand.

"Don't you want to tell me?"

"It's nothing I'm proud of." She put her head back to stare up at the black sky. "But I suppose I've paid for it enough by now that there's no point in still feeling ashamed."

He waited.

"I was eighteen when we met. I'd been out of school for a year, living with my mother in our decaying mansion in the Blackdown Hills. She was a hopeless drunk by then, and it was my job to take care of her. I can't describe to you what it was like. There was literally nothing to hope for; I lived closer to despair in that year than at any other time in my life, before or since." That was the truth, because as wretched as the years with Ben had been, at least she'd always had Michael.

"So Ben came along and saved you," Alex guessed.

"There were moments when I thought of

it like that. Not for long, but in the beginning."

"How did you meet?"

"It seemed like chance to me; later I learned it had all been rather carefully arranged. My best chum from school had taken pity and invited me up to London for her coming-out. It was my first debutante ball — but not Ben's, I found out. In fact, he'd already had marriage proposals turned down by two young titled ladies. The season was ending; desperation was setting in. He saw me as his last chance."

"He *told* you all this?"

"Later, yes. Of course, now it seems all of a piece, but at the time the cold-bloodedness of it stunned me. He'd been planning it for ages, he and his protégée."

"Protégée?"

"Yes — a fancy word for mistress. She was a widow named Mrs. Russell — Minnie. He actually introduced us once."

Alex swore.

"Ben was incredibly wealthy by the time he was twenty-five. He started out in the Chicago stockyards, prodding cattle along a chute to their deaths. Sometime you must ask him to tell you about the skull-smashing device he invented to speed things along. Anyway, he had everything he'd ever dreamed of except for one thing — social respectability. He wanted to be allowed into the elite. Minnie told him how to do it — take an aristocratic wife. Her name and his money, she assured him, would open all the doors of the Fifth Avenue mansions that had been closed to him before. She'd been around the block, as Ben would say, but she must have been nearly as naive as he was to think it would be that easy. But he swallowed it whole, and went off to England to buy himself a bride. He'd decided to limit the search to Great Britain," she added as an aside, "because he couldn't stand foreigners, and if he had to marry one he at least wanted one who spoke English."

"And he's *telling* you all of this."

"Yes, I've told you. So he found me. You can believe that I was perfect. A duchess's daughter, shy and biddable, reasonably well-educated. And *refined* — that was the great thing — as only sheltered English girls can be." She laughed softly. "I must have seemed like a creature from another planet to him. At first he couldn't even understand me when I spoke. I put him on his best behavior with my intimidating for-eignness and my strange formality. Can you believe he thought I was sophisticated?

We spoke at cross purposes, neither of us understanding the other. Attributing qualities to each other we wanted to find but which, as we would learn later, didn't exist at all. We were abysmally, categorically mismatched."

"What did you like about him?"

"Oh, Alex." She leaned against his shoulder. "I was so young. And so ignorant. I saw his stubbornness as drive. I saw his bullying and intolerance as energy. He was an American, and that made him foreign and exciting, a little wild. A man on the frontier. Oh, I don't know, I don't know. Maybe it was our complete oppositeness that appealed to me, if only for a little while — weeks, really."

They had reached the rocky end of the beach, where a tumble of sea boulders blocked the way between the woods and the water. They found a flat, dry rock away from the outrushing tide and sat down.

"He came to Somerset almost immediately after we met. I don't think I invited him; maybe my mother did. I can't remember that part. Anyway, he made a bargain with her with amazing speed. He offered her fifty thousand pounds right away, a sort of down payment on me, and then ten thousand a year for the rest of her life."

Alex had heard the "down payment" was twenty thousand; a part of him was glad she hadn't come so cheap. He took her hand and held it in both of his, hearing the pain underneath the cynicism in her voice.

"It was a fortune to her, a pittance to him. She told me to marry him. So I did. And part of the reason was to get away from her."

She paused, then sank against him, resting. He pulled her closer, not speaking.

"We were married in New York," she resumed finally. "The honeymoon was short; in fact, it really ended at the wedding ceremony, when most of the socialites he and Minnie had invited declined to attend. That was the first inkling he had that his strategy for self-advancement might have a flaw. Naturally he blamed me. We went to Italy after the wedding, Florence and Rome. That's where a lot of my girlish questions finally got answered. No, my husband didn't love me. No, I didn't love him. Our marriage was a business deal, and we'd both only begun to suspect how disastrous the deal was going to turn out to be."

"Did you become pregnant with

Michael immediately?"

"Very nearly. Thank God — I truly think Michael saved me from going mad. But first there were those awful months in New York, just after we returned from our wedding trip. A few invitations turned up, but they were from parvenues Ben had never thought of cultivating anyway, social climbers no higher on the ladder than he was. So he told me to be more *aggressive.* He ordered me — his eighteen-year-old bride, friendless in a strange country — to knock on the doors of the Drexels and the Whitneys and leave cards, issue invitations to the Bradley Martins for dinner and tea, ask Mrs. Henry Phipps to play bridge or to ride with me in Central Park."

Alex rested his temple against hers. "Poor Sara."

"Yes. It was dreadful. And needless to say, it was all for nothing. When I'd confess, in tears, the snubs I'd endured, it made him furious. He honestly couldn't understand where he'd gone wrong. He'd bought and paid for an aristocratic Englishwoman, by God, so it must be *my* fault, something I was doing on purpose to sabotage him. He . . ."

"Punished you," Alex guessed, grimfaced.

"We punished each other. We both felt angry and cheated, and so we waged war in our separate ways. Sometimes I'd start a fight with him on purpose, because it was the only thing that made me feel alive, if only with bitterness. I was a bad wife — am a bad wife."

"Oh, please."

"It's true, I'm most of the things he calls me — cold and unfeminine, selfish, super-cilious —"

"You're none of those things, don't be an idiot."

"You love me — you don't know."

"I know because I love you."

She wanted to laugh and cry at the same time. She didn't want to talk about Ben anymore. Alex didn't either. He slipped his hands inside her robe — his robe, which she wore with her drawers over his shirt: a fascinating ensemble. The robe came untied and she wrapped it around his shoulders, enveloping him and her in its big gray wings. "If you knew what this is like for me, Alex, my love, my love."

"I do know."

"No, you couldn't. To tell you all of that — to be with you here, to have the freedom to touch you like this —" Stupidly, she started to cry.

Nuzzling her wind-tangled hair aside, he put his lips on her tight, aching throat, soothing her, murmuring to her. She felt the blossoming of a bittersweet happiness inside. His hands slid to the sides of her breasts; his mouth burned where he kissed her. Everything changed, so quickly she could hardly follow her body's swift, unexpected combustion. "You make me lose my mind," she observed wonderingly. "I mean — literally —" It tapered away to nothing, just as she'd predicted, and she lost the power to speak words more rational than, "Alex, please, yes, oh God —" Her trembling arms circled his neck, still sheltering them with his robe; under it, he opened the buttons on her shirt and uncovered her breasts. She arched up, gasping, and pressed closer. Lifting her knee, she draped it over one of his in blatant, wanton invitation, hazily amazed at herself.

Cold and unfeminine, her husband called her. Alex dragged his mouth down her soft throat, feeling the surge of her pulse. He found her breast and suckled her slowly and steadily while she moaned and her nails dug into his back — a delicious pain she stopped inflicting, abashed, when he lifted his head and said appreciatively, "Ow." The skin on the inside of her thighs was softer than an infant's. "Sara," he whispered, "beautiful Sara. Have you ever made love outside, darling?"

She couldn't stop shaking. That was odd, because everywhere he touched she was burning. "I've never made love anywhere until tonight."

He kissed her eyes closed, her mouth open. Pulling her other leg across his lap, he bent over her until she felt the cold solidity of the rock on her shoulder blades. "I know just the place."

His hand stroking between her legs caused her to squeeze her eyes shut and sigh, "Do you ever."

He gave a throaty laugh. "No, on the sand — over there." He moved his head vaguely. "It'll be softer than this rock on your lovely backside."

"Are we on a rock? I thought it was a cloud."

He gathered her in his arms and stood up, suddenly out of patience and finished with finesse. She clung to him, in instant sympathy with his need for haste. She didn't care where he took her; it made her dizzy, but it was lovely to close her eyes, press her face to his neck, and let him carry her wherever he liked.

He didn't go far. The sand leveled off a

few feet above the tide line; he sank to his knees and laid her in a soft-looking place, lit silver by moonlight. A feverish urgency seized him when the loose folds of robe and shirt slipped open, uncovering her intoxicating nakedness. But his hands on her face were gentle, his voice steady when he told her, "I'm in love with you, Sara. This won't end tonight, it can't. You must know that. Say it."

She'd told him one lie already; her spirit rebelled at the thought of another. "Alex —"

"Say it."

She caught his caressing hands and held them tight. "I will always, always love you. That won't end. Ever."

He understood the distinction. But he was too lost in her now to continue the fight. Waves of desperate, debilitating passion stormed through him. He took her with fierce, nearly violent need, and surrendered.

"Give me my blouse, Alex. I can't argue with you with no clothes on."

"I haven't got — oh." He'd been sitting on it, on the edge of the bed. He pulled it out from under his leg and handed it to her — reluctantly. Since it was impossible to believe she was going to walk out of his life forever in a few minutes, he'd been enjoying watching her get dressed, not construing the charming spectacle as the end of anything. "I'm not arguing, Sara, I'm simply asking when I'm going to see you again."

She stooped to pick up her skirt, which lay in a dark blue heap beside the bed, and shook at the wrinkles ineffectually before stepping into it and doing the hooks up at the back. "This is either going to be very difficult or else it's going to be impossible, so —"

"I vote for impossible."

She put her hands on her hips. "Alex."

"What?" Her serious eyes sobered him; he stood up and went to her. "Missed a button here," he murmured, unbuttoning the one between her breasts. She looked down, then up, then smiled. But when he tried to slip his hands inside her blouse, she stepped away quickly.

"Listen to me," she pleaded. "Please help me to do this. It's so hard now — if you fight me it'll be a hundred times worse."

"Sara, why are you doing this? What's the point? Darling, if your conscience bothers you, I'm truly sorry, but you'll have to find a way to live with it. You can't leave me and you know it."

"You don't understand at all. This has nothing to do with guilt, it never has. From the day we met — no, I didn't like you then — from the *second* day we met I've wanted to be with you, be your lover. You're wrong if you think *I* think we've committed a sin together. What happened last night was — perfect. If there's a God, He was smiling at us. He *wanted* us to be happy."

"What's changed, then? Why doesn't He want us to be happy now?"

"Will you please just try to be —"

"*Leave* him, Sara," he broke in, exasperated. "Divorce him. Come and live with me, you and Michael. You won't be rich anymore, but you won't be exactly poor, either."

"God — Alex, if you think —"

"No, I *don't* think it's money that makes you stay with him."

"What, then?"

He said it gently. "Fear. Timidity. Fear of the unknown. I don't blame you, sweetheart, but you have to —"

"No!" She should *let* him think that of her, it was safer, much less risky. But she found she was too proud; she couldn't bear it that her beloved thought her a coward.

"It's Michael I'm trying to protect, not myself. You've never understood about Ben. I tried to tell you once, but you wouldn't believe me. No one would, it's too beastly. Alex, he'll take him from me, I'll never see Michael again."

"That's not true," he said flatly.

"It is true."

"Sara, that's just not reasonable."

*"Reasonable —"*

"Will you listen to me?"

"No, I won't, I can't! I already know everything you're going to say — that I've allowed my husband to terrorize me for so long, I've lost sight of reality, that he's only a man, that he can't keep my son from me on a whim, that I'm hysterical. Why can't you trust me?"

"I do —"

"No, that's not fair, I'm sorry. I haven't told you what he's capable of."

"Then tell me now."

But the task was too monumental. She felt helpless and inarticulate. She'd countered Ben's cruelty with stoicism for too long; her reticence was too ingrained. "I'll tell you this. When Michael was three years old, Ben took him away."

"What do you mean, 'took him away'?"

"I mean he disappeared with him for

twenty-seven days. Twenty-seven days, Alex! I didn't know where they were, or if I'd ever see my son again. Do you know why he did it? To teach me a lesson. I'd committed the unpardonable sin of threatening to leave him, and he wanted me to know what would happen and what it would feel like if I did."

"God, Sara, it must've been awful."

"It was more than that, it was —" But she didn't know any words to describe that time. "Almost from the beginning Michael's been the only weapon he could use against me. But it's a potent one and he knows it. He hoards it, hides it, lulling me — and then he strikes. It's true, Alex, you can't know! Sometimes he takes him away on sudden, unannounced trips — to taunt me and torment me, not because he wants to be with him. Or he talks about sending him to school in Europe — or last year it was New England. He's hired a nanny he knows I distrust and detest. But always the ultimate threat is to take him from me and never let me see him again if I try to divorce him. Because, believe it or not, in spite of everything, Ben still thinks that one day New York society is going to let him in. Pathetic, isn't it? But that makes divorce out of the question because the scandal would destroy him."

Alex reached for her, gripping her elbows. She'd already discounted everything he wanted to say — that she was letting her fear take over her rational mind, that Ben was a man, not some diabolical fiend who could spirit her son away whenever he liked. "Then we'll fight him," he said calmly. "You tell me he's been unfaithful. Unless you're afraid of scandal for yourself or for Michael, why not charge him with adultery?"

"Because he'd win. He's too smart to let that happen. I know, I know, it sounds crazy. But, Alex, don't you think I've thought of that? I could never prove adultery because he's always been too careful. And if I tried and failed, then there would be nothing to stop him from doing his worst. I can't take such a chance." Alex shook his head impatiently and started to speak. His disbelief finally unleashed her temper. "It doesn't matter what you think, I know what I know! Alex, let me go, I'm begging you, don't do this to me."

"What am I doing?"

"Whether you believe it or not, you're asking me to choose between you and my son."

"I would never do that," he denied hotly. "Never."

"But you are. And that leaves me no choice at all." She hugged herself, despairing. "Oh God, I was mad to come here. I'm sorry now. This was a mistake."

"A mistake?" he repeated, stiff-lipped.

"Yes, yes. I've only made it worse." She reached for him, touched his chest. "But I wanted to —"

"Mistakes can be corrected," he said jerkily, backing away. "This one fairly easily. Don't worry, Sara, I won't inconvenience you any further."

"Alex —"

"Hurry and finish dressing, it'll be light soon. I'll show you a shortcut through the woods. No one will see you." He pivoted, yanked the door open, and stomped out.

She wanted to lie down on the bed and sob. But there would be time for that later. Nothing but time, later. What kept her dry-eyed and upright was the knowledge of the absolute futility of tears or emotional storms now. They might afford a temporary relief — Alex might even come back and comfort her — but afterward nothing would change. She still had to get through the next half-hour of her life: she still had to leave him.

She found her jacket, slung over the post at the foot of the bed. After a long search, she located one earring under the pillow, along with a quantity of hair pins; the other earring was nowhere to be found. She went to the mirror over the dresser and pinned her hair up, standing on tiptoe, using Alex's comb. His clothes, his cologne, a laquered box containing his jewelry, a faded miniature of a pretty girl with a sad smile — his mother? — all the intimate objects of his life filled her with a poignant, desolating sorrow. If she could have known him, discovered his tastes and habits and quirks, been with him for just a little longer — but that bittersweet pleasure was denied her, and who could say it wouldn't have made this parting even more intolerable?

She swept the room with a last glance. Her cloak hung over his wardrobe door; she took it down and threw it across her shoulders. If only she had something to give him — a gift he could find later that would make him think of her. But she had nothing.

Outside, she paused at the top of the porch steps to look at him. He had his back to her, hands in his pockets, facing the sea. The sky before him had paled to gray and the moon was gone; the stars were winking out one by one. "I'm ready," she said, quiet-voiced. He turned. His face was indistinct, but she could see his pain and his lingering disbelief. "I didn't mean it was a mistake. You know I didn't mean that. I only meant —"

"Sara."

He came toward her, holding out his hand. She lifted her skirts and ran to him. Their embrace was joyful and sad and tinged with desperation. "Oh, my love. Please believe me," she begged, holding him close, "this isn't fear or willfulness, it's real. If I leave him, he'll ruin me."

But he still couldn't accept it. "If I talked to him —"

"*No. No.* My God — *Please,* Alex, promise me you won't."

"Sara —"

"Promise!"

She was shaking with the violence of her emotion. He buried his face in her hair, defeated. "All right. I promise."

Even though it was what she wanted, even though his words made her go limp with relief, they echoed in the hollow of her empty heart like a heavy door closing. Now there truly was no hope.

"Will you go home now, back to New York?"

"Yes. Otherwise —"

"I know. It's all right."

"Ben will be furious with me, but it's just too hard. Knowing you're here."

"Will you let me write to you?"

She shook her head, not trusting her voice. "Too dangerous," she whispered.

"You could write to me."

"Better not. I think it's better —" Her throat closed.

He could think of nothing to do but hold her. "I won't try to see you. If I hear we've been invited to the same party, the same lecture, I'll stay away. But it's bound to happen — eventually we'll see each other."

"I know it."

"I used to think that would be hell, the worst punishment of all. But, Sara — now I can't wait for the day when I look up and you're there, and it doesn't even matter anymore if you're holding Ben's arm or Michael's hand, because the real hell is going to be the time between now and then. I love you, Sara. I wish I could rescue you."

"You have. I love you."

"Try to be happy. If you ever need me —"

"Yes. And you. Alex, kiss me and then let me go, I can't stand this."

"No, I'm coming with you. But I'll kiss

you." He did, with such sweet, aching tenderness that he almost wept with her. "What a pair," he whispered. Her face was slippery with tears. He took out his handkerchief and blotted her cheeks gently. Then he had to kiss her again.

She clung to him for as long as she dared. But then it was time to go, and no amount of wishing or wanting could change that. "The sky, Alex . . ."

"Yes."

"You don't need to come with me."

"I'm coming." He led her around his house to the path he knew that would keep her out of sight until she was only a few blocks from home. Behind them, past the waves swatting the shore on the in-running tide, the fiery tip of the sun flamed through a pale haze on the horizon. It would be a beautiful day.

# Seventeen

Four weeks later to the day, at Rector's lobster palace on Broadway and Forty-third Street, Sara saw Alex again.

The day began, as so many of them did lately, with the nerve-wracking sound of Ben shouting. Since it was Saturday and he was working at home, the shouting erupted intermittently all morning, ensuring that the whole household stayed in a near-constant state of anxiety. Sara, who was trying to read Lauren's latest letter, got up from the desk in her own tiny office and closed the door to muffle the irregular outbursts of fury and frustration that had her nerves stretched tight. Better. She sat back down and continued reading.

"I'm aware that you tried to warn me, in the kindest possible way. Now I wish you'd been brutal. No — I don't, not really. It would not have done any good, for one thing. And for another, in spite of all that's happened, Sara, I don't regret any of it. I'm sure you think I'm mad, and perhaps I am, but I loved him deeply and with my whole soul — how can I regret that? You will say that he wasn't worthy of such feelings, but it hardly matters now. I felt what I felt, it's over, and I am changed irrevocably. I'm left to thank God that our affair had no *consequences* beyond my broken heart."

Indeed. Sara imagined Lauren's lack of contrition for giving herself to a faithless, hypocritical bastard might very well reverse itself in the event of a tiny *consequence*. She folded the letter and sat back, staring out the window at the yellowing leaves of the ginko tree. She was like Lauren, she supposed, because in every way but technically she'd gone to her lover a virgin. Unlike her friend, though, there were moments, such as now, when she deeply regretted it.

Each morning she awoke as if floating in a black, baffling fog of misery, wondering, *What is this grief?* And always she remembered, and always the blackness deepened. Except for duty, she might have let it smother her; but duty forced her to get up and to get through the days. She understood now, too late, that she would not hurt this badly if she had left Alex alone. By opening her heart and body to him, she'd exposed nerve and flesh and bone and spirit to a ruthless, toothed weapon that would not stop tormenting her, not for a second. When would it cease? When would this wound scar over and give her ease? To be able to live through a whole hour of time without thinking of him and so without suffering the biting pain of his loss, truly that would be a miracle. Surely the day would come — it must! no one could go on like this forever — but until it did, all she could do was endure.

The telephone startled her out of her dreary reverie. It was Paren Matthews, cool and abrupt as usual. "Have you finished the draft for my speech to the settlement council yet, Sara?"

"Yes, I finished it last night."

"Oh, good." He let a hint of unflattering surprise color his tone. "I'm glad your social obligations didn't conflict this time with your professional ones. When can I have it?"

Sara traced a stiff finger around the black circle of the mouthpiece. "I can bring it to you on Tuesday," she said evenly, "since I have to come in anyway for the history class. Or if you like, I can drop it in the mail. That way you'll have it on Monday." She ought to be used to his sarcasm by now. She didn't even blame him for it much; he had good reason not to trust her — she'd abandoned her settlement house work twice last summer, once without warning and both times for reasons that must seem contemptibly frivolous to him. Still, it hurt, because once they'd been friends.

"Yes, mail it. Who knows, something might come up on Tuesday to keep you away — a shopping trip, or a tea party."

"Damn it," she burst out, "that's not fair, Paren, and you know it."

First there was silence, then a sigh. But she would not discover today if it was meant to preface an apology, because at that moment there was a sharp click in her ear and then Ben's voice booming, "Hello? Hello!"

"Ben? I'm on the —"

"Sara? Get off the line."

"I'm speaking to —"

"Hang up, I said, I'm on the 'phone. Jesus Christ, this is *business*."

The bang of the earpiece made her jump. Red-faced, she tried an apologetic laugh for Paren's benefit. "I'm sorry, I'd better go. Ben's working at home today and he —"

"Right," Paren said shortly. "Mail the speech, Sara. Thanks for your time." He hung up on her almost as violently as Ben had.

She could have cried. She missed Paren's friendship. And Lauren's. And she missed Alex so much, she wanted to die.

She found her handkerchief and blew her nose, thinking of Ben to distract herself. Something was the matter with him these days. After weeks of nagging, she'd finally been allowed to make a doctor's appointment for him. The doctor couldn't find anything wrong, but in her opinion worry and overwork were making Ben sick. The precise nature of his problems was a secret, though, and whenever she tried to pry into it he exploded. Money and labor troubles, that was all she knew.

On Thursday, things had come to a head. She might not even have known why if she hadn't read about it in the newspaper on Friday. Without warning, all his bakeshop employees had gone on strike — along with every other bakery worker in the city, over nine thousand men, women, and children — for the cause of shorter hours, higher wages, and healthier working conditions. What had enraged him and sent him storming around the house like a rampaging bull wasn't the workers' demands, though; it was an editorial accompanied by a cartoon in the *Evening Post* — a conservative paper, notoriously unsympathetic to strikers — condemning the working conditions in all the city's bakeries and naming Cochrane bakeshops in particular as shameless examples of exploitation of the labor force by a rapacious capitalist looter. Ben's anger had been so terrible that Michael had hidden in his room with the door closed, for his father's fury terrified him; he reacted to it the way other children reacted to thunderstorms.

Now, even through the closed door of her study, she heard a fresh bellow of outrage. She stood up, angry herself. Really, this was too much. If she found Michael cowering again, she would confront Ben herself and put a stop to it. Somehow.

But Michael wasn't in his room. Nor in hers, nor anywhere else on the second floor. At times like this she was almost sorry Mrs. Drum was gone, or at least sorry she hadn't hired anyone to replace her. She'd left without notice while Sara was away in Newport. She had never completely understood why, beyond the fact that it had something to do with Tasha. But Tasha couldn't or wouldn't explain it to her, except to say, "She was a stupid woman. Stupid Mick."

She found Tasha in the red drawing room, reclining on the sofa and reading a fashion magazine. Her new hairstyle, Sara noticed uncomfortably, was an exact replica of her own. Tasha sent her a lazy smile, stretched like a panther, and resumed reading. Sara's jaw tightened; the languid spectacle released a spurt of hot irritation in her out of all proportion to the offense. "Have you seen Michael?" she asked sharply.

"Michael? No."

She was the only one in the house who seemed genuinely unaffected by Ben's rages, Sara realized. That annoyed her, too. "Will you please help me look for him?"

Tasha let her magazine slide to the floor. It was past eleven o'clock, but she still wore her *robe du matin,* as she called it, over a satin negligee. "I would like to, but it's time for me to go and dress or my tutor will arrive and find me in *dishabille.*" She got up, stretched again, and walked leisurely past Sara to the door.

Sara whirled. "Tasha, I would like to speak to you."

Tasha paused in the threshold, striking an attitude. "But have I not just said? I am in a rush. We will talk later, Sara." And she was gone.

Sara felt as much amazement as anger. It was clear to her by now that she had done Tasha no favors by letting her stay so long with no employment and no usefulness. Now she must deal with the situation — Tasha got more impudent and impossible every day. But what an unpleasant task it would be, telling her she must leave and find a place of her own. Sara had no energy for the encounter. With a troubled sigh, she realized she had just made a decision to put it off a little longer.

"Sheila, have you seen Michael?"

"No, ma'am," said the maid, looking up from the mirror-like surface of the table she was polishing in the foyer. "I haven't seen him since breakfast."

"I can't find him, and I'm a little concerned. Help me look for him, will you?"

They searched the house; they even went outside, although it had begun to rain, walking to either end of the block and calling him. Sara knew there was no point in asking Ben; he wouldn't know anything, he would resent the interruption, and Michael wouldn't have gone anywhere near him anyway. Finally there was nowhere left to search but the basement.

She found him there, huddled on a piece of canvas beside the coal bin, fast asleep.

No wonder he was tired. Last night a nightmare had woken him — monsters chasing him through terrifying streets — and she'd stayed with him until he'd finally gone back to sleep. It had taken hours.

In the dim light from the lone bare bulb overhead, she could see he'd been crying; his face was smudged with coal dust and the tear tracks stood out like dirty trails through a field of mud. Beside him was a crumpled piece of paper. She knelt down and reached for it fearfully, dreading what she would see. Lately all his art work was black and violent and heartbreaking. His interest in school had declined in the last month, yet he still did his work well. He was such a dutiful child, he broke her heart. And she was riddled with guilt, for she knew who had taught him this terrible stoicism.

But the drawing wasn't bleak and disturbing, she saw with surprise; peering at it in the dimness, she made out a picture of a beach — Bailey's Beach? — in bright blues and yellows. A man, woman, and child stood in the center, beaming and holding hands, all wearing red-and-white striped bathing suits. A happy family. He'd even drawn a dog at the bottom — Gadget, she surmised, from its short legs and long tail.

With a pang, she set the drawing aside and gently stroked her hand through Michael's silvery blond hair. His eyes opened. "Hello, you," she said softly. "You've been sleeping."

"Hi, Mum." He smiled, and her heart twisted.

"Look at you, what a mess you are. Were you rolling in the coal bin?"

"No."

"No?" She rubbed a particularly black cheek with her thumb. "You look it. Come upstairs and have a bath."

"I don't want to."

"I'll run it for you myself, not Sheila. And you can play with your new battleship in the tub."

A flicker of interest lit the blue-gray eyes, then died. "I don't want to go upstairs."

Sighing, heedless of the six rows of white braid at the hem of her red poplin skirt, she sat down beside him on the filthy concrete floor. "Daddy's not angry with *you*, you know." No answer. "Do you think he's angry with you?"

"I don't know."

"Of course he isn't."

"Why is he so mad, then?"

"He's angry with the way things are going right now with his work, that's all.

And when he gets mad, he yells. That's the way some people are."

"You never yell."

"Oh, sometimes I do."

"Hardly ever. That time in Newport when I let the frog sleep in my bed because it was raining, you yelled then. Remember?"

"Vividly."

He put his head on her arm. "I don't like it, Mum," he admitted. "I don't like to hear it."

"I know. But you have to remember that it's nothing to do with you. Daddy's angry at *things,* not people. He loves you." She'd told him that so many times; now, looking down into his pinched, unhappy face, for the first time she saw skepticism. It chilled her. She remembered what he'd told her a few days ago, and the sound of wonder in his voice as he'd related it — that Charlie O'Shea's father *picked him up and kissed him* every night when he came home from work. "I *saw* it, Mum," he'd insisted, amazed.

"Is this Newport?" she asked, pulling the picture toward her, surreptitiously wiping her cheek on his hair.

"Yeah. It's you and me and Mr. McKie."

She was so shocked, she couldn't speak. Intense guilt assaulted her because somehow, she knew, it was her fault that the man in Michael's smiling, ideal family was her lover instead of her husband.

"Why doesn't he come to see us anymore?"

"Because he's in Newport. He's still building our house."

"Does he still like us?"

"Yes. Yes."

"Can I write him a letter? I made something for him and I never got to give it to him."

"What?"

"It's a secret."

"Oh."

"Don't try to guess, okay?"

"Okay." Fair enough; whenever he had a secret, she always guessed what it was because he couldn't resist giving her such broad hints.

"Can I write to him, Mum?"

She hesitated. His devotion to Alex perplexed her. They'd been friends during the early part of the summer, but that was months ago. Michael was a child, with a child's memory and fickle loyalties, but he'd remained steadfast in his friendship with Alex. Was it because of something she was doing without realizing it, an attitude in her that he could sense? The possibility appalled her. And yet how could she say no to him now? It would be cruel to deny him this simple pleasure. "All right," she said slowly, "you can write to him if you want to." But she hoped he wouldn't; she hoped he would forget.

"It's cold down here, darling, and you really have to get cleaned up before lunch." They scrambled to their feet.

"Is Dad going to have lunch with us?"

How she hated the sound of fear in his voice. Meals had been a trial lately, with Ben growling and sniping at her, at Michael, even at Tasha. "No," she decided suddenly. "You and I are going out."

"We are? Where?"

"Mmm . . . Fleischmann's?" A squeal of delight. "And then we'll go to Union Square and listen to the street orators and browse for a while in Brentano's."

"Oh, *neat.*"

"And on the way home, if we *feel* like it and we're not too tired, we *might* stop in at Huyler's." Shocking over-indulgence, she knew, but she didn't care; she wanted to hear him laugh again.

But the mention of his favorite candy store made his grubby face turn serious. "Mummy, you don't have to — you know, worry about me so much. I'm really quite all right."

She laughed; it stuck in her throat before it could turn into a sob. Bending down, she embraced him. "I know you're really quite all right!" she whispered fiercely. The feel of his spindly little body was so dear.

He burrowed his grimy face in her neck and inhaled loudly — he loved to smell her perfume. "Mmmm," he breathed appreciatively. She held on until he squirmed away, remembering all at once that he was seven and getting too big for these sentimental displays. "I've named my battleship Invincible," he informed her, his voice deepening, as he ran up the steps in front of her. "After the knight's horse in the *Black Warrior's Tale*. Remember?"

"Yes."

"Mummy?"

"Yes, love?" They'd reached the kitchen.

"I don't need you to run my bath for me. I can do it by myself now."

Before she could answer, he ran ahead of her and disappeared into the hall, leaving her alone. She heard his light footsteps on the staircase. At the other end of the house, Ben was still shouting.

She almost didn't go to the symphony that night. The long afternoon with Michael had tired her, the thought of dressing again to go out depressed her, and she hated all the wearying subterfuge required to spend an evening with Ben in public. Unexpectedly, it was he who insisted they go, in spite of his foul mood and his almost sickly-looking fatigue. Vivaldi, of course, had nothing to do with it; Mrs. Conrad Sheridan had called in the afternoon and invited them to join her and her husband in their private box, and afterward to have supper with their party at Bustanoby's Cafe. Mr. Sheridan was president of the Nantauk Mercantile Bank & Trust Company. The obvious fact that the Cochranes were a last-minute afterthought therefore did not signify.

Ben slept through most of the concert. Watching him, his chin on his chest, hands limp in his lap, Sara noticed for the first time how much weight he'd put on. He didn't look healthy, though; his normally ruddy complexion was pale, almost pasty. And he must be tired indeed to fall asleep in Carnegie Hall, where he usually took such a deep delight in gazing about at all the gilded fractions of the Four Hundred and imagining that he belonged among them. But he looked heavy and uncomfortable in his evening clothes, the black bow tie around his starched collar seeming to pinch into the flesh of his thick neck. Tonight, as usual, he'd made her wear too much jewelry with her pale blue Callot gown. When she protested, he'd quoted his vulgarest hero, Diamond Jim Brady — "Them as has 'em, wears 'em." The ostentation embarrassed her; she felt self-conscious and foolish in her ropes of pearls and flashing jewels. But she flaunted no more than most and less than many in the crowd of braceleted and tiaraed glitterati around her, so she could console herself that at least she didn't look any gaudier than anyone else.

The concert ended. There were two other couples in the Sheridans' party, the Stanleys and the James Kimmels. Waiting for carriages to take them down Broadway to Fortieth Street, Mrs. Kimmel mentioned that she and her husband and the Louis Stones had gone to Bustanoby's last night and found it deadly dull, not the thing at all. Immediately the plan changed: they would go to Rector's, then, in Longacre Square, and eat lobster. That would be more fun anyway, because there was no telling who you might see at Rector's after the theaters closed. Ben's tired face brightened, and Sara knew he relished the thought of being seen at the city's supreme shrine of the cult of pleasure. When they were unhesitatingly shown to a *downstairs* table in the bright, crowded restaurant, his satisfaction was complete, for only those who had truly arrived were permitted to sit on the first floor; the less illustrious, if admitted at all, had to make do with one of the seventy-five tables upstairs.

By midnight there were no tables left for anyone, regardless of consequence. The din of voices and gay laughter crackled between the high mirrored walls, and the crystal chandeliers winked and gleamed in the reflected glory of a fortune in jewels and stunning gowns of hyacinth and heliotrope and canary yellow. Champagne flowed like a golden waterfall, and Sara watched in dull alarm as Ben's mood, under its influence, shifted from sullenness to feverish exhilaration. He couldn't stop talking, and his relentless, booming voice pounded on her nerves like fists. What was the matter with him? He rarely drank to excess in public, especially when he was with people he wanted to impress — he was too wary of losing control. But twice he told the same interminable story of his latest stock market coup to Conrad Sheridan, who could barely conceal his impatience, and three times he bragged to the Kimmels that his new box at Madison Square Garden had cost four hundred dollars. His laughter exploded incessantly, loud as cannon fire, harsh and inappropriate. Knowing how futile it would be to warn him, Sara kept silent, embarrassed for him, while a deep, throbbing headache began between her eyebrows and soon clouded her vision.

But she saw Alex before he saw her, in the gilded mirror opposite, beyond Jenny Stanley's ostrich-feather headdress. On either arm he had a woman; they could have been sisters, both tall, brunette, and queenly. He was remonstrating good-naturedly with the maitre d'hotel when another man, thin, bearded, and blond, joined him, casually taking the arm of one of the queenly brunettes and tucking it under his own.

Sara's blood surged giddily; she reached for her wine glass, unthinking, but her fingers shook and she had to drop her empty hand back into her lap. Impotent, she closed her eyes and ears to the din and the dazzle, searching for a handhold, for stability somewhere inside herself. Ben's thundering voice floored her, calling out, "McKie! Hey, McKie! There's my architect, Conrad. Know him? Finest firm in

410

the city. McKie!"

Colors swirled; sounds clashed and bludgeoned. She sat still, as if frozen in a violent dream, incapable of raising her eyes until she felt him standing behind her and the cacophanous bits of dialogue all around became recognizable as introductions and greetings. Did they all know Alex McKie? Ben boomed, taking over as host. The Kimmels did, from Newport. Tell the headwaiter to bring more chairs, there was plenty of room if they all squeezed together. Have a seat, have a seat! Who were these charming ladies? Floradora girls, two in the statuesque Sextette who danced and sang to wild applause every night at the Casino Theatre on Thirty-ninth Street. Ben, overcome with awe, sprang up and immediately gave the nearer one, Miss Sampson, his own chair. The blond, bearded man who was her escort raised his elegant brows and sent Alex a dry look. He was a sculptor, Sara heard dully; he and Alex had known each other since their student days in Paris.

The lady who still clung to Alex's arm was Miss Phelan. Sara automatically took the large hand she offered and gazed up, beyond a prodigious, satin-shrouded bosom, into a pair of sultry black eyes. The

411

two women murmured to each other, smiling falsely.

Finally Sara looked at Alex. He didn't offer his hand, but he bent toward her as if he would speak. But she spoke first. "She's lovely, Alex." Her light, congratulatory voice carried only to him. "And how nice for you that her charms aren't spoiled by any wearisome inhibitions."

She didn't look at his face, but his body straightened jerkily, as if reacting to a blow. Thick, suffocating waves of wretchedness buried her. She went blind and deaf until Ben's voice chiding, "Move, Sara," and his hand rudely pushing at the back of her chair brought her back to awful reality. He shoved a new chair between her and Miss Sampson, squeezed into it, and immediately turned his back on her to engage the striking soubrette in loud and animated conversation.

Time became a clever, grotesque enemy. Every hour she checked the diamond-and-ruby-studded watch she wore pinned to her bosom, only to discover that a minute had actually passed. The smell of hot fish brought her, again and again, to the brink of nausea. Alex was somewhere at the other end of the table; she didn't know where because she never looked at him.

412

Twice she asked Ben if they could leave; both times he didn't even bother to answer. The bearded sculptor, whose name was Blackman, spoke to her repeatedly and with great charm; but she could hardly follow his amusing stories, and she answered his questions in monosyllables.

And then it was simply not possible to go on with it any longer. She had to take hold of Ben's wrist to get his attention. "I'm ill, you must take me home." He started to argue; her hand tightened like a claw. "No, now — I tell you I'm sick."

She didn't realize how drunk he was until he tried to stand up. She reached for him — too late to prevent him from stumbling so hard against the table that dishes clattered along its whole length. His flailing arm upset water and wine glasses and knocked a lit candle out of the floral arrangement. Mr. Blackman was beside her in an instant, steadying Ben and speaking to him in calm, jovial tones, maneuvering him carefully away from the table. She said something apologetic and then something about a carriage to Mrs. Sheridan, whose appalled face stayed in her mind's eye for long moments afterward. Intent on helping Ben pull enough money from his purse to pay for the evening, she didn't notice Alex until he shoved money of his own at the hovering waiter and grabbed hold of Ben's other arm. Between them they got him out of Rector's, while Mr. Blackman held the door.

Fresh air didn't sober him so much as revive him, turning him from a confused drunk into a boisterous one. "McKie!" he cried, seeing him for the first time. Blackman's name eluded him. "You, y'know this guy? This's McKie, my architect. Building me the biggest goddamn house in Newport. Right? Right? Tell 'im, McKie, tell 'im how much the sonofabitch's costing me." He lurched against Sara, throwing his arm around her for balance. "Get a cab," Alex muttered; Blackman stepped off the sidewalk into the street.

"I'm drunk, Sare. How the hell di' that happen?" He pushed Alex away and draped his other arm around her too, leaning heavily. "Mm, smell good." He buried his face in her shoulder, humming with drunken appreciation. His hands fumbled at her waist. She stumbled and would have fallen from the weight of him if Alex hadn't pulled him off with sudden, hardly suppressed violence. "This's my wife, Sara. Oh yeah, you know 'er, I forgot. Know 'er mother was a duchess? Her bleedin' *grace,* fer Chris' sake." He laughed, then staggered again and swore. Sara didn't know she was crying until he pawed at her face. "Whatsat?" he mumbled, squinting at her.

A hansom pulled up in front of them, at the curb. Alex and Blackman put Ben in first; he landed with a thud that rocked the carriage like a boat in the water. "I'm coming with you," Alex said grimly, reaching for her hand.

She pulled it out of his grasp and backed up, blocking the door. "No. Thank you."

"But you need help. We'll both come —"

"You're very kind, Mr. McKie. I have servants who will help me."

He couldn't stop himself; he whispered, "Sara —"

She whipped around, feeling blindly for the step. The touch of his hands on her sides made a sob rise in her throat. She knew she was perilously close to disaster. Even so, when he reached for the door to close it, her stiff-armed grip held it open for a few more precious seconds. *I didn't mean what I said,* she told him with her brimming eyes, praying he would understand. *Alex, I love you.*

She sat back. The door slammed. Blackman gave the driver money; Alex told him her address. The coach jerked. Ben groaned and put his head in her lap, winding his arms around her knees. Her hand went to his shoulder. She patted it automatically while the electric griffin on Rector's yellow facade slid past the window and the hansom merged cleanly into late traffic on the Gay White Way.

# Eighteen

The mantel clock striking one woke Sara out of a light doze. But she didn't get up from the sofa, on which she lay in her beige striped traveling suit and high-button shoes. Hours ago she'd lit one candle and set it on the low marble table in front of the couch. Now she watched it sputter for a few seconds and go out, leaving her in the dark. Maybe she would stay here all night. Who would care? Michael and Tasha were asleep upstairs; they would never know. She'd left Ben this afternoon in Tuxedo Park; he would never know. Who cared what the servants thought?

She did. No, that wasn't it; she worried about what sort of woman she would have become if she stopped caring what the servants thought. So there was still hope for her; she wasn't completely lost.

She'd felt lost this afternoon. So lost that she'd had to leave the Kimmels' gay house party a day early and come home on the train alone. "I'm sick," she'd told Ben for the second time in eight days. But this time he'd refused to come with her; a weekend in Tuxedo Park with the likes of the William Whitneys and the Horace Duveens was a social opportunity he would not relinquish on any account, certainly not hers, probably not if she was dying.

Anyway, he wasn't stupid; he'd almost surely seen through her excuse. She wasn't ill, not really. But she was giving out. Breaking down. She couldn't do it anymore.

A noise she recognized as the closing of the front door echoed through the silent house. She'd locked it herself, hours ago. It must be Ben, then, using his key. But why would he be getting home now?

She sat up dully, wondering if she ought to go and greet him. What was the point? He would only make her explain why she had behaved so oddly as to fall asleep downstairs in her clothes, and she had no explanation. Better to avoid him.

But now she heard a woman's low laugh, and for a second her heart stopped. She stood up, stiff-legged. She heard a man's heavy footsteps in the hall, coming toward her, and the accompanying staccato of a woman's high heels. The door to the drawing room wasn't closed; two dark shadows loomed in the threshold. Sara stood frozen in place while the couple in the doorway merged, fusing into a black, indistinguishable silhouette. The rustle of cloth rubbing against cloth sounded loud in the silence, and somehow obscene. She covered her mouth with both hands when she recognized the woman's deep, throaty voice, purring. Because she couldn't speak, she reached down toward the end table and switched on the electric lamp.

Tasha screamed. But it was only half a nightmare, Sara saw, because the man wasn't Ben. He was a stranger, black-haired and white-faced, his mouth slack with shock. They both wore evening clothes. Tasha had on Sara's midnight-blue opera cloak and, under it, already unhooked at the bosom, her new crimson moire evening gown.

No one spoke for a full half-minute. At last the black-haired man cleared his throat theatrically and made a rather touching attempt to charm Sara with a smile. *"Madame, je suis navré, désolé!* This is most awkward. Perhaps I should go, *oui?"*

"Yes."

Tasha made a grab for his arm; for a second Sara thought she would try to detain him. But when he pulled away, she dropped her hand. The man made an ironic bow that managed to include both women, murmured something low and insinuating to Tasha, and escaped. A moment later, they heard the front door open and close.

Another silent moment passed. When she realized Tasha wasn't going to speak, Sara held out a helpless hand. "Where have you been?"

"To the opera, is it not obvious?" She threw Sara's cloak on the back of a chair and began to rebutton the front of her gown, her movements deliberately casual and unhurried.

"You told me you would stay with Michael while Ben and I were away this weekend."

She shrugged. "Sheila looked after him."

"That's not the point. You lied to me. And you brought a man into this house."

"So? What does that matter?"

She stared intently, but she could see no remorse, not even embarrassment in Tasha's hot, sullen eyes. She drew a long breath. This was partly her fault, she thought wearily, the payback for putting off the inevitable because it would be unpleasant. Now it was intolerable. "I'm sorry," she said quietly and, as much as possible, without rancor, "but it's time for you to find somewhere else to live."

Tasha faced her, a faint smile on her full red lips. "Oh, I don't think so."

"I'm afraid you must. There's no reason for you to stay here now. You need to find work —"

"*Work.*" She laughed in genuine amusement. "I do not work."

"No? How else do you intend to support yourself?"

"I intend to stay here."

"Are you listening to me? You can't stay here any longer. I offered to help you find a job once; I'm willing to help you again, if you want me to. I'll give you some money until you get back on your feet. But you must go. I'm sorry, but it's the best thing, Tasha, even for you."

"Even for me?" She bared her teeth and came closer, so close that Sara caught the high-priced scent of her own perfume. "So you will throw me out for *my* sake? How kind! Please to tell me, Sara, how is that best for *me?*"

She stared back unblinkingly. "It would be more honest." Tasha uttered a coarse word in a language Sara didn't understand, but she comprehended the sentiment perfectly. "I'm sorry," she repeated stiffly. "I

421

would like you to go tomorrow." She started to walk past her when Tasha grabbed her shoulder and twisted her back around.

"Do you do this because of Louis?"

"Louis?"

She made a rude, impatient gesture toward the door with her thumb.

"Ah, Louis. Yes, partly. To bring him here was a betrayal of my tru—"

"Hypocrite."

Sara went rigid. "There's no point to this —"

"Whore. How dare you judge me when you are the lover of a man who is not your husband? Eh? Yes, yes, you have no answer to that, have you, Sara?"

No, she had no answer; she was too shocked to speak. The opportunity to deny the accusation slipped irretrievably away as she went dead white and tried to draw air into her paralyzed lungs. "Get out of my way," she finally managed to grate through numb lips. "You're not welcome here anymore, I want you gone by morning."

Tasha struck her, a blow to the shoulder with the flat of her hand. Sara made a sound of amazed wrath, but the younger woman only stepped closer until their faces were inches apart. "No, I won't go. If

you try to force me, I will tell your husband about you and Mr. McKie."

"There's nothing to tell!" she denied
belatedly.

"Liar. You sleep with him, I know it. I
will tell your husband."

"No!"

"Tomorrow I'll tell him, I swear before
God, and he will throw you out. He will
keep his son and throw you out. I'll do it,
I'll do it!"

Sara believed her. Because she was not
an optimist — had never known any reason
to be — she saw it all happening, the fated
inevitability of it. At the same time, she
knew exactly what price she was going to
have to pay to escape it. But how could
Tasha know about Alex with such cer-
tainty? Was she herself that transparent, or
had Tasha only made an assumption, using
the standard of her own reckless morality?
She felt the fury and helplessness of the
trapped, and under that a keener anger
toward Tasha, not because of her
treachery, but because her dangerous
knowledge dirtied and degraded the one
honest act of love Sara had ever committed.

Backing away, she resisted the tempting
solidity of the chair behind her. Blood

pounded in her throat, her wrists. The possibility of actually fainting had never been more real; but Tasha had enough power already and she wouldn't add to her advantage by sitting down. "What is it you want?" she asked as calmly as possible. The instant flare of triumph in her adversary's eyes made her feel physically sick.

"I want a thousand dollars."

She almost laughed. There was a lesson in humility somewhere in the ludicrous distinction between the utter ruin of her life and the paltry cost of saving it. Maybe someday she would find it instructive. "All right," she said immediately.

"That's only to start. I would like it tomorrow, no later than noon because that is when I'm going shopping. You may come with me if you like — I have always valued your sense of style, Sara."

The conversation was veering toward absurdity. She snapped out, "What else?" to bring back grim reality.

"In fact, you will come with me, I have just decided — you will introduce me to your dressmaker at Longine's. What else? Oh, many things." She began to pace back and forth, her usually languid movements hurried and jerky with excitement. "On Tuesday, when you visit or leave cards at the homes of your acquaintances, I will accompany you. You will introduce me to everyone as your friend. Your very dear friend." She stopped pacing abruptly. "And I would like a party. In my honor. A sort of *debut*. You will invite many eligible men to this party, and" — she laughed coquettishly — "many ugly young ladies. Perhaps you may even wish to invite Mr. McKie; he is very handsome and soon to be very rich, yes? Well, we will see."

Sara's voice crackled with anger. "Even if I agreed to this, my husband would never allow it, you must see that. What you're asking is impossible."

"But I am not asking, and you will make it possible. Otherwise, it is I who will have to find *you* a job." She laughed again. "Delicious, is it not? Tell me, Sara, can you sew? No? Well, there are other things you could be — a governess, a whore. But we needn't speak of that yet." She folded her arms, savoring Sara's expression. "But where was I? Oh, yes. Tonight Louis and I made use of the Cochrane family carriage, which was most pleasant. That will continue. We enjoyed your box at the Metropolitan Opera as well, and will do so again, as often as we like." She tapped her lips with her forefinger, thinking. "I need the names of your milliner, your hairdresser, and your furrier. I will need money all the time. You can either give me cash or I can charge what I need to your accounts. I think perhaps a combination of these is best. Well? You are so silent. What are you thinking?"

She was thinking that if she believed she had committed a sin by loving Alex, this was undoubtedly the kind of retribution his grandfather would have wished on her. She wondered what sort of justice was at work when a simple act of kindness was repaid with heartlessness and perfidy. She marveled at how naive she had been to expect friendship, perhaps even gratitude, from a woman who must have detested her for a very long time. Aloud she said, "Do you plan to continue living in this house?"

"Oh yes, for a while. Later, after I am established, I will take a place of my own. Uptown, I think."

"How long have you been planning this?"

Tasha raised innocent brows and didn't answer.

"It won't work, you know."

She smiled a thin, nasty warning. "It had better work."

Sara shook her head. But it would be

futile, and maybe dangerous, to explain to Tasha that an immigrant gypsy seamstress had less than no chance of acceptance in society, even the lowest circle of it, and that if she thought it would work because the former Lady Sara Longford was going to be her sponsor, she would suffer precisely the same disillusionment Ben had suffered eight years ago. She might have felt sorry for Tasha — in spite of everything, she sometimes felt sorry for Ben — but Tasha's exploitation of her was more ruthless and even more calculated than her husband's had been, and Sara found she had no pity to waste on her.

But she had to know one thing. "Were you even raped, Tasha? Or was it all a lie from the beginning?"

Tasha stretched her arms out wide. "I am so sleepy. From all the excitement tonight, I think."

"Come, you can tell me. What difference does it make now?"

The catlike innocence disappeared and pure venom shone in her dark, lethal eyes. "I don't tell you anything. You are not so much the great lady now, are you? You're nothing, the same as me." She smiled, showing her teeth. "Or else we are both great ladies and I am the same as you.

Think about that. Perhaps we will be friends after all, Sara. But whatever we will be, I promise you we are going to be the same."

Sara shivered, chilled. She had the answer to her question, and more.

"Let's go to bed now," Tasha said, holding out her hand. "You look very tired. A long day, yes? Why did you come back so early from your weekend?"

Sara didn't answer, and she shrank from Tasha's outstretched hand.

"But wait — let us be clear. You agree to all this, do you not, Sara?"

She hesitated, not because there could be any doubt, but because she loathed the satisfaction Tasha would derive from her answer. "Even if I were willing, Ben won't allow these changes you're suggesting."

"Ah, but you will find a way to manage him, I'm sure of it. Tell me now, do you agree?"

"Very well." What choice did she have? "But only on the condition that you stay away from my son."

"What? What is this?"

"Don't speak to him, don't go near him."

"You are not to demand things from me!"

"Then we have no bargain."

"I tell you —"

"If you speak to Michael or have anything to do with him at all, I'll expose you."

"Why would I wish to speak to him? We do not like each other anyway!"

"Then you agree?"

"Puh! You do not tell me what to do."

So Tasha hated making a concession as much as she did. She found that pathetically consoling. "Yes or no. You must say, Tasha, or we have no bargain."

"Puh," she said again. "It makes no difference to me."

"You agree?"

"Yes! I have said so."

She nodded once and moved toward the door. Tasha sprang after her, so abruptly that she stopped in surprise, half-expecting some kind of attack. But Tasha only wanted to get through the door first. It was almost laughable. Almost, but not quite. Because the ridiculous incident was revealing. It gave her a sharp, bitter foretaste of what her domestic life was going to be like — if she was *lucky* — for a long, long time to come.

"Say that again, Alex? I couldn't have heard you right."

429

"I said I'm resigning."

John Ogden's eyebrows jerked up so high that his pince-nez fell off his nose and dropped in his lap. "What? No! Why?"

Since Ogden was too startled to offer him a chair, Alex took the liberty of draping one thigh over a corner of his desk and folding his arms. "I'm sorry to spring it on you like this, John. I guess it sounds sudden."

"I'll say it sounds sudden! What the devil are you talking about? We just made you a partner."

"I shouldn't have accepted that — I apologize. This hasn't been an easy decision, but it's been coming on for quite a while. Longer, I guess, than I even knew myself." He wasn't doing a very good job of this, he realized. Ogden deserved better. "I'm moving back to California, John. I want to try to go into business for myself and build a different kind of house from what I can build here for Draper and Snow."

"In other words, you want to throw your career away?" Ogden couldn't hide his consternation. "That's what you're saying, let's be clear about it."

"I don't see it that way."

"Alex, I *know* you. You won't make any

money out there on your own, so you'll be miserable."

There was no mistaking the insult, but Alex supposed he deserved it. "It'll be quite a change, that's for sure," he said mildly.

"Is that what this is about?" Ogden's eyes narrowed in suspicion. "More money? You could've just asked, you know, it would've been —"

"It has nothing to do with money."

"No? Look, if it's the Marshall Farley house that's bothering you, I could probably get you pulled off it. It's still early, I'm sure Ames would be glad to jump in and replace you if Farley would agree —"

"John — listen, I'm honestly not being coy or trying to drive up my price. I'm quitting."

The older man sat back in his swivel chair and gestured helplessly. "But why? What can you do out there that you can't do here — better, for more money and more prestige? If you go to California you'll be starting over, as if the last six years never happened."

"That might be true as far as my reputation is concerned, at least for designing the kind of buildings I've got in mind. But it's not true for my experience and my ability.

I don't regret a minute of the last six years — I couldn't have come to this decision without them. The firm's been decent to me from the beginning, and more than generous, and I'll always be grateful for that. But it deserves my best, and that's exactly what I can't give anymore."

"But *why?*"

He stood up. "It's hard to explain. More and more I've been feeling like an anachronism. The twentieth century's almost here, and I'm still designing buildings in a style that reached its peak a thousand years ago — *two* thousand. For a while I could do it, but not anymore. I feel as if I've given up architecture and gone into archeology. I'm finished with it, John, I can't do it anymore."

Ogden threw up his hands. "I don't understand."

Alex hesitated, frowning. "Have you got a minute? Come into my office and I'll show you something."

His new office down the hall from Ogden's was functional, hardly luxurious, but still a far cry from the noisy and always overcrowded drafting room. He went to his desk and drew a stack of drawings out of the bottom drawer. "Have a seat," he invited the other man, pulling his chair out from behind the desk. Ogden sat down, took the drawings from him, and hooked his pince-nez back on the bridge of his nose.

Alex went to the window to wait, bracing his knee against the low shelf under it and peering out at the falling rain. His ascension from drafting room to private office was still so recent, he hadn't had a chance yet to get tired of his view of Union Square from Sixteenth Street. The October day was dreary, but the incessant bustle of streetcars, cabs, carriages, and a hundred black umbrellas made it look almost gay, at least from this distance.

Six months ago he couldn't have given any of this up. In fact, by now he'd have already started wanting more — more praise, more power, more possessions, more feminine conquests. That's how he'd defined himself, evaluated his own worth — by toting up how much money he made and how many women he took to bed. Now he wanted only one woman, and Draper and Snow was just a building on Broadway where he came to work.

"Good God."

He looked around, smiling. "That bad?"

"Christ, Alex, no one's going to buy houses that look like this!"

"You've been in New York too long."

"Are you serious? Well — obviously you are."

"It's coming, John. Maybe not soon, but it's coming."

"Not in my lifetime."

Alex chuckled.

"Well, at least the partners will be relieved to know you won't be stealing any of our clients when you go."

"That's for sure," he agreed cheerfully.

Ogden stood up and came toward him, holding out his hand. "I wish you luck. God knows you're going to need it."

"Thanks." But he thought he saw grudging admiration in Ogden's bland features that was new. Before, he'd approved of Alex's work but not much of Alex; now that seemed to have reversed. The possibility pleased him.

"I certainly hope you'll stay in touch, Alex. Yours is one career I mean to follow closely."

"Yes, sir, I will."

"When do you plan to go?"

"I was thinking in a couple of weeks, if that's all right."

"I suppose so. Lucky for you the Cochrane house fell through, eh?"

He didn't answer.

"Well. See you around."

"Yes, sir. See you."

After he left, Alex sat down in the chair Ogden had just vacated. His hand went automatically to the stack of drawings on his desk and a wry smile tugged at the corners of his mouth. He hoped to hell he knew what he was doing; otherwise, Ogden was going to have the last laugh after all.

His smile faded slowly. He'd been looking forward to telling Ogden his news — or rather, to having told him. Now his temporary euphoria was dissipating. He had one more person to tell. He glanced at the telephone. If he asked to see her, she might say no. He couldn't say good-bye to Sara on the telephone. And he wanted to see Michael's face when he gave him his last gift.

He stood up, and grabbed his hat on the way out the door.

"Sara? Oh, pardon — you were taking a little cat nap?"

She sat up quickly, pushing her hair out of her eyes. "What do you want?"

Tasha came all the way into the bedroom and went immediately to the mirror over the dressing table. "Do you think this hat is quite correct with this dress? Madame

Bixiou insisted on it, but now I am not so positive."

"I asked you what you want."

She turned back, regarding Sara with upraised brows. "To tell you that Mr. Cochrane has called to say he will not be home for dinner. And so tonight, Sara, you are going to take me to the Waldorf Hotel, where I have wanted to dine for a very long time. I'll be back early — I'm going to Paquin's now for another fitting. Be ready at eight, will you?"

Sara didn't speak.

"Oh — I almost forgot. You have a visitor."

"No, I can't see anyone."

"Ah, too bad. Mr. McKie will be so disappointed."

She jolted to her feet. "My God — did you call him?"

"I?" She laughed. "But of course not. He is in the blue drawing room, Sara. I ordered tea and told him to wait for you. He looks very handsome today, I think. And rich. He looks — as your husband would say — like a man with lots of tin." She moved back to the door, expensive silk skirts rustling subtly. "I hope you enjoy yourselves," she murmured in her throaty, suggestive purr, and sidled out.

He thought at first that she was ill. She stood in the drawing room doorway clasping and unclasping her hands and smiling at him with a frail gladness that hurt him to see. "Sara? How are you? Have you been all right?"

"Yes, yes, I'm fine." She couldn't take her eyes off him. His being here was a miracle — she didn't care what had brought him.

She didn't look fine. She'd put powder under her eyes — he could see it, smell its fragrance — to disguise the dark crescents there, but she hadn't succeeded. Her lips were pale, her complexion paler; even her hair, freshly brushed, lacked the magic, satiny shine he was used to. Into the lengthening, disturbing silence, he said the first thing that came into his head. "I hardly recognized Tasha just now. What's happened to her?"

"What do you mean?"

"She looked different. And she seemed — I don't know — more sure of herself, somehow." And she'd stared at him oddly, almost as if she knew a secret. "She's never said anything about us, has she, Sara?"

The temptation to tell him almost overpowered her. But her situation was so sordid, so shameful, that she could never find the words to say to him that she was being blackmailed by a gypsy for committing adultery. More than that, she knew how he would react: with outrage and indignation and a thoroughly masculine need to rescue her. But she was beyond the possibility of rescue, and if he tried he would only make everything worse.

"No, of course not, what could she say? She doesn't know anything. She said you looked different too," she rushed on, forcing a smile. "She said you looked rich."

His smile was just as false. "I'm about to get a lot poorer. That's what I've come to tell you." There was no other way to say it. "Sara, I'm going away."

Her face crumbled before she could turn aside. She got her hands up to cover her mouth; miraculously, she didn't cry. She backed away and sat on the arm of the sofa because it was closest. She felt leveled, cut down, and violently determined not to let him know. Stupidly, as if it mattered, she asked, "But what about Eden?"

That shocked him. "You mean you didn't know? Ben's ordered work on it stopped indefinitely."

"No, I didn't know." She didn't care. "When did he do that?"

"Two weeks ago. The day after I saw you at Rector's."

"I'm not sorry. I hated it. Oh — forgive me —"

"For what? I despised it."

She took a deep breath, gathering herself. "Where will you go?"

"California. I'm going to try to set up on my own in San Francisco. Build houses there."

"Oh, Alex, that's good. I'm so glad for you. It feels right," she said truthfully, "and I know you'll succeed." But she was out of control; her face turned red and she had to stop talking. When she heard the maid coming with the tea cart, she jumped up and went to the window, keeping her back to the room.

Alex stood still, thwarted and helpless, while the maid fiddled with cups and napkins and uncovered a plate of sandwiches.

"Will there be anything else, ma'am?"

"No, nothing."

The maid sent Alex one quick, curious glance and withdrew.

She ought to turn around, pour tea, speak to him — she was making a mess of this! But she couldn't move. Couldn't. Not yet.

Alex couldn't stand it. "If you want me

to stay, I will. Say one word, Sara, and I won't go."

That made her whip around. "Don't say that. It can't have anything to do with me."

"It has everything to do with you."

"No, no, no —"

He went to her and took her hands, holding her still. "Yes. I can't lose you and my work at the same time. Sara, I need something."

"What do you mean?"

"Did you know that Draper and Snow offered me a partnership?"

"Ben told me. I was so proud —"

"It meant I'd have to keep building Edens for the rest of my life. If I could have had you, I might've done it — might not even have minded."

"Oh, no —"

"But without you, it's impossible. I hate Ben's house, I hate Kubla Khan —"

"Kubla Khan?"

"The house Marshall Farley wants now in Newport — I told you about it."

"I remember."

"Sara, I've got to have my work, and I can't do it in New York. So I have to go."

She nodded vigorously. "Yes, I see that. You have to go." She started to cry.

"Sara, don't." She tried to pull her hands

away, but he wouldn't let go. "I want to touch you, hold you. Can we go somewhere?"

She just shook her head. "Servants," she got out finally in a whisper.

He growled a vulgar oath. Because he was familiar with every variety of adulterous intrigue, he understood the need for secrecy. But now he loathed it because it degraded Sara, degraded them both. "Over here," he muttered harshly, "behind the goddamn door."

She let herself be led, and when he embraced her, pressing her against the wall at her back, she let him do that, too. The solid feel of him steadied her, even though they were both trembling. She closed her eyes and held him, and tried not to think that it was for the last time. "Darling, darling," she murmured, and that was for the last time, too. "When will you go?"

"A few weeks."

"Will you build houses like the one in the drawing you showed me?" He nodded. "Good. It was so beautiful."

"Did you like it, Sara?"

"Oh, yes."

"You asked me who it was for, and I lied and said no one. But it was for you. It was the only way I could think of to make love to you."

She let him kiss her — could not have denied him to save her life. Her lips were salty from tears; he tasted them on the tip of his tongue, cradling her face in his palms and moving her head slowly from side to side. His sweetness broke her heart. But her breath caught when his slippery fingers slid softly to her throat, her chest, and then inside the thin lapels of her Eton jacket. He stilled his hands on the sides of her breasts, holding her, while his tongue caressed her mouth open and entered her sleekly. She clutched him harder, moaning, feeling her own helpless seduction.

He had only meant to stop her tears and soothe her. But his need was too strong and he'd buried it too shallowly. "Come to me again," he whispered against her lips. "Let me love you. We can go anywhere, out of town if you like. We'll be discreet, no one will —" She tried to say no, but he kissed the word back into her mouth. "Please, Sara. Just once more. Don't make me leave you —"

"No, Alex. I can't, I can't."

He stopped asking. It was cruel to do this to her. She had always been stronger; now it was time for him to try to help her.

"Don't cry." He brushed her new tears away with his fingers and smiled at her tenderly. "I'm sorry, Sara. I'm such a selfish bastard."

"No, you're not."

"Yeah, I am. I've had it all my own way for a long, long time." But he couldn't think of anything he'd ever done that deserved a punishment this hard. "I shouldn't have come, I know it. But I couldn't say good-bye to you on the telephone —"

"No, no, I'm glad you came!" She took his hands and kissed them, pressed them to her hot cheeks. "I'm glad, and I don't care —" She broke off, and jumped in reaction to the distant slam of a door.

"Mummy!"

Alex stepped back and she twisted past him, fumbling for her handkerchief, patting her hair. "I'm in here, darling!" she called, and the forced gaiety in her voice hurt him more than anything had. She wiped her eyes in haste and squared her shoulders and barely got the handkerchief back into her pocket before Michael raced into the room, a canvas bookbag banging over his shoulder.

His face lit up in pure, guileless delight. "Alex!" he shouted, and made a run for him.

Alex knelt and caught him in his arms, hugging him. A rush of emotion swamped him suddenly and with no warning. He looked past Michael's shoulder at Sara, searching her stricken face for a clue to the unexpected depth of his own feelings for this boy. The skinny arms around his neck loosened and they both pulled back to grin at each other. He might have been looking into Sara's gray-blue eyes, so exact was the likeness. Michael's hair had darkened slightly, but it was still shiny, still as soft as corn silks. "Great heavens, you've grown a foot." He massaged one sharp-boned shoulder through Michael's jacket. "How's that collarbone?"

"All healed up! Is our house finished yet?"

"Not yet."

"Did you get the letter I sent you?"

"Yes."

"Did you like the picture?"

"I loved it."

Michael glanced back at his mother. "I sent him a picture I drew of his house, Mum." She looked puzzled. "His *dream* house. He told me everything it would have, and I drew it. It was a surprise, right, Alex?"

"Right."

"It had stuff like lots of light and ways to get outside and neat colors and everything."

Alex nodded, confirming it. "You did a beautiful job. I could almost build it just from the drawing." Michael beamed. "I've got a surprise for you, too."

"You do, really? What is it? Is it here?" Alex rose and went to the sofa, on which rested a small, square box of varnished wood. Blowing her nose, Sara saw that the box opened with a padlock through a metal hasp. When Alex took a key from his pocket and handed it to him with the box, she thought that it hardly mattered what was inside, and wondered how he could have known that Michael's favorite things in all the world — this year, at least — were boxes with locks that opened with keys.

But what was inside proved even more wondrous. It was a set of child-sized drafting tools: T-square, a compass, triangle, protractor, templates in all shapes and sizes, lead holders, brushes and erasers, even a miniature slide rule.

"Oh, boy!" cried Michael, and immediately began taking them all out of their neat velour receptacles.

"Alex, it's wonderful. Wherever did you find it?"

"I had someone make it." He screwed up his face suddenly. "Botheration," he cursed — for Michael's benefit. "Forgot drawing paper. Could you get him some, Sara?"

"Yes, of course. Tomorrow."

He crouched down beside Michael again. "Not sure when I'll be seeing you again, pal," he said lightly.

"Where are you going?"

"Out to California."

He didn't look up; his tone was casual. "Are you coming back?"

He couldn't bring himself to say no. But he couldn't lie and say yes. "Not sure," he repeated. "Could be."

"Can I come and visit you?"

Alex looked up involuntarily, and Michael followed his glance. Sara's eyes were too bright, her face flushed again. Michael looked away quickly, but she saw with her mother's knowledge that he already understood much too much. Politeness and an innate delicacy would keep him from saying anything more to Alex about visiting, for he would rather die than embarrass anyone. When she could speak she said, "California's a long way away. Maybe Mr. McKie wouldn't mind if you wrote to him."

Michael's voice was subdued now. "May I, Alex?"

"I hope you will. I'll write back. We could send each other pictures, of houses or whatever we want."

"Yeah. And now I can *build* your house for you — you know, a model."

"That would be great." He reached out and stroked Michael's yellow hair, then cupped his hand around the back of his thin stalk of a neck. "Take care of your mother," he instructed softly.

He took it as seriously as it was intended. "I will." Suddenly he threw his arms around Alex and hugged him. Sara saw tears squeeze past his tightly closed lashes, and she had to look away. A second later she went out of the room.

Alex found her in the foyer a few minutes later, waiting for him beside the door. Neither spoke. What was left to say? Only one thing. "I love you," in a whisper.

"I love you, Alex."

"Be safe."

"I will. I hope . . ." She trailed off. He put his hand on the door knob. Why were they putting each other through this again? Still, he delayed, and she was glad.

"I'll send you my address when I'm settled."

"Send it to Michael."

They smiled fleetingly, looked away.

"If you ever need me, Sara —"

"I know. And you."

He nodded.

She put her hand over his just for a second, whispered, "Good-bye," and stepped back.

"Good-bye, Sara." He pulled the door open and walked out.

She closed it immediately, not watching him out of sight. She stood still for a moment, then turned away to find Michael.

# Nineteen

She woke up disoriented, cold, and cramped, with a crick in her neck. It was morning, and yet the light was on — Michael's light. Then she remembered.

She'd fallen asleep in his bed hours ago, after soothing him free of the terrors of his latest nightmare. "Don't go till I'm asleep, okay?" he'd begged, and they'd drifted off together in the midst of her own yawn-punctuated story of the Pied Piper. The last thing she remembered was Michael murmuring in unison with her, "Great rats, small rats, lean rats, brawny rats. . . ."

She sat up, careful not to wake him, and pulled her robe more tightly around her shoulders, shivering a little. Only his face showed above the covers, serious as always, as if he had weighty matters to ponder even in his sleep. She ran a finger lightly across the satin hem of the blanket under his chin, recalling the halting details of the dream he'd sobbed out to her last night. They were all — he, she, and Ben — in the garden at Eden. She and Michael were picking flowers while Ben sat at his desk and talked on the telephone. The new maze was finished; Michael was dying to try it. "Go on in," said Ben from his desk. Michael ran toward the maze, excited — but suddenly he stopped.

"I wanted to go in, but then I got scared. Dad kept saying, 'Go in, go in,' but I wouldn't go in and he got madder and madder and he started yelling. So I went in, and I was in it, and there were these monsters waiting around all the corners. I wanted to run back and get out, but Daddy wouldn't let me. So I kept going because there was a lady at the end who would get me and save me." His swimming eyes widened. "It was *you*," he realized as he said it. "But I never got to the end, I never saw you, I just kept running and running from the monsters and Daddy yelling."

"It was just a dream," she'd told him, "just a terrible dream, and now it's over." She'd had no other words to console him, and she'd tormented herself then as she did now with the thought that she would never know if she'd helped him or hurt him by sacrificing herself to her pitiful burlesque of a marriage. But for as long as she could be the lady who would save him, she would never give him up to Ben, and ultimately it didn't matter how much of herself she lost in the process.

But she hated what she couldn't change, and she hated what was happening to Michael. Another child might react to his situation with rebelliousness or aggression; but Michael only paled, rarefied, grew more attenuated, more exquisitely self-effacing. It was his way of saving himself, she knew — to become invisible. But how she longed to see him throw a truly vile tantrum, or shout out some vulgar curse of his father's!

She got up from the bed and stretched stiffly.

"Mummy?"

"Go back to sleep a little longer. It's Saturday, you can stay in bed late if you like." She kissed his eyelids closed gently, straightened, and tiptoed out of the room.

Silently passing the closed door to Ben's bedroom, she slowed and then stopped, arrested by a sound. A voice. Not Ben's. Something clicked in her brain, a fatal, premonitory certitude. She could hear the slow pounding of her blood in her temples. She went closer. Forehead touching the door, looking down at her bare toes.

She heard a woman's high, rising moan,

451

and now Ben's gruff voice, low-pitched, asking a question. She saw her hand go out to the doorknob and begin to turn it. *Really?* a voice inside asked, eerily calm. *Is this what you're going to do?* The turning knob stopped. She could either turn it silently back and steal away, or she could press on the handle and push the door open. The significance of the choice paralyzed her because she knew it would change her life.

The voices beyond the door rose, high and low, taking turns, the exchange growing more rapid, the intervals of silence shorter. She wouldn't have understood that double cadence or known so well what it betokened before the night she'd spent with Alex. Her hand on the knob began to shake. Without a sound, her straightening arm pushed the door ajar an inch, two inches, three.

Enough to see the lovers in Ben's bed in three-quarter profile, oblivious to widening doors or anything else except each other. Tasha's dark hair streamed across her shoulders, hiding her face as she gazed down at Ben, her arms braced on either side of his pillow, and urged him on with vulgar, harsh-voiced inducements. The grip he had on her breasts looked painful.

"Want this, little whore?" he grunted, thrusting up in her, powerful thighs straining. "Do it, yesss," she hissed, riding him, grinding herself against him. She threw her head back and bared her clenched teeth, grimacing at the ceiling, while his hands slid to her hips and squeezed until his knuckles turned white.

Sara watched them with an altogether odd impassivity. Revulsion was her dominant emotion, not distress. Anger would come soon, but for now this shameful betrayal couldn't touch the core of her; she might almost have been watching the passionate acrobatics of strangers for all the power this act had to cut her.

Tasha thrust her hands under Ben's buttocks, humping him violently and grunting her explicit demands. But her stallion had gone lifeless beneath her, and at last she craned her neck over her shoulder to follow his slack-jawed gaze. She gasped, but almost immediately a subtle look of sly, vindictive triumph replaced the shock in her face. Curiously, that didn't surprise Sara, either.

She might have gone on observing the frozen tableau, waiting with detached interest to see who would speak first, but a noise behind her made her turn. Michael was coming toward her, scuffing along in slippers and bathrobe. If she'd been talking to Dad, maybe he could too, his smiling face as good as told her, especially since this time he hadn't heard any voices raised in anger between them.

She jerked the door closed on a reflex, slamming it, and moved toward Michael purposefully. What happened next was unpremeditated, her words unscreened, for once, by any mental censor.

"Listen, Michael, remember when you and I went to the Berkshires last year and stayed overnight with the Dearborns?"

"Sure."

"You just took one little suitcase and you packed it yourself, remember?"

"Yes."

"I want you to pack that same suitcase now — it's in the back of your closet — and put in enough clothes for a day and a night. Don't forget underwear and socks. Do it now, Michael, right now."

"Where're we going?"

"We're going on a little trip, just the two of us."

"Where?"

For the first time she faltered; she had no idea where they were going. "It's a surprise. Just do it, darling, and don't ask me

454

any more questions or it'll spoil the surprise."

His gray eyes clouded with worry — she could never hide anything from him. "Is it a good surprise or a bad surprise?" he asked anxiously.

"It's an adventure, and we don't always know what to expect from adventures. Now, hurry." She kissed him, turned him around, and gave him a little push. *"Hurry."*

He glanced back uncertainly and then scampered for his room.

Doubts swamped her as soon as he was out of sight. What if she was cheating him out of a choice he had the right to make himself? But he was only a child! He was sensitive, yes, uncannily acute, and probably wiser now than she would ever be — but he was still a child, and she had to take responsibility for him. Walking past Ben's closed and now silent door, she remembered with photographic precision the scene that she'd just witnessed, and it hardened her shaky resolve. She was leaving and she was taking Michael with her.

Fear and excitement pumped through her in equal measure as she pulled a small trunk out of her own closet and began throwing clothes into it at random. She felt like an escaping criminal — guilty, terrified, and exhilarated all at once. Where would they go? If only Lauren were back from Europe, they could stay with her. The elderly Hubbards would welcome them, of course, but Sara was reluctant to impose on them without Lauren being there. Well, no matter, they could stay in a hotel, at least until —

"What do you think you're doing?" She jerked up, startled in spite of the fact that she had known he would come, had even been expecting him. He filled the doorway, already dressed, his florid features blotchy with anger — or perhaps it was residual passion. "I'm leaving you," she said steadily. "I'm taking Michael with me."

"No, you're not."

"I'm divorcing you, Ben."

He laughed. "Like hell. For what?"

"Adultery. At last I've got a witness: myself." He came all the way into the room, his bulky body seeming, as always, to dwarf it. She didn't flinch or back away. But she was gripping a green tulle petticoat in both hands as if it were a shield. Through her teeth she asked, "Did you sleep with her all summer while I was in Newport?"

"None of your business. You might as well put that stuff away, you're not going anywhere."

"You're mistaken."

"It doesn't matter what you saw, no one's going to believe you."

"This time I'm willing to take the chance to find out."

She thought his face couldn't get any redder, but it did. Instead of shouting, though, he took a different tack. "You know what kind of a scandal this'll cause once it goes public? If you really care about Michael the way you say you do, you won't put him through that."

She hurled the petticoat on the bed. "You ruddy hypocrite! You don't give a damn about Michael's feelings and you never have. You don't care how a scandal will hurt him, you only care about how it'll hurt *you*." Her lips curled spitefully. "Think about it, Ben — millionaire tycoon caught by his own wife in bed with a Jewish seamstress. How do you think they'll like that at the New York Club?"

"You goddamn bitch —"

He moved toward her and she shrank back, hands raised for protection. "If you don't want a scandal, then don't fight me," she said fast, trying not to stammer. "It doesn't have to be ugly, we can do it quietly in another state, on grounds other than adultery. If we both —"

"Not on your life."

Again anger overwhelmed her fear of him. "Bastard! Bloody, hypocritical —"

"Who's a hypocrite?" he raged, hands clenched into white, murderous fists. "You try to do this to me, Sara, and I'll ruin you! I'll countersue on the same grounds!"

"What do you mean?"

"I know about you and McKie!"

All the blood drained from her face; her legs gave out and she had to sit down hard on the edge of the bed. Once again she let the chance slip away to deny it. Her mind was a jumble of nightmare dread. What did it mean? How would he use this new weapon against her?

"I've known for months," he crowed softly, fleshy lips curving into a smile.

"Months." She stared down at her limp hands. Revulsion twisted inside her. "You've known for months." He and Tasha were two of a kind, then, incapable of honest feelings or of straightforwardness about anything. She marveled at their *coldness*. She wanted out of this murk. "You don't deserve your son," she said quietly. "I'm taking him from you."

"No, I'm taking him from you."

"Hi, Dad."

Ben whirled; Sara shot to her feet. In the doorway Michael grinned uncertainly, dressed in his Norfolk jacket and knicker-bockers and holding his suitcase.

"Well!" Ben exclaimed heartily. "Got your bag all packed, have you?"

"Yes, sir."

Sara said, "Go downstairs and wait for me."

"That's a good idea," Ben seconded. "I'll be right down."

"Are you coming too, Dad?"

"Well, now, there's been a little change in plans. Your mother's not coming with us; it's just going to be you and me."

"No," Sara cried involuntarily. Fighting for control, she sent Michael a ghastly smile. "Go down and wait for me," she repeated, "your father and I have to talk for a few minutes." Michael didn't move. "Please, darling —"

Just then Tasha appeared in the door behind Michael. "Take the boy downstairs," Ben ordered, "and call for the carriage."

"Yes, Mr. Cochrane." She reached for Michael's hand, but he slipped away.

"Mummy?" He blinked fast to keep from crying.

Sara started toward the door. Ben stepped in front of her, blocking her. "Now, I said!" he bellowed, at the same moment he reached back with one hand and slammed the door shut in Michael's face.

She sprang at him and he hit her across the cheek with his open palm. She fell on the bed, stunned, but with enough presence of mind left not to cry out — Michael might still be close enough to hear. She tried to stand, but Ben hovered over her, legs spread, breathing hard.

"I thought we settled this a long time ago. You're never leaving me. I took Michael away once to teach you a lesson, but I guess you didn't learn it. This time he's going away for a long, long time, with me and his Aunt Tasha, and you aren't going to do a damn thing about it. Because if you do, if you make a *peep,* I'll fix it so you never see him again."

"For the love of God, Ben, you *can't* do this —"

"I'm doing it." He spun around, went to the door, and yanked it open.

Jumping up, she ran after him and caught him in the hall. "Please don't, please don't." She pulled on his arm to stop him. He pushed her off roughly and kept walking. Over the bannister she saw that the foyer was empty — Michael must be outside already. She threw herself between Ben and the stairs, blocking the way with her outstretched arms. "You can't have him!" she shrieked, pummeling him with her fists when he butted into her, forcing her down a step at a time.

"You want me to hurt you? Is that what you want?"

"You can't take him! Damn you —" She flung herself at him, screaming, nails raking across his cheek. She saw his hand fly backward, then whip toward her face. The blow was shocking; the force of it threw her against the wall. She lost her balance and fell down the last six steps to the hall below.

She lost consciousness, but not for long. When she could see past the shimmering gray cloud of dots blurring her vision, she made out Ben's white moon face frowning down at her, and she felt his big hands surrounding her biceps.

"You okay, Sare?"

She whispered, "Don't take him, Ben. Please don't take him."

He let her go and sat back on his haunches. "You don't give me any choice."

"I won't leave you, I promise."

"You're probably lying. I got to teach you a lesson, and this is the only way to do it."

"Ben —"

But he stood up and backed away from her, watching her until he reached the door. For a second she thought she saw regret darken his eyes, blotting out the spite. Then he was gone.

She got up slowly; she had to lean against the wall to stay on her feet. Bruised hip, sore ribs, bump on the head, she inventoried automatically; scraped shins, palms, elbows. Not serious. Limping, she made it across the hall to the front door and dragged it open.

In the street, the carriage was just pulling up. Tasha helped Michael inside, then got up behind him. Ben called to the coachman, "Grand Central," and climbed in too. Sara took two steps out onto the porch and stopped. Michael saw her; his small face in the window looked frightened and bewildered, but he smiled at her. He waved. She lifted her hand, but her mouth was trembling too much, and she couldn't smile back. The carriage rolled off.

She turned immediately and went back into the house. She crossed to the telephone and gave Alex's number to the oper-

462

ator in a shaking voice she couldn't control. "Sorry, ma'am, no answer." No — of course, it was Saturday, he wouldn't be at work. If he still went to work. Moving more quickly now, she went to her tiny study, found her telephone book, and gave his home number to a new operator.

"Hello?"

Somewhere in the back of her mind it registered that he'd been sleeping. "Alex, can you help me?"

"Who is this? Sara?"

No wonder he didn't know her voice; she hardly recognized it herself. "Ben's taken Michael, kidnapped him."

"What?"

"They've gone to Grand Central Depot in the carriage — Tasha too — and I have to stop them but I can't do it by myself. Alex, can you come here?"

"Yes."

"If you can get a cab and pick me up, I think we can stop them."

"I'll be there as soon as I can."

"Thank you." She hung up and ran upstairs to get dressed.

# Twenty

Alex opened the black hansom cab's door and leapt to the pavement while the vehicle was still moving. Sprinting up the steps, he lifted his hand, but the door jerked open under it.

"Thank God," cried Sara. She had been watching for him through the beveled glass sidelight.

He took her arm when she started away without another word, holding her, his other hand going to the side of her face. "Jesus God, what did he do to you?"

"I fell," she said automatically. No — the time for lies was over. "He hit me, and I fell down the steps. Come on," she pleaded over his numb curses, "we have to hurry." She hauled on his hand. "I'm all right, really. Come on!" She pulled him toward the hansom, gave the driver the destination herself — "Grand Central Depot, as fast as you can!" — and got in. Alex jumped up behind her and the cab jerked away.

They sat opposite each other, hunched forward, hands clasped. "I almost didn't wait for you," Sara confessed. "It took so *long.*"

"I'd have gotten here sooner, but we came up Sixth instead of Fifth Avenue, thinking it would be faster, and instead we ran into a mob."

"A mob?"

"The trainmen's union is picketing all along the Sixth Avenue Elevated, you can't get through." He squeezed her hands. "Sara, tell me what's happened."

"It happened so fast. I told Ben I was leaving him."

"Why?"

The obvious answer wasn't the answer at all, she realized. "I found him with Tasha this morning. In bed. I suppose it's been going on for months. It's why he wanted me out of the house all summer." Alex started to say something, but she shook her head. "No, but that's not really why I did it. I mean — it is, in a way, it's what brought it on. But it wasn't even a decision — I never really made up my mind to do it. All of a sudden I was doing it, and it felt so *right.* And yet — oh God, Alex, look what I've done," she whispered, horrified.

He could hardly stand to look at the deepening bruise on the side of her fore-head, the raw scrapes on her palms.

"Listen to me — whatever happens, you did the right thing. You had to leave him, Sara."

She stared back in misery, thinking but not saying that if she lost Michael, she would certainly not have done the right thing, and she would regret this day's decision for the rest of her life. She looked out the window. "Why are we going so slowly?" They were just turning onto Park Avenue from Thirty-fourth Street. "What's happening?"

Alex got up, opened the door, put one foot on the step, and leaned far out, peering north. There was nothing to see but carriages, carts, trolleys, and jitneys jammed front to back, moving a few feet, then stopping. "Can you see anything?" he called to the driver.

"Something's backin' 'em up," he answered laconically. "Can't tell what."

Alex resumed his seat, slamming the door.

"What did he say?"

"He doesn't know." He watched her twist her hands in her lap, teeth clamped on her bottom lip. "Ben's probably caught up in the same snarl," he told her. "We'll find him, Sara, don't worry."

She hardly heard. "When he took him

away the last time — I told you, remember?"

"Yes."

"He took him to a hunter's camp on the tip of Long Island. But he's much too clever to go there again. Unless we find them before they leave, I won't know where to start looking." She wouldn't even know where to go when they finally reached Grand Central — the Harlem Railroad depot, the New Haven, the Long Island —

"We'll find them," Alex repeated doggedly.

"I can't stand this." Every minute she almost jumped out to walk — surely it would be faster than this nerve-wracking crawl! — and each time the coach suddenly jolted forward, filling her with an agonizing burst of new hope.

Minutes later they crossed Thirty-eighth Street and the hansom came to a final halt. The driver yelled something; Alex jumped out of the cab. "What's that?"

"Can't go any farther, I'm turnin' off here and getting out. Might be them trainmen again, striking along Third and the Forty-second Street Spur into Grand Central. We can't get through."

Sara heard, and stepped down into the street with Alex. "Then we'll walk."

Alex paid the driver and ran to catch up

with her, taking her arm. He closed his mouth against all the reasons he could give for why she should turn back, knowing how futile it would be. At Thirty-ninth Street the sidewalk became almost as crowded as the street, with as many people hurrying toward them as there were pushing along beside them. "What's going on?" Alex asked a neatly dressed gentleman rushing southward.

"Strike! You can't get to Forty-second Street, there's hired strike breakers shoving everybody back down Park and Lexington. The Murray Hill Tunnel entrance is blocked so you can't even get into the station. I'm telling you, you can't go anywhere!" he called after them when Sara started off again and Alex hurried after her.

She scanned the cluttered avenue for signs of the Cochrane carriage returning south — "It's gray with maroon trim," she told Alex — but they never saw it. A patrol wagon full of uniformed policemen clattered northward in the southbound lane, bell clanging. The sidewalk crush worsened; Alex drew Sara to him and linked arms with her securely.

"You've got to go back." He had to raise his voice to be heard over the growing din. A man running behind them butted his shoulder and Alex bumped hard against Sara. She recovered and kept walking, pulling on his arm when she spotted openings between people ahead of them. "You heard what that man said," he persisted, "the station's closed. That means Ben can't get through either. If there are strike breakers up there, there's going to be violence. Let me go on by myself. You go up Fortieth to Fifth and go home, Sara, let me —"

"No. I have to find him. I have to find him."

That was all she would say, and he gave up.

"Let's walk in the street," she said, pulling on him.

He let her lead him over the curb, realizing it was probably safer in the street now because the crowd on the sidewalk was getting rough.

She twisted her ankle in her high-heeled boots on the uneven cobbles, but after a few limping steps the pain faded. The sound of shouting grew louder in the distance, but it was impossible to see what was ahead because of the stalled vehicles blocking the street. All at once the crowd on the sidewalk surged out into the street in a great, unruly wave, and a second later bright orange flames shot out of the sides of a wooden building fronting the sidewalk.

"Arsonists," Alex guessed grimly, shoving a way through the new crush with his shoulder.

Sara lost her shawl; her hat had been torn off minutes ago. Shouts mingled with the screams of terrified horses rearing and jerking the reins to the stranded carts and carriages behind them. Alarm bells rang frantically and incessantly. There was no such thing as lanes in the street anymore; police wagons battling their way north through the mob were as stationary as every other conveyance. From the three-story rooftop of a restaurant up ahead, two boys not much older than Michael hurled bricks at the crowd below. People leaned out of windows and hung from telegraph poles; below them the mob swayed back and forth from sidewalk to sidewalk. There were few women in the crowd now; those who were left were tough-looking, some carrying pickets declaring their support for the strikers.

"We can't get through!" Alex shouted, both arms around Sara's shoulders. "You have to get out!"

She shook her head violently. "Michael's

in there! *Could* be in there!" she shouted back. All of a sudden his grip on her tightened and he lunged sideways in an ungainly pivot; in the next second a wildeyed man in shirtsleeves swung a wide wooden picket down across his shoulder. Alex grunted. Sara registered the words "Fight Corrupt Bosses" before the man hoisted his sign to strike again. Alex twisted around, bracing, shielding her with his back, but the crowd intervened and the sign descended on someone else's head before the picketer was lost to sight. When Alex turned around, Sara was gone.

She could see him clearly no more than six feet away, a head taller than anyone around him; but it might as well have been sixty feet because of the densely packed bodies between them. "Alex! Alex!" He didn't hear. When he turned, she couldn't get her arm up to wave to him because of the crush. The beginnings of panic snaked through her. She shoved as hard as she could against the stiff, moving wall of people pressing her back, back, but it was futile; she was as helpless as a twig in a current of flooding water.

A horse-drawn jitney lay on its side on the pavement; standing on top, a man heaved paving stones at the helmeted guardsmen surrounding him, clubs raised. The crowd waded into the fight, Sara borne along with them helplessly. She saw a policeman's red, sweating face looming above her, his club raised high in the air over her head. She screamed; he saw her, wheeled, and brought the club down on the shoulder of the boy beside her.

Horses hauling another patrol wagon reared and plunged, so close she could smell their hot breath and see the terror in their rolling eyes. Men in the clogged street lunged for their bridles. A policeman with his feet hanging out of the tail of the wagon was hauled out by his heels and surrounded. The other guardsmen leapt out and charged the jeering crowd, night sticks striking right and left. Bricks and bottles flew from all sides. Something struck Sara between the shoulder blades and she stumbled, breath gone. On one knee, hands pressed to the cobblestones, she tried to stand, but at that moment gunshots rattled over the shouts and the turmoil, and panic swept through the mob. A man's hard thigh struck her shoulder and she lost her balance, falling. She couldn't scream; it wouldn't have helped anyway. A booted foot smacked into her hip. She rolled, throwing up her hands to shield her face.

"Lady, get up!"

She opened her eyes to see a huge paw of a hand reaching for her. She took it in both of hers and was jerked to her feet by an enormous black man with a beard; a button on his chest said, "No Wage Cut, Porters in Sympathy with Trainmen."

"Get outa here, lady, they're shootin'!" he yelled at her.

She pulled out of his grip when he began to lead her south, away from the violence. "I have to find my little boy!"

Shots rang out again. The big man flinched, mouthed, "Good luck," turned, and ran.

The crowd had begun to thin at the first shots, but groups still clustered in doorways, calling insults to the police and throwing stones whenever they turned their backs. Limping, her dress torn, hair loose, Sara staggered off northward. The stampede was over and the devastation in its wake was visible now. Broken pickets and bricks and boards littered the cobblestones, and the sidewalks were lined with broken glass. Smoke from a burning coal cart filled the air with acrid soot; the frantic neighing of stranded horses sounded from everywhere, pitiful and nerve-wracking. Sara scanned the wide corner of Forty-first Street, searching for anything familiar. Twenty feet away a man in shirtsleeves and torn waistcoat had his back to her, but she recognized the set of his shoulders and his tawny hair.

"Alex!"

He turned, and the raw anguish in his face changed to intense, heartfelt relief. They came together, oblivious to the people running past and the shouted orders of militiamen to keep moving.

"Have you seen him?" she asked helplessly.

"Not yet." He kept to himself what he had seen. "They must have gone back, Sara."

"But we have to look."

"Yes." He took her hand, and they began to walk against what was left of the still-fleeing crowd.

She saw the carriage before he did. On its side in front of the Park Avenue Oyster Palace, the lathered horses standing still in the dangling reins, exhausted. Five men hunkered behind it, hands braced on the edge of the roof that touched the pavement. On the count of three they all heaved, and the heavy carriage rose up on two wheels, teetered, and dropped onto the other two, bouncing gently. Sara dropped Alex's hand and ran.

"Stand back, lady, there's somebody in there," warned a policeman in uniform, reaching for her.

She eluded him, crying out, "Michael!"

Another policeman was yanking the door open. Michael looked out, white-faced, huddled on the floor between the seats. "Mummy?" He scrambled down unassisted and ran to her. Sara dropped to her knees in the street, unable to speak. His high-speed impact nearly knocked her over; she hugged him back fiercely and they both burst into tears. Alex stood beside them and watched their sobbing, swaying, wordless embrace.

"There's somebody else in here. Big guy. Somebody give me a hand."

Sara lifted her head, blinking to see past the tears as Alex and two other policemen returned to the carriage. Michael choked out, "It's Dad, he's really sick, I don't know what's wrong with him," just as the men lifted Ben from the carriage and laid him on the pavement beside the door. Sara stood up slowly, still holding Michael's hand. They walked together to the still, prostrate figure on the ground and knelt beside him.

"This your husband, ma'am?" She

nodded. The policeman said no more, but over Sara's shoulder he gave Alex a quick, bleak shake of the head.

"Daddy?" Michael faltered, touching his father's arm gingerly. Ben's face was the color of beeswax. "Tasha jumped out and ran away, Mum, but Dad said not to move, we were better off in the carriage."

"Sare?"

She looked down at Ben. He was sweating now, but still white as paper, pressing one hand to his chest. She covered his hand with hers and leaned over him.

"I wasn't going far," he said in a wheezy gasp, blinking up at her. "Wouldn't've kept him so long this time, either." She couldn't answer. "Sorry about Tasha. Jeez, that was . . ." He shook his head once. Finally he muttered, "Stupid."

"You have to rest, Ben. Save your strength."

He made a weak gesture of impatience with his free hand; for a second the old belligerence gleamed in his black eyes. But he was strong enough only to whisper. "Money problems coming."

"It's all right."

"Big problems. Might have to sell stuff, but you'll be all right."

"Don't talk, Ben."

"Maybe not a millionaire, but still rich as hell." His laugh turned into a desperate gasp for breath.

Sara looked up. The nearest policeman said, "There's a wagon on the way, ma'am."

Ben subsided, exhausted, face gray and clammy. Michael, weeping beside Sara, touched his father's hand with one finger just for a second, then jerked away, afraid. Sara leaned close to Ben and whispered in his ear. His eyes flickered open, but they were glassy now. She squeezed his hand and whispered again.

Ben took a slow, shuddering breath and fixed his gaze on his son. "Michael."

"Sir?"

He opened his lips, but only air came out. Sara stopped breathing, clutching his arm with all ten fingers. "Michael," he tried again.

"Sir?"

"Something I never told you." Now his breath was a grotesque rattle deep in his throat and his lips were blue.

"Yes, sir?" Michael quavered through his tears.

Ben finally said it. "Love you. Always have."

Michael's pinched face was transformed.

"Really, Dad? Really?"

But Ben didn't answer; his lashes fluttered once more before his eyes rolled slowly back into his head and his stertorous breathing ceased. He didn't hear Michael say, "I love you too, Dad." He didn't hear anything else at all.

# Twenty-one

"Mrs. Wiggs? Are you home?" Alex put his head in the door his landlady always left ajar in defiance of constant warnings from friends and tenants that anyone could walk right in and steal everything she owned, and peered inside the cluttered parlor. Plenty of furniture, knicknacks, gewgaws and bric-a-brac, but no landlady.

"Alexander?" came a call from beyond the beaded curtain between parlor and kitchen.

"Yes, ma'am."

A moment later Mrs. Wiggs bustled out, drying her hands on her apron. Her big, pink-faced smile collapsed when she saw the suitcase on the floor by the door. "I'll swan, you're really doing it," she said tragically, fat shoulders slumping. "Lighting out on a train on Christmas Eve. I swear, I don't believe you've got the sense God gave a flea."

"You're probably right. But my ticket says December 24, 6:37 P.M., so I guess I've got to go."

Mrs. Wiggs clucked her tongue, a loud, sharp sound connoting powerful disdain. "And of course nobody's ever *changed* a ticket to a more sensible day before. They never *heard* of that at the train station."

Alex smiled and shrugged but kept quiet, experience having taught him he was no match for his landlady's sarcasm.

She jerked her head at the suitcase. "That all you're carrying?"

"I sent everything else ahead."

"Hmph. You couldn't stuff enough *underwear* in that little bag for four days."

He grinned. "Quit griping and be nice to me. I want to remember you smiling, not scowling." To his astonishment, Mrs. Wiggs's eyes suddenly welled with tears.

His dismay was nothing compared to hers. She scoured her cheeks roughly and stuck out a damp, raw-boned hand for him to shake. "Well, go if you're going."

He squeezed her hand gently between both of his. "I'll write when I get settled, to let you know my address."

"If you want to."

"Will you write back?"

"Maybe."

"It's been a good five years. I'll never have another landlady like you."

"That's a safe bet."

He arched a brow. "Admit it — you're going to miss me."

"Hah. I wish you'd left two months ago when you said you were going to. Could've doubled the rent and now I'd be a rich woman."

Alex's smile grew fixed. He might as well have left two months ago, considering the way things had turned out.

"Least you've got a job to go to now. I guess that's something," she said grudgingly.

"I guess it is, if I want to keep eating food and sleeping indoors." In truth, he was excited about his new job. Thanks to Professor Stern — again — he'd been invited to bid on and had won a contract to design the new foreign language students' union on the Berkeley campus. His brain was buzzing with ideas and he was impatient to start work; he even had plans to hire an assistant draftsman — McKie & Associates' first associate. The commission he would earn was modest by Draper and Snow's standards, but considering that he was almost broke, he'd have taken even less.

He reached into his pocket and pulled out a flat oblong box. "Merry Christmas," he said, handing it to his landlady.

"My law, what've you gone and done?" Her scowl deepened; she took hold of the box as if it might contain spiders. "Do I have to open it now?"

"Unless you want to hurt my feelings."

"Hmph." She lifted the lid and stared down at the buttery-soft yellow cashmere scarf he'd bought her. She was silent for so long, he decided she hated it. He was sure of it when she finally looked up, eyes swimming again, and said, "Well, that beats all."

"You can take it back. I got it at Buckley's, I'm sure they'll —"

"Oh, hush up." She went to one of the cluttered tables the parlor was full of, this one covered with a pile of brightly wrapped packages. She picked out a square box covered in red foil, brought it back, and shoved it into his hands. "Here. Merry Christmas yourself."

"Do I have to open it now?"

Mrs. Wiggs's smiles were rare and worth waiting for. "Unless you want a kick in the shins."

Chuckling, he opened his present. "Well, well," he said softly. "Great minds."

"Like it?"

He lifted the yellow knitted scarf out of the box and draped it around his neck. "I love it."

"I was halfway done making it when it hit me that you won't have any use for it out there. Too hot."

"No, you're wrong, San Francisco's got perfect scarf-wearing weather. Really," he insisted when she looked skeptical. "It's cold as a witch's left tit about half the time."

"Go on with you!" She cuffed him on the shoulder, pretending his language shocked her — an old game they'd been playing for years.

"Thank you very much. I'll think of you whenever I wear it."

"Oh, pshaw."

He put his arms around her soft, stout body and hugged her. "I don't know anybody but you who says 'pshaw,'" he told her, inhaling her unique vanilla scent. "Never even knew how to pronounce it till I met you."

She pushed him away, fumbling in her apron pocket for her handkerchief. "Well, go on, then. Six-thirty, didn't you say? Better hurry up so you can sit on a train with a bunch of strangers on Christmas Eve." She blew her nose and glared at him.

"Take care of yourself."

"Oh, sure."

He backed out the door, feeling like

crying with her. "I'll write to you."

She flapped her hand. Her nose was bright red.

"Bye, Mrs. Wiggs."

"Go *on*."

He sent her a last grim smile. He was halfway to the front door when she called to him. "Ma'am?"

"You build beautiful buildings out there, Alexander, you hear me?"

He grinned, but his nod was solemn. "Yes, ma'am. That's what I hope to do."

Mrs. Wiggs waved and then disappeared through her door. She left it ajar.

Outside in the bitter-cold twilight, it was snowing again. He walked up Tenth Street to Sixth Avenue to look for a cab. If he hadn't already been feeling dejected, the undercurrent of excitement that ran through the crowd of overcoated pedestrians rushing along the whitening sidewalks would have done the trick. Everyone had somewhere to go, some marvelous, magical destination, and they couldn't get there fast enough. He watched a dozen black hansoms trot by, full of fares, before he wound his new scarf tighter around his neck and set off to walk uptown. He'd intended to stop at Fourteenth Street and find a cab there; but he kept walking, beguiled in spite of himself by the lights twinkling in the little gift stalls stretching the four blocks from Macy's to Siegel-Cooper's. Even the most garish, useless objects looked desirable tonight, cunningly displayed among the snowy evergreens and flickering kerosene lamps. Hawkers called out their last-minute bargains: brass paperweights, tiny Statues of Liberty, handkerchiefs and cheap bracelets and rows of striped peppermint canes. The smell of scorched holly and chestnuts flavored the frosty air. Two Salvation Army soldiers beat a drum and a tambourine on the corner at Twentieth Street, calling on passersby to give to the less fortunate tonight out of the spirit of Christmas.

"Train set for your little boy?"

Alex shook his head at an old man standing behind a long table covered in green baize, waving a feather duster to keep the snow off an elaborate labyrinth of tracks and trains and papier-mâché hills, tiny metal trees and fences, cows and farmers, ducks and dogs.

"Sure? Make a little fellow happy on Christmas morning."

"No, thanks, I haven't got a little boy."

"Bet you know one, though!" the old

man called after him.

He kept walking, but at the next corner he stopped, so abruptly the woman behind him smacked into his shoulder. "Excuse me," he muttered, his gaze fixed blindly on the cloud of slow, thick crystals blowing a miniature blizzard in the street lamp's silver halo. To his right was the awning-covered entrance to the Cunningham Hotel. The doorman, splendid in a royal blue uniform with epaulettes, eyed him benignly. "Is there a telephone in the lobby?" Alex heard himself ask.

"Aye, sure." His ruddy Irish face lit up when Alex handed him a dollar bill, just for opening the door. "And a merry Christmas to *you*," he called gratefully as Alex made his way across the red-carpeted lobby to the desk.

The telephone, the clerk told him, was in an alcove behind the potted ferns across the way. A bald gentleman with a drooping white mustache was seated at the little desk, talking into the instrument, and Alex's heart sank. But all at once the man surged to his feet, said, "Okay, so I'll see you at the Hoffman House in ten minutes," hung up, and rushed past him without stopping, murmuring, " 'Scuse me, merry Christmas."

Alex sat down and reached for the still-warm earpiece.

"Number, please?" asked the agreeable-sounding woman at central.

"Six-one-four-one."

"Thanks, I'll connect you. Merry Christmas."

"I don't understand you, Sara. You're the least prudish person I know."

"It's got nothing to do with prudery."

"Well, what has it got to do with? You won't explain it. If you would, I might be more sympathetic."

"Lauren, let's not have this conversation any longer." She bit back anything harsher, such as, *Your sympathy wasn't solicited,* even though it trembled on the tip of her tongue, and gestured toward the tea cart. "More coffee?"

"No. All right, I'll shut up."

"Thank you."

"But I still say you're being silly. If you *love* him —"

Sara stood up, walked across the drawing room, and sat down in another, more distant chair.

Lauren made a face and thrust both hands into her short brown hair, pulling it straight up in the air and then letting it fall. Her enormous green eyes flashed an apology. "Can I just say one more thing?"

"I really —"

"Just one, and then not another word."

"It won't —"

"Consider the possibility, Sara — not now but sometime, and don't wait forever — that you're doing this out of *habit*."

"What does that mean? No — I don't even want to know. Thank you, that's your one thing, now let's drop the subject. How do you like your new apartment?"

Lauren sent her a dry, knowing look and let the conversation shift. "I love it, of course. You'd know why if you'd come see it."

"I've meant to. I will soon, I promise."

"When?"

"Soon."

"How about tomorrow? No, it's Christmas, I have to go to my mother's. The day after? For lunch. You can bring Michael."

"We'd love to."

"Good!" Her vivacious face slowly sobered. "Tell me something, Sara. The truth. Do you think I'm a bad person?"

Sara's lips pulled sideways with impatience. "Why would I think that?"

"Because of the way I'm living."

"The way you're living?" But she knew

what Lauren meant. She'd moved out of her parents' house after her return from Paris four weeks ago, and now she lived by herself in a studio in the West Fifties, from which she took great delight in publicly advocating free love and women's suffrage, entertained gentlemen callers unchaperoned, befriended bohemian homosexuals, and painted shockingly large nudes in the Neo-Impressionist style. Lately she talked about giving up Anglicanism and becoming a Buddhist. Sara smiled, feeling suddenly old, almost grandmotherly. "No, I don't think you're a bad person. I think you're having the time of your life." Lauren grinned self-consciously. "But sometimes I worry about you. I worry that you'll get hurt."

"Then I'll get hurt," she retorted airily. "Life's too short to spend waiting for things to happen. If you want to be happy, you have to *do* something."

Sara blinked blandly, refusing to be drawn so soon into the old argument.

Lauren sighed, propping her petite chin on her knuckles. "You can live any sort of life you want to now. You're filthy rich and you're absolutely free. Do you know how lucky you are, Sara?"

"I have a very quiet life in mind."

"Yes, I know." It reminded her — "Did the contract go through for the house?"

She nodded. A Mr. and Mrs. Eustace Turnbull, the dewiest of the newly rich, had offered an unbelievable — to Sara, who would have settled for much, much less — amount of money for the New York house. Now she could pay off what Ben had owed on Eden and still have money left for the modest home she had in mind for her and Michael somewhere uptown, possibly on Central Park South. Ben's real estate investments would be sufficient to pay off his other debts, which arose mainly, she'd learned, from his failing slaughter-house empire. So about one thing he'd been right: she was no longer a millionaire, but she was still extremely comfortable.

"That's good; now you can start house-hunting in earnest. Have you heard anything lately from Miss Eminescu?"

"No, not since her letter. I don't expect to."

Lauren shook her head in awe. "The *nerve* of that woman!"

Nerve didn't cover it, thought Sara. Two weeks after Ben's death, Tasha had sent her a letter in a frail, shaky hand, postmarked from Mercy Hospital. Her legs were broken; she had internal injuries that might shorten her life; she was only just recovering from a serious head wound, and her face had been permanently disfigured. She understood perfectly well if Sara could not find it in her heart to forgive her for succumbing, after a long and terrible struggle, to her husband's relentless seduction. But if there was any charity left in her, now was the moment when it was most needed — for Tasha had no money at all, and although she was almost too weak to lift her head, the doctors said she must leave the hospital unless she paid them four hundred dollars immediately.

It hadn't sounded very plausible. Still, as much as she despised her, Sara hadn't been able to dismiss completely the possibility that Tasha's story might be true. So she'd telephoned the hospital. Miss Eminescu? Yes, she'd been a patient there. Her injuries? A broken ankle, bruises and contusions, a cut on the forehead that might leave a scar. She'd been released over a week ago.

"What do you think she'll do now?" wondered Lauren.

"Who knows? I'm sure she'll land on her feet somehow. I don't think about her." But she wasn't as indifferent as she sounded. That Tasha had been blackmailing her was a secret she couldn't tell anyone, not even Lauren; the tawdriness of it still shamed her, and she expected she would take that profound embarrassment to her grave.

Lauren raised her arms and stretched. "I'd better go soon. I have to get ready for Maximillian Amis's Christmas party tonight." A thought struck. "You could come with me, Sara. Max knows who you are, we've spoken of you often. Why don't you come? It's such an interesting crowd, I know you'd enjoy yourself."

Sara smiled and shook her head, glancing down briefly at her black faille mourning gown.

"Oh. I forgot. I guess it wouldn't look quite right."

"Not quite."

"What will you do, then?"

"Michael and I are going to trim the tree and give each other our presents. And then he wants *A Christmas Carol* again. He's never stayed awake past the first ghost," she explained fondly, "but this time he swears he's going to hear it all." Lauren's look was tender and — if she wasn't being fanciful — a bit pitying. "It's what I *want* to do," she cried, laughing. "I thank you for the invitation to Mr. Amis's party, but to tell you the truth, it's the last thing in the world I'd want to do tonight."

"Then you're in worse shape than I thought," Lauren snapped disapprovingly. Sara only smiled and shook her head again.

The telephone rang twice and stopped. Presently the maid put her head in the drawing room door. "A call for you, Mrs. Cochrane. Mr. McKie."

Color flooded Sara's cheeks, but she said without hesitation, "Tell him I have company, Dora."

Lauren jumped up from her chair. "No, I'm leaving." Her grin was huge. "I'll see myself out. Dora, will you get my coat?" Sara stood up much more slowly. Lauren went to her and took her hands. "Merry Christmas, Sara."

"You don't have to go."

"Yes, I do, I said so five minutes ago. Give Michael my love. And give my *very* best regards to Mr. McKie." She laughed at Sara's expression, then turned serious. "Take an old friend's advice and meet the man halfway. I don't even think you understand yourself why you're treating him this way." She kissed Sara's hot cheek, whirled, and tripped out after Dora.

Sara stared at the empty doorway for a

long moment, shoring up her defenses, alternately discounting and flinching from the truth of Lauren's last guess. With lagging steps, she went into her little study and sat down at the desk, pulling the telephone toward her. She lifted the earpiece silently and put it against her ear, hardly breathing. Knowing he was there made her heart soar at the same time that it filled her with anxiety. Seconds passed. She touched her tongue to her lips, closed her eyes, and said, "Hello?"

"Sara."

"Yes?"

"Alex here."

There was a clattering sound on the line; Sara said, "I've got it, Dora." She heard a click, and then the new silence took on an intimate tone.

Alex broke it quickly. "I'm calling to tell you I've decided to take your advice. My train leaves in an hour."

The bottom dropped out of her stomach. "I see."

Alex's palm tightened around the long stem of the telephone. "Is that it? That's all you can say?"

"What do you want me to say?"

"Well, I don't know, Sara. How about, 'Don't go'? How about, 'I want to be with you, Alex, because I wasn't lying when I said I loved you'?"

"Please don't do this."

But the desperate sadness in her voice couldn't stop him this time. "I got your last letter," he said briskly. "It was nice of you to finally take the trouble to write. But I have to ask you something. What did you mean when you said, 'The convenient death of my husband doesn't change anything'? Just what the hell is that supposed to *mean*, Sara?" He realized that if he were anywhere else but in a hotel lobby, he would be shouting. "Do you know how that makes me feel?"

"I'm sorry —"

"What do you think I am, some — *vulture* circling Ben's body, waiting to swoop down on the grieving widow?"

"Stop it, stop, please."

"Just tell me why you're doing this."

"I've told you why."

He gave a sharp, derisive laugh. "I thought maybe you'd come up with something more coherent by now."

Sara lined four fingernails against the edge of her desk, pressing until they turned white and made tiny indentations in the wood. "I'm sorry that you can't understand my reasons."

"You haven't got any reasons. You've got a lot of trumped-up, half-baked excuses that don't make any sense."

Silence. She sat in a cocoon of misery while Alex tried to get his temper under control.

"Does it ever strike you as odd that I saw much more of you while your husband was alive than I'm allowed to now that he's dead?"

"Alex — please. I want you to be happy. I want you to start your new life in California, just as you'd intended to do before."

"Before what? Say it, Sara. *Before Ben died*. And now explain to me how that doesn't *change* anything."

"It just —"

"It changes *everything!* There was only one thing keeping us apart, and it's not there anymore."

"It's much more complicated than that." But she couldn't go on, and the long, waiting quiet that followed was intolerable.

When Alex finally spoke, his voice sounded more tired than angry. "I've tried to understand you. God knows, I've tried to respect your scruples. Sara, I've been as patient as a mortal man can be, but I keep coming back to the simple fact that you're

496

behaving like an idiot and I can't seem to get past it."

"Really? Well, then, I guess there's nothing more to say," she snapped, anger finally sparking in her, too. It felt wonderful.

"You're deliberately sabotaging your own happiness, not to mention mine, and all for a lot of fatuous, nonsensical self-justifications that add up to exactly zero."

"Listen, Alex, I'm sorry I don't explain myself very well, but that doesn't give you the right to insult me."

He sighed. "Just tell me this — are you grieving for him? Is it that you've found out you were in love with him all along, and now you can't —"

"No, no, no, no —" She broke off, unable to talk past the lump in her throat.

"What, then?"

"I love you," she whispered. "I'll always love you. Let me go, Alex."

"*Listen* to yourself — !" He cursed monotonously.

"Please try not to be so angry with me," she pleaded hopelessly. "I know why you are, but I can hardly stand it."

"I'm not angry!"

"Oh, Alex —"

"If I thought we'd never be together, Sara, *then* I'd be angry. As it is, I just want to strangle you for wasting so much time." He heard her sniffling. "Don't cry. Look, I've got to go. I'll write to you when I get an address."

"It's better if you don't."

"I'll write to you," he repeated, stiff-lipped.

"I mean it, Alex. It won't make any difference." His fury came flooding back all at once, hot and explosive. "You and Michael have a merry Christmas, Sara," he all but snarled, and cradled the earpiece with a bang.

Sara jumped in sick surprise. She hung up and hugged herself, pushing back in her chair, ice-cold. *What have I done?* The shallow, round trumpet of the mouthpiece stared back at her like a huge black eye, mute and accusing. In a panic, she tried to call up all the causes and motives and justifications she'd been using to explain her actions to herself and, without success, to Alex. Like balky soldiers, they were hard to muster; she sensed mutiny in their surly reluctance to assemble.

Michael was chief among them, of course, as he had been all his life, the compelling influence and prime mover behind most of her conscious choices. His father's death had shattered him, fracturing the already tentative illusion of control he had over his life's circumstances. Since the accident he'd withdrawn even further into himself, in spite of everything Sara could think of to do for him, and his nights had been hellish ordeals riddled with dreams of terror and abandonment that left them both limp and demoralized. It was only in the last couple of weeks that he'd begun to show signs of recovery, a new independence she both welcomed and regretted, for she had needed his constant and comforting presence, especially in the early days, very nearly as much as he'd needed hers. But he was far from whole, he was still in deep mourning, and it was unconscionable to consider uprooting him in the midst of his grieving so that she could go off to California to be with her lover. The fact that she'd been strongly tempted to do it anyway increased her feeling of repugnance at the very idea. And even apart from feelings, his or hers, such an impulsive act would inevitably start tongues wagging, possibly ignite a scandal. Although she honestly didn't care about social consequences for herself anymore, she couldn't shirk the responsibility she had to protect Michael, who was too young to protect himself.

That was two reasons. She had others. Although she wasn't in "mourning," she was still in something — shock, possibly — from Ben's death. He hadn't been a monster, he'd been a man; with more flaws than virtues, perhaps, but still a man. She'd cast her lot with him for better or worse, and one didn't get over eight years of marriage in two months unless one was impossibly shallow. Or so it seemed to Sara.

Guilt, of course, played a part. If she hadn't actually wished Ben dead, she'd certainly wished him gone enough times over the years, and now he was. No matter that it was patently, blatantly irrational: she couldn't help feeling culpable.

But her strongest reason was the most irrational of all, which was not consoling and explained why she'd been careful not to mention it to Alex. It was simply the conviction that happiness wasn't really possible, not for her. She was unfortunately not among the lucky ones fated to find contentment in their lives. Healthy or not, she'd had that feeling for as long as she could remember; it wasn't reasonable to think she could escape it, just slip out of it cleanly now that circumstances appeared to have changed. She didn't trust appearances. One had to proceed along life's road with extreme caution because it was pitted with traps and unexpected catastrophes waiting for the blithe and unwary. And what looked like salvation usually turned out to be the deepest trap of all.

Besides, there was something *unseemly* about losing Ben and going immediately to Alex. The convenience and tidiness of the situation had a kind of cheapness that offended her perhaps overly refined sensibilities. She had been Ben's *wife*. She'd cheated on him once; she owed him a measure of fidelity now to make up for it.

There they were then, her reasons, in all their murky splendor. "Half-baked," Alex called them, and "nonsensical." Fine. That wasn't what bothered her about them. Something else nagged at the back of her mind, a lesson being communicated in an obscure intonation, *sotto voce*, vaguely taunting. She pushed the telephone away, straightened her pen set, lined up the corners of the envelopes in her correspondence holder — all to create a diverting background noise. But the voice wouldn't be silenced, and finally she heard its scornful message. Her reasons were impressive in their range and ingenuity, and especially their selfless and high-minded tone, the voice said, but they all had one thing in common — cowardice. She put her forehead on the edge of her desk and wept.

Michael found her that way a few minutes later. He'd been practicing "Silent Night" in the music room for the last half hour, in preparation for the private piano recital he was to give her after dinner tonight; the music had stopped a few minutes ago, she realized now — which ought to have alerted her to his imminent presence, but it hadn't. She'd been too wrapped up in her own wretchedness. She jerked upright when he put his small hand on her back and patted it gently. It was hopeless to try to disguise the ravages of her tears, but she did anyway, blotting her bloodshot eyes with her handkerchief. "Hello, sweetheart," she managed thickly.

"Are you crying because of Daddy?"

She shook her head with a wan smile.

"Then it must be because of Mr. McKie."

That sobered her. She stared at him, aghast.

"Do you like him more than you liked Daddy?"

She reached out to smooth back his hair, then straighten his collar, dithering. They never lied to each other. But how could she answer?

"I miss seeing him."

"Who, darling?" she asked, confused.

"Mr. McKie. He doesn't come to see me anymore."

"No, I know. He's going away."

Michael looked stricken. "Where?"

"To California. He was going before, remember?"

"Yeah, but —"

"He has a new job. He's going now. Tonight." She looked at her watch; a fresh wave of misery rolled over her.

"On the train?"

"Yes."

"Can we go and say good-bye?"

"It's better, I think, if we don't." Michael turned his head, but not before she saw the splash of tears on his cheeks.

"Will he come back?"

She shrugged, not trusting her voice.

"If he doesn't come back, I can never give him his Christmas present. Please can't we go and see him? Now, at the station? Please, Mummy?"

She shook her head miserably.

Michael brought his skinny, bunched-up fist down on top of her desk with an ear-splitting crash, toppling a vase of paper flowers and half a dozen picture frames. "Damnation!" he shouted, causing her to jump in astonishment. "Why can't we? Why?" When she didn't answer, he kicked the edge of her desk twice, hard. "You never say why!" he raged, and ran from the room.

She was so surprised, she almost went after him. Tantrums were as foreign to him as they were to her, and she wanted to see more of this new Michael. She wanted to know if this novel reaction was an aberration or a harbinger of things to come. She wanted to know whether she ought to feel worried or hugely relieved.

But she let him go, out of respect for his privacy. They would talk later. A deep, pervasive sorrow crept through her, making her ache, compounded by a loneliness so intense it was nearly intolerable. Why was she enduring this pain? She could say one word and put an end to her suffering, Michael's, and Alex's. Was Alex right — was she being an idiot? She felt as if she were treading a thin line between black and white, darkness and light. Always she had chosen the dark, repeatedly, every time but once. She'd believed it her duty, her personal moral imperative to do so. But whom would she hurt now by choosing the light? Her "duty" was making the two people she loved most in the world miserably unhappy.

She heard a thump and turned to see Michael maneuvering a very large and ungainly wooden object through the door to her study. He set it down on her desk without ceremony, knocking over more picture frames, her pencil jar, and her ink bottle, fortunately closed, in the process. "What is it?" she asked. A natural question, she'd have thought, but Michael took umbrage.

"Well, it's a pointed horseshoe arch," he huffed, his tone adding the "What do you think?" without saying it. "They built mosques with it in Cairo in the eight hundreds."

"Of course," she said feebly.

"It's Alex's present and I want to take it to him."

She looked helplessly at the pointed horseshoe arch, which bore, she thought, an uncanny resemblance to a colossal set of false teeth, stained brown. She looked at Michael. Slowly his expression of arrogant defiance — a new look, and absolutely fascinating to her — changed, softening to the sweet, gracious, tenderhearted lines she knew so well and loved so dearly. He stepped closer, put his hand on her neck. She reciprocated. Gray-blue eyes looked into gray-blue eyes. A message passed between them. Either could have vocalized it, but it was Michael who said first, "I love him too, you know." Then, "Can't we go see him, Mum?"

Sara felt humbled and exalted. "I didn't know," she confessed readily. "I should have. I just didn't realize." She kissed him and stood up. "We'll go and say good-bye. Did you know it's snowing? He'll be glad to see us." Michael, she could tell, understood the non sequitur perfectly. "Give me a minute to splash some water on my face." And fix her hair. "You call Mr. O'Shea and tell him to bring the carriage round right now, immediately. Tell him I said it's an emergency. Do you know the number?"

"Sure. Eight-oh-one-one?" he asked to be sure, beaming.

"Right. Then put your coat on and meet me at the front door. Okay?"

"Okay! Can I take my arch?"

"Well, of course. Alex can't go off to California without his arch." They hugged quickly, intensely, and then she flew out the door.

# Twenty-two

"Which one is it, Mum?"

Sara scanned the list of arrivals and departures printed in yellow chalk on the long double blackboard. "I don't see it," she muttered, biting her lips. "It's not here." She turned, searching the cavernous station for the information kiosk. All but two ticket counters were closed, and most of the people waiting on the shiny wooden benches were late commuters bound for home in Yonkers or White Plains or New Rochelle. The echoing station was ill lit and slightly smoky; a burnt, vaguely electrical smell mingled with the odors of coffee, overcooked pork, and disinfectant. Efforts to brighten the concourse with Christmas greenery had been defeated by the sheer immensity of the place, and the results were halfhearted and stingy-looking.

Sara spied the information booth under the huge clock across the way and pointed. "We'll ask that man there."

Even carrying his pointed horseshoe

arch, Michael was faster than she was, his hasty steps loud on the worn marble floor. But when he got to the desk, he forgot how to put the question.

"Where's the train leaving right now for San Francisco?" asked his mother.

A bald clerk in striped shirtsleeves and celebratory red bow tie smiled with infuriating calm. "There ain't one."

"There has to be!"

"Nope. Got one pulling out in a minute or two for Newark, Philadelphia, Pittsburgh, Toledo, and Chicago."

"No —"

"Got one leaving in twelve minutes for Atlanta via Washington, Roanoke, and Asheville. One just left for Boston by way of Hartford —"

"Chicago!" Sara guessed frantically. "He'll probably change there. Is anything else going west *right now?*"

"Well, let's see." He pushed his green visor back on his hairless head and thought, while Sara squeezed her hands together and Michael spun around in a frustrated circle. "Got a nonstop to St. Louis leaving in —" he squinted up at the great clock over his head — "four and a half minutes. Track 9."

"St. Louis," she breathed.

"Which one is it, Mum, which one? Hurry!"

It could be either, she realized, panicked. "Which track does the train to Chicago leave from?" she asked ungrammatically.

"Number four." He pointed behind her.

Number four was closer. "It's that one," she told Michael positively. It had to be.

The clerk called out after them, "You'll never make it, it's leaving now!" They kept running.

"Tickets?"

They braked to a halt at the turnstyle leading to the outdoor platform and Track 4. "We're seeing someone off," Sara explained hastily.

"Everyone's on board, the train's leaving, ma'am," said the sad-faced ticket collector.

"Please!" she cried. Michael looked ready to scream.

"Well, go ahead, then, but the train's leaving."

They rushed out onto the cold, snowy platform. "Look in the windows," Sara instructed. They sped along sideways, peering up at the high, brown, steel-sided train. The first cars were baggage cars and curtained sleeping compartments. Michael set his arch on the ground and started running, and Sara trotted fast to keep up in her high-heeled shoes. From up ahead someone yelled, "Board!" A whistle blew.

"Alex!" shouted Michael, leaping up and down and pointing at the window of the third lounge car. "Alex! Hi! Hi!" He turned to Sara as she reached him, panting, "He can't see me!"

"Oh, lord." She stood on tiptoe and rapped her knuckles against the glass. But there was too much train noise — he couldn't hear her. "Alex!" she and Michael screamed in unison. He was facing away, gazing across the car. At last the woman behind him tapped him on the shoulder and said something, pointing. He turned — saw them grinning up at him. His beloved face lit up in delight, and Sara started to cry.

He jumped up, squeezed out of his seat, and pointed to the door behind him. They nodded, hurrying back down the platform to wait for him. He threw open the sliding steel inner door and rushed down the two steep steps to the platform. Michael yelled, "Alex!" and hurled himself at him. Alex swept him up in a jubilant bear hug. Uncertain, Sara hesitated for a second, then threw her arms around both of them.

They stood that way, thumping each

other's shoulders and pressing their faces together, laughing and sniffling, until Michael squirmed down and ran off.

"Where's he going?"

"To get your present." She stepped back into his embrace with teary alacrity. "You were right, I was an idiot."

"No, no," he said gallantly.

"Yes, I was. God, you smell good. I wish you weren't going. Stay and have Christmas with us."

His arms around her tightened; he closed his eyes. "I wish I could."

"Oh, if only I'd done this sooner!" she wailed.

"What made you change your mind?" He smiled down at her with great tenderness, his fingers warming her cold cheek.

"Michael. I love you, Alex. And Michael does, too. And it doesn't take anything away from the feelings he had for his father. I hadn't understood that. Stupid of me — I should've known."

"I didn't have time to wrap it," Michael cried breathlessly, rushing up and setting the awkward wooden contraption at Alex's feet. Sara kneaded her fingers nervously, trying to catch Alex's eye so she could mouth the name of the gift over Michael's head. But Alex squatted down in front of it without looking at her.

"Well, well, look at this!" he exclaimed, with what Sara considered commendable, even award-winning enthusiasm.

"Can you tell what it is?" Michael prodded.

"Let's see." He turned it this way and that, narrowing his eyes. Sara cleared her throat, but to no avail; he wouldn't look up. "Looks like an arch to me. A pointed arch. Pointed *horseshoe* arch."

Michael crowed. Sara's jaw dropped.

"Board!"

Alex stood up, grimacing.

Michael grabbed his wrist. "Will you come back?"

"Definitely."

"Can we come and see you?"

"I hope so."

"I hope so too," Sara echoed, misty-eyed. She wanted to kiss him so badly.

Whistles blew at either end of the platform.

"Come soon," Alex said, reaching for Sara's hand. She nodded, squeezing back. "Michael, what do you think of the idea of your mother and me getting married?"

Sara went poker-stiff, but Michael grinned and looked down at his feet. "I think it's a good idea," he mumbled, shy.

Alex coaxed his head up with one gentle finger under his chin. "You sure?"

"Sure I'm sure."

"Great. Thanks, pal."

What astonished her was how casually Michael had accepted it — almost as if the idea wasn't even new to him. "What about me?" she thought to ask. "Isn't anyone going to ask me what I think?" Whistles shrilled again, angry and impatient. "I accept!" she clarified hastily.

Laughing, Alex hugged Michael, then Sara. He gave her a quick kiss. She tried to hold on, but he muttered, "Gotta go," along with a soft, explicit curse. Scooping up his present, he turned and got on the train. A deafening blast of steam sounded from the engine; far up ahead, a flagman waved a red lantern. The train jolted once and glided away.

They all waved. Alex yelled something. Sara cupped her ear. "What?" He shouted again.

Michael said wonderingly, "He says come now."

"What?"

Alex jumped to the pavement again and sprinted toward them, laughing. "Come with me now. Come on."

"Yes!" shrieked Michael, leaping up and

down on his tiptoes. "Yes! Can we? Can we?"

Sara stared at them as if they'd both gone berserk.

"Come on," grinned Alex. "Let's go." He started walking backwards, one arm stretched out invitingly. Michael followed, beside himself.

"But — Mr. O'Shea's waiting outside with the carriage."

They sent her pitying glances. "We'll call from Newark and straighten it all out," Alex said kindly. The train was picking up speed.

"All your presents, Michael — you won't get any!"

He looked incredulous, one hand on his hip. "Well, *I* don't care about that!"

Sara froze for two more seconds, then yelled, "Hurry!" She ran toward Michael, scooped him up under the arms, and shoved him at Alex — who whirled and dashed up to the next door, which was sliding by at an alarming rate, and deposited Michael on the steel platform. Sara ran fast on his heels, breathless with exertion and excitement. Alex grabbed her arm and half-lifted, half-hurled her up behind Michael. Racing now, because in four more strides there wouldn't be any platform left, he leapt for the high step, just as Sara and Michael made a grab for his coat and yanked.

He made it. No one spoke. All they could do was stare at each other in amazed disbelief while the train sped faster and faster, whistle screaming, and snow swirled past like furious white bees.

The forward inner door slid open and a uniformed porter faced them in the threshold. The surprise on his big, friendly face mirrored the same emotion in theirs. "How do? You folks got tickets tonight?"

"Uh oh. Oh no, oh no," fretted Michael, clutching Sara's sleeve, fearing the worst. It was easy to see whose child he was, she thought ruefully. "Have we got any money, Mum? Maybe Alex could lend us —"

"I've got money," she assured him, laughing.

"We got plenty of seats, and still plenty of compartments in the sleeping car," the porter said helpfully. "Not many folks traveling tonight. Where y'all going?"

"California," Michael answered importantly.

"By way of Chicago," Sara explained.

"Where we're getting married," Alex elucidated.

Sara felt herself blushing. "We'll see."

"She always means yes when she says 'we'll see,'" Michael confided to Alex in a conspirator's voice.

"I'll remember that."

The porter's face split from ear to ear with a white-toothed grin. "Well, ain't this somethin'? Y'all ain't even got any baggage, have you?" Sara and Michael shook their heads.

"Well, that's not true," Alex corrected. "We happen to be traveling with one of the finest examples of a pointed horseshoe arch I've ever seen." Michael giggled, pinkening with pride. Alex reached into his pocket and handed something to the porter. "Would you mind helping the young man to a seat near mine? And after that, maybe you could find a sleeping compartment for mother and son — not too far away from mine, either." He didn't wink, but he wanted to.

"Yes, *suh*. You just leave all that to me. My name's Lewis, and I'll be takin' care of y'all on this trip." He eyed Michael benignly. "Need a hand with that?" The swaying of the train made it difficult for Michael to walk with his arch in his arms; he relinquished it to Lewis carefully, then preceded him through the sliding door.

Following him down the aisle, Lewis

started to chuckle. Michael looked back. "*I know* they just want to kiss," he said with quelling matter-of-factness, and the porter's wide eyes widened further.

On the platform, Alex draped Sara's arms around his neck and pulled her closer, bracing his back against the fire door for stability. Snow reeled and eddied around them and a freezing wind howled, but they were warm against each other. "Is he right?" Alex asked. "Does 'we'll see' mean yes?" Before she could answer, he kissed her.

She sighed with her eyes closed. "Mm. Usually, yes. Not in this case, though, I don't think."

"Oh God, Sara," he groaned, "don't say that." He kissed her again, deeply, and again, until they were both breathing hard. He pulled away to see if he was getting anywhere. "Come on," he coaxed. "Marry me in Chicago. We'll find a justice of the peace, some sentimental soul who won't mind being rousted out on Christmas night. Michael can be ring bearer."

She smiled dreamily and shook her head. "I'm afraid not."

Alex frowned. "Reconsider," he advised, running his tongue along the fragile inner surface of her lips. She caught her breath when he nibbled her top lip between his, then tickled the roof of her mouth with his tongue.

"Unh," she breathed softly, deep in her throat, while his hand snaked inside her unbuttoned coat and stroked her stomach in possessive little circles. "Alex," she tried to say, but he kissed her again, and his mouth was a ruthless silencer.

He slipped his other hand in and cupped her bottom through her gown, pulling her up tight against him. He groaned again, not sure which of them he was torturing now. "I love you, Sara. Marry me," he mumbled, lips sliding wetly from her mouth to her ear, her throat. "Marry me in Chicago."

"No. Can't."

He ground his teeth. "Why?"

She put her hands on his hard chest and pushed back. "Because," she explained, breathless, "I'll never hold out that long. Alex, you've got to marry me in Pittsburgh."

His face stayed blank for the length of a second, and then he shouted out a loud, joyous laugh, hugging her ferociously.

They kissed. Kissed again. When his hands slipped naturally to her breasts she moaned, leaning into him heavily. "Possibly Philadelphia," she got out faintly, clutching his shoulders.

"They 'bout to serve dinner in the dining car, you folks feel like eatin'. The little boy 'lowed as how he was startin' to get hungry."

They jumped apart, pivoting to see the porter behind them — how had he opened the door so soundlessly? — and pointedly looking away at the flying countryside. Sara discovered she was holding her hat in her hand, and busied herself putting it back on. Alex cleared his throat, running his hands over his disheveled hair and combing his damp mustache with his fingers. They gave each other surreptitious once-overs, then discreet nods that said they looked all right, everything considered, and followed Lewis into the lounge car. Michael waved when he saw them; they waved back. Sara turned her head to the side and said through her teeth, "I hope you tipped Lewis generously."

"Why?"

"He saved us."

"From what?"

"A wedding in Newark."

Alex was still chuckling when they sat down, Michael wedged between them on the crack separating their seats. There was an empty seat for him across the aisle, but they weren't ready to be separated yet.

"This is so *neat*," he declared, one hand on Alex's knee, one on his mother's. They nodded in agreement.

All three turned to gaze out the window. Twinkling lights floated by in the snowy distance, but in the foreground all they could see was themselves, smiling at each other in the shining black mirror. They looked like a family.